About You

Also by Kaitlyn Hill

Love from Scratch
Not Here to Stay Friends

WILD
About You

KAITLYN HILL

Delacorte
Romance

Text copyright © 2024 by Kaitlyn Hill
Cover art copyright © 2024 by Ana Hard
Chapter opener art and ornaments by Olga/stock.adobe.com

All rights reserved. Published in the United States by Delacorte Romance, an imprint of Random House Children's Books, a division of Penguin Random House LLC, New York.

Delacorte Romance and the colophon are trademarks of Penguin Random House LLC.

Visit us on the Web! GetUnderlined.com

Educators and librarians, for a variety of teaching tools, visit us at RHTeachersLibrarians.com

Library of Congress Cataloging-in-Publication Data
Names: Hill, Kaitlyn, author.
Title: Wild about you / Kaitlyn Hill.
Description: First edition. | New York: Delacorte Press, 2024. |
Audience: Ages 12–18. | Audience: Grades 10–12. | Summary: "Indoorsy theater girl Natalie must team up with surly nature-lover Finn in an *Amazing Race*–style reality competition show set in the Appalachian wilderness—if they do not kill (or kiss!) each other first" —Provided by publisher.
Identifiers: LCCN 2023051904 (print) | LCCN 2023051905 (ebook) |
ISBN 978-0-593-65095-0 (trade paperback) | ISBN 978-0-593-65096-7 (ebook)
Subjects: CYAC: Reality television programs—Fiction. | Contests—Fiction. | Wilderness survival—Fiction. | Interpersonal relations—Fiction. | Great Smoky Mountains National Park (N.C. and Tenn.)—Fiction. | National parks and reserves—Fiction. |
LCGFT: Romance fiction. | Novels.
Classification: LCC PZ7.1.H5617 Wi 2024 (print) |
LCC PZ7.1.H5617 (ebook) | DDC [Fic]—dc23

The text of this book is set in 11-point Maxime Pro.

Editor: Hannah Hill
Cover Designer: Angela Carlino
Interior Designer: Michelle Crowe
Copy Editor: Colleen Fellingham
Managing Editor: Tamar Schwartz
Production Manager: Shameiza Ally

Printed in the United States of America
10 9 8 7 6 5 4 3 2 1
First Edition

For Sheryl and Phil Burns, my Mamé and Pawpaw,
who give me wild adventures and unwavering love

Author's Note

While this story is a romance with plenty of lighthearted fun and trope-y goodness, it also deals with some heavier topics, such as learning to live with an anxiety disorder and grieving the losses of a parent and a grandparent. Much of this is based on my own experience, and I hope I have portrayed it with sensitivity and care for the characters and for all of you.

The story also takes place in a special part of the world, along a section of the Appalachian Trail in the Great Smoky Mountains National Park. I've spent a lot of time in and around the Smokies my whole life, from wandering through gorgeous Cades Cove to floating in an inner tube down the Little Pigeon River, and I'm lucky to call the region of Appalachia from Kentucky to Tennessee home.

To supplement my personal experience, I did extensive research on the AT and GSMNP for the purpose of filling out the world of Natalie, Finn, and *Wild Adventures* and doing justice to the setting. Still, I have not personally hiked the Appalachian

Trail, and I'm sure there are nuances to the thru-hiker's journey that I've missed. I also took intentional creative liberties for the sake of what the plot and characters needed, particularly in playing fast and loose with national park rules, altering distances between some landmarks or points of interest, and inventing others from scratch.

So while I don't recommend using this book as a guide for backpacking the AT, safe camping practices, or really much of anything, I hope its inaccuracies can be excused for the *wild* fun of watching two people fall head over hiking boots in love.

I'm looking forward to
lying in the tent and reading
Danielle Steel.

—Jessica Simpson

Chapter One

My face is melting.

Okay, so not my actual face, but the layers of primer, concealer, foundation, bronzer, blush, and highlighter I spent the morning tediously applying, blending, and contouring, all so that I could look my best for my first day on camera. That backfired harder than my dad's ancient Ford pickup.

It's not even that hot out here, at least not for a sunny June day. Tennessee summers aren't exactly temperate—I remember as much from visiting my grandma in Pigeon Forge most of my childhood—but up at this altitude, with thick tree cover overhead, I'm in a mild, green, wildflower-dotted oasis. An oasis that's been the backdrop of a uniquely intense, high-pressure workout, as I've hauled my clueless ass around for the better part of an hour. That's my best guess at how long it's been since the *Wild Adventures* crew sent me off from the little mountain town where we'd first met with a GoPro camera, emergency satellite phone, hand-drawn map, and their best wishes. I quickly sought out the least threatening, most grandma-like local available and asked her to point me toward the Appalachian Trail.

Fifteen minutes later, Ethel finally let me leave the street corner with not only some overly complex directions to the trailhead, but also the life stories of all three of her grandchildren, and a plastic bag of strawberry hard candies from her purse. Between the exertion and the anxiety as I've tried to make up for time lost to that sweet, four-foot-eleven roadblock, I'm starting to move past "glistening" into "sweating like an overly made-up pig."

Reese tried to warn me about this, I think with a grimace as I step around a fallen tree branch. My best friend and I spent our freshman year at different schools—me at Oliver College in Boston, her at UW in Seattle—but as soon as I knew I'd been cast for this season of the popular reality show *Wild Adventures,* and that filming would take place along a stretch of the Appalachian Trail just a couple hours from our hometown in Kentucky, I sent out the distress signal. She made sure she was home for summer break in time to help get me ready and see me off.

She'd had all kinds of questions since hearing that I'd applied for this show in the first place, starting with "Huh?" and "Why?" The questions have only gotten more pointed over time, ranging from "You haven't even been camping before, have you?" to "You know filming a reality show is going to be pretty different from doing live theater, right?"

As if she's never taken some extremely out-of-character leaps and landed somewhere amazing. But that's a whole other story.

When she and I road-tripped down to Tennessee yesterday,

we stopped at REI in Knoxville for a few last-minute outdoor apparel and accessory purchases. This only reinforced how woefully underprepared I was for this experience.

"Are you sure you need a new makeup bag? Let alone one that big?" Reese asked, eyeing my selection with skepticism. "It'll take up, like, half your backpack. And you probably won't want to deal with the upkeep while you're out in the wild."

"I've made bigger sacrifices in the name of beauty," I assured her with unfounded confidence.

If she could see me now, she'd sigh out the most exasperated "Lordhavemercy" recorded in human history.

Reese *could* see me now, it occurs to me. Or see a recording of current me a few weeks from now, or whenever episodes start going up on UltiMedia, the streaming service that airs *Wild Adventures*. Panting, I come to a stop and rest my perspiring backside against a tree while I pull the GoPro out of its holster that the crew affixed to my small day pack—the only luggage I was allowed to bring to filming. It contains a few changes of clothes, toiletries, and a hefty cosmetics supply for which I'm already side-eyeing myself. As my one allotted "secret weapon," aka nonessential item, I have my e-reader, loaded with plenty of my usual romance novel fare, but also a couple AT info books. Per the rules of the show, I didn't bring any other gear or equipment for this outdoorsy expedition—not that I own any of that stuff, anyway.

When my breathing is marginally less wheezy, I swipe my arm across my forehead in a half-hearted attempt at shine control while I have the camera pointed at the ground. I'm still inwardly cursing the fact that I can't see what I look like right now, but I give a big smile anyway as I lift the GoPro to capture my first close-up.

"Hey, *Wild Adventures* fam! Natalie here." The show's team sent out an orientation package to contestants a couple weeks ago, including all the paperwork we needed to fill out and waivers to sign, along with a series of videos on best practices for filming my own close-ups. They also recorded my intro, where I gave a more formal "I'm Natalie Hart, I'm nineteen years old and a theater major at Oliver College" spiel for audiences. Hopefully it's okay to just operate on a first name basis now. "I *think* I'm making progress toward the first checkpoint, but I have to admit it's a little hard to tell with this map. Like, is that blob supposed to be some kind of landmark? Or did the mapmaker spill their coffee? How am I supposed to know when I've walked 'four hundred yards northwest'? Cardinal directions are not my strong suit—I only remember the sun rises in the east by singing the *Beauty and the Beast* song in my head, Mrs. Potts voice and all." Okay, too much of Real Natalie coming out from the jump. Let's dial back the rambling. "So, yeah, they totally didn't exaggerate on the 'adventure' part of this whole thing. But I'm trusting Mother Nature and the UltiMedia producers not to let me meet my untimely end on day one. Stay tuned to see if that trust is misplaced!"

Who says my theater background didn't prepare me for this? I'm crushing it in the role of Girl Who Isn't Kind of Lost Or More Than Kind of Concerned. I wedge the camera back into its holster so it can continue recording my progress, satisfied I've made enough of a face-forward update for this leg of the journey. Hell, if I don't get to the first checkpoint soon, there won't be a journey for me to continue on.

Per usual on a season of *Wild Adventures,* they dropped each contestant off in a separate location with a camera to film themself and a map to guide them to a checkpoint where the whole group will meet up to kick off the competition. The last contestant to arrive gets eliminated before things even truly get started.

I can't let that be me.

I've watched a few seasons of *Wild Adventures* over the years, and it's always fun. Each season, they plop down a bunch of people with varying levels of outdoorsiness in a different scenic locale and have them race to different checkpoints with their partners, competing in challenges along the way. Some of the challenges require more survival skills, while others are random location-themed activities. A camera crew does some of the filming, catching up with teams at all points in the challenges and spotlighting one or two pairs per episode, but most of the footage is captured by team members themselves using GoPros. Normally, there are competitors at all stages of adulthood who apply for the show with a friend, family member, or significant other. It's always seemed to me like a great opportunity to test a relationship—if you can get through *Wild Adventures* together, you can get through anything. If the challenges only open your eyes to your boyfriend's assholeishness, on the other hand, you'll have plenty of chances to knee him in the groin and make it look like an accident.

But this season is a little different. All competitors are college students, and we'll each be partnered with a stranger. And rather than the standard $100,000 cash prize, we'll be competing for $100,000 in scholarship money for each partner. They're calling it *Wild Co-EdVentures*.

Really.

When I saw the information about the open applications in my school's e-newsletter, it sounded like some kind of old-school, sexist, *Girls Gone Wild* mess and I was side-eyeing Oliver College for advertising it—until I saw the picture of a bearded mountain man type, hunched over as he tried to start a fire with sticks. Curiosity piqued. And when I read up on the details of the season, and that *prize,* well . . . there are worse ways to try to get money for school. And lord knows I need it, after the freshman year I had.

I shake my head to try and banish all thoughts of my hellish first two college semesters, refocusing on the soft give of the dirt beneath my feet, the swish of leaves against my exposed arms as I walk through a bunch of plants I hope to Dolly Parton aren't poisonous. The school year and all its failures are behind me now, hundreds of miles away. My parents are back in Kentucky, where I can't see the judgy eyes they're always glaring with. And somehow, miracle of miracles, I got picked for this opportunity here, high up in these ancient mountains. I would've enjoyed getting to do this somewhere farther from home—past *Wild Adventures* seasons have been set anywhere from the Australian outback to Patagonia—but somewhat literal beggars can't be choosers. Nowhere to go but forward, into this vast, green unknown, toward my fresh start.

If I don't die in a bear attack trying.

I hear a faint sound and stop in my tracks, wondering if I've jinxed myself by thinking the *B*-word. I don't have bear spray in this pack. Because I wasn't supposed to bring "gear." Whose idea was that, anyway? Maybe I can blind the bear with my setting spray, or hyaluronic acid serum?

The rustling grows louder and my pulse skyrockets as I crouch down, bringing my arms over my head like a weak-ass shield and wondering why I didn't read more about bear safety before coming here. Or even virtually crack open any of those Appalachian Trail e-books. Black bears are, like, the Smoky Mountains' mascot. Maybe I should have prioritized research before making sure my cheekbones would look nice from all angles, but no. I'm a fool. A fool unable to survive past the first hour alone in the woods, and—

"What do you think you're doing?"

The voice is human, not bear, though it *does* sound pretty growly. Slowly, I lower my arms and stand up straighter, turning in the direction of the sound.

A guy, tall and lanky, fair-skinned, with sandy brown hair cropped close to his head, is standing on the trail behind me. The combination of his dry-fit T-shirt, hiking boots, and those pants that can unzip into shorts and have a bunch of pockets up and down the legs gives off the impression of capital-*O* *Outdoorsy*.

Putting a hand over my pounding heart, I do what I do best: blurt out the first thing that comes to mind. "I thought you were gonna eat me!"

There are weirder first words to say to another person, probably. I don't know what they are, but I'm sure they exist.

"You—you *what*?" His tone only seems to grow more aggravated as his face scrunches up in confusion.

I throw my hands up as if he's the one being ridiculous here. "I thought you were a bear! You still might be some kind of freaky, woodsy serial killer. Lord knows angry white men are the scariest predators out there. But I have acid in my bag and plenty of people who'd be out to avenge me if anything happened, so watch yourself."

The guy pinches the bridge of his nose as if he might have a migraine coming on. "I'm not a serial killer, or—or an angry white man."

"Says the white man angrily," I retort, crossing my arms over my chest.

He sighs. "I'm . . . mildly irritated at most. And why do you have aci— You know what? Never mind. Are you lost or something?"

It's then when I notice it. The GoPro secured to the top of his backpack, just visible over his shoulder. It feels like the extra layer of anxiety-sweat brought on by running into a stranger in the middle of nowhere dries up immediately.

"You're a Co-EdVenturer!" I cry.

He takes a step back at my sudden volume increase and frowns. "That name is embarrassing."

"But you are, aren't you? I'm one too! Oh, thank god. Now I know you're at least able to pass a criminal background check." I clap my hands and give a little jump. "Oh, and that means we're going to the same place!"

He sighs again. I'm tempted to stick a balloon in front of his face, see how long it takes him to fill it up with hot air and exasperation. "Yeah, and do you know where that place is yet?"

I put a hand to my cocked hip. "If I did, would I still be standing here talking to you?"

"Guess not." He reaches into one of his many pants pockets and pulls out a paper folded into a tiny square. He unfolds it carefully and steps closer again, holding it out toward me. "What's your map look like?"

I slide mine out of the slim thigh pocket on my new sport leggings and try not to cringe at the dampness. Comparing the two drawings side by side, it's clear how we both ended up here—though we were dropped off in different spots, the shape of the paths drawn out on each of our maps becomes identical as it nears the X marking the first checkpoint location. We have to be really close now.

"Okay, so if we're right here," I point to the place where our two paths should meet on both maps, "we should just need to go a bit farther. . . ." I spin in a slow circle to orient myself. "This way!"

His brows knit together as he studies the drawings. "Are you sure it's not a little more"—his gaze flits up and he points a smidge to the right of where I've indicated, making a little clicking sound with his mouth—"this way?"

I shrug. "I haven't been sure of anything since I filled in my brows this morning and got them *juuust* the same shape. But I don't feel overly unsure about it either."

"I have no idea what to do with that," he mutters. He eyes me up and down slowly, but it isn't in any kind of interested or checking-me-out way. Rather, he just continues to look put off by everything about me, from the neon pink laces in my new hiking boots, to the leggings I picked out in my favorite shade of purple, to my gray workout tank with cutouts that show glimpses of my sports bra. He doesn't focus long on my melting face before clocking the single purple streak running through my brown hair, then returning to the forest beyond me with an eye roll so subtle I almost miss it. But I don't. I'm about to snap something at him—I don't know what—when he deflates and starts walking. In the direction *I* chose.

"Okay, let's try it," he grumbles as he brushes past me.

"What a marvelous idea!" I coo, turning to march behind him. "By the way, I'm Natalie. And you are?"

"Hoping I won't regret this."

"Charming!" I shoot my winningest smile at the back of his head. "Clearly you're not from my neck of the woods."

There's a pause, as if he's considering letting the conversation die there, but curiosity must get the better of him. "What makes you say that?"

"Manners are kind of a *thing* in the South. I'm from Kentucky, not far from these parts. Spent a lot of time in Tennessee growing up, actually. Do I get to know where you're from? Is that less personal than a name?"

Impressive that his sigh is so audible back here. I picture the imaginary balloon inflating.

"My name is Finn, and I'm from Vermont."

He pushes past a thin branch without holding it back for me, so it ricochets and whips me across the chest. I suck in a sharp breath and try to rein in my growing irritation. At the sound, Finn glances back, seemingly oblivious to how he's just switch-slapped me.

"What is it, another bear?" he snarks.

I ignore that. "I thought Ben and Jerry's countrymen were supposed to be friendlier. Is Cherry Garcia some kind of false promise about the quality of all Vermont exports?"

He faces forward again, maneuvering around a few trees in our path. I take careful steps as I follow, still getting used to this backwoods hiking thing.

After a long silence, I hear his gruff voice again. "Do you have even the slightest clue of what to do if you actually run into a bear?"

I cross my arms over my chest. Guess he wasn't impressed with my whole cowering-in-fear-and-threats-of-acid routine.

"Define 'slightest clue.'"

Finn scrubs a hand over his short hair, and I sense I might be getting another eye roll. "With black bears, if they don't see you, you can just back away slowly. But even if they approach you, they're probably only curious. You try to intimidate it by holding your arms up to make yourself look bigger and making a lot of noise, and it'll probably stop or back off, then you can back away. Worst case scenario, it starts to charge you, don't run.

That's when you fight back, preferably with bear spray before it gets too close. Surely we'll all be getting some with our supplies at the first checkpoint."

I nod as I process all this information, finding it . . . surprisingly helpful. Annoyingly so, since he's so grudging in giving it up. I sincerely hope I never need to use any of it, though.

"Okay, let's practice," I say decisively.

He looks at me over his shoulder, where I'm already standing on my tiptoes, my arms stretched high over my head. "I'm not stopping to practice this. We can't waste time."

I keep up the same walking pace, just doing so in my Bear Intimidation Stance. "What kind of noise do I make?"

"It doesn't matter. Talk to it, whatever comes to mind."

Time to test my loudest outdoor voice. *"FINN'S PANTS HAVE SO MANY POCKETS BECAUSE THEY'RE FULL OF SECRETS!"*

He jumps about a foot forward and I have to tamp down my giggle as I drop to walk on flat feet again.

"Was that really necessary?" he grumbles.

"I just want to be ready if the real thing ever happens. Okay, I've got black bears down. What about other types?"

Finn's shoulders rise in a brief shrug, his hands coming up to grip his backpack straps. "You won't run into any grizzlies out here. Good thing, because your best chance with them is to cover your neck and play dead."

Oh shit. I mean, that would've been my strategy with any bear before this conversation. But it isn't encouraging to hear.

I can feel my heart wanting to gallop away and I try to take deep, calming breaths. That's when Finn gasps.

"What?!" I whisper-yell. Before he says anything, I realize the path we've been walking meets another, much more well-trodden trail. Finn takes an abrupt left turn onto the new trail, giving a little pump of his fist at his side.

"See that?" he says, half-turning so I can see where he's pointing. On the side of the new trail is a tree marked with a slash of white paint. I nod in answer. "That means we're on the AT now. The Appalachian Trail."

I'm about to respond that I know what AT stands for, thank you very much (even if I didn't a few weeks ago), when I hear it. Voices carry to us faintly. When I peer past Finn, I see a break in the trees ahead and the vague, blobby shapes of people milling around.

"Well, hell if I'm not a better navigator than the disembodied voice of Google Maps Lady herself, huh, Finn?" I quicken my steps to walk beside him and keep pace with his longer stride, batting my eyelashes even though he doesn't look at me.

"Sure," he says.

"Now, now, calm down. I don't do it for the glory. All in a day's work for a humble woman of the wild such as myself. We all have different gifts to offer the world, and it just so happens that mine is the gift of being right all the time. You'll get used to it."

"I hope not," he replies woodenly.

I laugh as if he's made the funniest joke as we step into the clearing, and a bunch of heads turn our way. Cameras, too, as we approach the group of people around our age standing in a semicircle, facing a bright orange flag with the *Wild Adventures* logo on it.

It's real. Our first checkpoint.

Beside it and only slightly less orange in appearance is the host of *Wild Adventures,* Burke Forrester. I'm determined to find out if that's a stage name before I leave. Finn and I approach, a big smile splitting my face involuntarily. I steal a glimpse at Finn only to find his expression totally neutral, which I guess is the perpetually frowning person's version of a smile.

"Natalie. Finn. Welcome to the AT! I see your paths crossed on your way here—forming alliances already?" Burke's high-pitched voice is . . . not the same as it is on TV. It doesn't match the faux-tanned, burly-but-polished exterior, that's for sure. Is there such a thing as auto-tune in reality TV editing?

Snapping myself out of it, I give him a cheesy grin and say, "No such thing as too many friends!"

At the same time, Finn utters a flat "No."

Well then.

Burke just laughs, fortunately, defusing the potentially awkward moment as he brings his hands together in front of him. "Well, I'm pleased to share that neither of you are the last to arrive. You may join your fellow adventurers before me and get ready for your wild adventure to commence."

My whole body sags in relief, knowing for certain that I'm sticking around. The only sign that Finn feels the same is the relaxing of the wrinkle in the middle of his forehead. As I thank

Burke and turn to take my place with the others, relief simmers into adrenaline, eagerness. It's *really* real now, and I'm actually, definitely in.

There's no dress rehearsal for *Wild Adventures*. I don't have a script, and I've never set foot on a stage like this. But I want—no, need—that prize money more than any standing ovation or Tony award in the world.

And I'm ready to perform my ass off to get it.

Chapter Two

I wedge myself into the semicircle of fellow adventurers between a friendly-looking blonde who reminds me of Reese and a not-unattractive athlete type. High School Natalie would have taken a bite out of him in a heartbeat. Good thing she and her overly romantic heart have been left in the dust by College Natalie, who has so many bigger fish to fry.

I can still appreciate the view, though.

As I'm doing just that, surreptitiously checking out Mr. Gun Show in his very revealing T-shirt with cutoff sleeves, my eyes drift without my permission. To Finn, my non-ally, who is tossing a judgmental look in my direction as he takes a spot as far away from me as he can possibly get.

So he doesn't like fun, cool people who are good at reading maps. Good for him! No skin off my nose.

I glance at the girl beside me. She really does look like my best friend—cute, wholesome, girl-next-door vibes, down to the spray of freckles across her cheeks. A potential ally if I ever saw one.

"Hey, I'm Natalie," I say, leaning toward her with my warmest smile.

Her eyes flick my way, and my grin falters. Is she deciding whether I'm worth a turn of her head?

But no, benefit of the doubt. We're all nervous here and new to being on camera. I stay cheesing while awaiting her verdict.

Her chin angles my way, lips turning down at the corners. "Ally." Oh my god! Her name is literally *ally* pronounced differently. If this isn't a sign we're going to be best friends, maybe even teammates—"With an *i*," she finishes.

Ah. Okay, close enough.

She turns her head away again, so I lean back. It's fine—this is a weird environment in which to meet people.

"Where are you from?" I blurt out anyway before I can stop myself, because I just can't leave well enough alone. Can't let yet another person dislike me today without a clear reason.

Alli's still-downturned lips twitch, her brows pinching together. At this rate, all of my fellow "Co-EdVenturers" are going to need Botox before they turn thirty.

"Colorado."

I wait to see if she'll ask where I'm from, or look at me again, but nope. That's all I get.

"Oh, awesome. I hear it's beautiful there! I'm from Kentucky," I offer.

In return, Alli's eyes dart my way again before making a quick up-and-down assessment of me, much like Finn did. Then she *snorts*. A derisive little sound, capped off with a short yet highly judgmental "Oh."

My mouth drops open. I'm . . . befuddled. I've always been a girl's girl—not someone who's ever had trouble making friends of the female variety, always flying my feminist flag, Very Much Like Other Girls. And until college, I thought I was pretty good at making new friends. But when Alli angles her body away from me, I decide to leave this one be for now.

The more I think about it as we watch the rest of the competitors arrive, one by one, the madder I get. Mad that no matter where I go, no matter how little people have to base their judgments of me on, it seems like no one takes me seriously.

Not my parents, when I spent years working my ass off toward my dream of going to college for theater. They've both worked on a horse farm doing manual labor for their whole adult lives, so they see higher education as a waste of time and money and eagerly await the day I come back home to get a "real job." And not my classmates at Oliver, who I thought would finally get me like no one else had. Instead, they were unimpressed by a freshman who'd been good on a small-town stage and in performances in her grandma's living room, and in all the theater camps she went to in these very Tennessee mountains growing up, but was nothing next to former Broadway child stars.

And now, here, among a group of people who I'm pretty sure have also never been on a reality competition show in the wilderness before, I already feel like the last kid any of them would pick in gym class.

The soft thuds of another adventurer's jogging footsteps pull me back to the present before a girl bursts out of the woods. Counting in my head, I see that with this latest girl, there are now sixteen of us in the semicircle. How many teams are in a normal *Wild Adventures* season? Surely no more than ten. Are we close to the last arrival?

"Amanda," Burke Forrester bellows. His expression is stern as he faces the girl still trying to catch her breath in front of him. If he's making *me* this nervous, I can only imagine what she's feeling. "As you can see, many Co-EdVenturers have arrived before you."

Oh, damn. I can feel the discomfort rippling through the circle of us looking on, everyone shifting on their feet, adjusting backpack straps and not making eye contact with one another— and especially not with the poor gal on the chopping block.

Burke lets us wait a brutally long, awkward minute before he speaks again. "Unfortunately . . . for the remaining arrival, you are still in this competition as the last Co-EdVenturer to make the cut. Congratulations, Amanda!"

Her relieved "ohmygod" is a cross between a gasp and a squeal as she bounces in place. There's scattered applause from some of us surrounding her, the confusion and awkwardness of the moment not totally gone, but at least we have a little fore-warning before we have to watch someone's dreams get crushed.

Only a little, though, as the remaining straggler appears mere moments after the clapping has subsided. Sauntering out from the trees wearing, of all things, a cowboy hat and boots, the guy approaches the flag and our host as if he already knows his fate, so the elimination doesn't hit as hard as it might have otherwise. When Burke confirms for all of us that Cowboy is the last one to make it to the checkpoint and has therefore been eliminated from the competition, the boy lets out a very sad "yeehaw" and waves to the group before he's led away by a production assistant.

If my time on this show is ever cut short, I can only hope my exit is that iconic.

Despite the weird introductions with Alli and Finn, and the whiplash of these last few minutes, I'm practically giddy. It's not something I've felt much in recent months, and makes me think once and for all that coming here was a good idea. Even if I don't win the money in the end, this feeling . . . it's still worth something. Obviously I can't pay for college with good vibes, but they certainly don't hurt.

My cheeks *do* hurt from wrangling the massively toothy smile that wants to take over my face into a tame, closed-mouthed grin. After another break during which a PA dabs some powder onto Burke's nose and forehead—I wonder what brand, and if it's actually bronzer because how would they find foundation in that shade, and how it isn't melting off his face in the slightest—the cameras start rolling again.

"Co-EdVenturers," Burke calls out, voice echoing off the tall trees surrounding us. "It's my honor to welcome you all to this special season of *Wild Adventures,* taking place on the world-famous Appalachian Trail. As the longest hiking-only footpath in the world, the trail you've all started walking today runs over two thousand miles through fourteen states from Georgia to Maine. Each year, hundreds of intrepid outdoorspeople make the entire trek and join the two-thousand-miler club. But doing so takes the average hiker anywhere from five to seven *months.*"

At his pause and subsequent wide-eyed look he sweeps across the group, there's a quiet chorus of nervous laughter.

"Don't worry—we don't have the filming budget for that." Burke is met with more genuine, relieved amusement this time. "So in order to give you all the most impactful—if condensed— experience on your AT adventure, we've dropped you in the middle of the action. Right now, we're about one hundred and seventy miles from the AT's southern terminus, just within the boundaries of another of America's natural treasures, Great Smoky Mountains National Park. The park service has graciously allowed us to utilize this stunning segment of the trail for the duration of your adventure. It's all of our hope that while racing and competing, you will also be able to enjoy the nature and history of both the AT and the Smokies.

"All of us at *Wild Adventures* are very excited to have you, and I'm sure you're even more excited to get started. So without further ado, let's do just that! We'll begin by pairing off into teams, or finding your *co*-Co-EdVenturer."

Burke shoots us a cheeky wink, and I'm one of a handful who laugh at the quip. Alli and Finn are not among us.

"In the woods surrounding you, we've hidden backpacking packs, each containing a different selection of top-of-the-line camping gear and other tools for survival. These packs will be yours to keep. Each pack is marked with a luggage tag, which will match the tag on one other pack. The person with a tag matching yours will become your partner. You're welcome to look at what's in each pack and shop around, but I'd advise you to pick one as soon as possible and return here. There are sixteen of you and only fifteen packs out there. The sixteenth contestant will receive their pack at the next checkpoint tomorrow, so one team will only have half their selection of gear for the night. Are there any questions?"

Yes, I think. *Is my voice going to sound two octaves lower on TV too?*

All of us look from Burke to each other. I feel my palms start to sweat and wipe them on my leggings.

"All right, you may leave your things here while you search for your new packs." At this, we all remove whatever possessions we have on our person. I drop my small day pack to the ground. Buff Guy tosses his beside it, shooting me a quick grin before he starts bouncing on the balls of his feet. Alli bends her knees, setting one foot in front of the other like she's at the starting line of a sprint. I don't know what else to do, so I reach up to tighten my bun.

Finally, Burke brings his hands together, looking us all over with a smirk as he announces, "Ready . . . set . . . *adventure!*"

The group scatters in all directions, racing into the forest around us like the ground in the clearing is lava. I run to the first opening I see, not paying any real mind to the humans around me, only focused on finding a backpack. I imagine this is how Katniss felt as she ran for her life in the Hunger Games, ignoring the fact that my fellow adventurers aren't trying to kill me. As far as I know.

I scan my surroundings as I jog, ducking under outstretched branches and dodging overgrown bushes full of thorns. It isn't long before I spot it—a flash of bright blue between two trees.

That has to be a pack, doesn't it? I jog faster, though I'm pretty sure there's no one else around to get to it first, and adrenaline surges in my veins. I am so totally getting a pack today, just a few yards ahead now, and—

"*Oof!*" The involuntary sound escapes me as I trip over something and go crashing to the ground, landing on my hands and knees. But when I look down, there's no rock or protruding tree root, or anything but flat dirt. And when I look up again, I see the back of Alli's yellow tank top.

I gasp, a little breathless from the fall. "Did you . . . just . . . trip me?" I pant-yell, a thing I don't recall doing before in my life.

Alli swings the bright blue pack up onto her shoulder before turning my way with a look of completely faked innocence. "What? I would never!" she says in a high-pitched trill. I've seen enough shitty acting in my life to know better.

There's a rustling nearby and I turn to see a camera person emerge from behind a tree. If only they'd arrived a few seconds earlier, I could dramatically yell, "Roll the tape!"

But they didn't, so I can't, and Alli is still playing a mediocre harmless bystander.

"Okay, sure," I huff, knowing this is probably not the battle to pick on day one. "I'll go find another pack, then."

I'm about to push up to my feet when a hand appears in front of my face. My gaze travels up, and I see short, strawberry blond curls framing a freckle-covered face. A face I remember from the group gathered at the checkpoint. Her mouth is a flat, slightly impatient line, but her eyes hold too much sympathy for someone planning to kick me while I'm down, so I accept her help in standing.

"Thanks," I say, brushing dirt from my knees. I expect the other girl to run off, then realize she's already wearing a pack. Of course. Must be nice!

"Watch your step this time!" Alli's voice is as cloying as her fake smile when she jogs past us, back toward the clearing.

That's it. Her name is now Enemi.

With an *i*.

"That was ugly." The girl who helped me up speaks for the first time, a soft, familiar Southern lilt to the words. While I know she's probably referring to my fall, I'd like to think she means Alli's behavior. My grandma in Tennessee, Starla Lee Hart, loved to describe people as "acting ugly." Someone cut her in the Food City checkout line? They were acting ugly. The girl in first grade who told me my stuffed bear I brought for show-and-tell was for babies? She was acting ugly. Tennessee politicians? Usually acting ugly.

"You okay?" my helper asks, and it's only when I meet her eyes that I realize a sheen of tears is forming in mine. I know it's not from the fall, either—it's the potential of failure looming closer and closer, the thoughts of Granny Star, *everything*.

I force a smile, blinking away the evidence of anything but badass resilience. "All good! Thank you! I should probably, ah—"

I gesture a bit maniacally, indicating the woods all around us, and she nods and backs away, offering a short "good luck" as she goes. It's not the most enthusiastic delivery, but it's still the nicest anyone's been to me since Ethel with the hard candies. I should've checked her pack's luggage tag so I can try to find myself its match and lock down a partner who didn't seem to hate me on sight. As if I have any time to be choosy by now.

Frustration and my long-dormant competitive side, the latter of which I've tried to bury since it got me kicked out of intramural volleyball in high school for unsportsmanlike conduct, are what fuel me to keep looking for this damn pack. I pass three more people already heading toward the clearing with packs on their backs, and my hope sinks a little each time. But there are still others out here looking, which means there are still some to be found.

In the end, it isn't the color of the backpack that gets my attention, but the sunlight glinting off a shiny metal zipper. I probably wouldn't have seen it otherwise, as my brain was filtering the vicinity for "things that aren't green." This pack, which I pull from where it's half hidden behind a mossy boulder, is a very similar shade of Emerald City to its surrounding landscape, and the victorious laugh I let out as I sling it across one shoulder sounds fittingly Elphaba, post-*Wicked* transformation.

"Defying Gravity" would be an appropriate theme song for the ordeal of me wrestling my new luggage onto my shoulders for the first time, but I eventually get the monstrosity settled without toppling over. I start an ambitious jog in the direction of all the voices, but quickly find that a speed-walk is as much as I can manage with a big-ass backpack. What am I trying to prove, anyway? I already got the goods, and there's no reward for getting back to the clearing sooner.

When I emerge into the open space, all the Co-EdVenturers

who already have their packs are milling around in a cluster, humming like a swarm of bees as they compare luggage tags.

"Red and green plaid?"

"Red and green plaid!"

Two new teammates hold their tags toward each other in one hand while high-fiving with the other. A shiver runs down my spine as it hits me that I'm about to find out who I'm sharing this experience with—who I'm going to have to count on to help me win the money.

I swing my pack around to my front and find the luggage tag looped through its top handle. One side is plain white, but when I flip it over, I let out a happy squeak. Dark purple background with lighter purple polka dots. This has to be a good omen, right?

Unless Enemi has a purple polka-dotted tag, in which case I might have to try my luck at running back into the woods for a new bag.

"Yes!" The excited shout draws my attention and I look over to find the nemesis herself jumping in place and fist bumping the muscular guy.

"Dream team," he says back, and I feel my lip starting to curl up into something snarly before I force it back to a neutral line. Good luck to 'em.

I push farther toward the middle of the fray, which has grown by a couple more people since I returned.

"Anyone have purple polka dots?" I project in outdoor-performance-without-a-sound-system volume.

There are some murmurs in the negative as others call out

their patterns, and I assume my partner hasn't made it back yet. Not a great sign if they're struggling with the very first challenge of the whole competition. But I can be patient and understanding, maybe pull more than my weight if I have to, especially if my teammate is on the nice side of hapless.

But when a voice emerges from just over my shoulder, it's anything but nice, gruffly muttering, "You've got to be kidding."

Chapter Three

I whirl around to face Finn, whose eyes are trained on the luggage tag in my hands. Another quiet but definitely displeased rumble comes out as he lets his eyes fall closed.

"Did . . . did you just *growl* at me?" I ask with a disbelieving laugh as I set my free hand on my hip.

His expression stays stony as his eyes blink open. "We're teammates."

"Yeah, I gathered that from context clues and upset animal noises. Why is that such a problem for you?"

He sighs as if *I'm* the one acting like a nonverbal toddler here. "It's not. I just . . ."

"Think girls have cooties," I supply at the same time he says, "Don't think we're a good match."

I nod in mock understanding. "Because of the cooties."

Finn's face somehow gets even more stern. "Come on, let's be adults about this. You can't tell me you think we'll be compatible as teammates."

Whatever fragile hope I had left—of pairing with a partner who'd become my friend, making this experience a departure from the series of letdowns in my life recently, having some *fun*—shatters in my chest. But just as quickly, I imagine sweeping away the broken pieces. Using them to construct something new and stronger, a wall of stubborn positivity. His bad attitude isn't gonna be contagious.

"What I can tell you, Finn, is I don't know you, and you sure as hell don't know me. Some of us reserve judgment—or at least keep the growling to ourselves—until that's no longer the case."

No need for him to know my recent uncharitable thoughts about Enemi. But she was uncharitable to me first! What is with these people?

Finn runs a hand down his face and blows out a tired breath. "Right. Well, that's that, then."

He turns and walks off toward the spot where he left his stuff earlier, presumably to start transferring it to his new pack. I stay where I am, marveling at his ability to use five one-syllable words in a row to say nothing at all.

My irritation from earlier returns. I wish it was only anger that I felt. Anger I can deal with. But the buzzing in my body and mind intensifies, leaning more toward the anxious kind than the excited. It's like a stage light that won't stop flickering, growing harder to ignore the longer I try to pretend nothing is wrong. No matter what I do, I can't shake it off completely.

The anxiety is not new to me, but the label is. I'd felt almost cheated when I finally worked up the nerve to go to student health services to get checked out. The physical symptoms had been building up bit by bit since shortly after I started at Oliver—hands shaking too much to take notes with pen and paper, migraines and stomachaches taking me out of commission for entire days. I didn't connect them to the racing thoughts, these worries and fears and what-ifs on constant loop in my mind, up until the doctor was handing me a brochure about generalized anxiety disorder and advising me on finding a therapist. *You mean this is all in my head?* I'd wanted to shout. I didn't have time to deal with it, not with classes, homework, my part-time job at Body Wonderland that seemed to take up every free hour but that I desperately needed for money. I'm independent, strong, and capable, and have always handled my own shit. So I taught myself meditation and yoga with YouTube videos in my cramped dorm room, loaded up on essential oils for relieving stress and helping sleep with my Body Wonderland employee discount, and mainlined romance novels like they're water to get me out of my own head.

Sometimes it even worked.

School didn't get any better, to the point that I lost my biggest merit scholarship when I didn't make the GPA requirement, but that doesn't mean it never will. I haven't told anyone about my biggest reason for being here—my dire financial straits and how they got that way in the first place. As far as Reese and our other best friend, Clara, know, this is cool, fun Natalie, embarking on a cool, fun adventure to cap off an easy-breezy freshman year. To my parents, it's just another dumb decision in a long line of them on my part.

I still have hope that I can figure this condition out, master the never-ending buzzing and quiet the thought spirals, become kick-ass, in-control Natalie again. And I absolutely have to do it while I'm on *Wild Adventures*.

I don't know what the alternative is.

"Co-EdVenturers!" Burke Forrester's voice calls out, and I jump at the intrusion on my wandering thoughts. "Have we all found our teammates?"

Blowing out a shaky breath, I walk toward my day pack, knowing at least what I need to do in this moment. I unzip the top pocket and reach for my makeup bag, dipping both my hands inside so I can discreetly rub a lavender rollerball onto my wrists before closing it back up and transferring it to my new pack, starting to do the same with the rest of my belongings. While I'm at it, I bring one wrist up as if to scratch my nose, but really, I'm taking a deep inhale, followed by a long exhale and repeat. I'm calm. I'm unflappable. I'm in control.

Not of other people and how they'll treat me, of course, but I can control how I react to them. I don't have to get upset or hurt or let Finn or Enemi ruin my experience before it's even started. I've got this.

"Co-EdVenturers!" Burke Forrester calls out, nearly making me drop the pile of my clean, unfolded underwear I'm repacking. "If all the teams want to circle up over here, you'll each receive a map that will take you to your first challenge!"

I hurriedly finish the repacking job and swing my now even heavier new pack onto my shoulders before making my way to the group. I sidle up to Finn and bump him with my hip, my effort at a gesture of "Yeah, you're being a dick to me, but I can be the bigger, friendlier person, bitch." Unfortunately, he is the literal bigger person, so my hip hits him in the thigh. And since he was looking straight ahead and trying to pretend I don't exist, it catches him off guard and he jumps away as if dodging a fatal blow. Is he a theater major too? Because the drama is unmatched.

"Seriously? It was a hip bump, not a crotch grope," I whisper through clenched teeth as the other teams start to fill in around us. Cameras are capturing the whole thing, but I hope there's enough other activity and chatter going on for us to avoid drawing much notice.

Not for his lack of trying.

He gives me a withering look, but his cheeks seem a shade pinker as he inches back toward his spot beside me. Is this a step in the right direction? Flustering him into speechlessness?

I don't have time to consider it further before Burke Forrester is clapping his hands and speaking again. "All right, great job, everyone! So good to see our new teams find each other and really get this adventure going. Meena, it appears that you were unable to find a pack before they were all taken, meaning you and Cammie are working with half the supplies as everyone else tonight. But by no means should you count yourselves out! Today's challenge will test all of your abilities to work with your new teammate, relying solely on each other to survive your first night in the wild."

He scans our group with the cool self-assuredness of someone who knows he's spending the night with a bed and indoor plumbing. "One of the most exciting parts of *Wild Co-EdVentures* is its unpredictability. Having all the right supplies

tonight doesn't mean anything, for example, if neither team-mate knows how to use them. We've brought you all together as strangers, so I now urge you to do everything you can to get to know your partner, their strengths and weaknesses, and how those mesh with your own, in order to be most successful going forward. There's no time to waste. With that said, are we ready for your first team challenge?"

There's a chorus of *woos* and *yeahs*, and I cheer with them. At my side, Finn nods silently.

Burke grins. "That's what I like to hear. In just a moment, I'll hand out the maps for your first leg. These will get you to your team's backcountry campsite, where further instructions for the night await. If you successfully complete your tasks and make it through the night, your team will receive a map to the next checkpoint. The last team to arrive at the checkpoint will be eliminated. Any questions?"

When the only answer he gets is the ambient sounds of the forest, Burke pulls a stack of envelopes from the inside of his puffer vest. "All right, then. I have your maps here." He pauses, smirking. "What are you waiting for? Come and get 'em. Ready, set, *adventure!*"

"WHAT DO YOU think about Team Finnatalie?"

While the question is meant for Finn, I pose it to the camera and our future viewers with a wide, open-mouthed smile, wav-ing the fingers of my free hand around jazz hands–style. I'm walking through the woods behind my teammate, who holds the map we were given to our first campsite and seems to be looking down at it every thirty seconds or so, even though we're walking most of the way on the clearly marked main trail.

"Team names don't matter. No one uses them," says Bad Mood Becky up there.

I give the camera a good-natured—as far as I want viewers to know, anyway—eye roll. "Viewers use them! People will hashtag it and stuff as they watch." I gasp as something occurs to me. "Our fans can call themselves *Finnatalics*!"

There's a beat of silence as Finn takes in this stroke of genius, and I turn the camera forward to watch the back of his head for a while. This is the view it's been getting from its holster on my new pack for most of the hike, as our cameras are supposed to stay rolling from when we wake up until we go to sleep, except for our allotted ten minutes per hour of privacy when we get to shut them off. I'm glad the holsters exist, so it's not entirely on us to be amateur cinematographers. But it's also quickly become clear that if I want any footage of myself on the trail, I can't count on Finn's backpack cam to capture it.

"Why not just . . . Finnatics?" he asks, and I can hear the reluctance to engage with me in his voice.

I smile to myself. *Wearing him down already!* "Because, *Finn,* that's already a word and also it only noticeably uses your name. I'm not even part of the picture anymore."

"Wouldn't that be unfortunate," he murmurs almost too softly for me to hear.

Oookay, not worn down. "That's it," I sigh frustratedly, fitting the camera back into its home at my shoulder. I briefly wonder if I should be using my off-camera ten minutes, but find I'm too irritated to care whether I'm about to make myself The Drama of this episode. "First Team Finnatalie meeting commencing now."

Finn glances at me warily over his shoulder. "I didn't agree to that name."

"It was an executive decision." I wave the statement away.

"Oh, are you the executive of this team?"

"I don't know, Finn, is a fake important title what it would take for you to give me an ounce of kindness?"

Shocking my sweat-wicking socks off, he stops, then turns around, looking more confused than chastened. "I haven't been unkind."

That gets a laugh out of me. "I don't think there's a kind way to tell someone you think they're gonna be a shitty teammate."

He takes a step in my direction. "Hey, I didn't say you'd be—"

"Oh, I'm sorry, an *incompatible* one."

"Well, do you really disagree?" He's stepped in again, and I have too, and we're so close I'm surprised I can't feel the steam coming out of his ears, nose, probably eye sockets too. I notice, entirely against my will, that his eyes are a deep, dark chocolatey brown.

I throw my hands out to my sides, trying to hold on to my ire. "I don't know! I guess on principle, I'm incompatible with anyone who dislikes me so quickly for no reason. Tell me, who *would* you consider a compatible teammate?"

His frown intensifies and he crosses his arms over his chest.

"I don't know!" he echoes me. "Someone more . . . serious about being here."

The words land like a gut punch. I mean, I knew. I'm aware that's how people perceive me a lot of the time. But he doesn't have a clue how much being here means to me, how much I have riding on it. And I shouldn't have to tell him just to prove I'm "serious" enough.

My face must show the way the insult hit, because Finn seems to deflate a little. He brings his fingers up to the wrinkled lines of his forehead and massages. "We're wasting time." Right as he says it, I hear softly tromping footsteps approach, and a team of two guys passes us, giving awkward, no-hard-feelings-but-we're-passing-you smiles as they go. All the teams have slightly different off-trail destinations on our maps, and while we left the first checkpoint at the same time, we've naturally spread out while hiking at different speeds. Due to my partner's, ahem, tenacity, our team has stayed ahead of most others. Finn is clearly itching to get a move on and keep that lead, but he waits until the others are out of earshot to continue more quietly, "I don't dislike you. Can we just find our way to the challenge, please?"

I want to spit, but instead I push past him and walk onward, snatching the map from his hands as I go. "I don't know about you, but I feel like I'm knee-deep in a challenge already," I mutter.

We don't speak for a while after that. Still, I barely have time to say friendly hellos to the other hikers we pass, going both directions, even though I want to stop and ask everyone how much of the trail they've done, where they're from, and how they got here—you know, the basics. Finn is keeping a punishing pace, and we're not exactly on level ground. I can feel my feet shifting in their new trappings, all-important sweat-wicking socks and ankle-stabilizing hiking boots that cost most of my last paycheck. The sales guy assured me these were the most comfortable and secure option on the market, and when I tried them on and walked up and down the store's fake mountain incline, I believed him. But I've owned enough shoes in my life to know that no matter how comfy, most need breaking in—which I didn't have time for. Hopefully somewhere in my fancy new pack there are Band-Aids.

I try to just push forward, not letting Finn get too far ahead of me. Lest he think I'm not taking the whole walking thing *seriously*. It isn't easy, though, and I'm breathing heavily by the time we come upon a stunning overlook.

"Holy . . ." I pant out as I stumble to a stop, unsure what kind of blasphemy is worthy of this view. A few yards ahead, Finn pauses to take a look, too. I feel him glance my way while I continue to look out over the rolling ridges and mountains spread out before us, everything green and tree-covered as far as the eye can see.

A sense of awe I don't often feel sweeps over me. It's reminiscent of my first time seeing a stage show—the first time I can remember, at least, though I know Granny Star took me even before then. We sat in the very back, deep in the shadows where we couldn't possibly have been seen from the stage, but it felt like the performers were singing and acting their hearts out just for me. It's like I knew right then, in my too-earnest, too-hopeful little preschooler heart, that my life would never be the same.

I don't think this is the day I change my entire life path to be a naturalist or anything like that. But I feel the awe. The *Oh, shit, has this all been here all along? Just waiting for me to find it?* The sense of witnessing something so much greater than myself, and understanding that it can change everything for me, if I let it.

Of course, it also makes me think of my grandma. Yet again. What is this, the sixth time today? That's about five more than I'll normally allow. My Granny Star moments are usually limited to when I see my tattoo in the mirror—the one on my ribs that I got in an impulsive moment the summer after she died, with a shitty fake ID so my parents never had to know. It's an outline of a star and a heart interlocked, like she drew at the end of her signature. The brief physical pain of getting it was a welcome distraction from the deep, lingering emotional wound. The one that, if I'm honest with myself, has never really healed.

Which is why I try my damnedest to ignore it. But I should've known that would be hard to do, from the moment I learned we'd be in the Smokies on the AT. Not exactly in her hometown, but awfully close. It doesn't take a psychologist to anticipate this might dredge some shit up. My eyes struggle not to water against wind and emotion, but it's my partner's gruff voice that pulls me out of my feelings.

"You need water," Finn says. It isn't a question, and when I think about it for a moment, I realize he's not wrong.

"Do we have that?" My voice is embarrassingly breathless.

I mean, I shouldn't be embarrassed—I've been half running up a mountain. If only my teammate didn't sound cool as can be.

When I look at him, he's already lowered his pack to the ground and started digging through it. I take a few steps closer and he pulls out a metal water bottle, immediately passing it over to me. The heft of it tells me it's full, and when I crack it open and take a sip, it's amazingly, magically cold.

I finish a long series of gulps with a gasp. "*God,* that's good. Did they put a little something extra in there?"

Finn gives me a dry look, and I think he could use a sip of the good stuff too. "No. You're just dehydrated, and probably need food. Here."

I try not to let my surprise show at all this . . . caregiving. Maybe he just doesn't want to be held responsible if I fall off a mountain or something. After a little more rustling in his pack, he hands over a pouch of trail mix.

"Wow," I say as I accept it. "How on-brand."

He grunts. "Hurry up and eat so we can keep going."

Well, the caregiving was nice while it lasted. While I munch on clusters of nuts, dried berries, and M&M's, Finn extracts his own snack, a protein bar, then shuffles some things around in his pack before closing it up and shouldering it on. He backs away from the view to go stand on the trail again. Giving off such patient vibes. Such subtlety.

Only the trees can see my eye roll while I finish my snack and drink more water, and afterward, I'm significantly re-energized. Annoying that he was right.

Walking up beside him, I hold out the bottle like a stainless steel olive branch. "Thank you. I did need that," I admit. He only turns and stomps back down the trail, which I guess I prefer to a smug I-told-you-so.

I have no concept of distance or time after that, my thoughts meandering far more than the path. We only stop once more, when it begins to drizzle a little and I want to dig out my rain jacket from the depths of my pack. But after working up such a sweat earlier, I realize the feeling of the rain on my skin is more refreshing than I expected, and I end up carrying my jacket in my hands in case it starts to pour harder.

I take in all the trees and wildflowers around me, their leaves and petals sparkling with raindrops, and wish I knew enough about plants to identify any of them. My fingers itch to do a Google search and any number of other time-wasting things on my phone, but it's locked away in a production van somewhere. In exchange for our personal devices, which would be useless in a lot of remote areas with no service anyway, we got the classic *Wild Adventures* satellite phones. They look like a sturdier version of a toy cell phone I had as a kid, a brick of hard plastic with only a few buttons and a chunky antenna. One number can be used to speak to a producer in an emergency, one will send them our exact GPS location, and I assume the others are there because they don't make phones with only two buttons. I hope I never need to use this thing in an emergency, and maybe more importantly, that Finn doesn't need to on my behalf.

That cheery thought is interrupted by the man in question pointing off the trail to the right. "I think that's the marking where we turn and go northeast three hundred paces."

He holds the map up to show me the small red flag drawn on it, and the similar red flag hanging from a tree branch beside the trail.

"Looks legit to me," I agree, glancing briefly toward the brightening sky above. The rain is tapering off, which feels like such convenient timing, I'd swear the *Wild Adventures* producers could control weather patterns.

Feeling like I'm acting out a goofy pirate treasure hunt scene, I count my "paces" behind Finn, who I scarcely hear counting his under his breath. When I haven't quite reached three hundred, he stops abruptly. I walk straight into his back.

"Ouch," I whine, rubbing at my forehead where it hit his pack. I'll probably have the imprint of a zipper scarred onto me. Finn doesn't even seem to hear, though, before he's walking into a clearing where an orange envelope hangs from a tree.

Everyone's map is taking them to a different spot off the main trail, where I imagine they'll find their own orange envelopes with further instructions. Excitement hitting me, I skip forward to Finn's side as he plucks ours from the low branch, and I pull out my GoPro again to make sure I'm getting good footage of our envelope-opening.

"We found the campsite!" I cheer, pointing the camera at the envelope, then doing a quick sweep of the clearing around us. I use the hand not filming to help my pack slide down off my shoulders onto the ground. Immediately, my body feels two feet taller, like I can stand to my full height again unencumbered. I also feel forty pounds lighter, for obvious reasons. I wouldn't be surprised to open that thing up and find a bunch of bricks.

Finn pulls a piece of paper from the envelope and his eyes track over it, reading silently until I clear my throat and look pointedly at the camera I have trained on him. He grimaces— clearly the camera/filming part of this whole deal is an after- thought for him, as is the fact that he has a partner who wants to know what we're doing—but then reads aloud.

"'Challenge One: Fire, Food, and Friendship. Co- EdVenturers, today you'll try your hand at the basics of Appala- chian Trail life while learning to work with your new teammate. To survive on the trail . . . yeah yeah, enough provisions, safe camp cooking . . .'" He mumbles the last part, trailing off as his eyes dart farther down the page.

I clear my throat. "Whole thing, out loud please. Skip noth- ing."

He gives me a quick, narrow-eyed glower, but his gaze jumps back up to the top and he resumes reading. "'To survive on the trail, hikers must put careful thought into what they pack. They need enough food and other provisions to get by, but not so much as to put excessive strain on their bodies when carrying it. We've given you a randomly allocated set of provisions in each pack. Using what you have and what you're able to source from your natural surroundings, you and your partner will need to complete the following tasks: One, build a fire in your camp- site's firepit. Two, prepare a dinner out of the food supplied to you. Three, clean your food prep area and dispose of trash safely and appropriately. Four, build a shelter that will protect both team members from the elements overnight.

"'You may want to sit down with your partner and assess

your provisions before you begin, working together to complete the tasks as best you can while making note of what you are lacking. At the next checkpoint, you will get the chance to barter supplies with other teams and offload anything you feel you don't need. You will also be able to "shop" our *Wild Co-EdVentures* food stores and restock on food at every checkpoint.

" 'As you work through these tasks, spend some time getting to know your teammate. Your team bond will directly impact your performance on *Wild Co-EdVentures*, as you must rely on each other to survive and thrive. Do not waste any opportunity to nurture this important relationship. If your footage from tonight shows you have successfully completed all tasks, a crew will be by in the morning to deliver your go time and your map to the next checkpoint. Good luck!' "

I just imagine the last part was written with an exclamation point; Finn gives it no inflection to suggest as much.

"Woo, here we go! Fire, food, and friendship, three of my favorite *f*s around. Along with *Finn,* of course!" I turn the camera on myself with an exaggerated grin. "What do you say, partner? Should we see what's in these packs?"

I unzip my pack's top pocket and feel around it for the small, flexible tripod they gave each of us for filming when we're not hiking. With that in hand, I begin circling the clearing until I find a level-ish, clear-ish spot on the ground, then mount the camera there.

When I turn back to grab the rest of my stuff, Finn is gingerly removing his own pack, watching me as skeptically as ever. "You're really into the camera stuff."

I blink up at him. "You mean the filming for the show that's our entire reason for being here?" I shrug, finding a nice log in the middle of the campsite and dragging my pack that way so I can sit down and sort through it. "I guess I am. Someone's got to be, right? You can always tell as the viewer when teams aren't really into being on camera. They're just not as fun to watch. Haven't you ever seen *Wild Adventures*?"

He moves to sit a few feet away, dragging his pack there too. "Of course I have. I guess I just care more about the challenges than all the extra stuff, explaining what I'm doing, making one-sided small talk with a lens. It feels awkward filming myself."

"For me, it's all the extra stuff that helps me get to know a team and makes me want to root for them to win challenges. If, you know, they're doing more than just throwing moody looks at the camera."

He throws one of said moody looks my way before yanking open the top zipper on his pack and starting to pull things out. I do the same, and over the next few minutes, we arrange everything aside from our clothes and toiletries on the ground in front of us. And damn, can they fit a lot into two backpacks. The ache in my back worsens just from looking at all that I've been carrying the whole day without realizing it.

Between us, we could fill a pantry with dehydrated meals, protein bars, and packets of granola and trail mix. There's this rubber bag-and-tube contraption that Finn explains is a water filtration system, and two water bottles, one of which I've already half emptied. I remember a piece in the orientation materials about staying hydrated and not rationing water more than necessary, as production staff can change out your empty water bottles for full ones at each checkpoint or be paged from the sat phones to bring water in an emergency. There's bear spray, an airtight bear canister to hold our food and anything with a scent that could draw animals, two sleeping bags, one sleeping pad—another thing Finn had to explain, but is apparently like a mini air mattress—a hammock, a multitool, a tiny gas stove that we can use when we haven't been explicitly instructed to cook our food over a campfire, matches, toilet paper, plastic bags, Band-Aids, hand sanitizer, and more. To me, an inexperienced camper, it seems like we have just about all we could need. But . . .

"There's only one tent," Finn says, echoing the thought that just occurred to me. It was in his pack. Somehow, this feels like a shortcoming on my part, like I should have randomly selected a better equipped backpack. But what can I do about it now?

"Guess we'll have to get cozy," I answer, trying to sound optimistic even as it becomes more difficult with each minute I spend with this guy.

He stands and starts to walk away, but not far enough that I don't hear his quiet groan.

Chapter Four

"Are you sure there isn't *anything* else I can do?" I ask, fiddling with Finn's GoPro tripod.

"Not unless you have a time machine that can take us back to get packs with fire starters inside." He's crouched on all fours, carefully rearranging the sticks he's already arranged in three barely differing configurations, as if *this* is the particular twig tower that's finally going to ignite. He might actually know what he's doing, but I wouldn't know. Because much like how he won't let me help, he won't tell me anything that I don't drag out of him like I'm pulling teeth.

"You sure I can't take a crack at the tent?"

Finn shakes his head before I've finished voicing the question, eyes still trained on the fire. "We only have the one. Can't risk messing it up or breaking something."

I want to point out—again—that I'm a grown-ass nineteen year-old. Not a fumbling, incompetent kid. I can read setup instructions.

But honestly, I'm too tired to fight any more today. He wants to treat me like I'm useless? Guess it's just as well that I act like it. I can pick up my independent woman torch again tomorrow. Use it to set Finn on fire.

Maybe he would actually ignite, unlike everything else around here. Apparently it rained more than I realized from my pleasant stroll through the sprinkly mist. Or perhaps there was a single storm cloud hanging over our campsite in particular, dumping buckets of water onto everything as a fun little surprise for Team Finnatalie's first evening together. Whatever the reason, all our potential "kindling"—twigs, leaves, anything else flammable from the forest floor—is just soggy enough to give Finn a hell of a time trying to make it burn.

This wouldn't be so much of a problem if either of our packs had come with fire starters, or the fuel bottle needed to make our camp stove work, or even just more than one book of matches. I've heard Finn grumble about it roughly thirty-six different ways, because "in what world is that enough for weeks of backpacking?"

I feel useless, sitting here doing nothing, and wonder why I'm even letting him tell me what to do (which is nothing). I don't look his way as I head into the trees. "I'm gonna see if I can find any dry wood."

If he can hear me over his own muttering, he doesn't answer.

As I wander, I remember watching my dad make fires in our old wood stove when I was little, though he bought firewood and starter bricks at the gas station. I've seen campfires built on TV, read about it in books. Actually . . .

Stopping in my tracks, I squint up at the sky and mentally scroll back through my recent-ish library checkouts. It was a romance novel I read—I mean, no surprise—a romantic suspense, about a woman on the run from a hitman. I don't remember how or why she ended up in those unfortunate circumstances, but I do remember thinking that if I were her, I would've run to, say, an inconspicuous yet comfortable hotel somewhere, instead of into the mountains with little more than the clothes on my back.

But I digress. The point is, girlfriend was more of a camper than me to begin with, but she was also creative, and figured out all kinds of little tricks to get by in the wild. It wasn't too long before she stumbled upon a ranger station, and the sexy outdoorsman on duty ended up helping her outwit and survive the bad guys while they also fell into mad, passionate love. But she totally could have saved herself, too! And her ingenuity is now going to help me, Natalie Hart, build the best damn campfire these woods have ever seen.

Newly inspired, I focus on looking for spots shaded by boulders or brush, where there might be wood I can use that's been protected from the rain. It takes a while, but I get a decent armful of twigs and small branches. I also collect a clump of moss and dead, leafy things before heading back to the clearing.

Finn sits atop his folded-up poncho on the ground beside the campsite's metal fire ring, looking especially sulky as he stares at his sad, damp twig pile. His head darts up at my return and the skepticism written plain as day across his face only strengthens my resolve. *He'll see.*

"We're not going to start a fire using more of the same stuff," he says, making no effort to hide his annoyance.

"Not as dumb as I look!" I trill, sugary sweet.

"I never said you look—"

"Didn't have to. And you're not making any progress on your own, so why don't you let me give it a go." My voice this time is as hard as my expression when I glance his way, warning him to quit while he's not at all ahead. I crouch by the fire ring and drop my burnable bounty beside it, then make a move toward my pack, where my secret weapons await.

"Feel free to give me a little space," I call without looking at Finn. "I think wet blankets are more helpful in putting out fires than getting them going."

When I turn back toward the ring with my makeup bag in hand, he's standing a couple feet back, arms now crossed and a frown creasing his face. "What are you doing?"

I revert to extra-cheery mode. You know, for the Finnatalics. "I'm so glad you asked! I'm gonna show y'all a little trick for starting a fire in less-than-ideal conditions." I face one of our GoPros and wave one hand to indicate our recently rained-on surroundings before dropping to my haunches and unzipping my bag. "This is something I learned from a book, actually. *Hot on Her Trail* by . . . hmm, who was it?"

I pull out a few of the cotton pads I use for eye makeup removal, along with a tube of cheap lip balm I only use in dire chapped-lip emergencies. It's about to get sacrificed for the greater good—proving Finn wrong about me, whether we complete the challenge or not—but I'm not sad to lose it.

Not like anyone's gonna be testing the softness of my lips out here.

"Donna . . . something was the author, I think. But it has a guy wearing a Forest Service hat and no shirt on the cover—really steamy." I fan myself and wiggle my eyebrows at the camera, not letting myself look over for Finn's reaction before returning to my task and uncapping the lip balm. "But the heroine has to go on her own kind of wild adventure, camping and surviving in the outdoors for a few days before she meets the hero. And when she has to start a fire with a bunch of damp wood, she whips out her lip balm . . ."

I roll the tube all the way up before breaking off the waxy balm in my hand and setting the plastic part aside to throw away later. I hear Finn's sharp intake of breath and have to peek, pleased to see he's watching with rapt attention rather than doubt.

"And she tears off a piece of her cotton T-shirt for this part, but I don't know, I'm kind of attached to all the clothes I have with me. So I'm gonna try these cotton pads."

I continue to narrate as I work the balm into the cotton with my fingers, embracing the absolute gooey mess of it all, then clean my hands with a wet wipe. When I strike a match and bring it to the little pile of ChapStick-covered cotton, just as advertised in the book, it ignites easily and doesn't burn out right away. I have enough time to work with it, adding the moss and other small forest detritus for tinder, blowing softly to help the flames along, and soon starting to build a cone of twigs— definitely drier than the ones Finn found—over the burning bundle. When the fire spreads and keeps burning, I let out the breath I've been holding since Finn uttered the words "someone more serious."

I have to pay close attention to the fire and add more wood as needed for a while, but once it's really going, I let an antsy Finn step back in.

"Here we go," he mumbles to himself as he pulls the fire ring's attached grate over the flames. I resume my place as a bump on a log, the useless feeling from before replaced with smugness. But that only lasts so long, as I realize no "Sorry I doubted you" or "Good job, you secret survivalist queen" is forthcoming. Finn just moves on down the task list as though I didn't change the whole trajectory of our evening with my ingenuity, setting the pot from our camp stove atop the grate and pouring some water in. Once it's boiling, he opens two pouches of dehydrated vegetable soup and pours them in.

So inevitably, as he goes on closely monitoring our dinner and stirring it occasionally with a reusable spork from my pack, I find myself wondering whether what I did was all that ingenious. Maybe I'm just used to sucking at life as of late, so achieving the smallest thing feels monumental. If my partner's reaction is anything to go by, nobody else sees starting a lip balm fire as akin to discovering electricity.

When Finn says—again mumbling, again to himself—that our soup is about ready, I take it upon myself to bring over a couple of mugs for him to pour it into. Their appearance surprises him, he was so in the zone of Big Man Tend Fire Cook Food Pound Chest. But at least he says thank you this time.

We mostly eat in silence, except for when I give a brief, mostly false review to the camera about how delicious the soup Finn made is. We have some granola for a second course-slash-dessert, which is a stark example of what a turn my life has taken. I offer to clean up, but he feels the need to run that operation too, Finnsplaining about "leave no trace" principles and being aware of what scents and food remnants we're leaving for wildlife to find. Which, okay, are worthy and important things to share. But I don't have to like his tone.

By the time the sun is going down, I am fully over it. Over him. And more than anything, over the combination of time alone with my thoughts and together with all of Finn's, both of which have my anxiety rearing its neurotic little head.

"Can I go to the bathroom alone, or do you need to micromanage that too?" I finally snap, just as he's attaching the last hook from the tent wall to its corresponding pole.

Finn blinks over at me, his cheeks going pink as he opens his mouth to say something I'm probably not going to want to hear. I put a hand up. "Nope, that was a rhetorical question. I've peed in the woods before, and you already gave your spiel about it. You're not coming with."

I just remember to swipe a handful of toilet paper and a plastic bag as I stomp off. Part of the leave-no-trace stuff involves packing up your TP for later disposal, which, gross. But needs must. And at least I don't have to deal with any other bodily functions yet.

When that's dealt with—beyond the wildlife-safe, one-hundred-feet-from-camp distance, thank you very much—

I find that Finn is tying some kind of strap around a tree near the tent. I take it upon myself to start my nightly routine as I look on, beginning with a makeup-removing wipe. This'll be the first time in I don't know how long that a boy is seeing me without my cosmetic armor. Good thing it's almost dark. And, you know, that I don't care what Finn thinks.

"What are those for?" I ask as I scrub at one eye, then another.

Finn doesn't look my way as he wraps an identical black strap around another tree. "The hammock."

"Oh. Why do we need that?"

He begins unfurling the hammock from the little ball it's rolled into. "I'm sleeping in it."

My hand pauses its wiping mid-cheek. "You're *sleeping* in it?"

He nods, briefly glancing over before his eyes dart away again, as if he's caught me over here in my birthday suit. Which I suppose is not much more shocking than catching me fresh-faced. "You can have the tent. I'll be good over here."

My brows pull together. "I . . . You . . . Does that count as proper shelter from the elements?"

This feels like an easier question than "Am I really so disgusting that you won't share a tent with me?"

He shrugs as he attaches a carabiner on one end of the hammock to one of the trees by the strap, and then the other end. "It should. There's a rain fly I can cover it with."

His mind sounds made up, and I guess far be it for me to try to talk an unwilling guy into sharing my sleeping space. As darkness fully descends, we can finally shut off our cameras, but my routine gets more difficult. I do the best I can and just cross my fingers I don't wake up with a chin zit the size of an Appalachian mountain. The hum of my battery-powered toothbrush sounds overly loud and out of place, and I swear I can feel Finn's judgment from across the clearing, but cavities don't care how far from civilization you are. In the end, he only makes one pointed remark reminding me to pack out anything scented in one of the canisters we've set far away from the tent and hammock for the night. Does that count as restraint in Finn's bossy, domineering world?

Moving closer to the tent, I'm about to change into my pajamas as discreetly as I can. But as I go to strip off my leggings, it hits me that I'm still wearing my hiking boots. Haven't taken them off once since this morning. And as quick as the realization comes . . . so does the pain.

It's like my feet have realized, "Wait a second, these heavy-duty cages aren't just an extension of us now! And actually, we hate them! We mustn't be trapped any longer! FREE US!" I slump onto a log behind me, wincing at the biting twinges in my ankles and pinkie toes. Actually, as I untie the laces and loosen them enough to start easing my feet out, each one is more of a foot-shaped mass of ouch-iness. Surely that term is in a medical textbook somewhere.

I can't suppress my winces and whimpers as I finally get the boots off, then the socks, and examine the damage as much as I can. Blisters on each pinkie toe, for certain, and on the inward-facing sides of my ankles. There are plenty more at-risk spots, where the skin looks red and raw but isn't broken yet. I eye my discarded boots and socks with disappointment, muttering, "Y'all really let a girl down today."

I must be disoriented enough to expect them to talk back, because I'm not surprised when I'm answered with a gruff "No kidding."

Of course, my shoes haven't attained sentience and a grumbly voice. I turn my attention to the weak beam of light now glowing around me to find Finn, first aid kit in one hand and some kind of tablet in the other, coming to sit beside me on my log. He eyes my gross feet with the detached coolness of a paramedic, quietly counting to himself.

I venture cautiously, "What are you—"

"Looks like we have enough Band-Aids for the both of us, tonight and tomorrow. We'll restock at the next checkpoint. And hopefully get a real flashlight." Finn waves what I now see is an e-reader, which he's using as a makeshift light source with the brightness on high, then he sets it and the first aid kit on the log between us. He opens the kit and extracts exactly four Band-Aids—one for each of my blisters—then passes them to me. I accept, but my eyes dart toward his foot propped on the opposite knee as I register his "both of us" comment. It's not in great shape either, as far as I can tell, all of his ouchies revealed by the outdoorsy-looking sandals he now wears with the straps loosened. "I'd disinfect first, then Neosporin, then Band-Aid. Put fresh ones on in the morning, plus cover the spots that haven't blistered yet but probably will if you keep going without protecting them."

Surprised by what seems an awful lot like concern, I swallow any snarky comebacks about knowing how to put my own Band-Aids on. "Got it. Thanks." We both tend to our sickly little appendages in silence for a while, but I'm also taking in all kinds of new information in a peripheral observation, nonverbal way. Like how Finn already changed into his pajamas, dark basketball shorts and a thin white T-shirt. And how his newly half-bare legs are . . . different than I expected. More muscle to them, which I guess makes sense for someone who hikes a lot. He did imply he hikes a lot, didn't he?

"Hey," I say, causing his head to jerk my way mid-bandage-application. I gesture for him to finish before I continue. "Does this happen every time you hike? Or did you get new boots that need breaking in, too? Because if this is just the norm, that's gonna suck."

Finn doesn't look at me again, but I can still see his mouth turn down at the corners, the little stress line in the middle of his forehead looking stressier. "Doesn't happen every time. And my boots aren't new." It seems like he's going to leave it at that, but as he crumples up his Band-Aid trash, he adds, "It's just been a while since I've used them. I haven't gone hiking since— I mean, it's been a busy year. Haven't had time."

The cagey way he says all this has me rethinking my earlier judgment. He may be dramatic at times, but he can't lie for shit. I just don't know why on earth he'd lie about anything related to this.

"I'm, uh, going to try to get some sleep," Finn says as he gets to his feet and takes the dim light with him. "So. Good night."

"Good night?" I answer back, the word coming out more like

a question. With a shake of my head, I call out after him, "Sleep tight! Don't let the bed bugs bite! Wait, hammock bugs? Or any bugs? Lots of 'em out here. Well, you know what I mean!"

If a woman yells a bunch of nonsense in the woods but her teammate doesn't stick around to hear it, does she even make a sound? I'll undoubtedly get the chance to test this further.

Finished with my own self-doctoring, I pack up the first aid kit and resume changing into clean sleepwear before getting settled in my tent. The sleeping bag is nicer than anything I ever took to sleepovers growing up, and crawling in, I feel immediately ten times more comfortable than I have all day.

It doesn't last, though.

Almost instantly, I'm wide awake. Jittery. Anxious as hell. I situate myself as closely as I can to how I'd fall asleep in my bed, even as it's impossible to ignore that my usual pillow, mattress, and bedding are replaced by less ergonomic, more transportable stand-ins. My body won't relax.

In a tent. In the dark. Near a boy who seems to rate me somewhere near plastic bags of used toilet paper in appeal.

The peaceful forest around me sounds deafeningly loud, even more so than on our hike today. Insects humming, birds whistling, leaves rustling. A plane flying over somewhere far in the distance. I can even hear Finn sighing softly a few feet outside the tent, shifting as he tries to get comfortable in the hammock, the straps rubbing on tree bark.

My pulse picks up. The hairs on the back of my neck stand on end as the buzzing inside me rivals the sound outside in intensity. I grab my e-reader and can barely get my eyes to focus on the words, let alone my mind. It's full of questions and worries that multiply by the second.

What am I doing here? Is it always this loud outside? How many of these noises are actually concerning? Am I in danger? Is Finn? Did we clean everything up from dinner well enough, or is a bear going to smell our soup and come for us? What was that sound? And that one? Would I even hear it if a bear was coming, or not until it was too late? What about any other animal? Bears aren't the only predators out here. How am I supposed to sleep with all this going on? But if I don't sleep, will I be useless tomorrow? Even more useless than I was today? Is every night going to be like this one? How long can I keep this up?

For all that I was skeptical about Finn sleeping outside, it doesn't take long for the soft sounds from the direction of the hammock to taper off, suggesting that he's fallen asleep. Inside my lonely tent, I'm not nearly as lucky.

THE NEXT TIME I notice the birds chirping, I reach a hand out to slap the ground beside me. When I connect with a smooth nylon tent floor instead of my phone, consciousness creeps in and I realize this isn't an alarm I can silence.

Much to my disappointment.

Arching my neck, I peer out over the edge of my sleeping bag, which I've nestled into overnight, blinking against the dim daylight that filters into my shelter. It looks like the sun isn't even all the way up. What do these birds have going on that's so urgent?

I burrow into the bag again and close my eyes, trying to resume what, after a largely sleepless night, was finally a really good dream. I think it was about cinnamon rolls. I could smash a whole can of the Pillsbury Originals right now. My stomach grumbles.

Birds continue to chirp.

Damn. This isn't going to happen, is it?

But I refuse to admit defeat and continue to lie down, my eyes squeezed shut, my mind running a highlight reel of favorite baked goods. Until I hear it. The swish of artificial material, the sleeping bag or hammock kind, brushing against itself. Then comes a soft, rumbly groan that is unmistakably the other half of Team Finnatalie. I hear more rustling and the light padding of footsteps moving away from our little camp compound.

I'm definitely not getting any more rest, but is fake-sleeping still preferable to more Forced Finn-ship? I feel bad for thinking yes.

Giving him enough time to attend to whatever morning business he has, I wriggle out of my sleeping bag and try to roll it and the sleeping pad back into their compact, pack-ready form. When I'm done with cleanup inside the tent, I make my way into the sunshine.

"Morning!" I call as I walk over, sporting quite the Look in my pajamas and hiking boots. My hair probably resembles the nests that my fine, feathered, natural alarm clock foes live in.

Finn sits on a log with his back to me, but peers over his shoulder at the sound of my voice. He doesn't look sleep-disheveled in the least, already dressed for the day in a light green T-shirt and another pair of pants that could double as a storage unit. His hair is too short to even get messed up. I bet that's intentional.

"Mm-hmm," he says after taking a bite of a protein bar. I guess that means "good morning" in Antisocial Man.

"You sleep okay?" I pass his makeshift bench and head for my pack where it's propped against a tree.

"Mm-hmm," I hear behind me. "Good morning" again? Or in this language, does the term have multiple meanings? It will require more study.

He doesn't ask me the same thing back, but it's probably for the best. Since I got to have the tent while he was hanging like a bat between some trees, I don't feel like my inability to sleep well will garner much sympathy. Then again, would anything garner Finn's sympathy? Is that a thing he feels? Or does he operate on an emotional metronome, ticking back and forth between disdain and exasperation?

These are the thoughts that occupy me as I grab clothes for the day and my toiletry bag, then continue to dig through my pack for my own breakfast options. Where did those food rations go? I could've sworn—

There's a sound like a hollow drumbeat from behind and I turn to see Finn with one foot propped up on the lid of a round, transparent container. *Ohhh.* The bear canister.

"Food's in here," he says, eyeing me like I've forgotten something as simple as the sky being blue. Embarrassment threatens to creep in, but I tamp it down and lift my chin high, because really, what do I have to feel bad about? That I didn't remember every single piece of the overwhelming amount of new information I've had to take in over the last twenty-four hours? Not today, Oscar the Grouch.

I wolf down a protein bar, then find a tucked away spot to change my clothes and get ready for the day. The tent would provide more privacy, but it's too confining for my needs this morning. While I don't feel overly sticky and gross, or smell too bad yet, I still give myself a quick once-over with one of the body-cleansing wipes I packed while I stand behind a tree in my unmentionables.

It's a humbling experience.

All part of the journey, though! *I'm having FUN,* I remind myself as I head back into the clearing, now properly clothed. I cross to the log where Finn is hunched over, tending to his feet.

"Care if I join you?" I ask when I plop down a few feet away from him, as if he has a choice. He doesn't even grunt, just eyes me with skepticism as I set up my travel mirror in my lap and begin to attempt my Process outdoors. I start with another cleansing wipe, this one specifically for the face and with packaging containing a bunch of my favorite buzzwords, like *brightening* and *smoothing* and *purifying*. Next I layer on the serums, moisturizer, and all-important sunscreen. Once done, I pack all the bottles neatly back into my kit and begin to unload my makeup.

"There's *more?*" Finn murmurs softly.

"Takes a lot of money to look this cheap," I paraphrase Her Majesty Dolly Parton in an equally quiet voice back to him, keeping my eyes trained on the mirror as I dab concealer under my eyes. I don't actually think I look cheap, of course. But I've always idolized Dolly's ability to be unabashedly into taking care of herself. Looking good makes me feel good, and I look and feel my best when I put some effort in.

It's one of the things my parents have rolled their eyes at over the years, trotting it out as evidence that I'm superficial and spend my time and energy on frivolous things. Ignoring the fact that even if I take thirty minutes to do my makeup in the morning, I'll still be down in the stables mucking stalls on time, getting my hands and boots as dirty as everyone else. I'm not about to apologize for it.

Besides, I'm not even doing the full face for my time here. Just a little concealer—or a lot, if I keep sleeping as poorly as I did last night—some powder that contains extra sun protection, a touch of brow pencil, eyeliner, and tinted lip balm. I could be *so* much higher maintenance.

A long-winded sigh interrupts by internal self-congratulating. "I hate to ask, but—"

"Well then, don't, Mr. Finntastic," I offer cheerily in return, tilting my head from side to side to make sure the wings on my liner match. They're perfect. I can't believe I thought this would be hard!

"Is all of that really necessary?"

I cap my liquid liner and tuck it back into my bag before turning to face him, bringing one leg up on the log between us. With a solemn expression, I finally meet his judgy eyes. "In my years of experience watching *Wild Adventures,* I've observed that the teams who do the best are the ones who find their own unique ways to stay calm, focused, and competitive," I say with conviction. "You have your pants, which I imagine contain all kinds of survival skills and resources in their many, many pockets, and your resting bitch face, which intimidates the competition. I have my skincare and makeup routine, which allow me to feel like less of a forest gremlin and distract everyone with my hotness. Doubt me if you must, but my Sephora Rouge membership and I will be laughing all the way to the financial aid office with our hundred-thousand-dollar scholarship."

Finn's head drops, and his hands come up to cover his face in a way that almost looks like he's praying, but in fact, he's just rubbing at the lines between his eyes again. "Shouldn't have asked," comes his muffled mumble.

My smile is both proud and serene as I stand and bounce over to my pack to put all my things back in. And it turns out I finished not a moment too soon, as a producer with an orange envelope and a camera operator emerge into our clearing.

Showtime.

Chapter Five

"Hey. Hey, Finn. What is a tree's favorite month?"

I hear a grunt from where he's briskly hiking a few feet ahead of me.

"Nope, good try though," I say with a wink back at the camera behind me. "Sep*TIMBERRR!*"

The only sound aside from all of our footsteps through the forest floor is the muffled laughter of producer Carina and camera operator Hugh, both of whom are following us to the checkpoint today. When they'd arrived earlier, Carina had given us an envelope containing our next map and go time fifteen minutes later, which gave Finn and me just enough of a gap to stash everything back in our packs, tighten up our boot laces, and argue a little about whether it rained overnight. I didn't actually think it rained; I just wanted to see how worked up Finn would get. Flash forward to my poorly suppressed smile as he shout-explained the concept of dew.

I guess I'm partially to blame, then, for his poor attitude ever since. He's hogged the map, steamrolled me on the navigation front, and exhibited a promising future in competitive speed-walking. We aren't *quite* running to the checkpoint, though the pace my partner is setting suggests that he could do it, if he wasn't stuck with me.

This has meant carrying the entertainment portion of our team responsibilities on my back. I'm not the best at improvisation—I haven't had a ton of experience with it in my lifetime of acting. But the key to good improv, for me, is having a good partner to work with, someone you can bounce banter and ideas off of, who will be your "yes, and—" person.

Finn is more of a "no" or (tense silence) person.

It hasn't given me a lot to go on. And it feels like the silences have grown more pronounced the more I try to engage him. I can just imagine some editing room sorting through a bunch of footage from the hike with Team Finnatalie, in which it's entirely quiet save for the crunching footsteps and labored breathing of the crew and me. They'd surely insert some cricket chirping, or quirky music meant to emphasize the awkwardness between teammates. I simply can't allow it.

"Have I told you about hiking in the Red River Gorge?" I ask Finn. I know I haven't, but I'm trying to pretend this is a dialogue. At his vague negative-sounding noise, I go on. "It's this beautiful part of eastern Kentucky, where the Red River carved a big canyon system that's all covered in trees, and there's a ton of hiking and camping and stuff. My friends Reese and Clara used to like to go every summer and—okay, to be honest, they'd have to drag me along with the promise of Miguel's Pizza after we were done hiking.

"So there's one hike up to a big, sandstone arch called Natural Bridge, but since it's the most popular place for tourists to see, you can also take a sky lift to the top. A few summers back, Reese and Clar wanted to do the hike, but it was *so* hot and *so* humid in the middle of July, and I just could not. I told them I'd meet them at the top, and I bought myself a sky lift ticket and floated on up there. When they arrived sweaty and exhausted, I was chilling, enjoying the view with my still-cold water bottle. Work smarter, not harder, you know?"

All I get is an exaggerated sniff that could mean a lot of things, but I think I'm sensing aggravation.

"I wonder if there's a sky lift for any leg of this journey. I wouldn't be mad about it. Keep an eye out, will ya, Finn?"

We continue on like this for the whole two hours it takes to hike the almost-five mile stretch laid out on our map, Finn only occasionally speaking up to acknowledge my requests for water breaks. We pass or get passed by hikers heading in both directions, most of whom smile and say some form of hello, a few giving Hugh and his camera wary looks. But we never cross paths with another team, which could be a great sign or a terrible one. Either way, I try not to think about it.

When at last we hear voices up ahead, I squeal with both excitement and relief. It's like I've been onstage for the entire first act of a show with the most lines in every scene and a few especially aerobic dance numbers, and it's finally intermission.

I jog past Finn and all the way into the clearing, where Burke Forrester stands next to a *Wild Adventures* flag in front of a small stone building. I don't even register which other teams have arrived or what that means for our ranking, I just keep my eyes on the man who will hand down my fate—at least for the next twenty-four hours or so.

"Finn and Natalie," Burke says in his cartoon character voice. "Welcome to your next checkpoint! How was the first night of your wild adventure?"

"Oh, Burke, it was a delight," I enthuse breathlessly, slapping a hand to my leg. "Like an elementary school slumber party with my besties, minus plumbing, plus an added low-level fear for my survival at all times!"

Burke laughs and I smile as if the latter part was indeed a joke.

"So, Finn, you and Natalie are becoming 'besties,' then?" He points between my partner and me.

I look to Finn, who is now running a hand over his face in what I've come to recognize as one of his signature moves. He only sighs and shrugs in answer, so I jump back in.

"He might seem shy by day, but let me tell ya, boy, does this guy love him some pillow talk! Throw him into a sleeping bag, and bam, you won't get him to hush. I was like, 'Finn, please, I need my beauty rest,' and he was like, 'Natalie, you're just so easy to talk t—'"

"Okay, we get it," Finn cuts in, nearly making me jump back in surprise. "What place are we in? Do we get to stay or what?"

He puts his hands on his hips and eyes Burke Forrester like the guy just said there's a global shortage of khaki. Despite

Finn's hard expression, I don't think I'm imagining the pink tint to his cheeks. I bite down on my smile.

Burke looks less than pleased to be rushed, but it's only half a second before his professional host mask is back in place. "All right, we'll get to it, then! Finn and Natalie, you are the second team to arrive at this checkpoint. That means you will be continuing on *Wild Co-EdVentures*. Congratulations!"

I whoop and bounce on my heels, turning to Finn with my hand up for a high-five. "Not bad, partner!"

His lips twitch in something almost resembling a grin as his hand meets mine in a weak smack. We're waved over to the side, where the first team who made it here—Enemi and her partner, naturally—is waiting under what we learn is one of the AT's shelters for backpackers. Stone walls close it in on three sides with a roof over top and a dirt floor under our feet.

One by one, the other teams arrive and join us in and around the shelter, looking varying degrees of disheveled and exhausted. It turns out everyone completed their tasks last night, including the team with only one pack, so the team eliminated is the last one to make it to the checkpoint.

I feel a little bad as I join the others in giving the two girls leaving, Sam and Amanda, goodbye hugs, because I haven't spoken two words to either of them. Not that I really had the time to do so. Mostly, it seems like a shame that the team name "Samanda" didn't get a longer run.

But I resolve to make more of an effort to get to know everyone here, especially once we learn we'll all be camping together around the shelter tonight. Keep your friends close, competitors you want to ruthlessly defeat so you can win a college fund closer, and all that.

As Enemi's team's prize for coming in first, they each won a five-hundred-dollar shopping spree at a fancy outdoors store, so I'm feeling especially unfriendly where they're concerned. Meaning I should probably keep them closest of all.

I wince with each step I take toward the other side of the clearing once filming is paused, all the aches and pains catching up with me now that I'm not in go-go-go mode. When I get to a tree where I can offload my pack and prop it up, I groan with the relief of taking all this weight from my shoulders.

"What's wrong?" Finn's voice at my back catches me by surprise, and I spin to face him.

"What? Nothing!" *I'm totally fine and capable, just like you!*

"You just made a really unpleasant sound."

"Well, that's rude," I say, putting my hands on my hips. The movement makes me wince again. He doesn't miss it.

"Is your pack uncomfortable?"

I catch myself before I shrug. Not in the most shrug-friendly shape right now. "A little. But it's fine. Maybe my shoulders will go numb soon and I won't feel anything when I'm carrying it."

Finn's critical eyes sweep over me slowly, from my shoulders to around my hips, and while I feel about as unsexy as I ever have, a bizarre little shiver runs down my spine. But the conclusion he seems to draw from his perusal is not what I expect.

"Put the pack back on."

"Huh?" Does he enjoy inflicting pain? That's gonna be a hard no.

"Put it on, however you've been wearing it. I want to see if there's a way to adjust it so you won't be so sore."

Oh. Reluctant as I feel to agree, it's a good idea. So I bend and grab the straps, carefully easing it back on, mentally apologizing to my poor, abused shoulders. Then I'm distracted from any feeling but surprise, because Finn is reaching for my hips . . .

. . . and grabbing the waist straps on my pack.

Whew, okay. Chill out, Natalie.

"You're not even using these," he says, tugging on the wide, padded straps and making me take a stuttering step closer to him.

Flustered, I try to figure out what he means. "Well, no. I clipped them together yesterday, but they kinda just circled around my butt and didn't really serve a purpose, so I leave them unclipped now."

Finn starts to adjust the length of the straps, jostling me with each pull on them. "They didn't serve a purpose because you weren't wearing them right. And you have the shoulder straps too loose. None of it is fitted to you like it's supposed to be, both for comfort and to not destroy your body."

I look for the words to defend myself, but I don't really have any beyond, "Oh. I didn't know."

"I should've noticed sooner," he mumbles, seemingly to himself, as his eyes stay trained on his hands. Which are still moving all around my hip/pelvic region. I try to stand perfectly still.

"Okay, let's see if these work. . . ." His voice is a soft rumble awfully close to my ear as he bends to hoist my whole pack a few inches higher up my body, pulling the lower straps tight around my hips before clipping them into place. "Does that feel good?"

Oh? My? God??? Another shiver courses through me. *Indecent* is what it feels!

Finn takes a half step away, his eyes tracing back and forth from one of my hips to the other, and even though I know he's entirely concerned with the fit of the straps there, and also that there is barely a cordiality between us, let alone anything more *friendly,* it still seems like there should be some sultry background music floating out from the trees.

"Your hips are supposed to carry most of the weight and the shoulder straps should just keep it upright. Is this comfortable at your hips?"

I really need him to stop saying "your hips." It's doing things to me—making me hear his gruff, grumpy voice in a very different way. A way unbefitting of a teammate who doesn't like me all that much.

"It's fine," I grit out quickly, then shift from side to side and realize that it actually is. Not just okay, but a lot better already. Like, a totally different pack than I've carried the whole time so far. "It's much more comfortable."

"Good," he says firmly, and ope, the weird indecent feelings haven't totally left the premises yet. *Snap! Out! Of! It! Natalie!* His eyes rise to my shoulders, hands following as he grabs for one of the upper straps and starts to pull it tighter. "Now for these . . ."

I can't do much but stand there and flop side to side like a rag doll as Finn tugs the adjustable straps on one shoulder, then the other, then the first again. Finally he sets his hands lightly on my upper arms, then leans away to look back and forth at his handiwork. "Do those feel more comfortable?"

Before I can answer, his hands drop and he steps around me, presumably to look at the fit from my side and back.

"Looks good from back here."

"I bet you say that to all the girls," quips the devil on my shoulder who's apparently using me as a mouthpiece. My jaw clamps shut as soon as the words, so breathily, flirtatiously spoken, are out. I want to smack my own forehead. No choice but to own it now. "But it'll take a lot more than pretty words to get into my sleeping bag, big guy."

"Jesus," I think Finn says, but it's muffled by his hand running down his face. "I meant the pack. Looks good. In how it fits. Looks like it fits how it's meant to now, so you won't break your back and get us both sent home."

I laugh, feeling the tension and any other weirdness I was sensing in the atmosphere between us shifting back into nothing but fresh air. "Relax, Finn. I know you're not complimenting my ass, though it is objectively compliment-able. And you're right—the pack feels infinitely better already, so thank you for fixing it."

He gives a jerky nod of acknowledgment, and it feels like that's the last we're going to speak of it. Any of it.

Good, I think definitively. And if the word echoes through my head in the exact low, gruff way Finn said it, that's nobody's business but mine.

Chapter Six

"Co-EdVenturers!" Burke Forrester calls when we've gathered together to film a short, final segment for the day. He raises his arms in a two-handed wave and starts to back away from the shelter. "Congratulations on making it through to the next leg of your journey! I'll meet you back here in the morning. Enjoy today and rest up, because there's a lot of adventure ahead of us!"

We cheer and clap with hardly any prompting, getting the hang of how this goes. When the cameras are lowered from their operators' shoulders, though, Burke's entire TV-ready demeanor drops too. He doesn't spare the group another glance before barking out, "Where's the car picking me up? I need a beer."

I pull the sat phone out of my pocket. It's barely noon.

Some of the crew assembles a lunch buffet they appear to have brought out straight from a real kitchen somewhere, a couple of catering trays with gas heaters under them, no less than seven bags of different kinds of chips, and coolers with drinks inside. I zone out a little as I wait.

"Are you in line for food, or did you just choose a weird spot to practice your mannequin impression?"

My head jerks toward the voice, then to the food table and back, and I realize lunch has been fully set up while I experienced the human version of airplane mode. I blink and focus on the face of the person talking, paper plate in one hand. It's the girl who helped me up after The Trip Heard 'Round the Woods, her expression, like her voice, flat but not quite irritated.

"Oh," I say with a shake of my head, blinking again. "Sorry, lost in thought. I'll just . . ."

I pick up a hot dog bun and wave it at her, in case I haven't made myself look strange enough yet. But her mouth quirks up at the corner, a breath of fresh air after spending all this time with the stone statue that is Finn.

"No worries. I'm Harper. We were in too much of a hurry to cover that yesterday."

She holds out her free hand, and I shift my plate so I can return the shake. "Natalie. Yeah, thanks again for the assist."

"Of course." She gives my hand a squeeze before returning her attention to the food and starting to fill her plate. "So who'd you end up with as your partner? I can't keep track yet."

"Oh, I'm with Finn." As I reach for some plain potato chips out of one of the bags, I say a mental thanks to the hygiene gods for letting me be first in this line. So many grubby, unwashed camper paws are about to be all over this spread.

"Is he the tall, quiet guy? Kinda looks like he hates us all?" She spoons baked beans onto her plate.

My eyes track to where I last saw Finn settling down on a log and riffling through his pack. But now his pack is closed and he's just hunched over with his elbows on his knees, staring off into the woods. He looks accustomed to human airplane mode, comfortable without a phone to mess around with during any scrap of downtime. If he's not one of those people who uses a flip phone by choice, I'll eat the bark off one of the trees he hangs his hammock from.

"That's him," I answer cheerily. "I don't think he hates anyone, though! It's just . . . how his face looks."

Harper raises a skeptical brow as we both bend to choose drinks out of an ice-filled cooler. I'm a little too excited to see a Dr. Pepper, my caffeinated weakness. Twenty-three flavors, all of them perfect. When Harper straightens back up with a root beer in hand, she belatedly replies, "If you say so. I respect his energy, anyway. I *do* hate most people, but they see this freckle-covered baby face and feel compelled to either pinch my cheeks or tell me their life story. Often both."

I laugh as we head toward the circle of chairs set up around a firepit, where a producer is hunched over getting some flames going. A small table to the side holds skewers and hot dogs.

"Well, golly, am I blessed you talked to me first, then! I'll try not to tell you my life story in return." I take a seat and Harper eases into the chair next to mine. "No promises about the cheeks, though. They just look so damn pinchable." I pinch my thumbs and forefingers in the air in front of me like I can't help myself, and she gives me an unamused look.

We continue chatting as we eat and as others fill in the circle around us. Enemi's partner, who we learn is named Zeke, quickly proves himself to be one of the more outgoing among us, interrupting all conversations from time to time to call out a new person in the circle at random, shushing everyone else as he asks the chosen one to share their name, pronouns, where they're from, and something interesting about themselves. After a couple of these, I'm already fidgety, ready to volunteer for the next introduction so I can get it over with even though I've forgotten everything interesting about myself.

It's a helpful icebreaker, if lacking in creativity. It gets people talking, as we eat and cook hot dogs on skewers over the fire, eat some more, cook more hot dogs. There are quiet side conversations, and louder ones yelled across the crackling flames.

We all learn that Daniel, from California, is a competitive pole vaulter, and his teammate, Luis, has ten siblings. Evan, who I learn is Harper's partner, might rival Finn in "most outdoorsy person here" vibes, as they casually reveal that they've hiked most of the Pacific Crest Trail in segments over the past couple summers with their mom. When Zeke calls on Harper as "cutie with the freckles," I worry he might get to meet the business end of her hot dog skewer. But she lets him off easy with an icy glare before sharing that she's from Georgia and her last job required her to dress up in a hamburger costume.

I have about twenty follow-up questions, of course, including "Do you have pictures?" But I get to ask none of them right now, as Zeke has decided to start calling on people with no breaks in between.

"Purple streak!" he shouts.

"Oh, that's me." I pat down my hair where said streak is located, feeling like it's frizzed out to the side, all mad-scientist-style. "I'm Natalie, pronouns are she/her, from Kentucky, and . . . ooh, okay, I've been an extra in a movie."

That clearly invites more questions too, but it's best I don't go further into it. I was slightly more than an extra, in truth, because I had one line. But I was also seven years old, and it was a movie about a Triple Crown–winning horse filmed at a racetrack near my hometown, not anywhere in the vicinity of Hollywood. Sounds cooler the less you know.

The ongoing banter feels surprisingly friendly for an environment and circumstances that are competitive at the core. Even Enemi lets out a smile or two. It seems like it genuinely splits some cracks in her face due to unused muscles, but still.

Maybe everyone else is as eager as I am for company that's not their randomly assigned partner. But even as I think it, I'm checking over my shoulder to make sure Finn's still there, on a log on the outskirts of the circle. At first I thought he was just waiting for everyone else to get food before he'd make his plate and join. But then I saw him get his lunch and return to the log of loneliness.

He chose that, I remind myself. *There are open seats over here. He doesn't need me checking on him, let alone worrying about him.*

Zeke must not come to the same conclusion, because he suddenly shouts Finn's name. My gaze darts up to Zeke, then behind me to Finn and back again.

"It *is* Finn, right? Why don't you join us, man? Introduce yourself!" Zeke's clueless grin suggests he's never heard the word "*introvert*" in his life. Or "*no*."

I stiffen, unsure how this will go. But to my surprise, after a moment, I hear quiet footsteps approach. I don't dare look again, afraid I'll spook him—or worse, seem overly interested in his well-being. But I feel his tall, sturdy presence at my back, just behind my chair.

"Yeah, I'm Finn," he says roughly, then clears his throat.

"Great!" Zeke plows on. "We're all sharing pronouns, where we're from, and something interesting about us."

"I'm from Vermont, he and him, and . . ." He pauses, and I find to my surprise that I'm on the edge of my seat, wondering what Finn will think is interesting enough to share. "And I'm a vegetarian."

Zeke nods. "Sweet. Good to meet you, man. Let's see, who's left?"

I sense Finn slowly retreating to his spot, but I can't get myself to stop replaying everything he's just said, as if I'll find more significant pieces of his identity hidden in the word *vegetarian*. I add the fact to my mental catalog of Finn-formation—a pretty flimsy catalog, so far. More of mini-brochure.

"Are you ever planning to call on your *partner*?" Enemi's sharp voice claims all of our attention, as I'm sure she meant it to. I can't tell if the way she snaps at Zeke is a feisty brand of flirting or actual animosity. Really, how much animosity could they have built in a day of knowing each other?

Then again, it took me about twenty minutes to start thinking of her as Enemi.

While she tells the group something about her family lineage being traced back to the British monarchy—which, okay, *sure*—I feel something prodding at the back of my mind. It's a feeling like I was cut off mid-worry, hadn't fully thought through whatever I was becoming anxious about when I got distracted, so now I'm just residually anxious and can't remember the cause.

The bothersome brain itch won't let up as the afternoon goes on and most of the group continues grazing and hanging out. Harper, Evan, and I play with one of the decks of cards the crew put out for our use, during which I learn that Harper wants to be a psychiatrist (quite the departure from a hamburger) and Evan is a fellow theater kid (so they're not only a nicer version of Finn, but a nicer version of Finn and me combined). I also give them the—in my opinion, solid gold—team name of "Hevan," which Evan finds hilarious but Harps isn't quite sold.

It's when dinner comes around that it finally hits me, what's had me unsettled since lunch. The production crew taking over for the night shift brought all the fixings for a baked potato bar. There's butter, cheese, sour cream, chives, all kinds of meaty toppings, and—that's what snags my focus. Not a lot of vegetables happening here for my herbivore partner. Were there more at lunch? Mindlessly loading up my own potato, I think back to the first group meal. Hot dogs over the fire, baked beans that had ham in them. That would've left mac and cheese, cole slaw, and potato chips—not what I nor any concerned Southern grandma would consider a meal.

Once my plate is made, I loiter near the buffet table. Finn is at the back of the line again, and I have some suspicions to confirm. Harper eyes me with an appropriate amount of confusion as I awkwardly try to balance my plate and drink in my hands and eat my baked potato, all while standing up. Guess it's best that she get used to my oddities early on.

Finn clearly isn't used to them yet. When he finally gets to the end of the buffet, I make no effort to hide that I'm eyeing his plate. He pulls it closer to his chest with a wary look my way, but I've already seen what I need to see. Sure enough, the only things he put on his baked potato are butter and cheese.

"What did you eat for lunch?" I whisper sharply.

He looks to his plate, then off to the side shiftily. "I had enough," he murmurs, already starting to walk back toward his Log of Loneliness.

Well, this won't do. Especially when we've been hiking as much as we have, and this is supposed to be a chill, refueling kind of stop where we're not responsible for rationing our own provisions. And who knows what we'll be doing tomorrow? He needs more sustenance.

"Does production know?" I fall into step beside him, incapable of minding my business.

Finn only shrugs. Letting out an irritated huff, I peer around the clearing in the fading daylight, zeroing in on a producer walking toward the woods not far from us.

I veer off toward the woman. Finn's footsteps pound close behind me, his voice more of a hiss when he asks, "What are you doing?"

"Excuse me!" I ignore him and call out to the producer, my hand shooting into the air and waving like that of a third grader who's really gotta pee. She stops and looks my way, briefly glancing behind her to see if I'm beckoning someone else. "Yes, you! Over here a sec, please."

She looks cautious as she starts toward us.

"Whatever you're up to, it's not necessary," my teammate whisper-groans behind me.

"Hi there," I say when the producer stands before me and I give her a real nice-white-lady-about-to-become-a-nuisance smile. "I'm Natalie. Remind me of your name?"

"Ginger," she answers, looking between Finn and me like she's not sure what's scarier—his mad face or my happy one.

"Awesome. Listen, Ginger, it seems to have gotten lost in the shuffle somewhere that my partner here—oh, this is Finn, by the way"—I gesture to him and he gives a small, embarrassed nod—"is a vegetarian. He's also not a big crowds guy, so he waited till all of us carnivorous vultures had gotten our food to go through the line at lunch and dinner. I was hoping we could get our hands on some kind of alternate protein, more greens, anything like that. Do you think you could help make it happen?"

Ginger looks like a nervous witness on the stand. "Oh, I'm sorry we missed that, Finn. I—I don't think we have any other options on hand tonight, but I can make sure there are more vegetarian-friendly choices at breakfast when the morning crew comes up. For now, we have protein bars, trail mix, meal pouches . . . Do you think any of that can hold you over?"

She addresses the hulking, sulking figure behind me and I turn my gaze on him too, willing him to speak up for his needs. He looks only a little mortified.

"I'm fine," he says dully. "Don't worry about it, really."

I jump in before he can tell Ginger that he's not even *that* much of a vegetarian, or that he'll just eat some dirt if he has to, or anything similarly passive and ridiculous. "The breakfast plan sounds good—thanks a bunch, Ginger! So listen, can we count on you to get the rest of the crew in the loop? Meatless options at every group meal, and making sure there are plenty of vegetarian items in the food stores we'll have to choose from?"

"Y-yes, we can do that." She gives a shaky nod. "Anything else you all need?"

Finn looks like he's trying to Animorph into a roly-poly bug and tumble on down the mountain, far, far away from his meddling teammate.

"I think that's it for now. Thanks again, Ginge!" I aim a satisfied grin her way, hopefully conveying a peaceful vibe now that the problem has been addressed. Unclear if the nickname was a bridge too far. But she takes the out as soon as it's offered, scurrying off faster than a mouse at a cat convention.

"I'm not sure if you said her name enough times," Finn says, deadpan.

I scoff as I turn on him. "I think the words you're looking for are 'Thank you, Natalie. I'm glad I won't be facing malnutrition as the Final Boss of *Wild Adventures*.'"

A low grumble sounds in his throat, but at least he's un-roly-poly-fied himself, standing at his normal height once more. His eyes bore into me, and this close, I notice they're not just dark, endless black, but a warm brown that catches the sunlight and glows almost a caramel-y gold in places.

I blink. Why am I contemplating his eye color? And I haven't even gotten started on those lashes, which are—

"Okay, cool!" I cut off that train of thought before it can leave the station. "I'll just, uh, go back to others now. You know, all those potential new friends you've been avoiding."

I've made it a few feet away when I hear a quiet "Wait." I turn on a heel, unable to hide my surprise.

"Thank you . . . Natalie."

It's the first time that my name coming from his mouth has sounded anything but displeased. I feel a little flutter in my stomach. Then I want to kick myself because, god, could the bar be *any* lower? What's next, getting weak in the knees when he answers any of my questions with a complete sentence?

But okay, a "thank you" is good. I can accept that.

"Sure," I reply, considering him. I think for half a second about asking if he's doing okay. Why he's been so quiet and removed today—even more than yesterday, which I wouldn't have really thought possible. But I rein in the impulse. I'm done going out of my way for someone who gives me less than nothing in return. Well, except Band-Aids. And a properly fitting pack. And a "thank you." And he does look genuinely appreciative, if also a little sad, before he turns and walks to his log bench, takes a seat, and starts to pick at his potato.

Ugh. I look down at the plate I'm still clutching, my own potato that's getting colder by the second. Why do I want to take it over and sit down beside Finn, scoot close, pester and poke until he tells me what other problems of his I can solve?

No, Natalie. I start to turn back to the group sitting around the fire, but my feet won't follow the rest of my body. *But maybe . . . ? Just for a second . . . ?*

Before I've processed my own actions, my feet have carried me to Finn's secluded spot. He notices me just as he's pulled his e-reader from his pack, and his eyes start at my sandals before tracking up to my face, slow enough to make me wonder if he's—

"Are you ever going to eat the rest of your potato?" he asks.

Okay, so our minds are not in the same place. I huff as I sit down a couple feet from him. "I'm so sorry for putting your needs above my own for five minutes! I'll be careful not to do it again."

All I get in response is a beleaguered sigh before he props the e-reader against his knee and clicks it on, still chipping away at his own sorta-meal as he starts to read.

It totally doesn't bother me while I work on my food, which is indeed pretty cold. I'm not desperate to know what kind of stuff he reads, or thinking way too much about the fact that somehow, for two vastly different personalities, we both packed the same "secret weapon." It doesn't get ten times more intriguing when whatever he's reading brings him closer to actually

- 84 -

cracking a smile than I've ever seen. Could the book really be more amusing than me? Frankly, it's insulting. It's just not right. I'm not paying attention to any of it.

"What are you reading?" I ask, because I'm a lying liar who lies to myself.

Finn doesn't look my way nor even startle in the slightest, like he was waiting for me to ask. But he still waits, chews, and reads in silence for a few more moments before he replies.

"Have you ever heard of Grandma Gatewood?"

I pause, then say, "No . . . ?"

He points to his e-reader, looking down at it. "It's a book about her. She was a grandma from Ohio who became the first woman to thru-hike the AT solo in 1955, and she did it at age sixty-seven." He squints over at me. "You kind of remind me of her."

My face probably rotates through twelve different expressions before I settle on my jaw hanging open as I stare at him. "That . . . is so much to unpack out of so few words."

Finn simply looks back to his book as if he's resuming reading. But I'm not done here.

"I remind you of a 1950s grandmother? What, because I'm justifiably concerned you aren't eating enough?"

He gives a lazy shrug, and I watch a smirk play at his lips.

"If the hiking boot fits."

Chapter Seven

"I hope we're all appreciating the irony of looking for mushrooms in a place called Devil's Tater Patch."

"That's not a yes or no," Finn mutters, to which I maturely blow a raspberry back at him. A raspberry isn't a yes or a no either—the only words I'm technically instructed to say to my partner in this leg of the challenge—but I think any future viewers of this footage will understand.

If I thought Finn and I might've turned over some kind of new leaf last night, boy, was I mistaken. This partnership is the same antagonistic, dead-on-the-ground leaf it's been since the beginning, and Finn's mood really has me wanting to stomp down and make it crunch. Never mind the fact that my girl Ginger came through and there were plentiful fresh, filling vegetarian options on our breakfast buffet this morning. I didn't hear so much as a "thank you."

Now we're back on the trail with a map that led us to our team's assigned area for the "Fungus Among Us" challenge.

The instructions had us choose one partner to forage for three mushrooms of different varieties and correctly identify them. The other partner got the mushroom foraging cheat sheet, with photos and the basics of identifying each variety based on qualities in the cap, stalk, and spores. The forager can ask yes-or-no questions of their partner with the cheat sheet, but the other partner can't provide any additional help in finding or identifying mushrooms.

One guess as to who claimed the first job. And while he hasn't handled the lack of information especially well, he's still managed to find two of our three mushroom varieties. We'll find out if we got them right when we call a producer from the sat phone to come check our work.

"Potatoes sound so good right now." I decide to ignore Finn's last comment and keep up my running commentary. As long as I'm not giving him any information relevant to the task, I don't see the problem. "If we spot any, we should pick them up too. Ooh, I would kill for one of Taco Bell's spicy potato soft tacos. Have you ever had one?"

"No."

"*So* good. I swear, if all restaurants had options like that, I might just be a vegetarian too. Did y'all know Finn is a vegetarian?" I'm getting pretty good at carrying on a conversation with a camera, if I do say so myself, as I walk backward at Finn's side and talk to the GoPro on his pack. "Pretty cool, right? I've thought about going veg over the years, but I just . . . I don't know, I forget, and I blink and suddenly I'm halfway through a ten-piece McNugget meal. It's convenient to be a meat eater in our society, you know? I mean, I'm sure *you* know, Finn. So what made you go this route?"

"Uh, it's better for the environment," he says in a distracted murmur, head turning back and forth as he scans a brushy field around us while we hike, like it's one giant game of I Spy. I'm surprised he's even answering me, but I let him keep going, afraid if I breathe too loudly, he'll notice he's being cooperative on camera and stop himself. "Factory farming is shitty for animals, and for humans with all the unnatural stuff you end up consuming, and greenhouse gas emissions—wait, why are we talking about this?"

Damn. It was nice while it lasted.

"That's not a yes-or-no question," I answer, unable to help myself.

Finn groans, and I think I see a corresponding gray hair sprout on his head.

I manage to suppress my weary sigh as I follow his careful footsteps through the patchwork of grasses, weeds, and open dirt beneath us. If I have to deal with this stuff again today, at least I'm better rested. I slept alone in the tent, which was assembled by Finn before I realized he was doing it, and he took the hammock. Camping in the same space as the rest of the group—lots of other humans, therefore lots of cans of bear spray on all sides of me—I found my mind could actually quiet itself, and I slept like a rock.

Someone else on this team must not have had the same luck, or he just woke up on the surly side of the hammock. At the supply exchange and food restock with the other teams, his catchphrase was "We don't need that"—to all my suggestions of gear we could barter for and half the food I tried to put in my pack. I wanted to tell him that what we really don't need is his attitude, but figured that would only exacerbate the problem. We did get headlamps, fortunately, and an extra bear canister since, as Finn said, "you carry around so much scented junk." He'll be lucky if I don't smear some on his face tonight, then drop a trail of delicious scents to lead the bears right to him.

At the same time as I want to use him as bear bait, though, I'm extremely aware that our fates are tied. My wagon is hitched to his, for better or worse. Helping him, I think as I hear his grumbles and huffy breaths increasing in frequency, is helping me, too.

"Tell me what's in your head," I call out, the words surprising us both. From a few yards ahead, he peers over his shoulder at me, looking baffled, like I'd shouted *Make out with me!*

But he does finally stop walking and speaks. "I'm just—I feel like I've been looking for our third mushroom for hours. It's frustrating."

He did it! Expressed an emotion by stating it aloud! I want to give him a gold star on his emotional maturity progress chart.

"I get it. But you've found two already, so I know you can do it again." His shoulders still have a defeated slump to them, so my mouth keeps on running. "Hey, listen. When I was little, I was kind of, uh, scattered. Okay, don't give me that look," I say to his twitching lips, and they go still again. "Anyway, I used to lose things all the time, usually to the abyss of my messy room. And I would get so *mad,* angry to the point of tears, knowing whatever toy or homework assignment I'd misplaced was somewhere right under my nose, but I couldn't see it. My parents had no patience for me when it happened, but my grandma . . ." I look at pink wildflowers dotting the green expanse of forest floor, an involuntary grin pulling at my own lips as I remember. "If she was around, Granny Star would stop me in my tracks. She'd hold my hands—"

Before I can talk myself out of it, I offer my hands to Finn, palms up. His gaze darts from them to my face and back, and if I was any less sincere about this, I'd make another cooties jab. Finally, he slides his hands over mine, his palms warm and slightly rough. A little zap of awareness runs through me, one I don't let myself consider as I close my fingers over his in a loose clasp.

"She'd do this and say, 'Natalie. You're not going to find it because you've got the feelings fog clouding your vision. It's hard to see through, makes everything blurry, then the problem is so much worse. So let's close our eyes . . .'"

I close my eyes, hoping Finn takes the cue to do the same. As soon as I do, I'm a decade younger, in a different place with a different person.

"'. . . and we'll take a big, deep breath, one . . . two . . . three . . . four . . .'" I count on a slow inhale, and hear him do the same, hands subtly tightening their grip on mine. "'And let out the feelings fog, one . . . two . . . three . . . four.' One more time, okay? One . . . two . . ."

After I count out another deep inhale and exhale, I open my eyes, blinking away images of gray hair, rosy cheeks, and a mischievous smile with sixty-something years of laugh lines creasing the edges. I focus instead on the sandy lashes that flutter open. Finn looks marginally less frustrated, but there's a new emotion on his face, something I can't quite interpret.

"Think you can see any clearer now?" I ask, and it comes out in a near whisper.

"Maybe, yeah," he murmurs back, but the only thing his eyes seem to be taking in is me. Our gazes hold for a prolonged moment. But in a second, his focus is gone, as are his hands in mine, and I wonder if I imagined the intensity in the whole thing. Too swept up in the emotions of a cherished memory, maybe.

"We should keep moving," Finn says.

"You're right." I don't even wince saying the words! Growth. Giving him the most confident, optimistic smile I can muster, a final strike to try and banish the feelings fog for good, I add, "I bet you're about to find something, any minute now."

"Thanks for the vote of confidence," he says as he turns on a heel and starts walking again. "And, uh, for the fog clearing."

We walk on slowly, making our way out of the mountaintop meadow and into a forested area. Finn's gaze darts every which way as he looks for that last mushroom we need, and I keep quiet for once. I'm in the middle of closely perusing his oddly clean-looking form from behind, wondering how he seems to be avoiding pit stains and B.O. completely, unlike some of us, when his shout of "Aha!" startles me.

He crouches by a log with a bunch of mosses and plants growing over and around it. Mosses, plants, and, Dolly Parton bless America, mushrooms.

"I DON'T KNOW what you want to be when you grow up, Finn," I say, hurrying to keep up with his speed-hiking once more. "But I think you have a promising future as a truffle pig."

His short snort-laugh doesn't exactly disprove my point. "I'll keep it in mind."

My new bestie Ginger was the producer who'd shown up to check our mushroom findings, and I momentarily feared she might harbor a grudge from yesterday. But she quickly confirmed that we had, indeed, found a chanterelle, a chicken of the woods, and a bolete, then handed us our map to the checkpoint. We have no concept of where all the other teams are, if everyone else finished foraging hours ago or if we were the first, so all we could do was hit the trail and hope for the best.

Finn kicks up his pace another notch, and I think not for the first time that it would've been convenient to randomly pair with a partner with legs closer in length to mine. I can, however, acknowledge that I'm probably better off for having one who makes me push this hard. Makes me treat these hikes as the race for $100,000 that they are, even when my feet are screaming at me to take it easier. Regardless of whether I leave *Wild Adventures* with the money, at least I know I'll be leaving with some banging thighs.

After only a couple miles—and no, I can't believe that I've so quickly become someone who will put the word "only" with the words "couple miles"—we hear the voices and general commotion that let us know we must be close to the checkpoint.

Finn breaks into a jog, and though my every muscle moans and groans about it, I follow suit.

When the checkpoint comes into view, I take in more details than I can process at once, nearly stumbling in my attempt to do so. Like the fact that the orange *Wild Adventures* flag that marks every checkpoint isn't there, next to Burke Forrester. Some of the other teams are. But rather than everyone standing around the host in a semicircle waiting for each new arrival, the teams are each standing by what look like larger, fancier versions of the camp stove in my pack.

Finn looks equally bewildered beside me, and we both approach Burke Forrester, who is mischievously smiling as if he's playing a prank on us.

"Natalie and Finn," he says, rubbing his hands together in a decidedly criminal mastermind gesture. "Welcome to the next leg of your challenge."

Chapter Eight

I should have known, from my lifetime as a reality TV viewer, that today was too easy for me. They might as well call it "Part Two: Natalie Hasn't Suffered Enough Yet."

"Okay, this doesn't seem too bad," I declare without believing a word I'm saying. Finn and I are standing by our cooking station, where in addition to the fancy camp stove setup, we have a gallon jug of water and a fully stocked bear canister we haven't been allowed to open yet.

According to Burke, we won't race to the second checkpoint until tomorrow. Today, all my fellow non-forager team members and I are facing off in a camp stove cooking showdown. Using the ingredients provided in the bear canisters—including mushrooms that are *not* the ones we foraged today, though the viewing public will never know—we've been tasked with making a one-pot mushroom carbonara. Complicating things is the fact that I don't have the recipe—my partner does.

To add a fun, extra element of pressure, Burke Forrester

gleefully announced that he brought a friend out to help him judge our dishes—celebrity chef and certified smokeshow Seb Kelly. Yes, Seb is allegedly the nicest guy in the world, and happens to be a coworker of my best gal Reese at the cooking channel where she's worked for a year, Friends of Flavor. But he's also famous and talented and unsettlingly beautiful, and none of these factors are helping me stay calm and focused in light of what I have to do.

You're an experienced actress, I keep repeating in my head. *So, like . . . act and shit!*

My inner voice could work on her motivational messaging. But outer me keeps smiling, even if it's shaky. Even if I barely know what carbonara is, the other teams don't need to see us sweat before this thing even begins.

Finn, apparently, has none of those qualms.

"Have you ever even cooked outside?"

The sharp point in his question pierces my chest. It hits somewhere near the soft, squishy side of my heart that I don't show a lot of people but found myself letting him see today. After that, I thought maybe we were past cheap shots at my capabilities.

Of course I was wrong.

"No, I haven't," I answer as calmly as I can. Which, okay, is not very calm. "If only I'd had the opportunity to practice the other evening, while there was plenty of time and space to do so around someone with experience in it. Wouldn't that have been a big help to us right now, if he'd allowed me to participate in cooking over the fire that *I* got going?"

Finn drops the water bottle he's been holding with such a loud thunk, I almost think he put a little extra force behind it. "Right. I'm an asshole and it's my fault you came on a *wilderness survival show* without having spent a night outdoors in your life."

I swallow the lump in my throat and look down at my boots, refusing to let him see any more of my emotions. I'm all too aware that any other team or producer or Smokeshow Seb himself could be witnessing this little drama we're having, but I don't expect anyone else to willingly wade into the shark-infested waters of our team dynamic. Until they do.

"Nah, I think it's just your fault that you're acting like an asshole." My head whips up at the familiar flat tone, and I find Harper standing at the next station over with her arms crossed over her chest. It's clear she's refined the skill of overcoming her naturally sweet looks with that narrow-eyed, unimpressed scowl.

Finn looks so taken aback, it's like he really thought he was yelling at me in a soundproof bubble. He leans away as if afraid the girl half his size might advance on him, his face and neck taking on a red flush as his mouth opens to respond.

Unfortunately, I'll never know how he planned to save himself, as the producers choose that moment to resume filming. Burke officially kicks things off with an air horn that sends a whole flock of birds flying out of the clearing, and the humans on the ground descend into instant chaos.

"You got this, Harper!" I hear Evan call first thing from their spot the required ten feet away from Harper's camp stove station. So many voices are talking over each other all at once, and I already feel like I'm behind, or not understanding how this is supposed to go or something. Burke told us that we're allowed to ask our recipe-holding partner yes-or-no questions, just like they did this morning. They're also allowed three "saves" to correct us if we're doing something majorly wrong. But how does everyone else have questions for their partners already? Or are they all just getting a constant barrage of cheering and support?

My own partner's voice, which I haven't heard since an *opposing team member* defended me from his criticism, rises above the fray with his attempt at encouragement. "Forty-five minutes to go! No time to waste!"

"Inspiring," I mutter under my breath as I open my bear canister. I pull out all the ingredients provided to me, most of them as cold as if they were just removed from the fridge, and set them on the small prep surface beside the burner. Then I assess what I know.

Mushroom carbonara is a pasta dish, confirmed by the box of uncooked noodles. I'm also pretty sure a carbonara is the one where there isn't really a sauce so much as an eggy, cheesy concoction mixed in with the noodles. Eggs: check. Cheese: check. Whoa, maybe I *do* know what I'm doing.

"What are you doing?" Finn yells, interrupting my inventory.

I grit my teeth in what I hope to the cameras will look like a smile. "I'm thinking and planning, dearest Finn! Is that okay with you?"

I don't even register his answer, because it doesn't matter. It's showtime. At showtime, you have one job, and it isn't arguing with your costar on stage. It's putting on the damn show.

"Do I need to boil water for noodles first?" I shout once I've got my thoughts together enough to form my first yes-or-no question.

"Yes, you—" he calls back, clearly wanting to say more, but catching himself. The hundreds of boxes of mac and cheese I've made in my life weren't for nothing. I fill the pot about halfway with water, then set it on the burner.

Remarkably, I'm certain I hear Finn's sigh, even through the ongoing, much louder commotion of teammates yelling back and forth to each other and the occasional declaration from Burke Forrester that one person or another has used a save.

"I can't make the water boil any faster, bud!"

"Are you sure you have the stove as hot as it can be, and there isn't anything covering up the burner?" he yells back. Behind him, the producer on the other side of the camera closest to Finn raises a hand in the air and waves, pointing at him with the other hand.

"Finn," Burke Forrester bellows before I even understand what the producer was signaling. "You have used one save! You have two remaining."

"What?!" Finn's reaction comes out as a loud sort of croak that would be funny under other circumstances. "How was that a save?"

When I look down to search for any kind of temperature control on the stove, I realize my hands are shaking. Wonderful!

My body's timing could not be better. The smothering stage mom energy from the other half of my team is certainly helping nothing.

I vaguely register Burke's explanation to Finn that anything that could help the team member doing the cooking, even if phrased as a question, counts as a save. But I'm more focused on making this save count for something. A fruitless effort, as far as I can tell. When I lift the pot to check, the burner is completely uncovered, though I can see a metal flap that could presumably slide over the flames to reduce the heat. Otherwise, I find nothing that would keep the stove from heating up the water as fast as it can.

Maybe, I think optimistically, *this will teach Finn to shut his damn mouth for a minute and let me do my thing.*

Maybe, I decide ten minutes later, after he's used both remaining saves to offer suggestions as unnecessary as his first, I can use my mushrooms and noodles to spell out *HELP ME* on Seb's plate, and he'll whisk me away from this nightmare. Back to civilization and a Finn-free future and, if I'm lucky, Seb's kitchen, where he'll feed me consolation desserts.

It's a lovely vision, one I latch onto to keep myself from falling into complete despair as I mindlessly stir the pasta. Finn apparently needed to take a lap, after unintentionally using his last save to shout "Why are you cutting up the mushrooms?" He didn't even talk back to Burke this time, just silently stormed off to the other side of the clearing. Screw Natalie and any questions she needs answered from the recipe, I guess!

"How's it hanging over there?" Harper asks, and I look over to see her waiting for her noodles to boil, offering me a small, sympathetic smile.

"By a thread, basically," I call back. "You?"

"We're good." She glances at Evan, who has even more pity in their eyes when they give me two thumbs up. "So are you! You got this. And if he doesn't come back, maybe we can be the first *Wild Adventures* throuple."

That makes me laugh and helps bring my blood pressure down even more than a hot chef daydream. I'm not losing it. I haven't set anything on fire or poisoned anyone, and people who are not my partner still like me, dammit.

By the time I try a noodle and decide they're done boiling, Finn has returned, looking marginally less unraveled than when he walked away.

"Okay, so I probably drain the water out of the pot now, right?" I ask, welcoming him back with an opportunity to (a) correct me if I'm wrong, while (b) not breaking and rules or (c) making me feel like draining said water directly over his head. When he opens his mouth, I add, just in case, "Yes or no!"

His lips form a flat line, eyes narrowing for a moment before he nods. "Yes."

He can stay mad, but I'm not letting us get disqualified with a fourth save I don't need.

For the remainder of the cooking process, I pretend I'm Reese in one of her Friends of Flavor videos. I narrate everything I'm doing, rambling a bunch of nonsense to the camera about my favorite ways to prepare mushrooms when, in fact, I've never prepared mushrooms in my life. I confirm each step with Finn, who has finally gotten the hang of this yes-or-no-answer concept, but still has no poker face.

"What, is this not when I add the eggs?" I ask, holding the bowl I just cracked a bunch of eggs into frozen in mid-air when I catch his wince.

He shakes his head. "No."

I purse my lips, considering my stove station. "Do I . . . add the cheese first?"

He rolls his lips between his teeth and shakes his head again, brow furrowed so intensely I worry it might get stuck that way if I don't figure this out quickly. When I'm about to throw my hands up and dump the eggs in the pot anyway, Evan's voice rings out, louder than it's been in a while.

"Harp, you're going to want to turn the heat down so your noodles don't burn and the egg mixture doesn't cook too fast."

I don't know how everyone else is playing this thing, but I've had a hard enough time with managing my own station and communicating with Finn; I can't imagine how confusing it would've been to try to follow other teams' exchanges and snag any tips, even if that's a smart way to play the game. But something about Evan's slightly robotic delivery feels like it was meant for me to hear.

This suspicion is confirmed when I look to Harper's station, and see she's nearly ready to plate her carbonara, clearly having passed the step of adding eggs a while ago. My eyes dart between her and Evan, both of whom seem to deliberately avoid my gaze. *Fine, be that way,* I think as a swell of confused emotion rises in my chest and I lift my pot of noodles from the burner and slide the metal piece over it halfway to lower the heat. *But good luck avoiding my hug attacks of gratitude when this challenge is through!*

Though it seemed impossible for a while there, I finally end up with a pasta dish that appears edible and probably nontoxic. I do the best I can to plate it nicely on our collapsible camping dishes, swirling the fettuccine noodles to make a little circular pasta pile on each, dotted with the mushrooms I might or might not have needed to chop into smaller pieces. I garnish both plates with parsley, because there was parsley in my bear canister, and I haven't used it for anything else, so . . .

"This looks gourmet as *fuck*," I say reverently when I'm done, pointing with my tongs at the steaming plate-bowls. Then I remember my surroundings and grimace toward the closest camera. "Shit, sorry! I mean—oh, bleep me as you must, whoever eventually edits this. I'm just too excited."

When I chance a look at Finn, who's been quiet for a while, I'm surprised to find the ghost of a smile on his face.

When time runs out, Burke clearly relishes his chance to act like the host of an entirely different reality TV genre. "And time . . . is . . . UP, people! Step away from your stoves, utensils down, no more fiddling with the food!"

Live out those dreams, Burkey.

Finn and I each hold a plate of pasta while we stand with the other teams in the Signature Semicircle of Wild Co-EdVenturers around the folding table that's been set up for judging, covered by a red-and-white-checkered tablecloth. As Burke calls teams up one at a time to have their mushroom carbonaras tasted and critiqued by him and Seb, my palms start to sweat so much, I worry the plate might slip out of my hands. I can barely hear their feedback over the sound of my own heartbeat thumping in my ears, and my mouth has gone dry.

And for what? I ask myself, as if I've ever been able to reason with this bitch. *This isn't even an elimination yet! Worst-case scenario, you can tap into your inner track star and sprint to the checkpoint tomorrow!*

Finn has to nudge me with his elbow when it's our turn, because I don't immediately start toward the table with him. When I do, it's on wobbly legs that I hope get cropped out of the final footage.

"This looks delicious," Seb says.

Want to get married? I say back in my mind.

Burke and Seb both raise their sporks—because hard-core backpackers can't spare the space for even *one* unnecessary utensil—and dig in with gusto.

Finn must sense my nerves, because he gently bumps his hip to my side. If I were him from two days ago, my limbs would dramatically flail as I jumped a foot away from him in shock. But the me of right now must be truly desperate for comfort, whatever meager form it takes, as I follow when he leans away so my side just barely brushes against his and stays there.

I don't know if Burke Forrester has been making these same moan-adjacent sounds with every dish he's tasted, but I do know

I'll never unhear them. Seb, fortunately, uses words to express his thoughts, which I know shouldn't make me love him more, but the bar for men remains ever on the ground.

"This is really great, Natalie," he says, gently dabbing at the corner of his mouth with a napkin before offering me a smile, and I don't even ask him to say my name again so I can record it. "I love the saltiness, and you cooked the noodles to perfection. Thanks for sharing!"

We get no further feedback from Judge McMouthNoises at the other end of the table, but I feel more at ease returning to the edge of the circle. Maybe I *should* record Seb saying a handful of nice things, so I can replay them any time I feel myself spiraling, like an audible shot of serotonin. I'm even soothed by listening to his feedback for the remaining teams, no matter the fact that he compliments literally everyone and says nothing negative.

We're sent to the other side of the clearing while Seb and Burke confer over their rankings. Finn paces in small circles while I give Harper and Evan the hug attacks I internally promised them. Harper squirms and grumbles protests about how she's "not a hugger" and she "didn't even do anything," but her arms wrap limply around me all the same.

And in the end, the good guys win this one—Seb awards a pair of shiny golden sporks and the earliest go time for tomorrow to my carbonara comrades, Harper and Evan.

UNFORTUNATELY, THE GRATIFICATION of earning a respectable second place in a challenge is like having candy for dinner rather than a well-rounded, nutritious meal. It may fill you up and make you happy in the short-term, but your stomach will be grumbling again before bedtime.

It's not like I expected Finn to kiss my feet.

For one thing, they've been sweating in my hiking boots for three days now, and still have some healing blisters. I wouldn't let Enemi go near them right now, not even after she judgily told me in front of everyone around the fire circle last night that putting a purple streak in my hair was "brave."

So no, Finn needn't show his gratitude for my saving our asses, despite his best attempts to take us down in camp stove burner flames, in that way. But my stomach is grumbling for some kind of acknowledgment that he wasn't at his best today. A simple "sorry" would go a long way.

Hip bumps of solidarity are nearly forgotten, the tension between us as thick as ever while we hike the quick quarter mile to our campsite for the night. Finn silently begins setting up the tent, and I don't have it in me to put up a fight about letting me help. Honestly, he *should* be setting up the tent for me. Laying out my sleeping bag inside, putting a chocolate on my pillow.

I know it shouldn't be that big of a deal. But as I dig through my pack for all the stuff I need for the night, the pride in my accomplishment has worn off, and I just feel deflated.

I'm tired of not being recognized for what I can do—by my parents, by everyone at Oliver. Not being taken seriously can be motivating to a point, in a fuck-the-haters way. But spite is like an adrenaline rush for me—it wears off, and I'm left tired, trying to catch my breath, and looking around for someone to say, "Hey. You're good now. You can stop pushing so hard," and maybe most of all, "I'm proud of you."

Finn's known me for three days, and it isn't fair to pin all my baggage on him. But the way he's been treating me isn't fair either, and I don't have to be this constant sunshine, trying to give off enough light to make up for all his darkness. He can make an effort to be pleasant for a change.

I wander off to go through my nightly routine, the anxious energy building within me, the buzzing under my skin even stronger than that of my toothbrush. My mind wanders even further. Maybe I never get others' affirmation or pride because I don't actually deserve it. I'm not impressive or talented; I have a lot of dumb luck, like Harper and Evan helping me out today because they're nice people who felt bad for me. That's what really kept us in the game, isn't it?

The thought sets me off down darker mental paths as I finish cleaning myself up and changing into pajamas, my hands shaking, breath coming more erratically as I tumble through all the ways I'm not good enough to be here, at Oliver, any of it. By the time I'm crawling into my tent, my mind has run wild—fear of all the ways I'm on the brink of failing getting muddled with the fear of my current environment. I'm panting when I collapse onto my sleeping bag, and I bring a hand up to my chest as if I can slow the pounding of my heart. Why this? Why now? I'm not in any imminent danger. I know that. But also, *do I?* I don't have night vision or any other ability to see what all's out there, lying in wait beyond the flimsy tent fabric that offers no real protection. Shit, should I have brought the bear spray in here? But since Finn's sleeping outside, he should have it—he's the first line of defense. Is he aware of that, ready for it?

It all feels paralyzing—I'm not safe here, I know it. But I'm not any safer if I burrow into my sleeping bag, nor if I get up and leave the tent. What am I gonna do, run through the dark woods in my tiny pajama shorts until I reach civilization? It's all I can manage to lie flat and press my palms into the slick material of my sleeping bag, feeling the layers of stuffing and my sleeping pad beneath it. I try to breathe deeply, in and out, a lot like what we did earlier today. But my breath hitches at every noise coming from outside. I don't even feel able to discern which ones are just Finn moving around, or the wind in the trees; all of it sounds equally menacing, terrifying.

I wonder if . . . No, that wouldn't help anything.

Wouldn't it?

If I felt any more in control right now, I might worry about this giving Finn more ammunition against me. Not only will he think I'm useless, but that I'm mentally unstable, to boot. But when I was at school and having the worst of my doom spirals about my life and future, and everything felt so terrible I wanted to do nothing but lie on the floor and cry, one thing stopped me.

My roommate. We weren't exactly friends or anything, but something about the presence of another living, breathing human in the room, one who seemingly did *not* think life as she knew it was ending, was calming to me. Let alone the social pressure of "there's another person here and she doesn't know you that well, so you cannot be an inconsolable ball of feelings right now, get your shit together, Natalie Hart!"

I can do it. I *should* do it.

Before I can talk myself out of it, I call out shakily, "Finn?"

There's a long pause, during which I grab fistfuls of sleeping bag and release them a couple times, willing myself not to startle at every little noise. Is he out there? Did something happen to him between when I hightailed it to the tent and now? God, if I wasn't in here losing it, I could have listened for—

A throat clears. "Uh, yes?"

Of course, he's fine. I'm being ridiculous, I know I am. I think about saying "never mind," feeling my pulse slow a little already at the sound of his voice.

Not because it's his or anything. Any voice would do.

I squeeze my eyes shut and bite the bullet. "Do you think . . . could you maybe, ah, sleep in here tonight?"

Another long silence, but this time I know he's out there. He's heard me. He's deciding how to tell me "Hell no, you absolute fre—"

"In the tent?"

"Yes." It comes out as nearly a whisper, so I add in a stronger voice, "Yes."

What am I going to say if he asks why? Because I'm possibly nuts? Obviously he'll ask why—it's a weird request, with our tense partnership being what it is. But I don't know how to explain myself. Maybe I'll say I'm cold?

"Okay. Give me a second."

Surprise hits me, followed by a wave of relief. I hear the

swish of his sleeping bag and imagine him wriggling his long body out in the same caterpillar imitation I do every morning. More rustling as, I assume, he gets out of his hammock, the soft thump of feet hitting the ground. Then comes the *whirr* of the zipper being tugged, and in my periphery I see the tent flap open on the opposite side from the one I dove through not long ago, and the beam of Finn's headlamp shining in.

I keep my eyes trained on the ceiling, still feeling the buzzing under my skin from head to toe along with the vague sense that I'm not safe yet. It's like the world's most persistent cell phone alarm clock, this vibration running through my body and mind, and I'm never quite able to rouse myself to hit Snooze.

Finn doesn't say anything as he arranges his sleep setup in the tent, which suddenly feels a lot smaller than it did with just me in here. But rather than being cramped or claustrophobic, it has an instant calming effect. I can see, even without looking at him head-on, that he is safe and unconcerned about any of the fears running through my head. I'm able to bring my hands from my sides up to rest on my stomach, rising and falling with my breaths, which grow deeper and slower, little by little.

Once Finn settles in, I can feel his eyes on me, and I think I'm ready to meet them. It's mostly dark, but he's removed his headlamp and set it on the floor in the sliver of space between us, like a small but mighty lantern. He's lying on his side parallel to me, but with his head at the end where my feet are. Upper body propped up on one elbow, he eyes me with that characteristic wrinkle between his brows.

"Are you okay?" he asks when he has my gaze locked in his.

"Getting there," I say on an exhale, letting more of the truth show than a chill, daytime Natalie would probably like.

"Can I get you anything?"

Caught off guard, I start to shake my head no. But then a thought occurs to me. "Where's the bear spray?"

"In my pack right outside," Finn answers, adding without hesitation, "Want me to get it?"

At my nod, he immediately sits up and opens the tent flap again, leaning out to rummage through his bag before quickly returning with the red canister in hand.

"I'll set it down here by your feet, okay? Safety lock is on, so we're not about to spray each other in our sleep."

It's the gentlest I've ever heard his voice, and there's a little bit of a teasing tone at the end. It melts the roughest edges off the craggy ice wall that's been sitting between us all evening, maybe even since we met. All I can do is nod again as he gets back into his sleeping bag.

I don't know if it's actually gone quieter outside, or if I'm just less attuned to it all than I was in my panicked state. Whatever the case, I'm able to hit Snooze. A temporary reprieve. The buzzing has faded to a low hum, the feeling of imminent danger ebbed to the low-level wariness with which I live most of my everyday life.

Slowly, I sit up and crawl to the head of my sleeping bag before opening it and sliding inside. When silence falls again, Finn clears his throat.

"You good now?"

There's no judgment there, that I can detect, but I'm returning to myself enough to feel the self-consciousness over my episode creeping in. "Yes," I say quietly. "You don't need to ask again."

It comes out a little more cutting than I mean it to sound, so I add on, "But thank you."

He grunts in acknowledgment, and I watch as he sits up and clicks off the headlamp, plunging us into full darkness. I half expect the panic to kick back in, but nothing really happens. Mostly, I'm just exhausted.

I roll onto my right side, which is how I always fall asleep and just happens to now be facing Finn's shadowy, sleeping bag–covered form. My heavy eyelids fall closed, suddenly very ready to let sleep claim me. I can feel the haze settling in, the lingering jitters making way for thick, deep sleepiness. My mind is starting to do its thing where I'm half thinking real, sensible thoughts but also half in nonsense-dreamland.

Which is why when I hear "I'm sorry," I think I'm dreaming it.

But when Finn says it again, with feeling, my eyes pop open.

"I'm sorry about earlier, Natalie. I was out of line, saying what I did, not trusting you to figure things out for yourself. This evening or . . . other times. I've been an ass, and you haven't deserved it. I'm sorry. You did great today, not just on the cooking—though that was amazing and I shouldn't have doubted you—but in everything. You . . . you're a good teammate."

A confusing lump of emotion forms in my throat, shock mingled with satisfaction, validation, maybe even a flutter of embarrassment at the recognition, even if it's exactly what I wanted and then some. "Thank you. I, uh, accept."

"Okay. Good," he murmurs back.

The chirps of crickets and hum of cicadas and breeze through the trees are more like a soft, sleepy soundtrack to me now as I lie there, processing Finn's words, so sincerely delivered. I've nearly let sleep take me fully when semiconscious Natalie feels the need to add a slurred, slumberous, "I am a good teammate. I hope you treat me this nice during daylight from now on. Then you'd be a good teammate, too."

I'm convinced he's already fallen asleep when I hear nothing back, and that's okay. I can tell him again in the morning.

But then he answers with a quiet but certain, "I'll do my best."

It's the last thing I hear before drifting off.

Chapter Nine

The tent life might've made Finn a little *too* comfortable, because for the first time, I wake up before him.

I don't expect it, assuming when I blink awake that he's probably munching on his breakfast already. But when I stretch my arms over my head and sit up slowly, I see the human-sized lump still in a sleeping bag beside me. I check the clock on my sat phone, fearing we've both overslept somehow, but find we have almost an hour until our go time. We get to set off for the checkpoint five minutes after Harper and Evan's go time, with each team ranked below us in the cooking challenge leaving at five-minute intervals after that.

I look back at the guy on his side facing me, his upper torso and head out in the open. Sometime in the night, he appears to have taken off his sweatshirt, and now he clutches it against the side of his face. With the sweatshirt on top and sleeping bag underneath, his head is squeezed in a Finn sandwich. Wonder what that's all about.

My gaze travels over his features. No trace of Waking Stern Face exists now, with his long, light brown lashes fanned over smooshed cheeks, full lips parted and twitching ever so slightly as if he's forming words in his dreams. It brings a grin to my face—just for a second, before I realize that I'm watching Finn sleep and smiling at him like a super creep.

As if needing him to sleep in the tent with me last night wasn't humbling enough. I don't need him worrying that I've actually taken his apology as a confession of love and think we'll be exchanging promise rings woven out of pine needles.

Hell, I don't even know if he'll still be nice to me today—if he was just doing whatever it took to calm down his mess of a partner in her moment of weakness and in the light of day, when I'm not actively breaking down, he'll resume grumpy business as usual. Nothing I can do but wait and see.

I slip out of my sleeping bag as noiselessly as I can and exit the tent. Finn hasn't even flinched by the time I'm zipping the flap shut behind me. I make it all the way through my morning routine, clothes on and makeup ready, and am halfway through a protein bar breakfast before I hear a peep from him. And it just about scares the ever-loving shit out of me.

"Did I sleep too late?"

I whirl on him. "Well, damn, good morning to you, too!" I yell, as if my volume can make up for his previous lack thereof.

His head jerks back, eyes still blinking against the bright morning sun. "Uh, morning. What time is it? You're never up first."

Even though I thought the exact same thing upon waking,

I scoff. "Okay, rude, and we've only woken up together on two mornings! That hardly justifies a sweeping claim like 'never.' " His blank expression gives me nothing. "It's quarter to nine. I can pack up the tent while you get ready."

When he doesn't point out that it takes him approximately two minutes to "get ready," nor argue that he should pack up because he knows how it all gets put away correctly, I wonder if Finn actually meant everything he said last night. If he wasn't faking for the sake of my fragile mental state. Twenty minutes later, when we hit the trail promptly at our go time—map to the checkpoint we got last night in hand, GoPros rolling, our camp packed up and on our backs once more—I'm almost convinced this change of pace is actually going to last.

Not any change in literal pace—we're still hoofing it, and I feel a little like a corgi trying to keep up with a greyhound as I follow his lead. But I'm not even mad about sweating my ass off under the hottest sun since we've been here, because my teammate is actually talking to me.

"Did I overhear correctly the other night," Finn asks, "that you were an extra in a movie?"

I press a hand to the stitch in my side as we continue speedhiking uphill and try to hide the panting in my voice when I reply, "You did."

"What movie?"

I think about the last time I told someone this, a classmate in Intro to Theater at Oliver, because I thought it was a funny anecdote about my brief stint as a professional child actor. Then I learned I was talking to an actual former professional child actor, who'd played the youngest sibling in a big soap opera family since she was six months old. And who did not find my story funny.

Finn feels like a very different audience. "Uh, it was called *Racing Heart*? It was based on the true story of the racehorse called Million to One, who won the Triple Crown against all odds—including, if you ask me, a pretty cursed name. I was seven and Granny Star took me to the audition, where she got hired as an extra too. And keep this between you and me, but I even had a *line*."

The breath Finn expels sounds almost like amusement, but I can't see his face to tell for sure. "Why does that have to be kept secret?"

"I just want everyone here to treat me like a normal girl. Not to be swarmed by fans and the media." I'm totally channeling my soap-opera-child-star classmate.

"Of course." I smile at his ability to play along, even as a little wariness still lurks at the edges of my mind. Are we really having a friendly conversation like it's nothing? "So do you remember the line?"

"Of course," I echo, then clear my throat before delivering it in a small-child voice with the exaggerated Kentucky accent the filmmakers requested. " 'That sure is some horse.' "

Finn is silent for a moment before he looks at me over his shoulder, as if he was waiting on me to say more. When I don't, he says, "That's it?"

I nod. "I'm in the credits. 'Child at Racetrack Number Two.' "

"I hope you were fairly compensated for your hard work."

"Twenty-five bucks for the day," I say with a fond smile. "Granny Star took me to Walmart right after, and I spent it all on Polly Pockets."

He looks back at me again as we turn around a bend in the trail, and I nearly stumble at the sight of his smile. No teeth showing, but it still packs a powerful punch of *wow*. All twinkly eyes and a dimple in one cheek. No wonder he doesn't smile often; he's flat-out dangerous this way.

"Classic child star, blowing your paychecks with no eye toward the future," he teases. *Teases!* And without even a hint of actual derision. I'm aghast. Agog. Whatever *A*-something words can capture the weight of this moment and its effect on me.

Finn, apparently, has no idea what his casual banter is doing to me. Let alone his face. "You've mentioned your Granny Star a few times. Why do you call her that?"

This helps settle my heart rate somewhat. "Her name is Starla Lee Hart, and she came up with her own grandma name. It always fit her. She's an actress—I mean, was." That familiar lump forms in my throat. I'm terrible at remembering the past tense. But I don't want that word, *was,* to just sit there like a lead balloon, so I hurry on past it. "Worked at a dinner theater in Pigeon Forge, Tennessee, not too far from here, actually. She also did community theater productions on the side, and she's the one who got me to start acting, took me to all kinds of auditions with her. She was the only person in my family who understood me, who embraced all parts of me. I'm not quite sure who I'd be if not for all the time I spent with her growing up. Um." I give a nervous laugh. "You didn't ask all of that, but yeah. It was her name because she said so, but also because she was the star."

"Not asking doesn't mean I didn't want to know," Finn says, gentleness in his voice. It's a balm to the soft, tender parts of me that never expect to be heard and understood—especially not from this unlikely source. I almost want to check that he hasn't fallen victim to some rare Appalachian parasite, one that drains all the unpleasantness from its host's body. He continues without taking his gaze off the trail ahead. "I take it she isn't around anymore."

"Correct. I miss her," I add quietly and without really meaning to. I don't know the last time I said as much out loud, if ever. The vulnerability in just those three words is a shock to my system, and I react instinctively, trying to smooth it over. "But it's fine. It's been a few years, and she was sick for a while. People lose grandparents all the time."

When Finn stops, I almost walk into him, but catch myself with a foot of space left between us. His face is all frowny sternness again as he looks down at me. "None of that has to make it okay, or means you can't miss her."

"I . . ." I thought the appropriate words to tie up the conversation would come to me if I opened my mouth, but they simply aren't. And if I think about what he said too much longer, Finn will have to go search for a bucket to pour his puddle of a partner into and carry me the rest of the way to the checkpoint. So I change course, slapping a fragile smile over everything inside.

"Can we keep walking? We're going to lose that five-minute head start over the next team."

After one more lingering look that surely sees way too much, Finn nods, letting me walk ahead of him. He also allows me to change the subject entirely, even answering when I ask questions about his life. Answers on the shorter side, and definitely less emotional than the whole feelings dump I just let out, but I think that's best for both of us. I learn that he's an environmental sciences major with a focus on conservation, which tracks with pretty much every other thing I've learned about him so far. He's never been to New York City nor seen a Broadway show, which is a crying shame since he lives much closer to the holy land of theater than I do, but I guess people can have different priorities. When he tells me about his little sister, Frannie, the softness coming through his voice is so startling—and sweet—I nearly trip on my own boots.

I forget all about our cameras until he makes a passing, softly grumbly comment about how Frannie will probably be mad it took him this long to mention her on TV. I feel a twinge of disappointment, and something almost like regret, realizing that all the personal stuff I said might not stay between me, Finn, and the forest. But at the same time, it's kind of freeing. Having put a bunch of words I haven't let myself say, feelings I haven't let myself feel, so candidly out in the open.

Still, I grow quieter by the last mile of the three we have to hike to the checkpoint, whether from a new consciousness of the potential worldwide audience, or simply the fact that I don't have any more breath to spare to be cute and entertaining. Finn doesn't say much either, but I can see him looking from side to side, taking in the gorgeous mountain views all around us.

When we hear the voices of *Wild Adventures* folk, it's not a moment too soon. It's hot as balls out here, and between the sun, the speed-walking, and the conversation that distracted me from all of it the majority of the way, I'm a sweaty, heavy-breathing mess.

Burke Forrester's spray-tanned face splits with a smile as we approach. I see Harper, Evan, Zeke, and Enemi already here, but no other teams yet. Still, when Finn starts to run the last stretch to Burke, I feel obligated to do the same, finishing this marathon of a challenge off strong. When we reach the orange flag, I'm fully dripping in places I didn't know had sweat glands. Can my fingernails sweat? My inner ears? Something to investigate another day, when I've showered and my fingers aren't too sweaty to operate Google.

Finn is barely breathing heavily, but his face shines all over. So the guy does perspire, after all.

"Finn, Natalie, welcome to the second checkpoint! How was your night?"

As I'm calculating in my head what I could say, because my partner hasn't been especially chatty in these little interviews, he actually throws me a bone. Or his unpleasantness-feeding parasite does.

"Good. I got the most sleep I have so far," Finn offers. "Natalie almost had to wake me."

Did I? I just let out a winded laugh.

Burke gives a livelier, if over-the-top, chuckle. "Well, your rest paid off. You two have arrived in third place! Meaning you move on to the next leg of the competition. Congratulations!"

I feel myself sway, both relief and exhaustion hitting me, but an arm slips around my waist in the gap between it and my pack. I blink dazedly up at Finn, who is looking down at me with . . . concern? A different expression from the ones I'm more used to, like contempt and consternation.

"You okay?" he asks quietly, as though he doesn't want any of this to be a scene for the cameras. The echo of him asking the same last night sounds in my head, along with his commitment to try to be a better teammate. Is this just . . . that? Him trying to keep his partner standing up straight so he can stay in the competition? Or does he actually care about my well-being?

Does it matter?

I try to shake the thoughts from my head before meeting his eyes. "Fine. I think I just need some water."

Meena and Cammie, who came in fourth yesterday, run up to the checkpoint then. His arm still locked around me, Finn leads me off to the side where the crew has set up some camp chairs. With him this close, I'm suddenly hyperaware of how gross I am. My sweat is surely getting all over him. Jesus H, I haven't showered in days—if you don't count a rain drenching—while also doing more physical activity than my body normally gets in months. I can practically see the cloud of stink and filth around me, like that one Peanuts character no one wants to hang out with.

Pre–*Wild Adventures* Natalie would be too disgusted for words, probably mortified enough to toss a towel at Finn and run off, hoping to never see him again in this life. But it's amazing how fast my standards have changed. Yes, I'm still wearing eyeliner, and they'll likely be building snowmen in hell before that stops. But giving off a normal physiological response after trudging through a forest on a hot day with the majority of my body weight strapped to me? I can live with it. And something tells me Finn can too.

A towel would still be nice, though.

"Can we get some cold water?" Finn calls out to the nearby crew. I know he likely means for drinking, but pouring a whole Gatorade cooler over myself like a coach who just won The Big Game sounds *heavenly*. Or cannonballing into a nice, cold pool. As Finn unceremoniously pushes me into a chair, pack and all, the idea feels more fantastic by the second.

A water bottle appears before my face and Finn goes full dad mode, demanding that I drink half of it as he sits in the chair by mine.

"Bossy," I mutter, bringing the bottle to my lips for a sip.

"Not sorry," he answers. I smile around the mouth of the bottle, just a little.

I chug as instructed while one by one, the remaining teams check in. Zeke and Enemi somehow ran from their campsite fast enough to come in first again, passing the two teams with earlier go times before either of us had even hit the main AT, and I almost don't want to know what their prize will be this round. If it involves soap, I might get violent. Harper and Evan were next, and after us were Meena and Cammie, Daniel and Luis, then Karim and Max. Jay and Tia were ranked last in the cooking challenge yesterday, and once they showed up last to the checkpoint, Burke delivered the news that they'd been eliminated.

We say our goodbyes to them, and temporary goodbyes to Zeke and Enemi, who are off to get massages at a fancy mountain spa. I'm not at all a simmering pot full of jealousy, closer to boiling with every minute I spend in this unrelenting sun.

The rest of us are hanging out by the shelter, and we'll camp as a group once again tonight. While the others split off, some building their tents so they have a place to rest, others digging into the snacks brought out by production, I'm plotting.

"What's that expression for?" Finn's voice is wary as he approaches, carrying an open can of Pringles in one hand and using the other to pop the chips into his mouth.

I don't know what expression I'm making, but I know what the mission in mind is. "Where can a girl go to bathe around here?"

Chapter Ten

"Just when I'd started to think an e-reader wasn't the most useful secret weapon on the trail, the power of pocket-sized literature proves me wrong," I say as we lay eyes on the creek for the first time.

Harper, who had only needed to hear the word *swim* before joining this excursion, nods. "We'll have to get you repeating that on camera sometime. See how many e-reader sponsorship opportunities roll in."

It was Finn's idea to break out the AT info books I apparently mentioned at some point in my ramblings, back when I thought he was ignoring everything out of my mouth. Since *Wild Adventures* doesn't give us regular trail maps, we hit up my e-books to see about locating a water source. There are spigots at the shelters, which he did propose as an option—use one to fill a bucket or empty bear canister, and sponge-bathe out of it.

But I couldn't shake the desire to be surrounded by cool, refreshing water, dunk my head under, rinse all the stickiness away, and Harper felt the same. So we got producers' permission to take a little field trip in our camera-free, obligation-free downtime, and wandered until we found the nearby creek that was described in one of the books. We brought our sat phones in case we got lost, plus a few other necessities.

"Make sure you put all of that somewhere it won't fall in," Finn warns with a pointed look at my toiletry bag as he approaches the creek bank, waterproof hiking sandals strapped on and ready for action.

"Okay, relax, Captain Planet," I call back, taking in the scene before us. "Even if I *was* a monster who didn't care about polluting the environment with all my harmful chemicals, this is, like, three paychecks' worth of products. I definitely don't want any of it floating away."

I was envisioning a creek like the one that runs through the horse farm where I grew up—a small, gentle stream that trickles through a skinny ravine and only goes up to my knees at its deepest point. As a kid, I used to kneel down at its banks or wade around ankle-deep for hours, looking for fossils or other interesting rocks and trying to catch crawdads.

But this creek is much wider and looks deeper—definitely above kid Natalie's head, at least—and rushes over and around big boulders. The water is also super clear, which is helpful in my effort to trick myself into thinking it's shower-level clean.

"Why even bring it, then?" It's getting harder to hear him over the rushing water as he moves farther away and I look for a safe, dry spot to keep my change of clothes. Harper, who just wore a one-piece swimsuit, shorts, and sandals that look like a smaller version of Finn's, hangs her camping towel from a tree before shucking the shorts and hanging them too.

"So I can moisturize right when I get out of the water. It's most effective that way. I also might do some biodegradable shampoo and rinse action on land, if I'm feeling frisky. We'll see."

As I turn my back to both my companions, I'm pretty sure I catch Finn muttering the words "feeling frisky, what the hell" to himself, followed by the sounds of water splashing as he steps in.

"This feels a little like hanging out with my parents before their divorce," Harper deadpans just as I spot a dry, sun-dappled boulder that looks like the perfect stuff holder.

My cackle probably sends some fish scattering while I walk toward my target. "He's not divorcing me at least until we win this thing."

Just after I say it, I second-guess myself. I think I have a decent grasp of Harper's dry, sometimes darkly funny wit, but what if you're not supposed to laugh at the divorced parents of the friend you've only known a few days?

"So do you live with one parent, or alternate, or . . . ?" I turn my head slightly to the side so my raised voice will carry back to her, trailing off as I wonder if I've now taken things to way too serious of a place. "You don't have to talk about it if you don't want to, of course."

Harper's short laugh sounds closer, like she's heading toward the water too. "It's fine, it was a long time ago and we're all way better off since. I don't live with either, now that I have an apartment near school."

Duh, Natalie. I've reached the creek finally, slowly hobbling in my thin rubber flip-flops, but stop short of wading in. "We're all way better off," she said. Even though my parents are together, I can relate. I've always been hyperaware of the fact that they only got married once they knew they were expecting me, an antiquated sense of propriety rather than love driving the wedding that my mom and her more traditional parents pushed for. Granny Star always tried to tell me that both Mom and Dad loved and wanted me, but that was hard to reconcile with all the moments when one or the other would let something slip in their weariest moments, or in the heat of a fight, about the life they could have had. The unfinished end to the sentence being, "if we hadn't had Natalie."

There's no way they'd even still speak to each other if not for me. But me telling them they should divorce, that we'd all be *better off,* would only make them more determined to stay married forever.

"I alternated every other week at each of their houses in high school," Harper says, reclaiming my attention as she wades into my line of sight. "They lived close together. But I try to divide visits equally-ish. You can take the legal adult out of the custody agreement, but you can't take the custody agreement out of the legal adult. Isn't that the saying?"

"Something like that, yeah," I call back with a smile, grateful to find someone else who deals with the hard stuff through humor. She's now knee-deep in the water about ten feet ahead of me, so the temperature can't be that bad.

I wiggle my toes. After days in hiking boots, the freedom is refreshing.

When I take my first step into the creek, it's a few degrees past refreshing.

"*Shhhhitballs,* that's cold!" I squeal, but I don't jump back out. The only way I'll get used to it is to keep going. Eventually, my feet will be numb and I won't care what the temperature is.

"Welcome to the mountains," Finn calls from upstream. He's mostly hidden from me by a boulder but I can hear the smirk in his voice.

"I was starting to wonder if you'd make it in today," Harper adds.

"Hey, watch it—you're not allowed to get along with him if it means ganging up on me!" I stab a finger in her direction. They both snicker. I don't love where that's headed.

Reaching my chosen boulder shelf, I stand on tiptoes to place my clothes, travel towel, and toiletry bag there, then put my hands on my hips and consider my next move. I didn't pack a swimsuit and figured my sports bra and undies would be more or less the same. But now that I'm here, and Harper's in her practical swimwear, the assumption that I can just strip down in Finn's presence feels . . . bold. Should I see what he's doing first? If he wants to turn away or something?

I spin toward him. "Finn, what should—"

I choke on the rest of the question, whatever it was gonna be, feeling speechless. Feeling a whole bunch of other things, too. Because Finn is now visible, having waded into the middle of the creek.

And stripped down to his underwear.

Like it's nothing.

They don't reveal much more than swim trunks would. I just hadn't even readied myself for the fact of Finn *shirtless,* let alone . . . everything else.

"What should what?" he asks with a brief glance my way, clueless that he's being ogled. He goes back to his task of cupping water in one hand at a time, bringing some up to pour over the surprisingly broad, fit expanse of his bare chest, each arm that I definitely hadn't been giving enough credit when they were T-shirt–clad, up his neck, over the top of his head. It's ridiculous, like watching some outdoorsy *GQ* shoot happen in slow motion before my eyes. Dunking himself under water for two seconds would be so much more efficient.

I can't look away.

But then he meets my eyes again, confusion in his. That makes me blink back to the present, to where I am and what's happening. To Harper now wading past me, about halfway between where Finn and I stand. To how I was about to ask the Calvin Klein model in training if it's okay that I take my bonnet off and loosen my corset strings in his presence, because apparently I'm some kind of Puritan now.

"Oh, nothing." The words are comically high-pitched and a little wheezy, like my mouth is too dry. Never mind those liters of water I downed back at camp. Take me to the town square and slap a red letter *T* to my chest, because this girl is thirsty.

I've seen my fair share of hot, less-than-fully-clothed guys, in plenty more intimate circumstances. I can acknowledge that yes, my partner is one of the hottest, but he's also only recently stopped being actively hostile to me. Let's have some dignity and move right along. It doesn't have to be A Whole Thing.

Squaring my shoulders, I summon all the reserves of confidence and shamelessness buried somewhere under the humbling experiences of the past year. I remove my shirt and toss it up beside my fresh clothes, then pull off my leggings, already relieved to be free from damp, clingy cotton.

Finally, I wade deeper in. Goosebumps cover me head to toe by the time the water is at my belly button.

"I think we're swimming in melted polar ice caps," I say through chattering teeth, taking slow, careful steps. My flip-flops don't have the best traction on the rocky creek bed.

"There's the drama I was promised from a theater kid," Finn deadpans, arms crossed over his chest. As I get closer to him, I see they're goosebump-y too.

I gasp. "You *do* listen when I monologue about my life!"

"I listen to everything you say," he says to the water, cheeks going pink.

Harper is drifting beyond Finn now, her head visible just to the left of his shoulder as she gives me a meaningfully raised eyebrow. Which I ignore.

"Oh, sure you do," I retort. "You especially love my nature jokes, and when I talk about skincare. Honestly, I'm starting to wonder if you're obsessed with me-*eee* . . ."

Splash.

Before the last word gets out, my foot slips on a slick rock, and I go cartoon-character-on-a-banana-peel tumbling backward, windmilling my arms through the air before my entire backside hits the water. And a low, flat boulder beneath it.

I'm startled more than anything as I emerge from the surface, spluttering and coughing up water, rubbing it out of my eyes and face so I can see. Warm, strong hands grip my upper arms for the second time today, pulling me up. I slide again, still not able to find good footing, but fortunately this time, I have a softer landing. Smack against Finn's bare chest.

His hiking sandals definitely have better grip, as he stays standing and holds me to him. We're plastered together, front-to-front, chest-to-thigh, completely soaked and breathing heavily. Our gazes lock, our chests rising and falling against each other, and I don't know if I've ever felt this aware of every place another person's skin touches mine. It's a lot of places. One of his hands releases one of my arms and glides over to my back, rubbing a slow circle there that seems almost mindless as his focus stays on my face, tracking from my eyes to lips to cheeks that feel like they're on fire and back. I take in new details of his face up close, like the light brown fuzz on his cheeks, jawline, chin that's starting to move past stubble into beard territory, the faint smattering of freckles across his nose with one especially dark spot under his left eye, a small scar in his lower lip like it was split at some point.

"You good?" Harper's shout from a few yards upstream snaps both of us out of this stunned tableau. Finn blinks a few times, his head jerking back before he puts a foot or two of space between us. With the loss of contact, I return to myself. And reality hits.

"Fine!" I yell back to her, followed by a quiet, gracelessly blurted, "Mother*fucker*." I wince as I bring a hand to my left side, where my hip and butt broke my fall against the big rock underwater. I rotate my body to look down at the area that now throbs in pain, finding that it's already got an angry red patch marking the scene of the accident.

"Are you okay?" Finn asks, reaching out as if to grab me again but stopping himself mid-air. He lets his fingers slowly float the rest of the way until they just barely graze my hip, gently turning me so he can take a look.

"I've given you way too many reasons to ask me that in the past twenty-four hours," I grumble. "But I'll be fine. Just gonna have a big bruise on my ass. Good thing there's so much padding back there, huh?"

His throat bobs on a swallow and he gives a short nod. I don't know if he realizes he's agreed, or that his gaze looks like it's trained on said ass, even though he's likely meaning to check on my injury. Totally innocent. Totally lighting up my insides anyway.

"I didn't know you had a tattoo."

His words aren't what I expect, and I look down at the interlocking star and heart on my ribs as if I didn't know it was there either. "Oh. Uh, yeah. It's from my grandma's signature." A soft, self-deprecating laugh bubbles up. "God, I've talked about her a ridiculous amount since I've been here. I'm not, like, obsessed with my dead grandma. I just thought it was pretty and—"

Finn's fingers brush over the ink for only a second, and I can't hide my gasp in response. My eyes flick up to find his, serious and intense as they've ever been, but with something warmer there too. "It *is* pretty."

Harper's voice is closer this time when she says, "I take back the divorced parents thing."

I didn't even register the light splashing sound heralding her approach, but now she's almost even with Finn, with a look of amused speculation on her face. I whip around to stop displaying my backside like a museum exhibit, and Finn grips my elbow to keep me steady.

He clears his throat. "We probably shouldn't stay in here too long. You have goosebumps everywhere."

Harper snorts before ducking her head underwater, so I can't even give her an innocent look. Never mind the fact that I'm pretty sure these goosebumps Finn is concerned with aren't an indicator of the onset of hypothermia.

I take a bracing breath and nod, avoiding eye contact with either companion. "I'd better start enjoying it, then!"

With that, I plunge down into the creek, dunking my head under for a second before reemerging above my shoulders. The first thing I see when I open my eyes is Finn's rueful smile, and it's devastating. The three of us float there for a while with teeth chattering, making fun of ourselves for choosing this little ice bath. Finn stays closest to me, probably thinking I'm a fall risk.

I wonder if he feels as much of this . . . *something* as I do. Something that surely has to do with the real conversations we've finally been having, the moments of connection and understanding. But it's also this instinctive, unstoppable pull of everything in me toward everything in him, a recognition of attraction clicking into place. It clicked for me, at least. And I don't know if it can be unclicked. Like a seat belt of sexual awareness that I can't take off.

Okay, yeah, I must have hit my head in that fall.

I am just . . . not going there with Finn. There's no way! Yes, there's been a sneakily hot bod lurking under all that khaki. I mean, are those the kind of fit, solid-muscle thighs that hiking gives you? Because if that's the case, maybe I should go ahead and plan on doing the rest of the AT. His biceps aren't overly bulky but definitely indicate he's lifting something other than books and tent poles on the regular, too.

Oh my God, I must be stopped. I splash some cold water on my face, now grateful for the abundance of it at my fingertips. Through the drops coming off my eyelashes, I see Finn stand and take a few steps away, water coursing down his torso in rivulets as he looks out across the creek. *Ugh.*

This changes nothing about how I see my partner, nor how I'll treat him. If anything, the hotter a guy is, the more skeptical I am of him. My dating history might make that look like a lie, but all the dating High School Natalie did is what bred the skepticism. College Natalie knows better, at least about this one thing.

As I turn my head away from the view, I find Harper's eyes on me, too much knowing behind them. I narrow my eyes at her then lean back to dip my hair once more. The chill makes my scalp tingle. Much to my surprise, I feel pretty clean and refreshed as I stand up, shivering in the air that felt scorching not so long ago. Finn looks back to me, and the way his eyes stay trained on my face seems deliberate.

"Ready?"

"Yep!" I chirp, turning quickly so I can make a beeline for my towel and dry clothes. But his hand grasps my elbow, pulling me to a stop.

"Let's take it slow. Your water shoes suck," he says by way of mildly rude explanation.

"Well, excuse me for going the five-dollar-bargain-bin route on this one item. I didn't expect to be doing much creek bathing—or any at all," I huff, but I don't try to shake off his grip. In fact, I want to trap his hand there, keep it tucked against my side for the foreseeable future. He guides me all the way to the rock where my stuff is waiting. The way it evokes helping a little old lady across the street should really kill off any lingering sexiness around the experience, but somehow it doesn't. *We both just need to put our clothes back on,* I tell myself. *That's all.*

But it might not be all, unfortunately. On shore, I commence working a palm full of shampoo into my creek-wet hair, then flip my head over to rinse with a cup Harper fills for me with more creek water. When I straighten up and wring out the brown and purple mop, Finn is leaning against a tree watching, a bemused little grin pulling at his features.

"Not a word," I warn.

He holds his hands up, palms out. "I didn't say anything."

"You didn't have to, Dad," Harper snarks.

From there, it's a hilariously acrobatic process of drying off and changing into dry clothes behind my towel, which Harper holds up for me, involving a lot of flailing limbs and elastic snapping into place by way of a new sports bra, underwear, and shorts. Finn turns his back to us for most of it, thankfully. It's another ordeal for me to comb the tangles out of my confused tresses, then don a tank top. I half expect Finn to have gone back to camp by the time I'm done, but he waits. Idly perusing his surroundings like he could do it all day, because he's just the kind of freak who would watch the trees and sky to entertain himself even if he had other options.

It's not *un*attractive. Nor is the fact that when we return to camp and pack our things away, and I've found an open seat by the campfire, he approaches me with an ice pack in hand.

"For your, uh, side," he says, his ears looking a little red, but it could just be the firelight. When I stare, gaping, at the plastic bag with ice cubes, he explains further. "I filled it up from the cooler. I thought it could help with the bruising."

I shake my head and find my words. "Right. Wow, thanks, Finn."

Taking the bag from his hands, I shift in my camp chair so I can wedge it partly under myself, covering the area of my hip and butt that's aching. I look back up at him and his eyes flit from my hip to my face . . . and he smiles. A real one, small, but with a rare flash of straight teeth and accompanying crinkles forming around his eyes. My heart skips a damn beat.

AS THE SUN sets, some of us munch on s'mores while others set up yet-unassembled tents and begin to turn in. One of the producers staying here for the night breaks out a guitar and starts to play, and, well, one thing leads to another until Evan and I are leading everyone in show tune sing-alongs. Even when this earns an eye roll from Finn across the fire, it feels like a good-natured one—confirmed when he ends it with a wink at me that I feel all the way to my toes.

"My teeth are chattering again," Harper murmurs from her seat beside me when there's a break in the music.

"From the cold?" I eye her shorts and T-shirt. It's cooled off a little from earlier in the day, but I feel pretty toasty from the fire.

"No." She does a dramatic, full-body shiver in her chair. "From all the vibes between you and Finn."

My jaw drops, but I quickly compose myself and look at her like she's lost it. "I have no idea what you're talking about."

"Uh-huh." Her tone is desert dry. A log burning in the fire slips off the log it was resting on, sending up a wave of sparks. Harper points to it. "See? Even the firewood feels the vibes."

"You sound ridiculous," I mutter back, forcing an exaggerated frown onto my face even as the temptation to smile is strong. It has been all evening, as the whole group has hung out around the campfire and this time, Finn has been a part of everything. And *he's* smiled some, or at least hasn't looked miserable.

Luis and Daniel spent a while telling bad knock-knock jokes, trying to see who could get Finn to laugh first. He didn't let either win, but clearly enjoyed their attempts. Over dinner, Zeke peppered him with questions about the health benefits of vegetarianism, which probably got more words out of my partner in one go than I've ever heard, and may or may not have made me burn with jealousy.

Okay, so it's possible I've been a bit hyperfocused. But Harper's wrong about whatever teeth-chattering "vibe" she thinks she's picking up. This is a temporary condition I'm dealing with, courtesy of pseudo-skinny-dipping together and homemade ice pack gifts. And anyway, Finn is giving off no obvious indications that he's experiencing similar, crush-adjacent feelings.

Is he?

I feel less sure by the time the group is winding down for sleep. I saw Finn go to set up the tent earlier, but we haven't talked about sleeping arrangements tonight. I figure I'll address it after my nightly routine, since I'm not even certain what I want yet. He probably doesn't need to be in the tent with me, now that we're camping with the others again. Still, I feel the preemptive anxiety rolling in—the jittery feeling of "I don't know if I'm going to freak out this time, but since I freaked out last time, it's a definite possibility, and I really don't want to deal with those feelings." It makes my hands shake as I take my makeup off, brush my teeth. I know they're not shaking from *vibes*.

When I return to the clearing, though, I don't see Finn anywhere, nor is his hammock set up. Cautiously, I approach the tent, unzip the flap on my side, and . . . find him stretched out there in his sleeping bag beside mine, as if it's the most natural thing in the world, the glow of his e-reader shining on his face as he reads. A wave of relief nearly bowls me over.

He looks up at me as I crawl into the tent, the light of the tablet making all his handsome features clear. And when he gives me that smile again, it hits me just how much trouble I could be in.

Chapter Eleven

There aren't many instances in my life nowadays when being a Horse Girl comes in clutch. But today, the equine angels have smiled upon me, singing in a heavenly chorus, *"Natalie Hart, you are the baddest bitch in this competition!"* I can hear it, I swear.

That's right: at last, my moment to shine on *Wild Co-EdVentures* has arrived. Our challenge is horse-themed.

"That sure is some horse," Finn says as we stand outside the barn at Wallingford Stables, site of today's challenge, waiting on the crew to get set up for filming. His attempt at a Kentucky accent is probably the worst I've heard since I was on the set of *Racing Heart*.

The sip of water I've just taken from my bottle spews out between my lips. When I recover enough to speak, I smack his arm while he just stands there trying to bite down on his grin. "I told you my most famous feature film quote in *confidence*! Don't go throwing it around like you have the right!"

"Don't worry. If any fans try to swarm you, I can fight them off."

When Burke Forrester met us earlier this morning, he gave the whole group the same directions for hiking to the stables and no further information—especially none to explain what horses have to do with the AT. We hiked here as one big, sleepy group, with Finn insisting upon carrying my pack along with his own after getting tired of hearing me whimper in pain every time the hip straps bumped my gigantic bruise. Enemi was the first to suggest, as we all discussed it, that the stables are probably sponsoring this episode.

"I've heard of them before, in equestrian circles," she'd explained. "They have the money for it."

This was how I learned, much to my chagrin, that Enemi and I have more in common than I ever wanted to believe—though her "equestrian circles" are *sliiightly* wealthier than mine, judging from everything she went on about for the rest of the hike. She's even at school with an equestrian scholarship, which confirms my judgmental suspicion that she's not especially in need of *Wild Adventures* money. That's fine—I can't resent her for being born into money.

I *can* resent her for acting like her shit doesn't stink because of it.

I didn't even pipe up to inform her that I ride too, though I got more and more excited as we neared Wallingford Stables. I was trying to temper the feeling anyway, in case we arrived only to learn we'd be mucking out stalls and covering ourselves in manure as a natural bug spray or something equally, well, wild.

When Burke told us we were indeed saddling up and riding later today, ass bruise or not, I was ready. To. GO. Finn, however, was immediately horrified, having never spent time around horses in his life. It's the first time I've really felt more skilled at something than him—if you don't count, like, the skill of social interaction—and I could get used to it.

"So you think we'll have to, uh, go in the stalls with them?" His voice takes on a more anxious edge as we watch a couple of the crew powdering Burke's face and running a comb through his hair, usually a sign that we're about to start rolling.

I look at the cameras set up to face a few of the stalls where the doors have been propped open. Then I look to Finn's increasingly petrified expression. The guy who is unfazed by the potential of a bear run-in is totally freaked by these gentle, giant babies.

"Probably, but it'll be fine. They're sweet! Just don't sneak up on them, and stay where they can see you, not directly in front of or behind them."

"Why?" he barks, and I flinch at the sudden volume spike.

"Um, so you don't get kicked or anything," I say with what I hope looks like a totally chill, you've-got-this smile.

He is not buying it. "You said they're sweet!"

"They are!" I throw my hands up. "But I think I'm pretty sweet, and I still wanna kick people if they startle me!"

"Sweet is not how I would describe you."

I scoff. "Oh, really? How would you describe me, then?"

Yet again, Burke Forrester's timing is impeccable. "Co-EdVenturers! Are you ready to start horsing around?"

Finn answers "no" in a voice I can only, ironically, describe as hoarse. I decide I'll save that one to tell him later.

In light of my partner's fear, which I apparently only made worse, I take the starting position in the extended relay race Burke lays out for us. It involves a series of tasks in and around the barn—the first inside a stall with a horse in it—that culminate with both team members riding across a field to the finish line. Better if Finn has as much time as possible to prepare himself for close contact of the equine kind.

"Ready . . . set . . . adventure!" Burke rings a cowbell to signal the start of the race, and half of us sprint off the starting line and into the barn. I find the stall with a FINN + NATALIE sign hanging under another sign with the horse's name, Daisy. I slow my pace to enter without freaking out the stall's resident.

"Hey there, pretty gal," I coo at the beautiful palomino tied with a halter to the front of the stall. "Mind if I look around a minute?"

The horse blows out an exasperated breath not unlike one of my partner's favorite reactions. I take it as a good sign.

Somewhere hidden in this horse's living space—either in their food or water troughs, or the wood chip–covered floor that doubles as a giant horsey litter box—are three horseshoes. In the corner of the stall are a pair of gloves, a shovel, and a pitchfork, any of which we can use to search for our horseshoes. When we have all three, we take them to our partner for the next leg of the race.

I tug on the gloves first, then plunge my hand into the food trough, dragging it back and forth a few times and feeling for anything hard and heavy. No such luck. Peering over into the big bucket of water, I don't see anything there, either.

"Horse shit!" The words, more of a yelp than anything, come from the next stall over. I can see Zeke's head just over the wall, his face set in a grimace aimed down until he looks up and meets my eyes. "Horse shit. On my shoes."

I jump back into motion and turn to reach for the pitchfork, hiding my amusement. "Hey, that's what boots are for! You're a real horse handler now," I offer encouragingly.

"I think I'll stick with my cats," he answers with more despair than I've ever heard in his voice. "At least when I clean their litter box, I don't have to step in it."

I won't argue there. I use the pitchfork to start hefting up piles of wood chips and all the manure mixed in with them, sifting out the clean chips and hoping one of these shit heaps also produces a horseshoe. They've put more wood chips in here than the stall would typically have, a layer of them blanketing the entire floor a foot deep. All the better for hiding small objects.

It takes me several scoops to find the first horseshoe, giving a victorious whoop as I hang it on the nail holding our name tag before diving back in. The cheers of the team members outside the barn are a nice soundtrack, if I pretend they're all yelling for me. They're interrupted by the occasional victorious cry from someone inside when they find a horseshoe.

Years of mucking out stalls just like this one, clearing the old wood chips and waste and bringing in a new layer, have prepared me well. I'm usually in a rush to get it over with, meaning

I can wield a pitchfork like an automated weapon, my efficiency at scooping near machine-like.

When I locate our third horseshoe, naturally in the very last square foot of the stall that I scoop, I squeal with elation, then jog out of the barn to find Finn.

"Come on, this way!" He sets off from where he's been standing with all the others waiting on their partners, and I realize from briefly scanning the group that I'm the first one to find all the horseshoes. It puts an extra spring in my step as I follow Finn to the next stage.

Long, straight lines of stones mark off a "lane" for each team in the grassy field beside the barn, cameras and producers already set up to capture the activity. At the end of each lane is a metal stake in the ground, at which Finn has to toss our horseshoes. For each horseshoe he lands, we earn a hay bale. I'll stack the hay bales in any formation I can make that will help me climb up to reach a "tack shelf" atop a flat section of the barn roof, which holds everything we need to saddle up our horses.

"How's your aim?" I ask as he gingerly holds the first horseshoe between two fingers. None of our horseshoes were covered in manure, but I understand the aversion anyway.

"Guess we're both about to find out," he says, then tosses the flat piece of metal. My head whips around to see its progress, all the way until it bounces off the stake with a loud clang.

"Hey, that was close!" I chirp, bouncing on my feet and giving him a small clap. It's only when Finn looks down at me with a hint of amusement that I realize I'm *alllll* up in his personal-space bubble. Practically plastered against his side. I step back abruptly, dropping my gaze and muttering a quiet, "Sorry. Carry on."

Another toss, another near miss, but I don't barnacle myself to his leg this time.

With the third toss, he nails it. Barely even a soft clink as the horseshoe perfectly encircles the stake.

"YES!" I shout, jumping up and throwing my arms around his neck. He returns the hug, wrapping his arms around me and lifting for a moment. I'm laughing and breathless when he puts me down, and I stay holding on to his shoulders. Our eyes lock, and I feel it—another *zing* of something between us. Attraction, connection, whatever it is, it throws me off balance, and can't be dealt with mid-challenge. "Go get the horseshoes!" I say hastily. "We need more hay!"

As more teams join us in horseshoe tossing, the chorus of clanging is so loud, I feel bad for the horses just trying to live life. I also feel bad for Finn, for having a short partner who needs more hay bales to reach the shelf than, say, a seven-foot-tall partner would. And I feel bad for myself for being short.

At first, I tried stacking three bales directly on top of each other to see if I could magically climb straight up them. The experiment failed, as my weight instantly toppled them over. Now I'm working on a set of hay stairs, a layer of three bales on the bottom, two stacked on those, and one at the very top.

"One . . . bale . . . mooooore," I sing out to Finn from my perch atop my middle stair, to the tune of "One Day More" from *Les Mis*. "Another bale, another destiny . . ."

"What if you didn't sing right now?" Enemi snarks from the lane beside Finn, determinedly lining up her next toss. "That's the destiny I want at this moment."

"She's just mad we're behind," Zeke whispers. He's sitting on the two bales he's stacked beside mine, one over another. "Which wouldn't be the case if she'd shoveled shit around and let me throw the horseshoes. I'm, like, really good at it. At my school, I've won the championship in intramural cornhole for two years running. I even told her that, but she was all, 'Cornhole and horseshoes are not the same, and my skin is sensitive to hay.'"

As he goes on, I make the appropriately sympathetic noises at the right times and try to disguise how gleeful this rant is actually making me. Another team having conflict can only be good news for Finn and me, right? Please, someone, anyone else, take the interpersonal drama torch from Team Finnatalie. My arms are tired of holding it.

"Hell yeah!" Finn's cheer tears my attention from Zeke as Finn rings another horseshoe. I hop down and rush over to grab the last hay bale I think—hope—I'll need to reach the tack shelf.

I haul it up there as Finn keeps cautioning me to go slow, and be careful, and watch my step. I'm beginning to wonder if I should've claimed a hay sensitivity when, finally, I wrestle it into place and climb up. . . .

And I'm just high enough to reach the tack shelf.

From there, it's a blur as I single-mindedly focus on keeping our lead, carrying armfuls of bridles and blankets and saddles down, load after load, to where Finn now waits warily by Daisy and a second horse, Donald. They've been tied to a fence, their coats already brushed down and their shoes cleaned by stable hands. Finn is now tasked with using all the stuff I bring over to ready them for riding. He even has a list of instructions, to make it easier.

It quickly becomes clear that no part of this is easy for him.

"How do I know they're not going to kick me when I put stuff on their backs?"

"They won't!" I call back, climbing the hay stairs for what I think will be my last load. "Forget I ever said the word *kick*! You can do this, Finn, so get started!"

By the time I'm back, he's only gotten the saddle blankets on Donald's and Daisy's backs, and Zeke and Enemi are starting this leg with their two horses a ways down the fence from us.

"Finn, I'm gonna need you to channel your inner cowboy," I whisper urgently, mustering Finn levels of sternness.

"I don't think I have one of those."

"I think you do. He's just been trampled on your whole life by the unlikely pairing of your inner uptight professor and inner off-grid-granola-barefoot-naturalist . . . guy."

He stares at me in silence for a moment, until I give him a push toward the gear I've been draping over the fence. "Whatever, you know what I mean. Let's go! I'll talk you through it!"

And so I do, watching his ease with the animals grow, slowly but steadily, as he layers each new item onto the horses. I direct him to move that saddle back a little, tighten that buckle by one notch, make sure the bit goes in just right, and the reins don't get twisted up there. Finally, it's time to mount. I haven't seen anyone pass us on horseback to head down the field toward the finish line, so we still have a shot at winning this one.

I demonstrate for Finn how to mount a horse—foot in stirrup, swing your other leg up and over, basically—before he tries it himself. He gets it right away, only remembering once he's up on Donald's back that he is absolutely terrified.

"This is very much not like riding a bike," his shaky voice calls from behind me as we walk our horses into the open field, a teeny tiny orange flag a speck in the far distance. Donald is making a lot of snuffling noises back there, and his rider has yet to buy into my assertion that he's not going to die.

"It totally is!" I chirp back, winking into one of the cameras that are rigged to both the fronts and backs of our saddles, likely capturing all my least flattering angles.

"My bike doesn't have free will," he grumbles. "Or weigh a thousand pounds and have the ability to trample me."

Fair points, but not the time to agree.

Even as we're still racing—or fast-walking, which is all Finn can really manage—to the checkpoint, this is the least anxious I've felt since coming to *Wild Adventures*. These animals calm me like little else. My cousin Liv is actually a therapist who uses horses in her practice, helping kids work through trauma by letting them bond with the animals. It's only just occurred to me to wonder if that kind of therapy exists for adults.

You know, if I had time or money for such a thing.

For the time being, I'm trying to manage Finn's mental state more than my own, distracting him from his fear.

"Did you know there are almost five hundred horse farms in

Kentucky?" I say, projecting my voice to the back of my outdoor theater.

"No," he says, valiantly trying to hide the waver in his voice. "Why is that?"

"It's the horse capital of the world," I say, but as I think about that, I tilt my head to the side. Is that really the "why"? "Or it might be the horse capital of the world *because* there are that many farms. Kind of a chicken-or-the-egg thing, I guess."

It isn't even especially clever or funny. Not my best work by far. But the throwaway comment prompts one of the most magical things that's happened in this experience.

Finn laughs.

I almost fall off Daisy when I hear it. I turn my head, my jaw dropping as I find that it is indeed Finn back there, *laughing.*

"What?" he asks as his chuckling tapers off.

"You've never laughed in front of me before!" I am openly gawking.

His forehead creases. "No way. I definitely have."

"When?"

"Uh, I don't know? But I'm not a robot."

"Mm-mm." I negate him with a shake of my head before looking forward again. "I would have noticed if you'd laughed like *that*. It's so . . ."

"Oh boy," he mutters.

". . . jolly."

"Jolly?"

I nod. "You sound like a cartoon Santa Claus. Ho-ho-ho! I

didn't know you could even produce such a laugh without a red flannel suit and belly full of Christmas cookies."

Finn scoffs. "I do not laugh like that!"

Donald whinnies.

"He disagrees," I say. After a moment's pause, we both lose it.

Our laughter cuts off abruptly, however, when we hear hooves approaching at a rapid clip. I turn my head to see Enemi on a snow-white horse, blazing toward us like she's got a monster on her heels. But in fact, it's just her poor partner, doing his best to keep up with her pace despite how he obviously has no idea what he's doing. His horse is weaving at least as much as Finn's, but faster and looking more agitated about it. Zeke is attempting all kinds of soothing words, but they're canceled out by his continued efforts to make the horse go as fast as Enemi's.

"Out of their way," I call to Finn, steering Daisy as far clear of their path as I can before they reach us, and Finn actually manages to get Donald distanced too.

"Should we try racing them?" Finn shouts back once they've blown by, but his eyes are saying, *"Please don't make me race them."* Realistically, *I* could get Daisy up to a run, try racing Enemi to the checkpoint. But it's the team with both partners there first who wins, and I don't see how pushing Finn to do that will end well for anyone.

"I'm good with second place," I say before turning forward and keeping Daisy plodding along. To myself, I add quietly, "Especially if it means getting there in one piece."

As we go, slow and steady—and I try to tell myself that,

per the old saying, we have any chance whatsoever at winning this race—we have a clear view of Zeke's and Enemi's progress. Or Enemi's progress, and Zeke's increasingly wild detours, his horse taking him in big, wavy circles while he tries to rein it in. Enemi gets fed up waiting for him and brings her horse over, taking the reins to Zeke's horse and starting to lead it along by force. Zeke's horse doesn't like this one bit and looks more and more distressed, slowing them down enough that Finn and I actually start to catch up.

But not quite. Enemi, Zeke, and their horses make it to the orange flag at least twenty yards ahead of us. Enemi drops the other horse's reins and screams as she throws her arms up in victory.

And Zeke's horse rears up on its hind legs, throwing Zeke to the ground.

Chapter Twelve

The best part of surviving a near-death experience is getting to tell the story.

Over and over. In great detail. Considering different angles and possible outcomes and how great it is that none of those happened.

This is what I have to assume, anyway, given how Zeke is handling the aftermath of the horse-throwing. I can't completely blame the guy; it was scary as hell as a spectator, so I can only imagine what he felt. But after the medics came and declared him, miraculously, completely fine besides a little bruising, I was ready to be grateful for Zeke's durable skull and move on. Because I prefer not to relive the scary things repeatedly. But far be it for me, I guess, to tell our well-meaning resident himbo he's doing trauma wrong.

"He keeps leaving out the part where Alli called him a dumbass *while* he was being put on a stretcher," Finn murmurs from his seat next to me at one of the long tables in Wallingford Stables' dining hall.

I snort into my cup of Dr. Pepper, then put it down and try to do a cuter, classier laugh for the cameras filming B-roll to advertise how amazing Wallingford Stables is (#ad #sponsored). "Ha! Oh, Finn, you're so funny," I say with an exaggerated smile and what would be a hair flip, but I forgot my messy, creek-washed hair is up in a bun.

"Is he?" Harper asks, covering her mouth while she finishes a bite of spaghetti. "And was that a neck twitch?"

I turn my dazzle in her direction. "Oh, Harps. You're hilarious too."

"Okay, really." Finn eyes me with skepticism, turning his water glass in a circle on the table. I shouldn't have been surprised that from one of those soda machines with five million soda and flavor combinations . . . he chose water. "What are you doing?"

I let out a frustrated sigh but keep smiling, which probably looks more unhinged than a failed hair flip. "This is my chance to make my commercial acting debut as a generic hot person having a great time at Wallingford Stables. But since the acoustics in here are too shitty for mics, I have to really sell it with expressions and gestures."

Luis, sitting next to Harper, asks Finn sincerely, "Are we sure she's not the one who got thrown from a horse?"

My shoulders fall, and I let myself sink into bad posture to match my messy hair and the makeup I sweat off. Generic hot person, I am not right now. But still. "Am I not allowed to have a little fun? It's been a long day!"

We're all a lot worse for wear since this morning's hike. Apparently no one but Enemi and I had any horse experience, and most struggled through the whole challenge. Daniel and Luis, the last team to make it to the checkpoint, didn't get there until twenty minutes after us. The medics had mostly finished checking Zeke over, and the two stragglers were deeply confused, having been too focused on the race to notice the commotion.

Zeke's accident turned out to be Luis and Daniel's gain. The whole ordeal shook everyone up so much that producers, with Burke Forrester as bearer of good news for us Co-EdVenturers and the future audience, decided there would be no elimination at this checkpoint.

So here we are, one big, happy-ish, bone-tired family of people who still want to beat each other to win $100,000.

It should feel weirder, hanging out with the competition like this, especially as the group thins out challenge to challenge. But it's like once we reach each checkpoint, we all want to recharge more than anything, and being hostile or calculating with anyone else takes too much energy.

At the same time, I can see how making friends with your competitors can bring out complicated feelings. I learned while talking to Meena in the buffet line, for example, that the living-learning program she was in during her freshman year, which paid for her room and board and half her tuition, is being phased out. If she doesn't get more scholarship money, her family's going into debt with a ton of loans. Harper told me last night, revisiting our talk by the creek, that the only thing her parents still fight about is paying for her school. She's hoping to make that go away if she wins the money. Even Daniel got to me, as he told us on the hike about watching *Wild Adventures* as long as it's been airing, and dreaming since he was a kid of winning the whole thing.

How am I supposed to wish for any of these folks to lose so I can win? Do I really deserve it over any of them?

"Are you done?" Finn asks, making me realize I've been ruminating over my empty pasta plate for who knows how long. I grab my dishes and follow him to the return area, and gradually everyone else wraps things up in the dining hall. The crew leads us out as a group, Harper and I making faces at each other in the back of the pack and, rather interestingly, I catch Zeke making an entirely different kind of face at Harper when she's not looking. The moony-eyed kind. Maybe I can tease her about vibes later.

We're directed to our accommodations for the night—a full glamping experience in little bare-bones cabins dotted around the stables' property, with one set of bunk beds and barely enough room for two people to stand up in each of them. We also learn there's a laundry room we can use, so I immediately start a load with almost all the clothing in my pack. But best of all—there are communal bathroom buildings. With *showers*.

I take my sweet-ass, still-bruised-ass time, absolutely basking in the low-pressure stream of lukewarm water. There's a shelf on which I can set my entire toiletry bag, and I luxuriate in the chance to have clean hair and armpits and every other nook and cranny for the first time in almost a week. I'll never take indoor plumbing for granted again, I swear to Dolly.

I've never been so refreshed as when I step out of the steamy stall and head to the bay of sinks. I stand before a mirror for another half hour, applying various serums and even a "heavy-duty repairing and replenishing" mask. I've probably given this product the heaviest duty it's ever faced.

With my last pair of clean undies and pajamas on and my whole body basically having gone through its own spin cycle, I truly feel like a new me. I'm certain no one's ever looked as happy as I do when transferring clothes from the washer to the dryer after my shower rendezvous. When I return to the cabin afterward and find Finn—also freshly showered and clean-shaven, though he likely took a quarter of the time—sitting on its tiny front porch reading, he looks at me with a semblance of concern.

"You're making that face again," he says.

Feeling my own wide eyes and smile that shows every molar, I say, "What face?"

"The one from your commercial acting at dinner, where you look like a Muppet that stuck its finger in a light socket."

I put my hand on my hip. "What a uniquely offensive insult, sir! Ex-*cuuuse* me for feeling joy!"

He shrugs, unrepentant. "I didn't say it was a bad look."

I laugh as I enter the cabin to put away my stuff. When I come back out, Finn still sits there, hands clasped over his flat stomach, taking in the view of the sun setting over the pasture. I sit in the chair next to his.

"Was Enemi about to strangle Zeke with a fettuccine noodle at one point, or was I seeing things?"

"Was who about to strangle Zeke?" Finn's forehead scrunches up.

My eyes widen, realizing my slip. "I meant Alli."

He gives me a dubious look, which I avoid by staring straight ahead.

"I don't know. But I'm more curious about why she's your enemy."

"All right, Mr. Eagle Ears, congrats on your stellar auditory comprehension," I say, giving him fake-impressed jazz hands.

"It's 'eagle eyes.' I don't think eagles have good hearing," is his reply.

"I said what I said!"

I peek at Finn out of the corner of my eye.

He smirks.

I sigh.

"It's just a nickname I call her in my head, because she was kind of a dick to me, and that was even before she tripped me while we ran for the same backpack, and yeah, it's a whole thing. I'm not great at burying hatchets. But it's fine."

He seems to consider this. "She doesn't seem like the most agreeable person in general. I'm sure it wasn't personal."

"Maybe, but I hate when people say 'It's not personal' or 'It's a problem with them, not with you.' Like, sure, but if they make you feel like shit regardless, what does it matter whether it's got anything to do with you?"

"True," he says, sending a brief, speculative glance my way.

"I guess the idea is that maybe it'll feel less shitty if you know you haven't done anything wrong."

I shift in my seat. "That almost makes it feel worse to me. Because then I'm powerless. If being a nice person doesn't make people reciprocate that niceness, sometimes it's like, why do I even try? Is it all pointless, so I should be an asshole whenever I feel like being an asshole?"

Finn leans forward and props his elbows on his knees, looking me square in the eyes. "Are we still talking about Enemi?"

Oof. He's right. But do I want to go there with him right now? This peace between us still feels tenuous, and I don't give out my trust freely. I think I want to test the waters in his creek first—see if he's ever going to divulge anything deeper about himself, give *me* any trust. I stretch my legs out in front of me, sinking down in the camp chair.

"Maybe not. But enough about me and my hatchets. Can I ask you a question?"

I can see his shoulders tense. "Will you use said hatchet on me if I point out that you just asked me one?"

"My weapon of choice is my biting wit, so no."

Finn nods slowly. "Okay. Well, go ahead, then."

Steepling my fingers under my chin, I cut an appraising look his way. "Why did you apply for *Wild Adventures*?"

His brows rise, though I don't know why. What did he think I would ask, what his purpose in life is? How many partners he's had, and if he's into women? Perhaps, in particular, women with multicolored hair and little to no filter? My cheeks heat at the thought. Definitely don't need to go that route.

"Besides my lifelong dream of becoming Burke Forrester?" he asks with mock sincerity.

"Well, that part's a given," I say.

A small smile crosses his face as he looks down at his hands, but soon after it's replaced by something more melancholy.

"I grew up watching the show with my dad. It was the only series we consistently kept up with, as ridiculous as we both found it some of the time. Reality TV, right? It's silly, and my mom made fun of us, but we loved it. Loved sharing it."

My gut clenches as I note that he's speaking in past tense.

"For years, we talked about trying out for it as a father-son team when I got older. Maybe when I was in college or after graduating, as a 'welcome to adulthood' celebration. I mean, if they even picked us—obviously odds were slim, but we always talked about it like it was a sure thing, just waiting on us to fill out the application. Then a couple months into my senior year, my dad got sick."

Finn pauses to swallow heavily. I feel like my heart is in my throat, and I pull my knees up to my chest and wrap my arms around myself.

"So yeah, that didn't go well. His cancer was stage four when they found it, prognosis was bleak. He actually made it longer than expected, till the month before I went off to school."

When he pauses again, I can't stop myself from shifting my chair closer to his, reaching out to put a hand on his shoulder and give it a strong squeeze. "Oh, Finn. I'm so, so sorry."

Finn nods his hanging head, and when he lifts it again, I

see his eyes are shiny. Of course I'm a goner then, my own eyes prickling with tears that I don't want him to see.

"Yeah. Thanks." His voice is firm. "I almost didn't leave for UVM, thought about deferring for a semester or a year, even. But my mom didn't want that for me, and she was in such a rough place—I mean, still is, sort of—that I'd do anything she told me to. And obviously, it was at UVM that I found out about this Co-EdVentures thing, and thought it was kind of a sign. So even though I hadn't been camping since Dad got sick, I decided to apply in his honor, and the rest is history."

He sits up straight then, and I pull my hand back, scrambling to disguise my leaking eyeballs and get my shit together. But it's no use—he obviously sees, and his face, which wasn't especially cheery to begin with, falls further.

"Aw, Natalie, no. Don't—it's okay. I'm okay. Or—" He scrubs a hand over his head roughly. "I'm not, but I am. I didn't mean to make you feel bad."

"Stop it!" One of my hands flaps maniacally in his direction. "Don't feel like you have to console me. I'm just really sorry for what you and your family went through—continue to go through." I wipe most of the remaining tears from my eyes and cheeks with the back of my other hand, not even sure what the right words are to say here. I've never known someone who lost a parent this young. Finally, I settle on, "That is so completely shitty."

God, Natalie. So eloquent, so helpful.

But to my surprise, Finn huffs out a quiet laugh. "Yeah.

That's about the best way to describe it. Shitty like nothing else I've dealt with."

I swallow heavily. "I'm sorry for making you talk about it." Something else occurs to me then, and I cover my face with my hands, muffling the next words. "Oh god, and for going on about my dead grandma as if it's the worst loss that's ever happened to anyone, when you've been dealing with this."

"What are you even saying?" Fingers gently wrap around one of my wrists and tug, bringing my hand down. I don't look at Finn but let him pull the hand between our seats, let his warmer one engulf mine in a firm grasp, interlacing our fingers. "First of all, I don't know if you've noticed by now, but you can't make me talk about anything I don't want to talk about."

That gets a short, sniffly laugh out of me. But I still feel bad for bringing up something hard for him. And self-centered for how much I've dwelled on Granny Star, every single thing out here reminding me of her, when my own partner has faced much worse.

"It helps me to talk about it," Finn continues patiently. "Even if it also hurts. And if I'm talking to someone who's been there too, no matter what their loss looked like, it's even more powerful. Loss and grief put you in the world's shittiest club, but once you're there, once you know what it's like, you can't un-know."

I nod slowly, the words ringing so true. No matter how much I've downplayed it, told myself Granny Star was old, lived a long life, people lose grandparents all the time, and it shouldn't be that hard, none of those things change the fact that her death changed me as a person. Changed how aware I am that at any time, you can just lose someone who feels essential to you and never get them back. There's no returning to when I didn't know, didn't think about it every single day.

"So yeah, I did my share of trying to stay strong and 'get over it.' I've had to learn to let myself dwell in the darkness when I feel like it, share the good memories when I have them—it's all part of processing and grieving, and not something either of us needs to feel bad about."

I'm just a little saltwater fountain over here now, a steady stream flowing down my cheeks, dripping off my chin. Whew, this has gotten real heavy, real quick. Since I brought us into the dark place, maybe it's my job to get us back to the light.

When I think I can speak without totally embarrassing myself, I say, "Who knew this deep well of emotional intelligence was hidden under all the grunting and growling?"

His grin is small, a little rueful. "Lots of therapy. Keep it to yourself, though. I have a reputation to uphold."

"Secret's safe with me." I smile, face forward, and let my head fall back to look up at the evening sky. "Maybe I'll get around to therapy one of these days. If we win this hundred thousand."

"How are those two things related?"

I consider how much to give away with my answer. But at this point, so many of my cards are on the table, I might as well lay down the rest of the hand. "Money. Time. I don't have either."

Finn hums thoughtfully. "Isn't that the college experience?"

"Yeeeah," I hedge, "but I think I've pushed it to the limits.

Which is why, as any reasonable person would, I applied for *Wild Adventures*."

"Oh, good!" Finn gives a short laugh, with only a trace of his Santa Claus guffaws from earlier. "I was hoping I wouldn't be the only one dumping my baggage out in the open tonight. Should I get the popcorn?"

"Nope. If you leave for even a moment, I might lose the nerve for story time." It doesn't come out like a joke, and I guess it really isn't.

"By all means, then, proceed."

I sigh and let my head roll sideways so I can see his face, all open and encouraging. And damn, so handsome. "Well, at the risk of sounding like a shallow bitch, I'm here for the money."

Finn gives me a sardonic look. "Yeah, yeah," I go on before he can get a word out. "It's true, though—I need the scholarship. My parents couldn't pay for my school, even if they were willing, which they're definitely not. So I applied to every funding source out there and got it mostly covered. My retail job accounts for my other expenses including, more recently, all the random camping shit I bought to come here." I laugh as I nod toward the cabin's interior where our packs sit.

"Anyway, it turns out that college is hard. Who knew? Not just the classes, but the social aspect, trying to eat and sleep enough, all kinds of challenges I didn't see coming. I developed what ended up being really bad anxiety, and probably could've used therapy or even medication, but it just felt like one more thing I didn't have the capacity to deal with, so I didn't. My grades took the biggest hit and I lost my merit scholarship, so I've been scrambling to make up for it any way I can. I've casually watched *Wild Adventures* over the years and, I mean, like you've said, it isn't exactly in line with my skill set. But all I saw were the dollar signs, and I've somehow made it through so far. Probably thanks to you, for the most part. I'll do everything I can to try to get us to the finish line, whether it looks like I'm doing the best job or not. If I can feel more secure about money going into next year, I have to believe more of the other stuff will improve too."

Finn looks contemplative, his gaze moving over my face for so long that I want to cover it again, then realize he's still holding my hand. Does he notice?

"Natalie . . . ," he begins, and my chest tightens. "Any of the times I implied you weren't cut out for this, I really was being an asshole. In all honesty, I respect you even more for how out of your wheelhouse it is. You're giving it your all at every moment, and that's gutsy as hell. No matter what I've made you believe, I couldn't have come this far without you either. You're amazing." He gives my hand a squeeze, his deep brown eyes staring into mine like they can see straight down to my nervous wreck of a soul. "And I'm sorry you've had such a hard year."

I blink rapidly, feeling the emotion creep in at the corners of my eyes again, but not willing to look like a weepy freak just because a boy said nice things to me. "Well, uh, thank you," I murmur after a long stretch of heart-squeezing eye contact. "That's . . . very nice of you."

"Just the truth." He pulls his hand back and looks away, and I feel a chill run through me with the loss of both forms of contact.

This night with this guy has solidified it—there is so much more to him than the grumbly grump I first saw, or who he allowed me to see. And the more I get to see beneath the surface, the more I feel for him. Without intending to, I let out a dreamy sigh.

Finn side-eyes me, raising a single, questioning eyebrow. "Yes?"

I whip my head forward, belatedly trying to salvage my cool. Way belatedly. "You're just . . . really different than I thought you were, those first couple days."

After a moment's hesitation, Finn replies, "The feeling is mutual."

"In a good way," I add.

"A very good way," he agrees.

I'm glad it's too dark for him to see what's surely the expression of a smitten fool on my face. The silence stretches long enough that I think we're done talking for the night, and I consider ways to gracefully say "This was a lovely heart-to-heart, but I gotta go fold my clean underwear and mentally unpack every single word you've said to me" when Finn adds one more thought.

"And listen, Nat. We're going to win you that scholarship money. Whatever it takes."

Chapter Thirteen

Somehow, the night in a bunk bed is less comfortable than the ones I spend sleeping on the ground. I honestly think I wake up with new bruises from tossing and turning on the thin foam "mattress," if you could even call it that. Though I'm sure I also have the horses to thank for my soreness.

Whatever the reasons, I'm groaning and moaning like a crotchety old bag of bones as I rise from my slumber and crawl out from my bottom-bunk cave. Then I shut myself up real quick upon finding that Finn is still fast asleep on the top bunk. Same as when we've woken up in the tent, he sleeps on his side and clutches his sweatshirt—freshly laundered along with the rest of his clothes—to his head. I wonder again what that's all about. Is he most comfortable that way? Is it just a habit? It's pretty cute regardless, making his normally hard features look childlike.

But after our talk on the porch, I have a whole new understanding of the intense, guarded quality to those features. The guy has been through some shit. I don't know what it's like to have a good relationship with a parent, but to lose that, and at such a young age, seems unthinkable. I have the urge to wrap him up completely in a mega version of his sweatshirt, squeeze him tight as if cutting off his air supply will soothe his grief.

Unfortunately that's when Finn decides to wake up. His eyes pop open abruptly, giving me a real jump scare.

"Are you watching me sleep?" he asks groggily, blinking a few more times against the morning light peeking through the cabin's one tiny window.

Pretty obvious that I was, yes. "No!" I cross my arms over my chest. "I was having a really good daydream about burritos. Your face just happened to be in my line of sight."

His mouth tips up on one side and a warm, gooey feeling settles in my stomach. He's giving those more freely every day, but each one still feels like a gift I want to tuck away in my pocket.

God, when did I become such a sap? And over *Finn*? No, this ain't happening. Panic starts to replace the warm gooeyness and I turn away quickly, hoping he won't see it.

"I'mgonnagogetreadyinthebathroom," I say in a rush while grabbing my toiletries and a change of clothes, then scramble out of the cabin like it's on fire.

I try to savor these fleeting moments with a mirror and running water, but I'm distracted by my own thoughts. I mean, what the hell, Natalie? This is an irresponsible level of interest, the likes of which I'm pretty sure I haven't felt since starting to date my first boyfriend in seventh grade. Normally when I'm into a guy—or when I let myself be into them, pre-Oliver—it burns hot and fast. It's an attraction that's mostly physical and we both know it, and when it inevitably flames out, I'm never left heartbroken because my heart was barely involved.

Finn is already so different. But this crush feels doomed for a multitude of reasons, starting with the fact that he's my partner, followed by how neither of us has time for any distractions from winning this competition. And even if we did, he probably doesn't have any interest in me, given his general "Ew, Natalie" aura for most of our time together.

On the plus side, I am a stone-cold, outdoorsy fox today. My freshly laundered shorts show off my newly smooth legs. The pit stains on my tank top's arm holes are gone. My winged eyeliner is immaculate. My superclean, conditioned hair is smooth and shiny, so I've only pulled half of it up into a ponytail, displaying the purple streak to its best advantage.

When I make it back to the cabin, the difference does not go unnoticed.

"Wow," Finn says like it's nothing, like the word combined with his raised eyebrows and the way he looks me up and down isn't lighting up my insides like a Christmas tree. *Ho-ho-ho, indeed.* "You look . . . renewed."

Not quite the same effect as *beautiful, gorgeous,* or *hella fine,* but better than an electric-shocked Muppet.

"Why thank you," I say with a mock curtsy. "You know what they say. Look good, feel good, hike good."

"Ancient Appalachian proverb," he agrees with a nod.

After a filling breakfast, we get our map back to the AT and the site of the next challenge, with several possible paths to get there, and all take off as teams. The path Finn and I choose to hike, along with Karim, Max, Harper, and Evan, isn't especially rigorous, but you wouldn't know that from my achy body's reaction. Fortunately, everyone else is sore after yesterday's ride too, whining about it as least as much as I am. I don't let Finn carry my pack this time, even when he offers repeatedly, declaring that I can't let him ruin my trail cred.

That he accepts this as a good reason makes me like him even more.

I'm realizing the hikes pass much more quickly when we're in a bigger group. The route we chose from the stables to the challenge site is about five miles, and with more than enough time until the filming start time the crew gave us, we keep a moderate pace and stop together when anyone needs a water break.

The vibe is easy, our banter comfortable. Karim wins my undying love and respect as he details his plans for launching a boutique jewelry line called Ice Karim, inspired by a lifetime of people thinking his name is "Cream." Max briefly tries to get a round of the Alphabet Game going, like we're on a road trip, before realizing there aren't any billboards, license plates, or much else with letters on it out in the forest. Evan and I duet on what we agree is the best song from *Frozen 2,* "Lost in the Woods," even as Finn grumbles that we're bringing bad karma to the hike. I'm just glad it feels like our good spirits are restored, though none of us really knows how Enemi and Zeke are faring.

When we make it to the destination on our map, we find

ourselves in a flat, open space atop some cliffs with gorgeous panoramic views of the mountains, where we learn we'll be camping tonight. We get to stop and take it in while the crew readies for filming and passes out sandwiches and assorted fruit for lunch. Just as we're wrapping up mealtime, Burke Forrester arrives, looking fresh as a daisy. No way did he hike here from the stables.

We gather around him at the cliff's most scenic edge, cameras rolling again. It's only now that I realize how windy it is up here, or maybe the breeze is just picking up. My hair blows into my face, sticking in my recently applied lip gloss and reminding me why I've mostly done away with lip gloss since I've been here.

Our host beams, his hair so still it has to have been gelled within an inch of its life. "Co-EdVenturers! Welcome back to the Appalachian Trail. Feels like coming home already, doesn't it?"

I wonder not for the first time if Burke has actually hiked the AT before. I've seen little evidence to suggest he considers it so homey.

"I'm excited to have you all together today for the next part of your challenge, which we're calling 'Helter Shelter.' This all about making do when a place to rest your head is hard to come by. In the early days of the AT, permanent shelters weren't as plentiful or well-maintained as they are today, and many thru-hikers relied on their own ingenuity to build lean-tos and other safe places to sleep each night. Even for the modern hiker, the wilderness is unpredictable. We want to channel these early hikers, testing your ability to adapt under less-than-ideal circumstances and create your own shelter."

I shoot Finn a wide-eyed look, but his expression doesn't mirror my concern. He just gives me a subtle nod, as if saying "We got this."

Not sure where he gets that idea, but his confidence isn't unattractive. *Dammit.*

"You can use anything from your packs except your tents, and you *should* use plenty of materials found in your natural surroundings. Get creative! You will have two hours to work on your shelters, but you won't be able to make alterations after that, so you'll need to ensure yours will adequately shield both partners from the elements and stay standing overnight. I'll be judging the suitability of your shelters in the morning. Without further ado . . . Ready, set, adventure!"

Some of the other teams immediately run off into the forest, taking me back to the Great Backpack Scramble of day one. I'm about to do the same, not even sure where I'd be running to, but Finn's hand clasps mine and keeps me in place. A small gasp leaves my lips, and I tell myself it's the surprise of his hand rather than the feeling of his skin touching mine.

Very chill.

"I think we should start by finding a good tree we can build around. How does that sound?" he asks.

My eyelids flutter, and I'm annoyingly preoccupied with the way he hasn't released my hand. Is this just a thing we do now? But more importantly, he immediately asked my opinion on how we should execute a challenge. I could make a big deal over it, and a couple days ago, I might have. But for once in my life, I don't feel like choosing sass.

"Uh, yeah, that sounds good to me," I answer with a nod.

"Good." He gives my hand a quick squeeze before waving for me to follow him farther into the woods as he slings his pack onto his shoulder.

It quickly becomes apparent that I have no idea what constitutes "a good tree." I think I'm learning how Charlie Brown felt in his Christmas special, when all his friends roasted the shit out of him for his dinky little sapling. Finn is, fortunately, gentler about it.

"Let's look for one with a wider trunk that we could lean branches against," he says about the thin birch I first point out, way too proud of myself for the new tree identification skills I've gleaned from my AT info books.

At my next attempt, a big oak tree: "That might be a little *too* wide, if we want to tie anything around it to secure it, you know?"

"Maybe one that's a little less"—he holds his forearm out at about a forty-five-degree angle in front of the beech tree that *is* rather lopsided— "Leaning Tower of Tree-sa?"

A shocked laugh sputters out of me at the joke. "Finn Markum," I say amid unstoppable giggles, pushing back the hair whipping chaotically around my head. "Was that a *nature pun*?!"

His cheeks go pink. "I think you know the answer to that," he says sheepishly, turning to resume scanning the forest for our perfect shelter tree.

"I know, I just—I kind of can't believe my ears," I continue in wonder.

"Well, be-leaf it," he replies with no inflection, not looking my way as he walks off.

I stand there gaping for a second before jogging to catch up with him, more surprised laughter bubbling up. "Are you kidding me with this!"

"Nope. This tree will work." Finn comes to a stop in front of the sturdy trunk of a sugar maple, its lowest branches hanging at about his height.

"I'm sorry," I say, holding up a hand as I bend at the waist to try to contain my hysteria. "I'm gonna need a second before I can focus on the challenge again."

He drops his pack and kneels to start digging through it. "Pine by me."

"*STOP*," I wheeze, the belly laughs coming out full-force. "Who even are you right now? Has this awful dad humor been lurking right beneath the surface all along?"

Finn shrugs as he pulls out his rolled-up hammock and the straps used to hang it. "I'm normally more of a subtle, blink-and-you'll-miss-it joke guy, but I'm trying to branch out."

"Oh! My! God!" I skip to close the few feet of space between us, then grab him by the shoulders and give him a shake. "Real Finn, if you're still in there somewhere, blink twice. Better yet, growl a passive-aggressive insult at me. I'm concerned aliens have replaced you with a Finn look-alike who learned human communication from a dollar store joke book, and I don't know if production will still let me win without my original partner."

Something about that finally breaks him. The serious mask slips completely, and not only is he smiling—with teeth!—but he lets out that deep, rumbling laugh. And doesn't stop. I have to sit down beside him as his laugh gets me going again, and we're both leaning against the tree, clutching our stomachs. It's not even that his puns were that funny—god, they weren't—but it's like some last bit of tension between us has finally broken down, and I think we both feel it.

"Whew, okay, we should really get to it," Finn says breathlessly, slowly getting to his feet before holding out a hand to help me do the same. I grasp it and, not expecting him to pull me up so swiftly and easily, stumble toward him a step, putting a hand to his firm chest to stop me from crashing into him yet again.

"Don't worry," I say breezily, giving his chest a pat as I take a step back. "We have *plant*-y of time."

The wordplay ridiculousness goes on for the rest of the afternoon as we build our shelter, even as it proves more challenging than expected, with the wind repeatedly blowing down anything we set up. Nearby, I sense other teams getting frustrated, hear voices rise and many a frustrated groan. But it's like Finn and I have built a little force field of good spirits, one I couldn't have imagined as a possibility days ago. We collect downed branches to make a lean-to structure against the tree trunk, calmly discussing our approach until every so often, one of us works in a new nature/tree/forest-related pun, and we're lost to the giggles again.

For some reason, the cheesiness of this back-and-forth with Finn does not make me feel like puking. Not in the least. Which shows that something is seriously wrong with me. Did he really look *that* good with his shirt off? Is there some kind of syndrome you can develop from being isolated with one other human in somewhat extreme circumstances in which you start to mistake the most basic signs of human decency as attractive qualities of a potential mate? I think I have that.

But I'm also feeling less and less inclined to find a cure.

Chapter Fourteen

By the time our two hours are up, Finn and I have proven to ourselves that we totally could've survived all this time without our tent. Tents are for the unadventurous. The conventional, inside-the-box thinkers.

Our shelter is badass. It's built from fallen branches and sticks no bigger than my arm leaning against the tree at an angle to form a little upside-down cone. Finn wrapped the hammock straps around the trunk and the top of the sticks for extra stability. And over the top of it all, we've draped the hammock itself as a roof and gigantic windbreaker.

The camera crew that stopped by every so often to film our progress is almost certainly convinced Finn and I foraged some psychedelic shrooms. They've never seen our team communicate that much, let alone laugh till we both have the hiccups. And it certainly wasn't the general vibe of the teams today. The wind was our common enemy. Daniel and Luis's shelter is already half collapsed by the time we're gathering around the campfire for dinner.

The collective mood has darkened since this morning, it seems to me, while we build our own burritos with campfire-cooked ingredients. I'm tempted to get another sing-along going but can read a metaphorical room. I'm glad to see, at least, that Finn has plenty of filling veg options to eat, and even though I totally lied about having a burrito daydream this morning, the meal is highly satisfying. Afterward, we all sit around the fire, eating our feelings in the form of "mountain pies," which are essentially s'mores ingredients folded up into leftover tortillas. The marshmallow-chocolate combo is a classic for a reason. Zeke makes an absolute massacre of the three he consumes, the lower half of his face covered in a big ring of chocolate by the time he's done. This, at last, breaks some of the tension, everyone dissolving into laughter when he turns to Harper and asks so innocently, "Do I have anything on my face?"

I'm grateful for the levity, and when I see the secret smile Zeke tries to hide behind a napkin, I suspect the big guy knew exactly what he was doing.

When we all split off and turn in for bed, sleep comes easier than I expect. I settle into a comfy spot in my sleeping bag inside our little lean-to, shut my eyes, and drift right off before Finn's even put his e-reader away, apparently too worn out to anxious-spiral about anything.

Unfortunately, I'm woken up some unknown amount of time later by the soft howl of the wind. Normally I'd roll over and go right back to sleep. But I can't once I realize that Finn's sleeping bag is empty beside me.

Most likely, he just went out to pee. It's still pitch-black outside, and I don't feel rested enough for more than a few hours to have passed. He'll come right back, I'm sure.

That's what everyone whose partner goes missing in the woods thinks, a voice in my brain whispers. I decide to wait up until he gets back. Not that I could fall back asleep now, anyway. My heart is racing too much, my mind running through all the ways Finn could've met his demise on the other side of these dead tree branch walls. Walls that feel like they're closing in on me, tighter with every minute he's gone.

After a beat, I dig out my satellite phone and check the time. You know, for when the police ask me later. 1:58 a.m.

To occupy myself, I find my headlamp, turn it on, and survey our small shelter space. His sleeping bag is here, boots are gone. Sweatshirt he always has over his head when he sleeps is sitting on the sleeping bag along with his e-reader.

I check the time. 1:59. *Cool, cool, cool.*

I don't want to sneak up on the guy while he's doing bathroom business in the middle of the night. In fact, I don't really want to leave my semblance of a safe haven at all. But how shitty will I feel for the rest of my life if he's somewhere out there, incapacitated, about to become a family of black bears' midnight snack, and instead of helping him, I spent the whole night twiddling my thumbs and playing the world's dullest game of I Spy with his belongings?

It's time to put on my Brave Girl Britches. Before I can talk myself out of it—which would be so, so easy—I shimmy out of my sleeping bag, tug on my boots, and step outside. And instantly get full-body chills. So I duck back into the shelter and grab the first warm thing I see, which happens to be Finn's sweatshirt.

Totally because it's the first thing I saw. Not because I am a simple woman who, when presented with an opportunity to wear a hot guy's sweatshirt, will take it every time. I pull it on, the worn, soft cotton immediately soothing. It smells like Finn and the forest, which is when I realize those scents are almost interchangeable to me. Fresh air and campfire. I pull the collar up over my nose and breathe it in like it's my new lavender rollerball.

I'm fine. I'm safe. I don't have a childish fear of the big bad woods that hasn't gone away after a week out here.

With the dim light from the lowest setting on my headlamp illuminating the way, I head toward the rocky overlook where we ate and hung out as a group earlier. I scan the woods from side to side as I walk, watching out for anything that resembles a tall human.

No luck . . . until there is. My whole body slumps with relief when I see the back of Finn's *Eat More Plants* T-shirt. He's sitting on the ground near the edge of the overlook, broad shoulders hunched with his arms resting on his bent legs in front of him. I focus all my attention on his familiar form as I approach, on the fact that he appears safe, whole, unharmed. I take a couple long, deep breaths, in and out, but still feel antsy. This feelings fog is chronic.

He must hear my boots approaching, because he suddenly sits up straight, spine going rigid, and . . . wipes at his face?

"Enjoying the view?" I joke as I plop myself down beside him and click off my headlamp. Then, as my eyes adjust, my chest tightens. Because Finn's face is tear-streaked, and he doesn't look okay.

Before I can ask, though, he answers, voice watery. "I am, actually. Good night for stars."

I realize that I haven't even really looked. So I turn to see what he means, and it's like the entire sky is suddenly open before me. An endless expanse of deep blue-black dotted with masses of glittering stars. More than I've been able to see in a long time, maybe ever, even at home on the farm.

"Whoa," I say on an exhale.

"Best part of camping," Finn whispers back. It's like we're afraid to be too loud, to make any sudden movements and scare the stars away. I am, at least. Things as perfect as this night sky surely can't last.

"Really?" I murmur back. "I think it's carrying around my own used toilet paper."

He snorts. "A close second."

We sit there without speaking for a while, watching the stars like a movie with the night noise of the forest as a soundtrack. I'm wondering if he's going to tell me why he was crying—why, I think from my peripheral vision, he still is—or if we're both going to pretend it didn't happen. Of course, I've never been great at subtlety.

"So did one of the stars insult your backpacking wardrobe?

Because I'll beat them up for you. I really will. The khakis have grown on me."

I steal a glance at Finn and find his face creased with quiet laughter as he swipes more tears from his cheeks.

"The stars didn't do anything to me," he says on a sigh. "I, uh, I couldn't sleep. Got to thinking too much about my dad. Thought I'd come out here and visit with him."

Oh. I still, not wanting a single fidgety movement of mine to distract from whatever he needs in this moment.

"I don't know what I believe happens after you die," he goes on in his low, calming rumble. "If his spirit is still out there somewhere, if he's watching from on high or whatever. But what I do know are my memories with him when he was alive. We used to camp a lot in the Green Mountains. We'd go year-round, but the best times were clear summer nights when the sky would get dark and absolutely fill with stars. I'd stay up long past my bedtime, Dad and I pointing out constellations to each other. Do you know many constellations?"

Startled at being invited into this walk down Finn's memory lane, I have to think about it for a second. I vaguely remember taking a field trip in elementary school to a planetarium in the next town over. It's been a minute. "Hmm, I know the guy with the belt, and a couple of ladles that are also bears."

Finn laughs. "Right, yep. Those are the official names."

"I also know I'm a Scorpio," I add with an air of superiority. "And—wait, when's your birthday?"

"December twenty-seventh."

"And that you're a Capricorn."

"Now you're just showing off."

I hear the smile in his voice and smile back into the darkness.

"Well, my favorite constellation is Ursa Major—the Big Dipper, aka the ladle that's also a bear," he continues. "I think at first I liked it because it was usually easy to find, and we'd try to locate it first, but then my dad . . . he kind of made it a whole thing. The big bear was him and the little bear, or Ursa Minor, was me. I guess it means even more to me now."

I feel a lump in my throat, and it's getting harder to keep my smile and voice from wobbling. "I take it you found the Big Dipper out here?"

If that's an answer any old one-time-planetarium-visitor should know, Finn doesn't act like it. He just nods and leans back to rest on one elbow, pointing with the other out at the sky. "Over there. See the four corners? And the handle . . ." I follow his finger and sure enough, I see it. "It's made up of circumpolar stars—always visible in the Northern Hemisphere. Barring, you know, trees in the way, or light pollution or whatnot. So I knew I'd probably see it if I went stargazing here, I just . . . hadn't. Until tonight."

I nod, leaning back onto my elbows beside him. "You hadn't, because it makes you think of your dad?"

Finn seems to consider it, then shakes his head. "No. I guess I just hadn't felt like it. I don't have to avoid things that make me think of him, because honestly, I'm always thinking of him. It's pointless to try not to. But I don't always feel so . . . despairing about it anymore? Like, I can get through my days without feeling like I'm swimming through a thick cloud of grief at all times. I can feel happy. But then something will hit me in a certain way, and I'm pulled under again and have to just ride it out. Tonight is one of those."

I hear him sniffle, and without thinking too much about it, I reach out to offer his own sweatshirt sleeve. He gives a sad chuckle. "I'm good, thanks." He exhales heavily. "Today was a really good day, and sometimes I think the good days are weirdly harder. When things happen that I wish I could tell him about, or that I wish I could experience with him, and I just get so mad and sad and heartbroken all over again that none of that is possible."

He isn't trying to wipe away the tears now. It's humbling, the fact that he's telling me any of this, let alone letting me sit in the sadness with him. "It's times like this that I wish I believed in heaven. That would probably be so comforting, to think I'd get to see him again someday if I play all my cards right, spend eternity together. But I settle for talking to the Big Dipper. Rage crying under the stars." He shrugs. "There are worse ways to cope."

"Definitely," I say with my own sniffle. I don't want to wipe my gross tear-snot on his sweatshirt, so I pull my T-shirt hem out from under it and use that to dry off my face. Not that I'm done with the tears and snot yet. "You could be putting up an unhealthy mental wall to prevent yourself from thinking about your person or dealing with their loss at all for, oh, four years, until you suddenly realize you can't put it off anymore and it's been making you really sad all this time anyway and you should maybe do something about that before you emotionally implode. It's good you're not doing that."

Finn nudges me with his elbow. "You say you put a wall up, but you got a whole tattoo in her honor. You've gotten yourself to theater school, like you dreamed about with her. You've been keeping her with you, even if you feel like you pushed her memory out completely for a while there. Grieving also requires us to go full survival mode sometimes."

I swipe at my cheeks again, forgetting this time and using Finn's sleeve anyway. "Survival mode, huh? Who says I wasn't prepared for *Wild Adventures* after all?"

I smirk at him playfully, but Finn's smile back is a little weak.

"Natalie, about that. I need to apologize to you," he says, voice solemn.

His pained gaze turns to the stars as he rubs a hand over his head. Wanting to ease whatever's making him feel bad, I almost ask, *"For all the puns earlier?"* But I refrain.

"I know I've been . . . difficult to work with. To put it lightly." A quiet laugh huffs out of him. I look back up at the sky again, not wanting him to feel the pressure of my gaze. "I'm really sorry for all of it. It took a while to realize how much it's been affecting me—the difference between my past hopes and expectations for *Wild Adventures,* my dad being here with me, versus the way things have turned out.

"I was never gonna come here and just . . . have a fresh, fun, dad-free experience. I've been constantly thinking of how x, y, and z would have been different if I was doing this with Dad. So I think I was primed to not like you because you aren't him.

Everything about you that was or is different from him was like a personal offense. When all along, in reality, so many of those qualities are what make you incredible. You've been the most accepting, open, down-for-whatever partner, or companion, or friend I could've asked for. I just wasn't asking for anyone but him."

I feel his gaze turn to me again, so I look back at him. "So . . . yeah. I'm sorry, and it's completely my shit to keep working on, and I never should've punished you for that."

Well, fuck.

The tears in my eyes spill over, tracking down my cheeks and blurring the sky behind Finn into an abstract painting of darkness and light. I definitely wasn't expecting this tonight—or maybe ever.

"I . . . Thanks, Finn," I say, trying again to hide the wobble in my voice. "That makes complete sense to me. Grief is a uniquely awful experience, and I bet everyone going through it says and does things they aren't proud of sometimes."

Finn sits up and reaches out a hand to me. I accept it, and he gives mine a squeeze. "And I'm sorry I keep making you cry. I'll try to stop being such a downer."

I laugh in spite of myself. "No, no, you didn't—I'm not crying because of you." I tip my head from side to side. "Well, I am, but I'm not. I just hate it that your dad isn't here and you didn't get to do this with him. I'd give up my spot in a heartbeat if it meant you could have that. You should've had it, and it's not fair that the universe or cancer or whatever we want to blame took it away."

My eyes stay locked on his.

"But also, it's . . . I don't know that anyone's ever apologized for taking something out on me that isn't my fault, even though now I understand where you were coming from. It means a whole lot."

It's an understatement, but I think he gets that. With so many of my issues with my parents, it's clear the way they treat me—their resentment, bitterness, whatever—comes from their own unhappiness. It took me a long time to get to that realization, and I'm not sure they ever will. And it seems like a hell of a long shot that they'll ever acknowledge it to me. I can already feel the way Finn's apology is healing something in me, patching up holes in my belief in my own worthiness of kindness, care, love.

His throat bobs, his eyes scanning my face for a long moment before he nods. It solidifies this new level of understanding between us, one I didn't know I was missing, but that changes everything irreversibly.

Before long, we decide to head back to the shelter, each probably five pounds lighter in saltwater weight. It feels roomier than before, like a physical burden between us has been cleared. I return Finn's sweatshirt ever so reluctantly, but I don't even need it. I'm more comfortable than I've been anywhere, with anyone, in a very long time.

Chapter Fifteen

Finn and I are so close to a challenge win, we can taste it.

It tastes an awful lot like my own salty sweat dripping down my face as we haul ass through the forest toward the next checkpoint.

"Come on, Hart. Run like there are front-row tickets to *Hamilton* in it for you," Finn calls from where he jogs a few yards ahead of me. We left with the earliest go time today, but not by much, and it's impossible to tell how close anyone else has come to catching up in the three miles since then.

Before Burke came around to rank our shelters this morning, I scoped out the competition's shelters, a confusing combination of feelings swelling inside me as I saw that Daniel and Luis's was basically a pile of sticks scattered over their sleeping bags, and neither Meena and Cammie's nor Karim and Max's had weathered the breezy night much better. Those teams made up Burke's bottom three, and he took his sweet time "deliberating" before declaring Harper and Evan third place, Enemi and

Zeke second, and Finn and me first. We could barely bask in the glory, with only five minutes until our go time and another five minutes until the next team's. Finn made it clear right away that even though we got the earliest start, he doesn't want us to get comfortable.

Boy, am I not getting comfortable.

"It's not 2015, Finn! Without the original cast, and when there's a filmed version I can watch whenever I want?" I yell back, pressing a hand to the cramp in my side, just over my pack's waist strap. "You're gonna have to do better than that."

"Okay, uhhh . . ." I'm selfishly glad to hear he's winded too. "*Mamma Mia!* onstage with the movie cast performing it?"

The groan I release is obscene, the words that follow slipping out against my better judgment. "It is *so* hot when you pay attention to me."

Do Finn's steps falter, or am I seeing things? "It's, uh, what now?"

"I said it's so hot out!" I call back a little cheekily.

He heard me the first time, though, and throws a pink-cheeked, gorgeously stern look over his shoulder. "You should know by now, I'm always paying attention to you."

For the remaining couple miles, we don't see Zeke and Enemi nor anyone else in the competition on our path down the main AT, so unless they've cracked teleportation, we might actually have a shot at this one. When we finally see Burke Forrester and an orange flag appear between brush and tree trunks ahead of us, it's nearly as exciting as a Meryl Streep stage performance would be.

"Tell us something good, Burke," I pant as we stumble to a stop before him, throwing my arms out wide. Even though none of the other teams are here, we never know when a fake-out or surprise twist is coming.

The host flashes his shiny veneers at us. "You've gotta give me something good to tell you, Natalie!"

I give him a snarky, raised-brow look. *Just hand us our fate already, buddy.*

"All right, all right." Burke waves a hand like we can quit begging him. "Finn and Natalie, after a near miss at victory in the 'Horsing Around' challenge, you built the top-ranking shelter. As you have now arrived first to the checkpoint—"

Unexpectedly, a weight comes down on my shoulders. I flinch before Finn pulls me into his side, then can't hide the smile that comes to my face.

"—Finn and Natalie, you have won this challenge!"

My pterodactyl screech could be heard where the trail begins up in Maine. Burke even jumps back, but I barely register it as strong arms wrap around my waist from behind and lift me into the air.

"We did it, Nature Nat," Finn says on a wild laugh, his barely stubbled cheek pressed to mine. My stomach swoops and I laugh too, clutching at his forearms in a chaotic attempt at hugging while being manhandled.

"Hell yeah, we did! Eat our trail dust!"

Finn is still chuckling as he sets me down and I turn to put my hands on his shoulders, smiling at him as I bounce up and down on my toes. I can't imagine being much happier than this if we won the whole thing.

Burke interrupts our celebration with his sound effect machine laugh. "Congratulations, you two. Want to hear your prize?"

I tear my eyes from Finn's and whirl around, having almost forgotten anyone else was here. Let alone that we get a prize beyond winning the challenge. I clap my hands. "Oh, do tell!"

"Your team has won a night's stay at the Blue Smoke Lodge, where you'll get to enjoy a five-course dinner at their Michelin-starred restaurant, accommodations in a deluxe suite, and amenities such as a full-service spa, outdoor hot springs pools, cinema, bowling lanes, mini golf—"

"*MINI GOLF?*" I bellow, and Finn startles at my back. Much quieter, I glance guiltily between him and an alarmed Burke Forrester and add, "Sorry. Big mini golf fan."

The host nods slowly, still eyeing me like I'm foaming at the mouth rather than simply expressing my excitement for miniature sport. "Well, whenever you're ready, you can load up and the crew will take you over."

I am not exaggerating when I announce to everyone in the vicinity that I was, in fact, born ready.

"**THANK GOD WE** have easy access to a bathroom tonight. With this many beverages, I'm gonna have to pee so many times. My pack couldn't hold all that TP."

Across the white linen–covered table from me, Finn chokes on his sip of water. When he regains his composure, he shakes his head mournfully, but there's humor in his eyes. "Shame your time on the trail has come at the cost of your capacity for civilized dinner conversation."

I tip my glass of sparkling cider—a bottle of which our dutiful waiter, Jamie, set up in an ice bucket beside our table, a champagne substitute for the underaged—at him. "Bold of you to assume I had that capacity to begin with."

His mouth curves up in a smile that I feel like a zap of electricity. I look down into my bowl of risotto, pretending to focus hard on scooping up a bite when I'm really just trying to hide whatever ridiculously giddy thing my face is surely doing.

The few hours since we arrived at Blue Smoke Lodge have been a kind of culture shock, with the culture being that of rich people. As soon as Finn and I stepped out of the van, cameraman Hugh started filming our reactions for the little segment they show of the winners enjoying their prize after a challenge, which doubles as an ad for sponsors like Blue Smoke Lodge. A bellhop escorted us—along with a couple *Wild Adventures* crew members staying in a suite next door—around the grounds, as we oohed and aahed over the views and hot springs pools and generally luxurious surroundings. My responses were mostly genuine, but I had to hold in my laughter as Finn robotically delivered the line a producer fed to him about how our victory was sweet, but the swim-up ice cream sundae bar looks even sweeter.

Then we were led to our suite, where more performances

of amazement ensued. It has two bedrooms with a king-size bed in each, divided by a living room that could fit twenty of our closest friends for a movie night—if we weren't using the hotel's *private cinema,* that is—and twenty more at a long dining table with an adjacent kitchenette. Hugh and his camera left for the day while the producers left for their suite next door, giving Finn and me the chance to clean up in our own bathrooms. They also gave us, much to both of our surprise, our phones for the night. Finn instantly proposed that we not look through them for at least the next few hours, to just "enjoy this experience." I agreed, which says a *lot* about how much has changed since I've been here.

Except for the small exception of accessing my music. I turned the phone on and navigated to the app I wanted through narrowed eyes, goofily trying to keep myself from reading any of the missed messages and notifications that popped up. I picked a playlist, then relished in the ability to hear something other than the great outdoors and my own thoughts under the ginormitude of the waterfall showerhead. I become a very happy Eeyore dancing under my hot and soapy personal rain cloud to the musical stylings of The Chicks.

Things only got more ridiculous when I emerged, wearing a fluffy white hotel robe and running a comb through blissfully clean hair, to find a selection of clothes from the hotel's boutique had been dropped off with a note telling me to take my pick for my dinner attire.

Upon entering La Villers sur Mer, Finn and I could immediately see that our trail gear would've caused us to stick out like a couple of sore forest gremlin thumbs. The waitstaff are all in pristine white coats with gold buttons down the front, each carrying a white napkin over one forearm and giving a little bow each time they leave our table. I think I cleaned up pretty well in the dress I landed on, a gorgeous lilac-colored number with a fitted bodice and flowy chiffon skirt that hits just above my knees. It felt very Cinderella's-glass-slipper-ish, the fact that a producer found such a perfect dress for me in a perfect fit *and* my favorite color.

And damn if Finn doesn't look like a painfully perfect Prince Charming. Upon seeing him for the first time, leaning against the suite's couch as he waited for me to head down to dinner, I made another noise that probably should've been embarrassing. Something along the lines of *urrrgggffhh*. He's in a blazer that has no right to fit as well as it does off the rack, over a light blue button-down and—because, even fancied up, the man has a brand—khaki pants. Much nicer, skinnier khakis than his hiking ones, and with only the standard amount of pockets. He's also shaved again, showing off that sharp jawline to perfection.

Needless to say, I'm doing great at keeping this crush under wraps.

"Need a top-up?" Mr. Business Casually Wrecking Me asks, eyes twinkling as he reaches for the cider bottle.

"Fillah up, bah-tendah." Apparently my new act-natural coping mechanism is bizarre accents. Finn laughs, though, so that's worth plenty of unhinged behavior. The whole dinner has been full of laughs.

It's also been full of me asking when we can play mini golf.

"All right," he says over dessert, bringing his napkin up to swipe away some of the berry compote topping from our crème brûlée. I definitely had not been picturing myself licking it off. "What's the deal with you and mini golf?"

I sit up straighter in my seat, savoring the last of the sweet, custardy cream treat on my spoon. When I look his way again, his eyes are on my mouth around my spoon. *Very* interesting. I give it one last slow, indulgent lick . . . in the name of science. He clears his throat abruptly, eyes darting away as he reaches up to tuck a finger into his shirt collar and tug it around, and I finally register his question.

"Oh. Uh, I don't know, I just really enjoy playing it? And I guess it's kind of sentimental." I set my spoon down and start straightening all the remaining dishes and utensils around me. "My family didn't take a lot of vacations growing up. It's just my parents and me, and their jobs never allowed for much time off, nor could we swing any fancy getaways on our budget. I spent most summers with Granny Star in Pigeon Forge anyway, which was all the getaway I needed. But Mom and Dad always managed, for one weekend in the summer, to come down to the mountains and visit with us. Gatlinburg, Pigeon Forge, that whole area in the Tennessee Smokies, some of it's touristy as all get-out, but it was my Disneyland. And you can't go more than a block or two without seeing a mini golf course. My parents enjoyed it, so it became our thing on their mountain weekends, trying out all the different courses—pirate golf, hillbilly golf, volcanic island golf, whatever we could find."

I smile into my cider glass as I take a sip. The bubbles tickle my throat as I drink them down, then I shrug before continuing. "I've told you already that I don't have a great relationship with my parents, but even as I got older, when my grandma was gone and things at home kind of worsened, those trips were still special. We still went for a weekend every summer when we could. And mini golf was still our best family time, when we laughed together and could joke around and just play. I'm grateful for that."

I pause before looking up at Finn with an awkward grin. I imagine he was expecting more of an "I was on the golf team in high school" rather than "Let's revisit my childhood trauma," but that's the Natalie Hart Special, I suppose. And maybe he's come to expect that after all, because he's just watching me with that intense, warm brown gaze, taking it in.

"So what I'm hearing is you're about to destroy me in mini golf," he finally says, dry as can be.

My head falls back on a laugh. It's the response I didn't know I wanted at the moment—not dwelling on the Daddy-and-Mommy Issues, just bringing things back to the light on this night when I want to celebrate and have fun.

"One weekend per year of playing lots of mini golf doesn't make you a pro," I answer.

His eyes narrow, but they also glint with humor. "Yeah, and that is not a denial of the fact that you, specifically, are really good."

I wink. "Guess you'll have to find out for yourself."

We've completely lost our bearings since the initial tour of the lodge, so we get directions from the restaurant's maître d' to the mini golf course right beside the main building, mutually deciding not to change from our fancy getups yet. I haven't felt this pretty in a while, and I plan to get some mileage out of it. I'm also just too eager to let anything slow me down.

But then something does. The Closed sign hanging on the gate to the mini golf course.

"Noooo!" I wail. I would sink to my knees in despair, but I have enough sense left to not want to ruin my dress. "This is like expecting Leslie Odom Jr. to host the Tonys, but they replace him at the last minute with James Corden."

Finn is genuinely distraught as he looks from the sign to me, rubbing a hand over his head and bringing the other to rest on my shoulder. "I don't know what that means, but it must be bad."

"The worst!" I cry.

He sighs as he looks back to the Gate of Letdowns. Then his hand leaves my shoulder and he takes a step toward the course, expression turning more determined than defeated. He walks a few feet in one direction down the tall fence that lines the perimeter, then pivots to walk a few feet the other way. He eyes the fence and cranes his neck to peer into the space beyond it, where the course presumably stretches out under a dusky sky.

"You know what?" He turns to me, hands on hips. I meet his eyes warily. "I bet we can hop the fence."

My head tips sideways as I try to determine if I heard him correctly. "I'm sorry, I thought you just suggested hopping the fence."

"Yeah," he says back.

"Breaking into the closed mini golf course."

"Uh-huh."

"You, Finn Markum, Mr. Leave No Trace, so rigid I've wondered once or twice if your spine could be used as a yardstick."

His mouth forms a thoughtful sort of frown. "One could argue this is the best time to put the leave-no-trace principle to use."

I find that I can't disagree.

Chapter Sixteen

Moments later, I'm watching Finn's especially fine backside stretch out its tight khaki confines as he hauls himself over a mini golf course fence. In way less time than I would've expected, his fingertips leave the top railing and he drops out of sight, the thud of his feet hitting the ground—at least I hope that's what it is—the only sound I hear.

"Piece of cake," he whispers a moment later from the other side.

My journey is not so simple. Granted, I'm lacking pants, Finn's height, and his weirdly high enthusiasm for doing crime. But I'm certain I look ridiculous as I scrabble for purchase against the fence posts.

"Do you have Spider-Man's sticky hands or something? How did you do this?" I grumble. My head is the only part of me on the other side, and I'm not sure the rest is gonna get there at this rate.

"Do you want my help?" he asks with obvious eagerness, his hands already reaching toward me.

"Obviously!"

"Give me your arm—no, like, reach all the way—there you go . . ."

Thus ensues the most awkward, fumbling sequence of grabbing, pulling, stretching, and ultimately falling the rest of the way over and completely on top of Finn. He lets out an *oof* on impact but fortunately, it isn't followed by his skull connecting to the ground. His hands are gripping my waist as I lay splattered over most of his body, my skirt definitely tossed up enough to reveal my entire ass, but he won't be able to see that from the tangle of my hair covering his face.

I reach back to pull my skirt down on instinct, then toss my hair over my shoulder and out of his rapidly blinking eyes. They connect with mine, and for a second, we're in an absurd freeze-frame. Everything goes still, and it's just our faces a breath apart, our hearts beating in matching staccato rhythm, the warmth caught between every inch of skin we have pressed together. It's the creek swimming all over again but horizontal, and while we're definitely more clothed, I feel much more exposed.

It's the things he knows about me now, let alone the things he doesn't—how aware I am of him, body and heart and soul, and how much I've grown to want it all. I think for a moment about kissing him, pressing my hands to his chest and scooting just a touch farther up so my lips could meet his. I wonder if he's thinking the same.

Then the shoe drops. Literally, one of my new, thick-soled

wedges chooses that moment to fall from my foot that has apparently been hovering over Finn's shin, because when it lands, he sucks in a pained breath. That gets me moving, and not in the climbing-up-Finn's-body direction.

"I would say I'm sorry," I say, a little breathless as I try to stand without doing further damage, "but this was your idea, so."

Finn sounds more winded than he ever has on the trail. "I accept your lack of apology." I watch him stand and assess his injuries, then he flashes a crooked smile my way. "The mini show must go on now, right?"

My heart resumes its own fall over a metaphorical fence, at hyperspeed with no ground in sight.

Once inside the forbidden mini golf land's borders, it seems everything else is ours for the taking. The small shed where we would check in and pick up balls, putters, and scorecards is unlocked and we have our pick of the loot. I take a glittery pink ball while Finn takes the rainbow polka dots, then we both grab clubs and are on our way.

The course is threaded through trees and shrubs that make it feel like we're in our own little forested world far away from the hotel, but there are enough floodlights scattered about that we can still see clearly. We're both comfortable enough with the seclusion to stop whispering, and I find my prior nerves about getting caught melt into excitement. *Mini golf! With Finn!*

"Break a leg," he says as I line up my shot at hole one. "That's theater speak for good luck."

I look back at him with a warning in my eyes. "Let's not push our luck on the breaking limbs thing tonight."

I put an extra unnecessary wiggle into my hips as I take my putting stance, all too aware of his gaze behind me. I pull the club back, bring it softly but swiftly forward, and connect with the ball . . . sending it in a quick, straight line into the hole.

"Hole in one!" I whoop, then put a hand over my mouth as if I can retroactively shush myself.

"Yeah, yeah. 'One weekend a year doesn't make you good,' my ass," he grumbles as he sets up his ball. Feeling smug, I let him take his shot in silence, and another, and another, giving him a score of three as we move to the next hole.

"Yeah, so I also dated a golfer," I reveal casually as I prepare my putt at hole two. "He worked at a golf course and would sneak me out on a cart after closing to make out under the guise of 'giving me lessons.' Terrible kisser, but actually a pretty good teacher. Especially with putting, because he could do the whole 'Here, like this' schtick and wrap his arms around me."

Finn's grunt—a surprisingly displeased sound—comes right as I swing, and my aim goes wild, sending my ball ping-ponging between the barriers on either side of the long, straight path to the hole. It rolls to a stop, not at all where I intended for it to go. I frown as I walk toward it and plan my next move.

"How long did that last?" Finn's question is infused with an innocence so over-the-top, it has to be fake. *Veeery* interesting.

"Oh, probably no more than a month or two. The kissing didn't improve as much as my golf swing, which was a deal-breaker."

With my attention more focused, I make my next putt,

sending the ball on a slow roll right into the hole. "Two!" I cheer with a celebratory spin, my skirt flaring out around me.

"Glad it taught you something," Finn grumbles.

I think the subject has been dropped as we wander through the shadowy maze of shrub-lined walkways to the next couple holes side by side, stopping to play each one, continuing to mess with each other—me teasing Finn for his weird putting posture, Finn bemoaning the several lucky shots I get despite taking wilder swings than I normally would, all due to him flustering me and throwing off my game. But I'm surprised when he brings up my long-forgotten sophomore summer boyfriend again as I'm taking a crack at getting my ball through the blades of a windmill on hole six.

"So, have you, uh, dated anyone since golfer guy?"

I dart a look his way and find him staring off at the lagoon sparkling under the moonlight in the center of the course, seemingly nonchalant, but the pink tips of his ears give him away. I bite down on a smirk and refocus on the putter.

"Oh, plenty." Swing aaand—*crack*. My ball hits the windmill and bounces back, rolling almost all the way to me. I reposition it and get ready to try again. "I dated a lot in high school. Wanted to see what all was out there, I guess."

The noise Finn makes is a more thoughtful, less grunt-y grunt. After a couple more tries, my ball finally makes it through, leaving me with a score of six for the hole. Finn takes his turn and it's his luckiest yet as, even with tensed up shoulders and overly wiggly arms, he sinks it in two.

"*Was* out there?" he asks as we take an arched stone bridge over a gently flowing stream toward hole seven. "So you haven't dated in college?"

Our eyes meet when he lets me pass him walking over some paving stones meant to look like lily pads at the stream's bank, and he briefly rests a hand on my back, a touch so fleeting I could believe it was the wind as much as a person.

At the green, I crouch to eye the meandering tunnel our balls will have to travel through on the way to a big, pastel painted castle at the other end. "Haven't had time or inclination," I answer as I rise. I hit my ball, hearing it bounce and reverberate in the tunnel, an echoing *boiiing*. "Ugh, are you kidding?"

I circle the structure for a moment, then, deciding there's no other way, lie down on my stomach and start to push my club through the opening in an effort to nudge my ball out the other side. I quickly find this is an awful lot like trying to use my club to nudge a needle out of a haystack. Continuing to jab at it does me no good, as the ball is past a curve in the tunnel that my putter can't angle around.

"Why's that?" Finn's voice is closer than I expect when it reaches me. I sigh, dropping my club and retracting my arm before rolling onto my back. He's kneeling at my side, expression open and watchful. His shirt has gotten more rumpled with the night's adventures, a few buttons undone. It's all *really* working for me.

He's the box of brownie mix that catches your eye when you're up for a midnight snack—it's been there all along, but suddenly looks more delicious than ever before, and you can't remember why you didn't indulge earlier.

You also might regret it in the morning.

"Why so curious all of a sudden?" I ask, trying to push brownies and other temptations far from my mind.

Finn lifts a shoulder at the same time as he turns his kneel to a sit, then lies down beside me on the squishy artificial turf. "I guess it's like . . . like the dam is broken." His voice is soft but carries to me easily. "The more I learn about you, the more I find myself wanting to know everything."

Something in my chest tightens then releases on a rush of fizzy, shimmery feelings. I look up at the stars overhead, less visible with the floodlights nearby and the glow from hotel windows beyond them, but still there. Still the same stars we gazed at from the top of a cliff last night. "Everything, huh?"

In my periphery, Finn shifts, and there's a sudden but subtle heat at my side. Has he moved closer?

"Mm-hmm." He's definitely closer. "You're kind of hard to pin down, you know? I thought you were one thing when I met you, and not all of that was wrong—you're fun and funny, loud and unfiltered, bold and outgoing. But you're also so much more under the surface, and you keep a lot inside. Even more than you've let on to me, or maybe to anyone."

That is certainly not where I expected him to go. The buzzing beneath my skin kicks in, my heart beats faster, urging me to move, evade, run. But there's something different about the buzz right now too, something unexpectedly like excitement.

Like I've been waiting for this. For someone to wonder the very things he's wondering. For someone to see all of this in me.

I've gotta say something before I chicken out or reason myself into shutting up. So of course the first words to come out are a clumsy, impulsive, "My insides are really not as cute as my outsides."

Instantly I cringe at how I've managed to sound so conceited-yet-fucked-up in so few words. My mouth opens and closes, but Finn speaks first.

"I don't believe that. And if your insides are even half as beautiful as your outsides—like everything I've seen so far—I'm already in so much trouble."

My soft gasp hangs in the air between us. "Wh-what does that mean?"

"It means . . ." He pauses, a few seconds that feel like hours. "It means my teammate is strong, brilliant, big-hearted, and . . . and beautiful from the inside out." He sucks in a deep breath and sounds like he's holding it when he continues. "And I really, *really* want to kiss her."

A flicker of feeling ignites in my tender heart, equal parts warm comfort and hot desire spreading into all my buzzing limbs and extremities. I know I'm not having a panic attack, but I also can't quite breathe.

Still, I somehow manage to turn my head to face Finn and gasp out the words, "That's . . . troublesome?"

My smile threatens to take over my entire face, but I hold it back, not quite ready to believe in what's happening.

He props up on an elbow, his big brown eyes, dark as the

night sky, now boring into me. "I've been telling myself it is, though I can't quite remember why at the moment."

His breath teases my lips as he speaks, we're so close. It's a whisper of a suggestion at what could be. His scent wraps around me, the hotel's eucalyptus soap mixed with a lingering note of campfire smoke.

"How long have you and yourself been discussing the matter?"

He swallows heavily. "A while."

I bring my hand up and bite down on my thumbnail as I consider him. I'd be huffing the hell out of a lavender rollerball if I had one right now. But I don't, which is probably why I just keep blurting things out.

"Me and myself have had similar talks."

Finn's nostrils flare, eyes brightening ever so slightly. "Have you?"

"Mm-hmm." I watch his gaze drop to my bottom lip where my thumb presses against it. "Consensus is I've been wanting to kiss my teammate too, whether it's in our best interest or not."

"It feels like my best interest tonight. Maybe the best interest of all time." There's a hint of teasing in his voice, but his quickening breaths tell me he's plenty serious, too. He reaches up and takes my hand from my face to wrap it in his hand, his thumb pressing into my palm and stroking back and forth.

My reply is more exhaled than spoken. "Can't say I disagree."

Finn's response is to lean forward as I tilt my face up, inching closer so slowly I could scream, before he finally takes my lips with his. Though I knew it was coming, the kiss surprises me. It isn't awkward or tentative, like first kisses with a new person so often are. It feels at once wildly exciting and perfectly familiar as our lips connect in a firm, lingering press.

When he starts to pull back I find myself trying to follow, but quickly see he wasn't really going anywhere. His mouth returns to play over mine, lips slightly parted, and I welcome the change. Both my hands reach up almost of their own accord to cup his jaw and pull him closer so he leans more of his chest onto mine. I want it all, as much of him pressed to me as I can get. He lets me position his face just how I like, in the perfect spot for me to deepen the kiss.

It's fiery, exploratory, and achingly gentle in different turns. One of Finn's hands comes to my hair, sifting through before sliding down to grip the back of my neck. His other leaves a path of sparks in its wake as it runs down my side, across my stomach, to my hip and back again, seemingly unable to land on just one place to grab, wanting to claim it all. And god, do I want that, too.

I slide one foot up closer, bending my leg at the knee to rest against Finn's hip, caging him in, and it has the unintended effect of sending the skirt of my dress to pool around the very tops of my thighs. Finn isn't expecting this when he coasts his hand down without looking, and I feel the surprised grunt from the back of his throat when he connects with bare skin. I've been wanting to taste his grumbly sounds nearly as long as I've known him, and they're every bit as delicious as I'd hoped, causing me to tighten my grip in his hair.

Still, he's able to pull his head back for real this time, breaking our connection to let his gaze travel down my body. My ensemble is starting to look as disheveled as his, but still not nearly as wrecked as I feel.

"Natalie . . ." My name scrapes out of him in a hoarse voice, and I feel a flush of pride that I've gotten him just as undone.

"Yes?" My chest rises and falls rapidly.

He squeezes his eyes shut and gives his head a brisk shake before looking back up at my face. Both his hands on me give a single matching squeeze before landing flat on the ground on either side of my head.

"That was . . . This is . . ." I watch him give up on searching for words. "Wow."

My answering giggle is cartoonishly high-pitched and breathy, but I can't find any shame. There's no room for anything but good vibes inside me, a witch's brew of happiness, desire, attraction, relief, all bubbling together.

This is happening, and it *is* wow. Who the hell would've thought?

"Right back at ya, stud." I reach up to give his chest a pat, then leave my hand there, wondering why I didn't explore more of this territory as we kissed. Something to remedy next time.

Finn's brows shoot up, cheeks going adorably even redder than they already were. "Stud?"

His voice cracks on the word, which I only find more endearing. *I'm a goner.*

"You heard me. Who knew you had"—I dart a look up and down his body, meaning to encompass his entire sexy essence right now—"all of *this* in you?"

Finn lets his chin drop, shoulders trembling with laughter as he shakes his head again. When he looks back up, he groans softly.

"See?" He nods toward me. "So much trouble."

"Yeah, right back at you, mister."

He sits back and climbs to his feet, brushing his hands against his pants as if they've collected any actual grass from their spot on the green. I pout like a petulant child, still flat on my back down here, trying not to be too dazzled by the way he's now positioned so the lights—from the hotel, the stars, and the moon—form a perfectly angelic glow around his perfectly gorgeous head. *So* much trouble.

"So yeah, this has been fun and all," he teases, trying hard to look sincere, but even he can't completely hide his smile tonight. "But I kind of have a mini golf game to win."

I make a huffy, offended sound and would like to keep throwing a fit down here until he shuts me up with his lips. But I know it's probably ill-advised to continue this where we are, so I take the hand he offers and allow him to help me up. When I'm standing, he crouches again, deftly knocking my ball out of the tunnel using his own and allowing the game to resume.

With some modifications. The winner of each hole now gets a kiss from the loser—which really means we both stay winning. When Finn loses the first couple times, he tries to keep me in check, giving brief, relatively chaste pecks.

So obviously, I start throwing the game. I take one wild swing after another, dragging it out to six to eight shots before getting the ball in at every hole. Finn knows exactly what I'm up to, but doesn't change up his play to match my absurdity. Nor does he stop me from giving him his winner's spoils however I please—pushing him up against the sparkly, fairy-tale-esque cottage to kiss him slow and deep after hole twelve, making him sit on a bench shaped like a giant butterfly so I can straddle his lap for our kiss after hole fourteen.

No, he takes everything I throw at him, even as it's plain to see his composure fraying by the minute. When we've finally finished hole eighteen, I'm barely able to brush my lips to his before he's pulling me toward the entrance, stopping only to drop our clubs and balls in their home before we're back at the fence and he's boosting me up with his hands on my hips.

As I'm about to cross over the top, giving Finn the closest close-up of my backside yet, I hear him say on a happy sigh, "God, I love mini golf."

Chapter Seventeen

Life is just a little *too* good when I wake the next morning, wrapped up in Finn like we're a couple of curly fries fused together by the deep fryer. The night stayed giddy and breathless and oh so romantic as we laughed and speed-walked our way back to our suite and spent the rest of our waking and sleeping hours together. We kissed and cuddled for hours in my big hotel bed, both in our pajamas, all my makeup washed off. We'd brushed our teeth side by side, and for the first time in my life, I felt the temptation to kiss someone with a mouth full of toothpaste foam. I disgust myself. And when eventually the passionate makeouts turned to soft pecks, tender touches, and long, sleepy eye contact, we curled into one another and drifted off.

It's felt like we're in a suspended reality, here at this resort I could never afford, only a short drive away from the trail we've been on but mentally in a different world. Of course, I can't completely shut off the voice in my head wondering if this is going to backfire, if Finn will wake up this morning regretting it, if he's only into me because I'm the only option around, if taking our relationship to this new level will distract us from the competition, and a million other things. But I try to tell her to pipe down for now—to not bother me while I'm on my vacation, and I'll get back to her in a matter of hours when we return to the AT.

All I've wanted to focus on is how incredible it feels to lose myself in Finn's arms, to experience this kind of closeness and intimacy with another person. And as glorious and intoxicating as it was to explore each other and feel his hands and lips roam all over and let my own do the same to him, it was somehow just as wonderful when we slowed down. Every bit as dreamy lying next to him, sharing a pillow even though there are five more in the bed going unused.

So it's only restoring some balance to the world when I drag myself out of bed and stumble to the bathroom, and before I can even wipe the tired, goofy smile off my face, I realize that I've started my period.

Mother Nature, you petty bitch.

She doesn't really visit me monthly—hasn't done so consistently since I was sixteen and started birth control. More often, it's every two or three months, and by my calculations, I figured I was safe enough to not pack tampons for *Wild Adventures*. Of course that was a mistake.

"Uuuuugghhh," I groan, forgetting there's another human not far from the other side of the bathroom door. A human I only recently started kissing.

"Everything okay in there?" comes Finn's scratchy morning voice, sounding like he isn't out of bed yet. And now might stay there forever, afraid of whatever Situation I'm having on the toilet. *Wonderful! Could I be any more alluring?*

"Fine! I'm fine. Stay where you are." Okay, now it definitely sounds like something horrifying's going down in here. There are times it would behoove me to be less dramatic.

I craft the makeshift toilet paper pad all period-havers learned in middle school before heading out to wash my hands in the sink—and face the hot guy who is probably no longer interested in me, now knowing I have bodily functions.

"Everything is actually fine," I reiterate as I towel my hands dry and turn to face Finn, who sits up in the bed looking sleep-rumpled and absolutely gorgeous, if a little concerned for my bowels. I put my hands on my hips, a power pose for the news I'm about to deliver. "I started my period."

Finn's face clears with relief for a moment, then takes on a look that's more sympathetic than anything. "Oh. Well, that sucks. Can I get you anything?"

My shoulders, which I didn't even realize were tensed, relax and my hands fall to my sides. Of course he passed the test he didn't know he was taking, and didn't get weird upon mention of the *p*-word. Of course I shouldn't expect any guy to, given that it's not the 1950s and we don't have to hide our "monthly visitor" like a scandalous secret anymore (even if some politicians live in denial of such truths).

"It's fine." I shake my head and cross my arms over my stomach.

"So you said." Finn's mouth ticks up in one corner as he continues to watch me.

I roll my eyes and force myself to move toward my backpack in the corner, to look like I have a purpose other than standing in the middle of the room feeling awkward. Why do I feel so awkward? "Because it is! I'll just see if we can, like, stop by a drugstore on the way back to filming. I didn't come prepared for this. But I'm gonna shower now and get ready to go and it'll be—"

"Fine?" There's humor in his voice, and I consider throwing a hiking boot at him.

"Exactly," I say instead, then gather my change of clothes in my arms and stomp off to lock myself in the bathroom.

As I bask once again in the utter bliss that is a hot shower, I try to examine my weird feelings. Has getting my period just thrown everything out of whack? Is this the hormones talking? Or am I having regrets about kissing Finn? With how happy I felt waking up with him, I can't even lie to myself about wishing it hadn't all happened. But should I have taken it slower, not pounced on him the way I did? Is he having regrets? Is this going to make everything weird for the rest of the competition? Either with tension because we like each other, or tension because we actually don't and just had a moment of weak impulsivity?

So much for shutting the inner voice down. That bitch is noisy. My chest tightens, and I'm so busy running through the zillions of questions, possibilities, what-ifs, that I can't even make myself step back and examine how I really feel. My mind is still muddled and messy as I stop the shower, towel myself off, and get dressed for the day—turning back into a leggings-clad pumpkin now that midnight has struck and the ball is over. Will Finn still look like Prince Charming by the light of day?

When I reemerge into the bedroom, I get my answer. Not by looking at the guy in person, as he isn't there—probably getting ready in his own room, if I had to guess. But sometime while I was showering, he left me a present, now laid out on the bed we slept in. Inside the bag from the hotel gift shop, there's a travel-sized pack of pads, one box of tampons, and a little bag of sour gummies. Beside the items is a note scrawled on hotel stationery.

N—

I know everything's fine, but I thought this could help until we get to go to a drugstore. Sorry if the candy is a cliché—I won't be offended if you don't eat them, but you said you always choose sour over chocolate. You also don't have to use any of it. Just wanted you to have it in case.

—F

Okay, the tears in my eyes are definitely some hormonal period bullshit. But it's still such a thoughtful gesture. So much of the awkward uncertainty in my mind and heart fade away in the time it takes me to unpack the gift and read his note once, then a second time. *Total* Prince Charming move. You know, if Prince Charming lived in the modern age and could acknowledge that Cinderella menstruated.

I utilize the gifted supplies, then lie down on the bed and stuff sour gummies in my face. My eyes flick to the clock, finding I have a half hour until the producers requested we meet them at breakfast. So with a deep, bracing breath, I reach for the thing I haven't touched since my shower last night—my phone.

Scrolling through the push notifications is the most surreal reminder that the world is still turning outside the bubble of *Wild Adventures*. Everyone I know—knew way before Finn or Harper or anyone else out here—has a life they've kept living while I've been out of contact. Reese and Clara have blown up our group chat, per usual, and I don't even try to catch up there yet, knowing it'll make me too homesick. The people kind of home, not a place. The notifications from socials are mostly comments and likes from people I don't care about, responding to my vague posts about taking a technology hiatus.

I know I shouldn't open my email even before I do it. The little envelope icon is the one that gives me the most anxiety of anything on my phone, because it's where all the shittiest stuff comes through. Emails from professors, my advisor, and, most stressfully, financial aid. But I can't help the impulse to clear out the little red bubble hovering there, with a number I hope is mostly representing the near-daily advertisements about whatever sales Body Wonderland is having.

I tap, and my stomach sinks as my inbox appears.

OVERDUE PAYMENT

OVERDUE PAYMENT: SECOND NOTICE

OVERDUE PAYMENT: THIRD NOTICE

Jesus H, what I'd give for a fifty-percent-off body wash supersale to interrupt all the angry capital letters from Oliver College Financial Aid Office filling the screen. My vision blurs, my pulse picking up as the stress I've been doing my best to block out comes rushing back in, all but drowning me.

Of course I hadn't forgotten my dire financial straits, but I sure as hell was trying. I throw my phone toward my pack across the room, and it lands on the carpeted floor. Bummer that it doesn't sound like it shattered, that the screen will still show me those recurring reminders of my failure if I pick it up again. I don't know what to do except sink face-first into a cushy hotel pillow, and let out a long scream.

It's a little bit cathartic, even as it obviously solves nothing. My reality is still waiting for me, when I'm done with this little "reality" side quest. The reality where I have a payment for the fall that's already overdue, three more years of tuition to cover, and a job to go back to and a school that hasn't been especially kind to me, and I don't get to just put on a pretty dress and have a five-course meal and defile a mini golf course with a gorgeous guy on any random night.

My chest is tight, my breathing frantic as I stand and pace the room. I turn my phone off and stuff it into my backpack to take back to Carina the producer, as if it's the problem here. The action helps to lull me into comfortable denial, as does applying lavender oil to my wrists and sitting on the bed, attempting a few meditation techniques I'm out of practice with. But by the time I'm finished, and scramble to get ready to head down to breakfast, I'm still uneasy, and the cramps starting up in my uterus aren't helping. I'm kind of grateful when I leave my bed-room for the suite's common area and find that Finn's door is open, his room already empty. More time to get my shit together before I see him again.

"Morning!" I chirp when I enter the breakfast area by the lobby, approaching the table where Finn, Carina, and the other producer, Emir, are already eating.

"Oh good, you made it!" Carina smiles up at me.

"Of course!" I plop my pack down by the chair beside Finn's. He peeks my way briefly before returning to shoveling eggs in his mouth, and I'm not sure what I read in the look. I gesture to everyone's plates. "So what's good?"

With the producers' advice to check out the waffle bar and omelet station, and no further input from an extremely food-focused Finn, I head off to peruse the buffet. I've nearly filled up my plate and am adding some fruit salad to give me the illusion of caring about my health despite my powdered-sugar-and-syrup-covered waffle and chocolate croissants—plural—when I bump into someone I didn't notice at my side.

"Oh, sor—well, hey there!" I smile up at Finn, genuine warmth and contentment flooding me. This is all I needed, the thing that can banish all the scaries from my mind. His expression is more subdued, but unlike at the table, he allows a small grin to break free.

"Hi." He clears his throat, then refocuses on the fruit in front of us, picking up a single grape at a time and placing them meticulously on his plate. "I, uh, just wanted to check in, since I didn't see you again after I—yeah. I'm making sure I didn't overstep. With the stuff from the gift shop. If you didn't want or need it, it's okay, I didn't mean to be weird or make you uncomf—"

I still him with a hand over his as he reaches for the tongs in a bin of pineapple chunks. "Stop that, goober. Look at me." He does so but warily. I squeeze his hand like his whole existence is squeezing my heart right now, and give him a smile that I hope carries even half the affection I feel. "Thank you, seriously. That was a really nice thing to do. I already ate all the gummies. Judge me if you must."

His shy half smile is everything. "I would never."

Rolling my eyes at that, I go on. "Yeah, right. But thank you again. And hey, while we're here . . ." I look around to ensure Carina and Emir are still at the table, paying us no attention. "We didn't really talk about, like . . . how to go forward. I mean, not that we need some kind of DTR conversation right now, god no, but—"

"DTR?" Finn asks, brows pulled together.

"Define-the-relationship," I say before jumping right back into the topic at hand. "But for the purposes of the show, and being around other people, I just . . ." I shrug, wishing I'd thought any of this through for more than two seconds before I decided to air it out loud to Finn. But I'm here now. "Are we teammates who kiss now? And are we letting people know that?"

Now Finn looks like he's trying not to laugh. Good, I've taken the mantle of awkwardness from his shoulders. So happy to offer this service. I narrow my eyes and he stands up straighter, deliberately clearing the amusement from his expression.

"Okay, we're talking about this. Got it. Uh, well . . . Is it too predictably nineteen-year-old-straight-guy of me to say I'd really like to be teammates who kiss now?"

That gets a real laugh out of me, one probably too loud for the quiet morning atmosphere in this breakfast area.

"Maybe predictable," I whisper when I've composed myself, "but we're on the same page. So that part's a done deal. But maybe we, I don't know, keep it quiet for now? It's just that this is new, and people would have questions—lots of them—and it could become a whole storyline on the show, which is a lot of pressure." I set my plate down on the counter so I can literally wring my hands. "It's not that I want to hide how I feel about you. It just seems way easier to keep it between the two of us to start. To not let other opinions and stuff in when we don't have to just yet, you know?"

I peer up at him, nervous he's going to be offended that I don't want to be with him out in the open, or argue back. But to my surprise, he nods, looking totally sure of himself. "Agreed. Let's not let any more complications in than we have to."

My eyes widen. "Did we just agree on something, completely and without extensive discussion?"

Finn gives me a skeptical look before going back to his careful fruit collection. "The fact that this surprises you so much is a great testament to what a strong couple we make."

"Careful there, buddy." I pick up my plate and turn to start back toward the table, tossing over my shoulder, "You're wading into DTR territory."

Chapter Eighteen

Finn turns out to be quite the capable actor in the role of Calm, Collected Guy Who Has Not Kissed The Hell Out Of Natalie, just as I'm crushing the role of Calm, Collected Girl Who Didn't Melt Down Over Her Email Inbox This Morning. We chatted and laughed with the producers over breakfast—well, Finn didn't do much of the latter, but I'm selfishly glad I have the monopoly on his ridiculous *ho-ho-ho*s—then piled into a van and headed back to the trail. I was even able to take advantage of the good cell service before we had to give our phones back, googling "what to do if you get your period while camping." The results were surprisingly helpful in mentally planning some practical aspects of my next few days.

Back at the clearing where the rest of the group is waiting with Burke Forrester, ready to kick off our next challenge, it's both like a month has passed in twenty-four hours and like we never left at all.

"Finn, Natalie, welcome back!" Burke bellows once cameras are rolling. "How was your getaway? Relaxing?"

Yes and no, I think, a little shiver running down my spine as I remember the heart-pounding experience of getting acquainted with Finn's lips, hands, body. But I also slept better in that big, cushy bed than I ever have or will in a tent.

So I answer with that part. Some of the others groan and call out their envy, so I grimace and try to look apologetic. I don't think I pull it off.

"Well, I'm glad you've been able to rest and restore your energy, because you're gonna need it for today's challenge!"

Burke, bless his plastic little heart, is not exaggerating. We get our maps for the first leg and set off with gusto, all the teams packed close together as we hike to the next challenge site on the main AT. I don't know if it's the night away coloring my perception, or maybe how poorly things went for most everyone during the shelter-building challenge, but it feels like there's a new bite in the air today, some extra layer of intensity and competitiveness between the remaining pairs. It could just be because there are fewer teams remaining—Enemi and Zeke, Karim and Max, Meena and Cammie, Evan and Harper, and Finn and me—and this is usually the point at which *Wild Adventures* picks up the pace, with more strenuous challenges and more frequent eliminations. That $100,000 is closer than ever.

But in the middle of it all, Finn and I are jog-hiking through the forest like a couple of happy Smurfs. It's a little absurd.

"Okay," I say, pressing a hand to the stitch in my side. Hard to say if it's from the jogging, the laughing at Finn's Burke Forrester impression, or my body doing its semi-regular preparation for the baby I don't want in this decade. "(A) Can we slow down for a few, please, just a little, so I have some reserves left by the time we make it to the actual challenge?" I step to the side of the trail to lean against a tree, reaching up to click off my GoPro for the ten-minute-break privilege I haven't used often. I nod for Finn to do the same, and once he does, whisper, "And (b) you're gonna need to grunt or grumble something at me at some point while I'm filming today, or else viewers are gonna think you've been body-snatched."

Finn leans on the tree beside me, not seeming to care about the gap between us and the rest of the teams widening as they keep walking. We know this challenge doesn't hinge on the order we arrive at the site, as long as we all make it by the given start time, so we don't need to out-hike anyone on this leg. He takes a sip from his water bottle, reminding me I should do the same, and stows it back in his pack before replying. "I haven't been *that* bad." When I just raise an eyebrow at him, he goes on. "Anyway, aliens couldn't touch this body. It's for your hands only."

I spew the entire sip of water I just took onto the dirt in front of us. Finn's laughter mixes with my hacking and coughing, echoing through the trees. When I can breathe again, I smack a hand against his taut stomach.

"You have got to warn me when Saucy Finn is making an appearance. My fragile being can't handle it!"

He swings an arm around my shoulders and pulls me to his

side, pressing a quick kiss to my temple. It's so brief, so casually affectionate, and so *so* nice that I've lost my breath in a wholly different way than a moment ago. Definitely worth letting the others walk on without us.

"Your feedback has been received and will be passed on to Saucy Finn for future reference."

My lungs don't feel quite capable of taking a full breath for the rest of our hike, but I might just have to accept that as normal around Finn now. He has me on my toes, off my game, giving me butterflies like no one else has since my first middle school crush. And he makes it look so effortless.

It takes a conscious effort to force my mind back to the competition. My whole reason for being here. Not the guy holding the map alongside me and how good his forearms look while he does it.

My attention is easily reclaimed, however, when we make it to the tall, concrete structure that has clearly been commandeered for a *Wild Adventures* challenge. I have to tip my head all the way back to see to the very top. It's about the height of my four-story dorm at Oliver, and looks like some kind of observation tower, capped with a round platform that looks out over the trees. People are up there, presumably hikers and tourists taking in the views from half of the platform, but the other half is empty, save for a couple familiar-looking *Wild Adventures* crew and a bunch of ropes that hang over the edge, equally spaced from one another and trailing all the way to the ground. My stomach lurches, not loving where this is heading.

We circle up with the other groups around Burke Forrester

and the crew, who must've jet-packed over here to beat us hikers, and the camera operators start filming.

"Welcome to Kuwahi," Burke announces. "This is the highest point on the entire Appalachian Trail, at an elevation of 6,643 feet. Today's challenge is all about embracing that peak, the height to which we've all climbed."

I look up at the tower again with a grimace.

"Behind me is the Kuwahi fire tower, built in 1959 by the National Park Service. It serves a variety of purposes, from allowing park rangers to spot forest fires to collecting data about unique weather patterns in the area. And at a height of fifty-four feet, it allows visitors to see views that, on a clear day, can be up to a hundred miles away. But we won't be enjoying the scenery just yet."

Has Burke's smile grown more menacing with each challenge, or is it just me?

"Our challenge is called It's Raining Co-Eds. Each member of your team will put on a harness and helmet, and receive a rain gauge that can hold ten inches of water. Taking turns with your partner, you will each climb up a ladder shared with the other teams to the top of the fire tower, fill your gauge with water, and hold it as you rappel back down the rope designated for your team, trying not to spill. Back on the ground, you'll pour your water into your team's bucket, which will hold eighty inches of rainfall—the annual average here—when filled to the orange line. Continue climbing the ladder, getting more water, rappelling down, pouring into the bucket, until the bucket is filled. The order in which teams finish will determine the order of your staggered go times to hike to the checkpoint tomorrow. Any questions?"

Yes, who the hell thinks of challenges like this?

It's a free-for-all once Burke gives us the go-ahead. Everyone scrambles to grab a harness and helmet, put them on with the help of the trained climbing and rappelling professionals who will hopefully lessen our chance of dying, and get one member of each team racing to the top of this tower. Zeke is first on the ladder, swiftly but carefully making his way up. Meena is a few rungs behind him, and Max just got his harness clipped into the mechanism on the side of the ladder that'll keep us from falling. I'm last in line, thanking my lucky stars that while I have a lot of fears, heights aren't one of them. I can't say the same for Harper, though, as I realize her small body is trembling while she waits her turn.

Her feet don't move closer to the ladder's base as Max begins to climb.

"Harps?" I prod softly. I know paralyzing fear well. "You good?"

"No," she says back, voice wobbly for the first time I've ever heard, barely audible through the cacophony of cheering and encouragement from competitors on the ground and the spectators watching from the part of the overlook still open to the public. I know a fierce competitor shouldn't get stalled by this, should say "screw friendship," jump in front of Harper and get a move on, but it feels wrong. Finally, she steps forward. "But Ev's scared of heights, too, so we're shit out of luck."

With that, she allows the crew member to hook her harness onto the ladder and takes her first step up. I can only gape while I wait to start behind her. *That* is badass. And brave. And oh damn, it's my turn, and am I sure I'm not afraid of heights?

As I begin to climb, I confirm that I'm not. I wish my anxious brain was sensible enough to have such a valid fear. Instead, it's decided to panic that I'll forget how to climb a ladder midway, that my foot is gonna slip on one of the rungs and cause me to twist my ankle, or hit my face on the rung above me as I step up, and just like that, I'll be out of the competition. All very reasonable injuries to worry over, I know, but I can't stop thinking through them.

So of course, after I finally make it to the top and collect my water, my rain gauge–holding hand is a shaky mess when I rappel back down.

"I'm sorry," I say to Finn when I dump my first tube of water in our bucket, and it only measures five inches.

"It's all good," he says as he jogs toward the ladder for his turn. "We'll get the hang of it."

And he does quickly, coming down his first time with eight and a half inches of water and managing to get ahead of Karim and Max as Karim clumsily tosses his water over the edge while clipping onto the rappelling rope, some of it splashing a couple producers on the ground. He has to unclip and get more water before starting down, putting him behind even a clearly petrified Evan.

My next turn, I do better with six and a half inches, while Finn has an almost-full gauge on his second try. But the third go-around, I fumble while pouring the water into the bucket, nearly losing everything I came down with.

On my next turn, so close to filling our bucket, I feel the pressure as I start up the ladder. I've had to stop focusing on what order we're all in, as I can't tell how full everyone's buckets are or how much water they're spilling each time or who's lapped me when I wasn't looking. I try to focus on doing the best *I* can and tuning out all the mayhem around me. Going up the ladder is still the hardest part, and the rungs shaking every time someone new starts climbing behind me makes it all the more nerve-racking. As a result, I'm all the more careful with each step I take.

"You're doing great, Nat," Finn calls from the ground. He doesn't sound like he's yelling, but his rumbly voice is distant enough that I'm probably pretty high up. I wouldn't know, as my eyes won't focus on anything but my hands and feet.

"You're welcome to go faster any time, though. Seriously. Totally an option," a grating, higher-pitched voice chimes in. Enemi, living up to her nickname today.

I'm choosing to ignore her, mostly out of inability to multi-task. Finn, apparently, is not.

"Hey, shut it. She's not moving any slower than your teammate."

I nearly miss a rung in surprise.

Enemi scoffs. I'm pretty sure, anyway, though she could've just choked on a bug. Wouldn't be mad about the latter. "And as you might have noticed, I'm pushing just as hard for my teammate to pick up his pace."

"That's between you and him," he barks. "Just leave mine alone."

I almost gasp out loud. *Mine.* I know the word is literally referring to me as *his* teammate. But the heart-eyed fool within me wants to hear it a little differently. I should probably splash said fool in the face with some fake rainwater. But what's the harm in letting myself be a teensy bit smitten, if only deep down on the inside?

Actually, I don't want the answer to that.

At the top, I continue to ignore the stunning vista from Kuwahi, single-minded in filling up my rain gauge and getting it to the ground. I hold it close to my chest in one hand as a crew member helps me clip my harness to the rope, and I use my free hand to guide myself down. Every ounce of my attention is on keeping this water as steady as possible, and my descent is extra slow in the effort to do so.

When I pour what's left into the bucket on the ground, it's worth it.

"Fifty-one inches!" I cheer. "If we can get three more almost-full, we'll get there!"

Finn doesn't even point out that he can do mental math, thank you, as he's running away. We've come so far.

He quickly and gracefully climbs the ladder and reappears a few moments later to bring his full rain gauge down. As I watch, I try to take deep, calming breaths, to press my palms flat to my thighs in the hopes that they'll decide to be steady. I take a drink from my water bottle, because the Big Water agenda is always telling me it solves everything. Why not try?

Finn nails it again, then gives me a pat on the back as I head off for what I hope is my last trip up. The contact, while brief, sends a surge of pleasure through me. He's on my team, literally but also more than that. He believes in me. And he should, because I've totally got this. I repeat it to myself, my racing heart, and my wobbly ankles the whole way up.

At the top, I hear cheering that I'm pretty sure is Enemi; she only makes sounds that joyful when she's won a challenge. *Dammit.* I fill my rain gauge and prepare to rappel down once more, but once I'm clipped to the rope, I notice Harper standing by her rope beside mine, clutching her rain gauge close to her chest. She looks out toward the view but I don't think she's really seeing it, every muscle in her face tense as she takes slow, deliberate breaths.

I'm so close. I should finish this out and check on her later. But I haven't forgotten what she and Evan did for me in that cooking challenge, and how she's been just the kind of steady support I've needed from the start, before she knew anything about me, before Finn was giving me any of that.

"Harper," I say, and her head jerks my way, her expression still hard and unsettled. "Let's go down together, okay?"

Her breath whistles between her gritted teeth, and she seems so frustrated with herself as her eyes drift to the side that my heart breaks a little. "It should get easier after doing it this many times, shouldn't it? I need to get my shit together. I spill, like, half the water every time."

I reach my hand out on instinct. "Let me take your water too, then. Come on."

Harper's shoulders slump, her chin dips, every inch of her emanating embarrassment. "You don't need to do that. I—I'll get there."

"I know I don't have to, but it's probably my last chance to offer and your last to take me up on it, so." I try to look flippant, like I couldn't care less if she lets me return the generosity she's extended to me. "What'll it be?"

My descent is a blur, two full rain gauges clutched in one of my hands, and I only vaguely register Harper starting her way down beside me with two free hands and nothing to stress about this time but getting to the ground. I pass off one of the gauges to a confused Evan then run to my own confused partner and our bucket, pouring the last of my water to get us to roughly seventy and one-quarter inches. It all comes down to Finn.

So of course, he delivers, and we finish in third behind Zeke and Enemi and Meena and Cammie. When we get the official stamp of approval on our full bucket, Finn picks me up in one of his tight, squeezing hugs again, but this time, it's a struggle not to wrap my legs around his waist and kiss the smile from his handsome face.

In fact, I find it hard to resist that impulse even when he's not hugging me, all through the end of the challenge—where Karim and Max narrowly beat out Harper and Evan—to setting up our campsite a while later in a nearby clearing with the other teams, and the campfire dinner with the whole exhausted group.

My craving for Finn's affection is briefly sidetracked by affection from a different source, when Harper and Evan catch me in a two-sided hug sandwich while I'm assembling a s'more for dessert. I don't feel entirely deserving, considering they still came in last place, but who am I to look a gift hug in the mouth, and all that? Especially from Harper, known Not-A-Hugger, who tells me she's making the exception for "these extenuating circumstances." The embrace makes me feel warmer than the fires I find myself near most nights. It also makes me realize how much I've been aching for this kind of platonic affection, which I had gotten so used to growing up with my two best friends. Not just out here on the trail, but for most of the past year.

I'm tapped out of energy, both emotional and physical, by bedtime. But looking at my partner, thinking of our entire day together and all the time we haven't spent kissing since leaving the hotel, I'm struck again, intensely, by the *want* coursing through me. Want to be near him, hold his hand, press my face into his neck, feel his grip on my waist, and so. Much. More.

I'm buzzing as much as my electric toothbrush when I finish my nightly routine and go back toward our tent. The area we're camping in is more wooded than some of the others, and I'm glad we're separated from neighboring tents by several trees on all sides. Not that I'm planning on mauling Finn or anything, but even whispered sweet nothings feel risky when all that stands between you and another team is a little thin nylon and two feet of air.

"You in there?" I ask softly into the darkness as I start to unzip the side flap. There's no headlamp or e-reader glowing from inside, but Finn never takes longer to get ready than I do.

"Yep," he answers. "Been making the bed."

I give a confused laugh as I pull the flap open and crawl inside. When I grab for the top of my sleeping bag, it doesn't pull down as easily as normal.

"What did you . . . ?" The material swish-swishes as I feel around, followed by Finn's stifled laugh when I connect with his torso under the bag.

"Stop, stop," he chuckles, and his hand reaches out to clasp mine and halt its roaming. "I, ah, zipped our sleeping bags together to make one mega bag. I thought it might be kinda fun, but also know it's goofy and might not be comfortable for the whole night, and it's okay if you don't want to keep it this way."

I hope it's too dark for him to see my unstoppable toothy smile. Talk about goofy.

"Uh, *obviously* we're keeping it," I squeak as I scramble to the top of the mega sleeping bag and slide my feet in. Finn unzips it part of the way and helps me wriggle down next to him before zipping us in. "Well isn't this cozy! We're like . . . like two hermit crabs sharing a shell."

I can barely make out the amusement flickering across Finn's face when he says, "I don't think hermit crabs do that, do they?"

"Okay, two joeys in a mama kangaroo's pouch."

He winces. "So we're siblings? Yikes."

"All right, fine," I huff. "If you insist on being this way, we'll go with two peas in a pod. My mistake for trying to be original."

His hand finds my waist, slides around to my back and pulls me in to rest against his chest. I bring an arm up to loop around his neck and idly run my fingers through the short hair on the back of his head.

"I don't think you could be unoriginal if you tried," Finn whispers. Then finally, his lips are on mine.

A strange kind of relief flows through me as it feels like we pick up right where we left off. Like our chemistry and connection wasn't a fluke spurred by a luxurious getaway from our real lives or, I don't know, the romantic power of mini golf. It's still here in our tiny tent and every bit as magical as before.

When we pull apart to catch our breath, Finn rolls to his back and I rest my head on his shoulder like it's as natural for us as poking fun at each other. His fingers toy with the ends of my hair while I trace small circles over his chest with my pinky.

"You know," I whisper sleepily after a while of listening to nothing but the sounds of the forest. "King beds are nice and all. But there's something to be said for pea pods."

Finn's laugh is soft and just as weighed down with tiredness. "Hermit crab shells."

"Kangaroo pouches." I smile as my eyes fall closed.

But I'm jostled a few minutes later. I see Finn reaching for the sweatshirt he always puts over his head while he sleeps, subtly enough that I know he's trying not to wake me, and I frown. "Why do you need that?"

He practically jumps through the tent roof. "Shit, I thought you were asleep already!"

"Almost, but I felt you sneaking away and got curious. Are you freaked out by forest noises too?"

I can faintly make out the tense lines of his face as he re-situates himself in the sleeping bag. "Not really. Is that why you wanted me to sleep in the tent with you that first time?"

"Yeah," I admit, but it doesn't feel as scary given all the other things he knows about me already. "Wait, we're not talking about me. What's with the sweatshirt?"

There's a long pause before he deflates a little, blowing a heavy breath toward the ceiling. "I don't know how to tell you this, Natalie, but . . ." He stops long enough for my heart to seize with fear. "You snore. Loudly."

Now I'm the one to flail-jump in shock. "I—you—why didn't you tell me sooner?!"

Finn rubs a hand over his head. "I don't know! It's mostly fine when I cover my ears with something, and I didn't want you to worry about it."

"Well, a lot of good that did both of us! I'm so sorry, I didn't know. I mean, I know I used to, but I thought it had gone away because I asked my roommate about it once and she said she never heard anything, but maybe the air quality is better at Oliver or there's less pollen up there or something, and being back in the South for the summer, it must've come back. I should've expected as much, I guess. Or *you* could've just *told me,* but—"

"Nat." He reaches over and finds my hand in our cocoon, linking our fingers together. "It's not a big deal. Seriously. This is why I didn't want to tell you. And anyway, I've gotten comfortable sleeping this way. I'll probably start doing it when I'm back home too."

I can hear the crooked smile in his voice and I huff out an exasperated sound in response. This just won't do.

"Hang on," I bark. I stomp out of the tent, ignoring his protests as I walk to my pack and dig through it for my toiletry bag. Inside, I grab a couple cotton pads. Who would've thought these would come in handy for so many situations out here?

"Here," I shove them at Finn when I'm back in the tent. "Ball these up and stuff them in your ears. You can tear them in half if they're too big. Just—quit doing the sweatshirt thing. If you're going to suffocate yourself with your own outerwear, I don't want it on my conscience."

Finn tries to stifle his laughter, shaking his head in a what-am-I-gonna-do-with-you way. I've gotten that head shake a lot in my life, but never has it looked so very adoring. He tears one of the cotton pads in two and balls up each half before placing them in his ears, just as instructed. Mission accomplished, I lie back down.

"I'm still mad you didn't tell me," I grumble as I roll onto my side so my back is facing him. "This isn't over."

My eyelids are already heavy again when I hear Finn's sleepy murmured response, feel his arm wrap around my middle and pull me closer as he tucks himself behind me. "Good. I hope it's not over for a long time yet."

Chapter Nineteen

I wake up on the wrong side of the mega sleeping bag.

Not in a literal way; Finn and I are curled so closely into one another that there are hardly even sides, just one central cuddle puddle. But emotionally? The side couldn't be wronger. The second day of my infrequent periods is the most consistent thing about them, in that my cramps are always the worst and I am one moody bitch. It seems that's no different out here, despite the soothing atmosphere of the great outdoors, the fact that I slept like an apparently noisy rock, and the hunk of a man snuggling me all night.

I wake up irritated at the world anyway. At the sun for shining so brightly before my eyes are ready to adjust to daylight. At the bugs and birds and other forest musicians for being so damn loud and keeping no rhythm with each other, just a cacophony of buzzes and caws and chirps and hoots. At myself for caring so much about my skin and appearance that I require a two-hundred-fifteen-step regimen every morning and a whole separate one at night. I do it anyway, of course, skipping zero steps of my slightly pared-down routine I've had for all of *Wild Adventures* so far, but I'm grumpy about it the whole time.

I can already tell it's gonna be a long day.

"Are you giving us the maps, or what?" When I snap for the first time, it's at Burke Forrester, of all people. He's lollygagging something awful as he teases today's race to the checkpoint, going on about the bridges we cross in life and how even when it feels like you're close to the end, there are always more obstacles to tackle. I, for one, am ready to get the hell on with it. Especially since each team gets to start five minutes apart, in order of when we filled our buckets yesterday. Finn and I will be third, leaving right in the middle of the pack, and I'm not taking anything for granted.

Burke, of course, has no sense of urgency. He looks at me with offense—maybe even a little disgust at my audacity—until he covers it with his polished host mask and a false chuckle. "Somebody's in rare form today, huh?"

Finn puts a hand on my lower back in a gesture that, if I'm giving him the benefit of the doubt, is probably meant to remind me he's there supporting me, and we'll make it to the checkpoint in time. But it also feels unpleasantly close to a calm-down-you-hysterical-woman warning.

Still, I bite my tongue, enduring the rest of the Burke Forrester Metaphor Hour until he finally hands over our maps and Zeke and Enemi set off for the checkpoint, starting the five-minute countdown for Meena and Cammie, ten for Finn and me. We confer over the map, deciding it looks like a pretty straight path up the AT. Finn asks how I feel physically and if I think I'm able to jog again, and I try not to take offense. I know he's trying to be considerate of the fact that I'm on my period, and if said period wasn't making me hate everyone and everything at the moment, I'd probably appreciate the consideration. So I don't bite his head off, and assure him that I'm fine to jog. Whether or not I'm lying remains to be seen.

Finally, Burke gives us the whistle to start toward the checkpoint. I let Finn go in front, determined to meet whatever pace he sets.

I quickly find that to be an ambitious goal.

"Shit, fuck, damnation, sonofa—"

"Okay back there?" Finn calls over his shoulder. I thought the curses I've been letting out with each pounding step of my boots were too quiet for his ears. My volume meter must be out of whack along with everything else, including the knives that have started stabbing at my lower abdomen as we've jog-hiked.

"Peachy," I groan back. If he's heard the rest, I might as well give up the pretense of okay-ness.

Finn slows his pace and walks backward in front of me like a campus tour guide I kind of want to kiss, kind of want to kick in the shins. "We can slow down a little. The later-leaving teams are probably well behind us, so we have a buffer. No need to make you miserable."

It's far too late for that, but a nice sentiment anyway.

"I'm fine. I'll be even better if we're not the last ones to the checkpoint. Let's just keep going."

Of course, it can't be that easy. We're almost to the checkpoint when we come up on a creek. It's marked on the map, so it isn't entirely a surprise, but what *is* surprising is the sign that blocks off the bridge crossing the creek—one that says *CLOSED FOR MAINTENANCE.* It's bright orange and written in the *Wild Adventures* font, which, combined with the fact that the bridge looks perfectly fine, leads me to believe it actually means *CLOSED TO GIVE CO-EDVENTURERS ONE LAST PAIN IN THE ASS.*

"Well, what do we . . . ," I start, but turn at the sound of voices over the rushing water a little farther downstream. Finn starts walking that way and as I follow, we see Meena and Cammie through the trees, appearing to levitate their way over the creek.

Of course they're not really, but it takes more frantic blinking on my part to make out the rope under their feet, a second clutched in their hands, as they shuffle sideways toward the other bank. A camera operator and producer on the other side cover the action.

Finn spots the orange envelopes hanging from a tree first, takes one, and tears it open. " 'Co-EdVenturers,' " he reads. " 'The Appalachian Trail, like all of life and the great outdoors, is unpredictable.' Okay, I'm skipping some of this. . . . To get to the checkpoint, we have to cross by these ropes. One to stand on, one to hold onto for balance. If we fall, head back to the start and try again." He folds the paper and envelope and stuffs both into one of his pants pockets. "Ready?"

Watching Meena and Cammie as he's read, I've already bitten my lower lip too hard and made it bleed. My arms are wrapped tight around myself as if I can physically keep my raging insides together. I try to run through the rational, reasonable facts in my mind—that the water doesn't look very deep, so I'll be okay if I fall; that *Wild Adventures* wouldn't let us do anything *too* life-threatening because it would really be bad if someone died on their show; that Meena and Cammie both just touched down on the opposite bank without falling once, and look pretty chill and happy about it. Zeke and Enemi aren't even here, so I assume they've already sped across.

But my anxiety has counterarguments to all of that. It might be shallow, but there are rocks everywhere. My bruise from the last time I fell in a creek out here is still there, in its yellow-green stage. I signed a bunch of waivers before filming started that I'm pretty sure exempted the show from any responsibility if I *do* die, and it would probably make for some record-breaking ratings. Zeke and Enemi both look like they've been training for *American Ninja Warrior* since childhood, so their success means nothing for how I, Anxious McShakyhands, will perform.

"Nat?" Finn puts a hand to my arm and I flinch away in surprise. Also in the hopes that he doesn't feel the light sweat that's broken out over my whole body, not from the hike here, just from the aerobic activity of worrying.

But this *is* a performance. I can treat it that way. Act like I'm fine, and manifest it into existence.

"Yeah, sure. Why don't you go first?" I smile, or think I do. Finn's answering skepticism indicates I might not be the most convincing.

"You don't want to cross together like they did?"

I release my grip on my own arms and try to subtly wipe my damp palms on my shorts. After seeing how much the other team bounced the entire way across, and eyeing the skinny rope that is our makeshift bridge, no, I don't especially want to have our combined weight on it. And it might help me to take another few minutes to compose myself.

I don't get that many, though. When I convince Finn to go on ahead—which doesn't take much, as he's very aware we're on a time crunch—he starts across like an experienced tightrope walker. Seriously, the guy should consider quitting college to join the circus. I'm certain it takes him no more than one minute to cross the length of the creek and jump smoothly to the ground on the other side, then turn to face me with an easy smile.

"You're up!" he yells.

The extra time only gave me more space to worry. My heart is galloping in my chest. Full Kentucky Derby underdog, going for the race of her damn life. *My* damn life. Which might be cut short by a rocky creek in the very near future.

"F-Finn?" I choke out, voice shaking, eyes on the water rushing over boulders under some parts of the rope crossing. I'm conscious of the camera operator moving closer to the creek, probably zooming in to capture every bead of sweat rolling down my forehead, but I'm too swept up by panic to keep up any performance of cool.

"What is it?" Finn calls back.

"I don't know if I can do it." I flick a glance up to his face and catch his expression of *oh shit* before he quickly schools it into fake confidence.

"You totally can. You kidding? Rappelling was way scarier."

He doesn't know how scared I was then, too. Already seems to have forgotten that my shaking hands could've cost us the whole challenge. I feel the trembling in my extremities, the buzzing spreading through my limbs. I tuck my hands against my sides, but the tremors amplify through my rib cage.

"I had a helmet yesterday, Finn!" I cry.

"See? This must be safer, if we don't have to wear helmets." The *gotcha!* grin he sports makes his face look all too punchable.

"Not what that means."

"Well, it kind of is. The fall isn't far, and—"

"You did not just 'well, actually' me at a time like this!"

"I—what?" I can't believe we're having this conversation across a creek, but I'm too worked up to stop now. He stacks his hands atop his head and I only spare a moment to notice the nice things it does for his arms because I'm now not only freaking out about crossing the ropes, I'm also annoyed at my partner.

Finn is the one to deflate from his puffed-up posturing first, arms dropping back to his sides and volume of his voice lowering with them. "Nat," he says on a sigh. "What do you want me to say? What do you want to do here? We don't have unlimited time to decide, you know?"

I stare back at the ropes, not feeling any surer I can haul myself across them. I register another team jogging up from the closed bridge, Zeke and Enemi. Where the hell have they been? I assumed they'd kept their first-place reign of terror, but they must've gotten sidetracked, or taken a wrong turn somewhere. Now they're going to make up for lost time while I flounder uselessly. I feel the threat of tears at the backs of my eyes. No. *No,* I'm not doing this right now. And I'm absolutely not letting anyone else see.

Blinking quickly, I crouch and mess with the laces on my boots, ensuring I don't have anything to trip over. Then I stand, just as Zeke is grabbing an orange envelope from the tree off to my side. "Okay, I'm heading over," I shout.

"Are you sure?" Finn calls back.

No, but he clearly doesn't want to hear that at the moment. And he's right—we don't have all the time in the world. What other option do I have? Hell, Meena and Cammie are probably halfway to whatever nice hotel stay they win for this challenge. Though in truth, the best prize would be not having to participate in any more activities involving serious risk of life and limb.

"Yes," I say, more forcefulness to it than I feel.

I take a few deep breaths, then approach the ropes, putting my hands on the top one. I am gonna eat this creek for breakfast.

MY BREAKFAST HAS never made me so furious.

"FUCK!" My shout echoes through the trees, along with the loud splash as I hit the water a second time.

I maintain that the first time was Enemi's fault. She and Zeke argued over waiting until I was across to start their trek, but against his protests, she hopped right on before I was even halfway over the creek. Her shaking of the ropes immediately made me lose my balance, and I dropped down, the only blessing being that I landed on my feet in waterproof boots.

This time, I wasn't as lucky. I did land on my feet, but unsteadily, and fell to my knees in the shallow creek. One got cut on a rock and both my palms are now scraped up with rope burn. As I trudge back to the bank, I let out a groan-scream that's likely as painful to everyone's ears as it is to my throat. Zeke gives me a sad, apologetic smile as he shuffles his way across the ropes.

When I'm almost to the starting point, Harper and Evan step on, one after the other, taking the Meena-Cammie tandem-crossing approach. And while I'm pleasantly shocked to see they overtook Karim and Max somewhere, they're still knocking Finn and me down one more notch in the standings.

Finn, a little more urgency in his encouraging tone now, shouts over, "Hey, you got this, okay? Take a breath. You can do it, Nat. Just stay focused, hang on, keep your balance—"

"What do you think I've been doing?" I yell. Harper startles midway across the rope, giving Evan and her both a little bounce.

Finn must have some sense of how unhelpful his advice is. It's every woman and her bleeding hands and knee for themselves out here. But the frustration and desire to be done with this already are starting to grow stronger than the anxiety. I feel less shaky as I climb up again, just after our friends have made it to the other side. I try not to hold the rope with the most scraped up parts of my palms, but it's still painful. The pain makes me almost dissociate, block out everything except moving forward so I can stop holding this rope and treat what hurts.

"Natalie, you're doing great," I vaguely hear Finn say. Well, that's good. Some encouragement, unprompted and without any extra attempt at motivational speaking or telling me what to d—

"See, you can crush this stuff when you really push yourself!"

My steps falter but miraculously, I don't go down. Does he think I only just started *pushing myself*? That my very real anxiety has actually just been, what, me not trying hard enough to be chill?

"And no pressure, take your time. Just want you to know Karim and Max are right behind you and they're the only team left after us, okay? But we're ahead and you can do this."

No pressure! Take my time! Sure!!!

I bite down on the frustrated beast-scream I want to unleash. Does it seem like I'm anything less than fully aware we're in the last two teams?

I feel the rope bounce, and don't look to see if it's Max, Karim, or both bearing down on me. I do pause for some of the initial bouncing to settle, and apparently this is all it takes for Finn to decide it's Yes Pressure time.

"Nat! It's now or never! Do you really want this to be what loses us the hundred K?"

When I hear the splash, I first think it's from me again. Woman down, brutally felled by her partner's complete lack of faith in her, that she was stupid to think ever went away. But I'm still on the rope, holding on for all I'm worth—which may or may not be one hundred thousand dollars. Finn probably leans toward not.

It's frustration and spite that push me forward without responding. Even as my fingers hurt, even as I kind of want to cry for reasons both identifiable and not, even as my whole body quakes with lingering nerves or perhaps a dash of fresh rage, I keep on.

When, at last, I set one foot on the solid ground at the far creek bank, Finn reaches for my waist and hauls me the rest of the way down, pulling me into a hurried hug. I don't return it, though he doesn't seem to notice before dropping his arms and pulling me by my red, roughed-up hand the rest of the short way down the trail to the *Wild Adventures* flag and a clapping, smiling Burke Forrester.

I barely register Burke's words, just the fact that we are *not* the last team. He and Finn talk back and forth about the challenges today and yesterday. I would add my two cents, but I don't think I'm human anymore. By my scientific calculations, I'm a barely sentient blob made up of thirty percent exhaustion, twenty percent open wounds, fifty percent mad-sad, the ratios of the former to the latter changing by the second.

The mad is partly directed toward my teammate. The guy who's been so encouraging and supportive, a good ally at plenty of points in this journey, even more than an ally at others. His impatience with me, the patronizing, all of it stung.

More than that, though, I'm mad at myself. Because Finn

was right, ultimately—I could have been the reason we got sent home today instead of Max and Karim. My anxious, screwed-up brain, which I thought was doing so well in this experience, has turned on me as the challenges have grown more intense. It's getting in my way as it always seems to do in the end, making it painfully obvious to everyone that I'm not cut out for this stuff.

And why did I ever think this wouldn't be the case? Even if I had my shit together mentally, it's not like I was ever going to be physically strong or outdoorsy enough to not only keep up, but beat out everyone else in a fierce competition for $100,000 that I really fucking need.

I probably deserved to lose today. This feeling intensifies as I watch Karim and Max make it to the top and approach the checkpoint, defeat evident in every inch of their bodies. I have to turn away as Burke hands down their fate and Max starts to get emotional about how much this experience has meant to him, my own eyes stinging once again.

Finn and I are still here, but it doesn't feel like we have much longer. And it really doesn't feel like any kind of win.

Chapter Twenty

The dark clouds gathering over our campsite tonight are a little too on the nose, if you ask me.

I wouldn't ask me much right now, though, as I can feel myself being an absolute witch to everyone who tries to engage in conversation. Especially Finn.

"Want seconds of anything?" he asks as he stands from his camp chair beside mine, on the outskirts of the group gathered around the fire. "I'm going back for more mac and cheese."

I have half a mind to ask him to bring the whole pan of it over here, but I know that's just the side of me that likes to eat my feelings, so I shake my head no. He gives me that lost puppy look he's perfected lately, but heads off toward the food table without another word.

He's been so extra nice to me ever since we almost lost the challenge today, offering to carry my pack, doing all the tent setup himself, helping bandage my gross, bloody hands and knee, now trying to shove food at me in penance. But what he hasn't done is apologize for anything he said. So I've given him nothing in return.

Though I do have this thought, like an itch at the back of my brain I can't scratch, that he wasn't really in the wrong to get a little impatient. I would be, if I had to deal with me as a partner. Someone who is her own biggest obstacle, getting in her own way time and time again. Have I been kidding myself, thinking I was ever a good teammate? Was today just the culmination of weeks of Finn wanting to tell me to get my ass in gear, try harder, do better? Can I blame him so much if it was?

Everyone must realize that I was not made for a show like *Wild Adventures*. I am as indoorsy as they come. Shit, I'd have been better off going on *Good Chef/Bad Chef* or something, and I scarcely know how to boil a pot of water. There have been moments when I believed I was getting the hang of things, or that my random knowledge based on romance novels and horse farm life have come in handy. But did I actually think I had a chance of winning the whole thing, back when I signed up for all this? Was I thinking at all?

These are the questions that consume me on a loop, as everyone else goes on eating, talking, and laughing together. Others include "How much money could I be making if I'd kept my job at Body Wonderland, stayed in Boston, and went up to full-time hours for the summer?" and "How much will I be able to make if I go back there and start working, say, next week?" and even "Which benevolent talk show host should I write a letter to, asking if they want to sponsor my college career?"

This brainstorming feels a little more productive than the complete self-loathing I want to sink into like a too-hot bath that'll turn my skin all red. But it also feels as pointless as the rest of this, as paralyzed by my own incompetence and hopelessness as I'm feeling right now.

"How we feeling tonight, everybody?" booms a voice I didn't expect to hear again today. We all turn to see Burke Forrester approaching, backlit by the setting sun, a camera close at his side. *What the . . . ?*

There are confused murmurs of "Good," "Great," "How are you?" in return, and Burke gives a small, fake chuckle. "Glad to hear it! But I bet you're all wondering why I'm here."

More murmurs of agreement with that.

"I've come with a surprise for you all—a little something to help the morale around here as our competition heats up and you're all feeling the pressure. Any guesses what it is?"

A dozen ridiculous guesses float through my mind. *Look under your camp chairs!* You *get a tent-sized memory-foam mattress!* You *get a new car that you can drive to our next checkpoint!* Meena and Cammie won lifetime entrance passes to the national parks system as their challenge prize today, plus a camping hammock from some luxury outdoors brand that advertises with *Wild Adventures.* More merch from them, maybe?

Instead, Burke pulls from his backpack a single, large tablet. What, are we all supposed to share it?

"Everybody come closer," he says, a grin spreading across his face. We do as we're told, some pulling chairs around him in a semicircle while others stand behind us. Finn stands directly behind my chair, brushing my shoulder with his hand, only for a second but it still makes me shiver.

I'm not really staying mad at him, am I?

Satisfied with the setup, Burke turns the tablet toward himself, tapping around a few times. When he turns it back to face us, a middle-aged white woman fills the screen. A couple seats away from me, Enemi gasps, a hand flying to her mouth and her eyes instantly shining.

"Hi, Alli girl," the woman says with a smile like her daughter's, if the latter had more soul behind it. "It's Mom!"

Even through tears, Enemi manages to sound like textbook Bitchy Teenager when she says, "God, Mom, obviously I know it's you. What are you—how is this—what's going on?"

Her mom has an infectious laugh that even makes me smile. "I just wanted to give you a little pep talk, let you know that you've got this! I'm sure you're doing amazing, sweetie, and I can't wait to watch you shine."

More sniffles from the blond bully's corner. If we keep this up for very long, it's going to make my grudge harder to hold. "Thanks, Mommy," she manages.

"You make me so proud every day, so keep going out there and kicking butt, okay? I'll see you when you get home, but don't hurry back. Love you, sugar monkey!"

Sugar monkey? I think I tamp down my incredulous expression before I look over at Enemi again. She doesn't seem embarrassed in the least as she and her mom exchange goodbyes and tears pour down her cheeks. Who knew she could produce such a human substance? I have to look away, lest my icy heart thaw.

Burke taps around to pull up another video call, this one featuring an older Black man who we soon learn is Cammie's grandpa. It goes on, each call from home somehow sweeter and more moving than the last. Maybe it's partly the period hormones, but I'm having a hell of a time keeping my eyes dry.

Then a pretty white woman with long, gray-streaked brown hair appears on screen. I wouldn't recognize her off the bat, but the girl next to her is a dead ringer for a younger Finn, if Finn had a pixie cut and his deep brown eyes were naturally smilier. My heart gives a squeeze, and almost without my willing it, my hand reaches up over my shoulder and clasps his. He holds on so tight, it hurts my rope burn, so I shift my grip to be more comfortable. I can feel him shaking, and know if I was to look his way, I'd lose it before his family members said a word. So I keep my eyes on them.

"Hey there, Finny! How is our favorite guy?" his mom says, already swiping a tear away.

"Hi, Mom," he says, not trying to hide the emotion in his voice. "Hey, Frannie. I'm good, how are you guys?"

"We miss you!" Frannie chirps.

"We do, but we're so happy for you, bud," his mom interjects. "We just hope you're having the best time on this—well, for lack of a better word, adventure. We are prouder than you know, sweetheart, and I know without a doubt that your dad would be, too."

"Thank you," Finn manages with shaking breath. "I—I think he would."

"Of course he would. You're smart and creative and you've

always been great at tackling each new challenge with dedication and courage. I see more of Dad in you every day—" His mom has to pause, and a stoic Frannie puts an arm around her shoulders. "I'm sorry, I don't mean to be too sappy. Point is, you're following through on both his and your dream, and even if you come home tomorrow, we hope you still feel pleased with all you've done and the amazing person you are."

"But try not to come home tomorrow," Frannie teases, and Finn and I, along with the whole teary group, laugh.

"We'll do our best," Finn says with a squeeze of my hand, and I wave to the screen with my free one.

"Is that your partner? Hi! We can't wait to watch you two together!" His mom gives me an enthusiastic wave, and Frannie smirks at her as though to tell her to chill. She doesn't give Finn or me time to respond, which is fortunate, as I have no clue what to say right now. "Have fun, stay safe, and we'll see you when we see you!"

Finn tells them he loves them and they say their goodbyes, and when I look over at the rest of the group, there's not a dry eye in the woods. Burke connects the next video call, and I finally chance a look back. Our clasped hands still rest on my shoulder, Finn's white-knuckling mine in a way that isn't sustainable for my circulation, but I won't say anything just yet. Especially when I see his face, tracked with tears that he isn't even bothering to wipe away. His chin trembles as the moisture collects under it and drips onto the ground.

I try to be subtle as I pat under my eyes with my sleeve, facing forward again to watch the rest of Evan's greeting from home. Apparently I am absolutely wrecked by proud, loving families expressing said pride and love. Duly noted.

As I watch, I realize I'm the last one left without a call. Nerves kick in for the first time, rumbling in my stomach, tightening my chest. What are my parents going to say? They barely know what I'm doing here and definitely don't care, let alone feel proud of me for it. And how the hell did *Wild Adventures* even get in touch with them? Were my folks nice about it, or is it another strike in the Natalie Is A Huge Burden column in their black book of all my faults? How is this going to be anything but the most awkward call ever?

When Burke turns the screen back around, I no longer have to wonder.

"Nat! Our love, our life!" Reese squeals. Clara and Reese's boyfriend, Benny, crowd into the selfie cam frame on either side of her.

"Natalieee," Benny sings in a strange opera voice, and Clara, the most camera-shy of us all, waves. "You're aliiive!"

Reese covers Benny's mouth with her hand. "And we are not at all surprised by that!"

"You're not?" I force a laugh over all the mixed emotions rioting in me. "I kind of am."

"No way! You're *such* a badass at everything you do, so of course you'd be the same out there. You take anything life throws at you and make it your b—best experience yet."

Clara cuts in as Reese makes an awkward, almost-cursed-on-camera face. "Personally, I'm impressed at how well you appear to have kept up your makeup routine."

"Obviously," I say with a smirk, hiding as many of my feelings as I can behind the façade of sass. Total Natalie move. "How are y'all?"

"Same old stuff around here, plus Clar came to visit," Reese says.

"Is that your partner behind you?" Benny asks, and I nod. "Man, I'm sorry for your luck. It must be rough, and if you need to talk about it, I'm—"

"Oh, hush, Norberto!" I snap. He's hitting a bit too close to the mark. "I know a lot of good places to bury a body now."

"I take it back." Benny waves his hand at the camera as if to clear the record. "Can we cut that whole exchange in the final episode? I did not consent to her use of my first name in front of the viewing public!"

"As we were saying," Reese enunciates slowly, cutting her boyfriend a sharp look. "We are really proud of you, and impressed by how far you've gone, and please come back soon. I mean, win the money first, then hurry on home so we can love on you and maybe throw a parade in your honor. That seems appropriate, right?"

"Not only appropriate, but necessary," Clara agrees with a decisive nod. "Okay, keep being incredible!"

"I love y'all," I mumble through my inevitable tears.

"We love you!"

"See you soon!"

The screen goes black, and the group in the woods breaks into emotion-drenched applause and excited chatter about how wonderful that was. I clap somewhat mindlessly and think I manage a semblance of a smile, but I'm no longer feeling the same uplifted, good vibes of everyone else.

It *was* wonderful to see my best friends' faces. To hear they love me and think I'm amazing and kicking ass in the competition—even Benny, who only teases because he loves me—however unfounded I think their confidence is.

But it's not lost on me that I'm the only one without a family member sending a greeting from home.

All at once, I'm back in the lobby outside my high school's auditorium, where everyone gathered after our theater productions to greet the cast, give out flowers and hugs, share praise and congratulations. Everyone's families and closest friends and even randoms from school who just felt like seeing the show. But for me and those close enough to know me, there was always a glaring absence in the group. My parents. They didn't come to any of my shows in my whole high school theater career. At first, there were excuses—not being able to get away from work, or the more vague "things to do." Eventually, those broke down into, *"Another* show? Didn't you just wrap up the last one?" and "Where do you think all this is going? No one actually makes it as a professional actress."

I heard the message, loud and clear: we don't believe in you, we're not interested in what you're up to, and we're not going to waste our time pretending otherwise.

Same story now. I know they don't understand why I wanted to do this. I know they are possibly the last people in the world who would want to be on TV for any reason. But I also know I'm so damn tired of making excuses for them, and that none of the excuses lessen the hurt.

Granny Star would have been there. Granny Star would have video called me, even if she'd had to go to Best Buy and get a webcam to attach to her ancient desktop computer. It's times like this that her loss feels that much more painful, and I don't know if it'll ever be less so.

I have to remove myself from the others as our evening wind-down resumes. I grab my toiletry bag and find a stump to sit on in a quiet spot in the woods. With the soft hum of conversations around the campfire in the background, I go through my nightly routine, trying to focus on each action in a meditative way—I feel the cool makeup-removing cloth against my skin, smell the light, chemical-y scent they call "unscented," taste my minty toothpaste foam.

It kind of works, but I find myself feeling sad more than anything. As a last-ditch effort, I dig out one of the sheet masks I brought and haven't gotten around to using, this one labeled as "serene green tea and eucalyptus." Sure, I could use some serenity.

After unfolding the thin, cool green sheet and patting it down on my face, getting the nose, eye, and mouth holes all lined up right, I lean back against another tree beside my stump and close my eyes. I try some deep breathing because it seems like the serene thing to do.

In, one, two, three, why don't my parents love me. . . . Out, one, two, three, I don't know but if they can't love me how could anyone else. . . . In, one, two, I almost lost us the whole competition today because of my scaredy-cat brain. . . . Out, one, I suck at this, I suck at school, I suck at being a person a lot of the tiiime. . . .

Okay, this isn't working flawlessly. I give up on suppressing the thoughts and just let them run away from me, with me, in circles around me, closing in tighter and tighter. At some point, I halfway hear my name in the distance, but don't make any moves to open my eyes or find where it's coming from. I stay put on my stump, clearing my skin while letting my mind get messier than ever.

"Natalie, are you ou— *Holy shit!*" My eyes pop open at the exclamation and I find Finn standing there with a hand over his heart, gasping for breath.

"What?" I ask, trying to sound as chill as the mask was supposed to make me feel.

"Your—" He waves a hand in a circle to indicate my whole face. "You scared me half to death. Not what anyone wants to run into in a dark forest."

Oh, right. The mask.

Still, I'm a little affronted by his reaction. I cross my arms over my chest. "Well, I didn't especially want to run into you either, thank you very much."

He sighs, shifting his weight to his left foot and crossing his own arms while he looks my way as if he doesn't quite know what to do with me. "Come on, Nat, that's not what I meant. You've been gone for a while and I was getting worried. Well, to be honest, I've *been* worried ever since we finished the challenge today. You haven't been yourself."

"I think I've been a little too much myself. That's the whole problem."

His head jerks back, expression incredulous. "What are you talking about?"

I take a moment to peel my mask off first. If we're getting into this, I don't need the indignity of looking like a demonic ghost.

"You've known it since the beginning, Finn," I say, not making eye contact as I ball up the used sheet between my bandage-covered palms. "I'm not cut out for all this stuff. I'm not outdoorsy or athletic or even all that adventurous. I'm weak, but good enough at fooling people into thinking I'm strong. Incompetent, but I fake being a badass bitch who has it all handled. It might win people over or get me far enough in the beginning, but eventually everyone sees the truth. Clearly you have."

Finn steps closer. "Okay, whoa, where to even start with that. Natalie, when have I given you the idea I think you're anything but amazing?"

I raise a brow. "Uh, most of the time we've known each other? I know, I know, it was different for a while there. But today, I completely lost it in the challenge and you knew it. You were frustrated with me, and you were probably right to be. I just lost my shit and couldn't get it back together, and I almost made us lose."

"No, that's—no. Stop." He crouches beside my stump so we're eye level. "I'm sorry I was too intense today. We both know I can be a dick. I shouldn't have gotten short with you, or said those things, and I'll do anything I can to make it up to you. Including not speaking to you like that again. But that's all on me, it's not—you didn't do anything wrong. It's valid to be afraid of something that's objectively pretty scary and that you haven't done before."

"Is it also valid to be too afraid to sleep in a tent by myself at night?"

"I mean, yeah?" Not the most confident answer. He rubs at the back of his neck as if he's holding a lot of tension there. "What are you trying to convince me of, here?"

"That I can't handle this!" I blurt out. "And it was ridiculous to think I could."

Thunder rumbles somewhere in the distance, but Finn doesn't bat one perfect eyelash. He reaches out and I allow him to take one of my hands in his. His grasp is soft, his thumb caressing my wrist the same, but when he speaks, the words don't match that tone.

"Well, tough shit."

I blink, offering a less than eloquent, "Huh?"

"You can tell yourself that all you want, but it's not true and you're not going to convince me. The only times you've struggled are when you've gotten too much in your own head."

My jaw drops. "Oh, so my biggest problem is me? If I can just get over myself or, I don't know, outsmart my anxiety, I can win this thing? Great! So glad you've cracked it!"

"Nat." He sighs. "I know it's not that easy. That our brains can tell us all kinds of bullshit, and there's chemical stuff at work that we can't just 'outsmart' and go on about our day. But you can change your thought patterns, try thinking about all the ways things can go right instead of how they can go wrong."

This conversation is making my head hurt, and I rub at my temples. "Telling myself how great I am isn't going to just magically make me capable of winning the money. I could be *making* money as we speak, had I not decided to come on a mystical forest goose chase for the minuscule possibility of a scholarship. I could've worked this summer like a normal human. How many times have my parents tried to tell me? But here I am, nutty Natalie, choosing the least practical path available."

Finn stands and paces back and forth a couple times before facing me again. "What good does thinking about that do you now? Obsessing over *should've, could've, would've* has the potential to screw yourself out of an amazing experience *and* winning a lot of money, and if you don't care about that for you, then care about it for me. Care that you'd be screwing me out of it too."

My stomach plummets to the forest floor, and I feel suddenly lower than the thousands of microorganisms that my AT e-books tell me live in the dirt. That's the last thing I want at this point, to ruin Finn's chance to win. And I know it's exactly where I'm headed.

But then he gives me whiplash as he steers this speeding train of a conversation in a different direction.

"Should we go over all the amazing things you've done here?" He sounds frustrated still, but also defensive. Of *me*. "Building fires, riding horses, assembling tents, rappelling down a fire tower repeatedly, hauling a backpack that's bigger than you across whole mountains? Let alone keeping both of us going when my bad attitude makes me want to give up. Making me laugh, brightening my days, turning my world upside down on a mini golf course—any of that ring a bell?"

Even as I'm still fighting the anxiety current that wants to pull me under, his words make my stomach do a flip. I'm not used to this, someone working so hard to convince me that I'm awesome. It's not familiar or comfortable, and I don't know how to respond.

Finn's gaze tracks over my face, probably trying to determine if he should continue his praise dump. I don't want that to happen, so I give him a small smile and hesitant nod. "It rings a bell."

"Good," he says, kneeling before me again. "Can you believe me when I tell you how great you are, then, and how lucky I am to be with you? I'm already begging on my knees but I can lie flat on the ground if I need to."

My smile grows against my will, and I even let out a small laugh as I shake my head. "No, the nice hotel people just did your laundry. Don't destroy their hard work so soon."

The double sleeping bag feels less cozy and exciting when we crawl in tonight, and more like a really tough setup for hiding my true feelings. I've never been so conflicted, so warmed and comforted by someone's support and yet still so sure that I'm causing more problems for either of us than is necessary. I curl up against Finn but my thoughts are too scattered to the emotional hurricane winds for much kissing or cuddling. I'm already past the worst of my period, but thankful for the convenient excuse of cramps when I roll away from him. It's only a few inches between us but I wonder, as Finn pops his earplugs in again, if he also feels it like a sign. One representing the gulf between us, our lives, our futures, that will only get wider from here.

Chapter Twenty-One

One of the first things I do after a restless night under rainy skies is drop my toothbrush on the ground. A bug is trapped in the toothpaste-covered bristles, surrounded by soil and dead leafy bits, buggy legs barely twitching with life, and all I can think is *same*.

I'm still sure that I shouldn't be here, that it's only a matter of time before everyone sees it once and for all. Maybe today is the day I go home. I'll be sad, of course, and I dread figuring out how I'll afford school now. But I guess I won't be all that surprised. Mostly, I'll feel even guiltier that Finn got paired with me. I keep hearing him in my mind on repeat, telling me I'm screwing over his chance of winning. Asking if the rope crossing was really how I wanted to lose a hundred K. Even if those were throwaway comments in the heat of the moment, they were fair. He deserves better, someone who can stay focused and optimistic and not be their own worst enemy in this thing. If there was a way for him to stay and win the money without me dragging him down, I just know I'd take it.

He can tell I'm off, too, though maybe he thinks it's still my period. This might actually be the one instance in the history of the world in which I've wanted a man to think I'm in a bad mood because it's my time of the month. Better that than us having another conversation about getting my shit together, a thing I am categorically incapable of doing at this point.

But I am capable of trudging on into the next challenge with the eagerness of one walking to the guillotine. The ground squishes beneath our boots as all the teams surround Burke Forrester in our usual semicircle. He looks oddly solemn today, and combined with the gray, misty sky and the very few teams left on either side of Finn and me, it's not helping my own inner doom and gloom.

"Co-EdVenturers," Burke says, voice matching his expression. "You and your teammates began this journey as strangers. Unlike most of our seasons, you didn't come in with a familiar partner, someone you know and with whom you are prepared to tackle every obstacle. You were paired at random with a fellow student, each of you from completely different backgrounds and experiences, and together you have faced the most intense, fast-paced adventure of your lives.

"For some of you, this has gone better than it has for others. Close friendships have formed, strong bonds that will endure long after you've left these woods. And in other cases, well . . ." He gives us an awkward grimace. "You may have spent time pondering how best to push each other off a mountain."

The group laughs just as awkwardly, no one looking directly at Zeke and Enemi. I feel my nerves begin to buzz, the half of a bagel I had for breakfast not loving its new home in my stomach, wondering where this is going and if perhaps Burke can read minds. Specifically, mine from the last twelve hours.

"At this stage and with the unique setup of this season, we are offering you an opportunity that we've never offered before. You will all have the option to change partners."

I'm pretty sure every one of us remaining lets out a gasp or some form of *"WHAT?"* Burke tries to look serious, though his eyes glimmer with the delight of throwing a sufficiently shocking curveball. He holds up both hands palms-out. "Now, wait a moment. Before we get any further into how this will work, you will all be blindfolded. We want everyone to make their decision based on their personal wants and needs, without any influence from their partner or others. You will not be allowed to confer with each other over the choice, even in nonverbal ways."

My wide eyes meet Finn's beside me. Just as we've been told not to communicate nonverbally, I have a split-second to see . . . I'm not exactly sure what on his face. Uncertainty? Panic? Even a preemptive apology? I know he tried so hard to convince me he wants to be by my side, but that's when there wasn't another option. Surely he sees the gift he's been given here. A free pass to ditch the dead weight. The one screwing him over.

He deserves to take it. Still, I'm a tumble of about seventy-two different emotions. Producers file in from either side of the group, tying blindfolds around our eyes. Ginger, my old pal, appears at my back.

"Ready?" she asks with an encouraging smile.

I nod even as I'm unsure if that's true, and she wraps the piece of fabric loosely around my head, securing it over my ponytail.

"Okay," Burke continues once all our eyes are covered. "You will now be handed two signs. The one in your right hand says *switch* while the one in your left says *stay.* These are what you will use to signal your choice when I tell you to do so. The catch is that both partners must choose to switch in order for a switch to be made. If they answer differently, they will default to staying partners. Additionally, if only one team chooses to switch, there will be no other options of teammates for them, so they must remain together. Are there any questions?"

While I'm unable to see, I can feel the tension rolling through the group in waves. This changes everything. Even if, in the end, the circumstances aren't right for any teams to switch partners, the whole dynamic will be altered by knowing *anyone* wants to switch.

A heavy weight settles in my gut as I know what I need to do. What Finn, if he has any sense of self-preservation, will do. And even as I want this for him, know it's for the best, it makes my heart ache.

I tell myself that it's been good, what we've had, though it feels like we've only just gotten started. It becomes clearer every day that I'm a mess, probably the kind who shouldn't be getting into a relationship anyway, on top of being a shitty teammate. This is an easy out from both partnerships, isn't it? Out of sight, out of mind, out of heart and tent and damned shared sleeping bag.

"Remember," Burke's serious voice calls out again. "Right to switch, left to stay. We will start the clock now, and you have one minute to hold up your choice."

I can practically hear the Final Jeopardy music in my head, prodding me to wager all my money. That's really what this is, when it comes down to it. I'm wagering my money, in a way. I know I'm not going to be the winner in the end, making my exit a merciful one. One that allows Finn a chance to Ken Jennings his way to the $100,000 he deserves.

He just needs to choose it, too.

For once, the forest is quiet, even the wind pausing to see what happens next. The fate of this season of *Wild Adventures*. When Burke alerts us that the minute is up and we can remove our blindfolds, I can barely hear him over my own heartbeat in my ears. While my right hand holds the *switch* sign upright and steady, my left hand shakes nearly too hard for the task of dragging the piece of fabric off my head.

When I do, the first thing I see is Finn's boots, which have taken a couple steps into the circle and now angle toward me. My eyes drag up his long form, pausing next on the sign he's holding up. In his left hand.

Stay.

I let my own sign of choice fall, my gaze darting before I

can stop it to my partner's face, the one that's looked at me with everything from mild irritation to emotional vulnerability to tender affection. What I see in it now is new, but utterly unforgettable. In those deep, dark eyes is a feeling of even deeper, darker betrayal.

Chapter Twenty-Two

No one has ever worn a tree-climbing harness quite like Finn wears a tree-climbing harness. It's a combination, I think, of the surprisingly muscular thighs hidden under those khakis, the not-surprisingly tight backside I've spent plenty of time watching in front of me on the trail, and, oh yes, the smoldering glare his handsome face is now permanently set in.

That last one's my fault. As I adjust the straps on my own tree-climbing harness, I go over the past couple hours in my mind.

My second mistake, after raising my right hand instead of left in the first place, was the next thing I'd said to Finn post-Swapportunity. A hastily blurted out, "Why didn't you do what I thought you were gonna do?"

It was a flurry of chaos in the wake of The Big Switch. Or The Big Switch That Wasn't. In the end, only Zeke, Enemi, and I opted to switch, meaning there was no other team for those two to swap partners with, so all teams stayed as we are. Basically causing a bunch of drama and hurt feelings for nothing—nothing but the good TV that comes from drama and hurt feelings.

Finn's scoff made the trees shake. "Have you listened to anything I've ever said to you, Natalie?" he'd near-shouted, out in the open for the cameras and Burke Forrester and god herself to hear. "How did you possibly think I was going to choose to switch?"

"Of course I listen!" I'd pleaded back, scrambling to justify my choice and also to make us less of a spectacle. "You said I've been screwing you out of a chance to win this, and you were right. You deserve to go on with a partner who can help you win."

"That's not—I didn't mean it like—" He let out a frustrated sigh-groan. "I was trying to tell you that you're capable of winning, that you have done amazingly already, and not to let all that other noise in your head get in the way now."

I'd clutched at my tightening chest. *That other noise in my head* is my feelings and concerns and anxiety, Finn. It's not all stuff I can ignore. I can't grumpy robot my way through life like you can."

Finn shook his head, already starting to walk away. "No, there you go again. Filtering out what I'm actually saying, picking and choosing what words you can patchwork together into the lies you want to tell yourself. You know I support you, believe in you, will validate you to the end of the AT and back. But what am I supposed to do when it never seems to stick?"

"Finn . . ." He waved a hand before sulking off and has been avoiding me ever since. Which is a tough job when "ever since" involved a brief, tense lunch, then hiking four miles as a big group to the site of our next challenge. The vibes were the weirdest they've ever been, even for the two teams that both chose *stay,* all of us hiking with a few strides between each person. Finn stayed at the very front, back in his comfort zone of not engaging with anyone.

We arrived here, a place called Newfound Gap, to find a cheerful Burke Forrester demonstrating absolutely no ability to read a room. He'd explained that since today's challenge requires a bit more specialized skill, the crew was going to help us don the equipment and practice using it before we began filming. Thus, the harnesses. We've each been able to practice using them to support ourselves in shimmy-stepping up and down tall hardwood trees.

It's nerve-racking, to be sure—plenty of opportunity to fall to my death, even if the professional arborists say the whole point of the harnesses is to prevent that. But I'm trying my best to keep it together, for Finn's sake more than anything. He's officially stuck with me now, and I want to do right by him more than I want to *be* right about my own incompetence.

I'm also motivated by Harper and Evan, the two people with a track record of not handling heights well, but who have already shown they're determined not to let it stop them today. The tree climbing only takes us to half the height of the observation tower, but I still want to cover my eyes the first time a nervous Harper goes up.

Nerves that prove unnecessary when she comes back down with a smile on her face.

"That was much better than the other day," she declares. "I trust my own legs way more than I trusted that rickety ladder or piece of string I had to slide down."

Evan's verdict after they try it is similar, which is extra reassuring. Team Hevan is once again doing more good for my mental state than either member of Team Finnatalie.

Producers call for us to circle up, requiring Finn to stand next to me at last. Does he feel the electric charge in the foot of air between us, like I do? Or is that just steam coming off of his body from his fiery fury at me?

"Co-EdVenturers!" Burke says once we're filming. "Welcome to Newfound Gap, the lowest pass over the Great Smoky Mountains, straddling the Tennessee–North Carolina state line. We're standing on storied ground, as on September 2, 1940, President Franklin D. Roosevelt came to this pass to dedicate Great Smoky Mountains National Park while he stood with one foot in each state. So in today's challenge, 'Newfound Knowledge,' we're going to honor the park's great history and legacy by testing your trivia skills—and hugging its trees."

I smile at his description of tree climbing, but it's the fakest smile I have to offer. A Burke Forrester smile, a performing-on-opening-night-when-you-have-food-poisoning smile. And my stomach feels just as uneasy.

Burke goes on to explain the challenge, in which each team will be assigned to a different tree with a platform secured to its trunk about twenty-five feet off the ground. On every platform is a stack of wooden blocks with trivia questions on them. One at a time, teammates will climb up to the platform, being careful not to topple the block stack. Once you reach it, pull a block out of the stack, anywhere but the top row, and call the question out to your partner on the ground. If your partner gets it correct, climb back down and let them take their turn. If they miss it, pull another block. The first team to correctly answer five questions without toppling their stack of blocks wins. If your stack falls, your team must rebuild it and start over completely.

This sounds stressful enough on its own, but then we learn it's an immediate elimination challenge, with the last team to get five correct answers going home.

I've used my lavender rollerball sparingly, what with all the warnings about scented things attracting predators. But I roll it halfway up each forearm while the camera crew gets set up by each tree, taking long inhales with it right under my nose, to boot.

"It's going to be fine," Finn grumbles at my side, making me jump. "Ginger says the questions are multiple choice."

"Oh good," I sigh, words laced with sarcasm. "We're absolutely crushing it with choices today."

A growly noise is his only response before he walks away.

When the challenge commences, Finn climbs up first, and his ease sends me straight back to our mini golf course break-in. Seems impossible that it was only days ago.

"Okay, Natalie," he yells down when he has a block in hand. "Great Smoky Mountains National Park gets how many visitors per year? (A) Two million, (b) seven million, (c) twelve million, (d) fourteen million."

I actually think I know this one. It was in one of my guide-books, wasn't it? Because the number surprised me, as did the fact that it's the most visited U.S. national park. I'm pretty sure it's twelve million. But it could be fourteen. The two and the four are so close together, it's confusing.

God, just like that, I'm back in a classroom at Oliver, ter-rified of being called on because I never seem to say the right things. Finn will be so mad if I get the very first question wrong. Hell, I'll be mad at myself.

"Natalie!" he shouts. "You know it or you don't and you make a guess. Either way, let's keep going."

His glare would be more intimidating if it wasn't mixed up with so much concern for me. I make a snap decision. "D) Four-teen million."

Finn turns the block over and my heart turns over with it when his lips twitch in a hint of a smile. "That's right."

Relief flows through me as he pockets the block and heads back down, but the tension ratchets right back up when I start climbing. I'm still unsure about this whole harness situation, but I'm trying my best to keep calm and smell the lavender. In my periphery, I see Harper spider-monkeying her way up her and Evan's tree, bolstering my courage.

When I get to the platform, the block I pull out is in the very center of the Jenga-like tower. "How many native tree species are represented in the park?" I read out. "(A) Forty-five, (b) one hundred thirty, (c) seventeen, or (d) one hundred."

I really wouldn't know this one. It feels both like there are a zillion trees around here and like they all run together. I definitely read up about more than seventeen kinds on the AT as a whole, but—

"(B) One-thirty," he answers almost immediately. My brows rise when I flip the block and find he's right, and we are starting off two for two.

The trend doesn't last. On Finn's next time up, I don't know that Horace Kephart is one of the fathers of the national park who a nearby mountain is named after, as opposed to the three other old-timey white guy names to choose from. But Finn keeps his cool as he pulls another block, and I *do* know that the native people who originally lived on this land were the Cherokees. Granny Star was very interested in correcting any "revisionist history" I learned in school, which, as it happened, was a lot.

On my next turn, with the prompt of "Great Smoky Mountains National Park houses the greatest diversity of this animal in the world," Finn incorrectly guesses lizards instead of salamanders.

"Ahh, I don't know which block I can pull next," I say mostly to myself as I eye the dwindling stack.

"Oh, so *this* is a difficult choice," Finn mutters. He's seemingly talking to himself too, but something tells me he wanted me to overhear.

"Really? We're doing this now?" I'm back to yelling, block tower forgotten as I put my hands on harness-covered hips. The cameras below hurry to cover both Finn and me, surely picking up on a good storyline about to go down. On the ground, Enemi, Meena, and Evan all turn their focus from their partners to send wary looks our way. I would be self-conscious about it, but my surly teammate has all my energy and attention.

"No, dammit, just pick a block!"

"Urrrgghhhh!" I roar my frustration. I start to go in for a block, but my hands are shaking like a street sign in the background of a hurricane broadcast. But instead of flying off and knocking out an unlucky weatherperson, they'll knock over the blocks and lose both Finn and me our hundred thousand dollars.

I'm not done talking. He opened this door, so I know he isn't either. Even if he's trying to shut it again, I'm wedging my beat-up, quaking little fingers in and pulling.

"I didn't want a new partner, Finn," I shout back. I don't want this to be a group discussion, but I can't come back down until we get a question right. And I can't keep holding on to what I need to say. "I wanted to give *you* the chance to have one!"

Finn's hands go to the top of his head, fingers lacing together as he tips it back. "I never wanted that. In fact, I remember telling you in the past twenty-four hours that I only want *you* as my partner. I don't know how I could have been clearer about that. So you weren't doing any favors for me."

"Just because it wasn't what you wanted doesn't mean it wouldn't have been the right thing for you!"

His laugh is humorless. "Why is it so hard for you to believe that you're the right thing for me? That you're the best thing that could've happened to me from coming on this ridiculous show?" The words make my breath catch in my throat.

"Finn," I squeak out, voice weakest it's been all day.

"Leave it, Nat. We need to get through this challenge. See?" He gestures to where Harper and Evan are jogging over to Burke Forrester and the orange flag with their arms around each other's shoulders, apparently having collected all five blocks first. I feel the adrenaline kicking in, a surge of urgency and competitive spirit spreading out through my veins. He's right that we need to focus. We've had too many close calls already.

I do my best to recenter myself on the task and steady my hands, pulling a block from near the top and barely stirring the stack as a whole. Finn answers this one, about the meaning of the Cherokee name "Kuwahi"—"mulberry place"—with surprising ease. When he goes up again, I waver on the question of the single most visited attraction within the country's most visited national park.

The choices are Laurel Falls, Cades Cove, Kuwahi, and the Rockefeller Memorial. I rule out the Rockefeller Memorial, because I didn't know it existed until today. Apologies to the Rockefeller family. Kuwahi could be the one—I mean, highest point of the whole Appalachian Trail. Nice observation tower, when you're not having to rappel down from it.

But it's Cades Cove that's calling to me. I remember going a few times with Granny Star, this beautiful oasis just outside the touristy hubs of Pigeon Forge and Gatlinburg. And in addition to stunning natural beauty, it had *lots* of visitors, a slow-moving parade of cars rolling down its loop road even on weekdays, forever making my grandma wonder aloud whether anyone had jobs or went to school anymore. It feels right.

And more importantly, I see Enemi starting to climb her tree, Zeke yelling, "Last one! Let's go!" That does it.

"Cades Cove!"

When he gets to the ground, we run over to the flag, and our second-place finish is official. We don't hug or high-five. Finn is a frown away from the most sullen I've ever seen him, back when we first got paired up. But this time, I don't know if it'll get better.

"**YOUR PARTNER JUST** growled at his half-eaten veggie burger before throwing the rest into the fire. You know anything about that?"

I look up at Harper from my perch. Like Finn only a few long days ago, I've settled onto my own log of loneliness at tonight's campsite, apart from the rest of the group around the fire. Harper's features shift from amused to worried at whatever's on my face.

"He's mad at me because I tried to switch partners," I say, crunching my uneaten potato chips between my fingers over the plate on my lap. It's the bubble-wrap-popping kind of therapeutic, in that it's not very helpful but gives me something to do with my hands.

"Oh good, because that's what I really wanted to ask about, but I didn't want to just dive right in," she says, taking a seat a couple feet down the log. "What was up with that?"

A sad smile pulls at my lips and I brush chip crumbs off my

fingers before leaning back onto my palms. "I thought it's what he would want, too."

"Why? Weren't you all friends at this point?" Her usually flat tone is animated enough to suggest I've truly baffled her.

I consider how much to divulge. Finn and I had decided at the hotel that we wouldn't tell anyone we were teammates who kiss, not wanting others' opinions or TV cameras involved in this brand new thing. But if the thing isn't even a *thing* anymore, does it matter? I've always told Reese and Clara every detail of my relationships from start to finish, and now that a similar, if newer, friend has sort of kind of asked, it's occurring to me how much I want to spill. So with a sigh, I begin.

"We were possibly a little bit more than friends."

If I'm expecting a dramatic pause or gasp, I'm let down. Harper's reply is instantaneous. "Whew, I'm glad that's out there, because I totally thought so, but I wasn't going to make you talk about it if you wanted to pretend otherwise."

I'm the one who gasps now. "Harper!" I gently swat her arm, catching her mischievous eyes and unrepentant smile. "From now on, why don't you just come right out with what you want to know, okay? In fact, if you have anything else on deck, now's your chance."

I wait a few moments with my most patient, expectant face, and she seems to think about it before shaking her head. "Nope, that was all. Carry on. More than friends and stuff."

So, I tell her everything. The whole progression of Finn's and my relationship, from its glacially chilly beginnings to the fiery peaks of mini golf and hotel beds, all the way to when I threw a bucket of cold mountain creek water on our undefined more-than-friendship today. I don't go into everything Finn and I have revealed to each other, but I do let her in on my anxiety issues, how they started during the school year and have followed me all through this experience. Harper seems to get the gist. And she's observed plenty on her own, more than I could've realized.

"Oh, I knew it was gonna happen from that day we went swimming. You guys have it all—forced proximity, grumpy-sunshine, there's-only-one-tent. Romance was inevitable," she deadpans.

"I didn't know you were a romance reader too!"

"Of course," she says. "All the bad bitches are."

A good point. But I replay her words. Were we really inevitable? Should I have seen it all coming?

"I don't think I've been very sunshiny recently." I draw a circle in the dirt with the toe of my boot. Add two eyes and a frown. "Maybe that's our problem. Now we're just grumpy-grumpy."

"You didn't ruin shit," Harper retorts. "Hard as you've tried to. Pushing him to get another teammate and all. How did you ever think he would choose switch?"

"I've been holding him back!" I cry. "We both know it! He said as much when he more or less warned me that we were going to lose."

When I look over at her, Harper is shaking her head, looking thoughtful. "I wasn't there for the conversation, of course, but it sounds like he also told you how awesome you are and how much he likes you. But obviously the hurtful stuff is going to burrow deeper in your brain. And because you, like me, have anxiety, you're going to overanalyze any criticism to hell and back until you've convinced yourself it's way worse than it actually is, and *you're* way worse than you actually are, and everything is terrible and there's no hooooope . . . Am I on the right track?"

My mouth hangs open. "I—it's not—" I blow out a defeated breath. "Maybe. You have anxiety too?"

"Of course. All the bad bitches do."

That gets a real laugh out of me, and she smiles before continuing. "I've learned to manage it all right—moments of losing my shit at the top of an observation tower notwithstanding—and from what it sounds like, it's still pretty new to you. But I promise it doesn't have to be so terrifying and control everything in your life forever. Your brain's not a broken thing to fix, it just has some extra features to figure out. If you want, when we get out of here, I can tell you about finding my therapist and experiences with medicine. But I also know people who swear by meditation and mindfulness stuff." She shrugs. "Point is, you don't have to navigate it all alone."

My crying reflex is on a hair trigger right now, and that's what sets it off again. Through halting, weepy speech, I try to convey that I'm not crying because I'm sad; it just means a lot that she's there for me. I don't think she understands half the words, but Harper pulls me in for a hug that's warmer than anything I'd expect from someone who definitely told me she wasn't into hugging, letting me get the shoulder of her *Unlikable Female Character* shirt all wet and snotty and a little mascara-stained.

"I can get these out," I say when I've composed myself, pointing to the black smudges. "Let me take it home with me after this, and I'll ship it back to you."

Harper dismisses this with a hand wave. "Not important. You feeling better? Healthy release of emotions done you some good?"

"A little," I sniffle. "Thank you for letting me dump all this on you and being so nice to me. You didn't have to do, well, any of it. I mean, we're technically competitors. You could've been like, 'Fuck you, I hope you *do* have an anxious breakdown that knocks you out of the running!'"

She looks at me like I've sprouted a second head. "Well, that would make me a horrible person. And an even worse friend."

"Ugh, and there you go again!" I say, voice getting all watery once more. "Calling me your friend like it's nothing."

What follows is another crying jag, and more of my half-coherent ramblings about how it's been a long time since I've made a new friend and I was starting to think I was un-friend-worthy now. Then Harper sharing her own story of a rough transition to college, but how things started looking up by the end of freshman year as she found her community, then me pestering her about Zeke's increasingly obvious crush on her, her assuring me it is not returned and she's not dating until after med school. I'd love to see if she sticks to that. By the end, I think we're both emotionally spent. Maybe physically too, as her yawns are growing more frequent and contagious.

"I guess we should get some sleep," I say eventually, as night sets in around us. I peer over my shoulder to the other side of the clearing, where Finn is still sitting in a chair by the fire with his back to me. Scattered in a sparse circle with him are Enemi, Zeke, and Evan, the other remaining Co-EdVenturers after we said goodbye to Meena and Cammie today.

"He and I have done a real role reversal, huh?" I turn back to Harper. "Mr. Campfire Casanova over there being social all night long."

Now she's frowning. "Uh, he's been reading a book the whole time. And I told you about the angry veggie burger sacrifice. Not exactly chill vibes coming from his neck of the woods."

Oh. I sigh. "Well, I don't know what I can do at this point."

"Plenty," Harper says with her easy, understated confidence. "But how about you start with not letting yourself think you've screwed everything up forever? Start realizing that you're in the top fucking three. Semifinals of *Wild Adventures*. And that all relationships have issues, especially brand new ones born in stressful circumstances. But you two are gonna rally and get to the happily ever after."

"How?" I ask meekly.

She throws her hands up. "Do I look like I know?"

"Honestly, yeah! You've seemed so sure about everything else in this romance!" I throw back.

Her lips quirk up. "I don't know how, but I have a strong feeling you'll work it out. Give him space, since he seems to want it. Collect your thoughts and feelings, and when the time is right, you kiss and make up." The side-eye she gives me is knowing and mischievous. "And zip your sleeping bags back together, you freaks."

Chapter Twenty-Three

"Are you ready to be challenged in a way you've never been before?"

God, no, why, is what I want to groan back at Burke Forrester when he poses the question in the morning. Have I not been challenged enough the past couple days? Including last night, when Finn set up his hammock while I was off doing my bedtime routine. I returned to find the tent and my sleeping bag sitting out, sad and alone, in a space a couple yards from the two trees with a sulky man cocoon suspended between them. When I set them up and settled inside, also sad and alone, I could still see the light of Finn's headlamp. I swear it shone through my eyelids when I closed them and tried to sleep, casually driving me to Edgar Allan Poe character madness. *The Telltale Headlamp.*

So yeah, Burkey Burke. Every bit of *Wild Adventures* has been a challenge like none I've had before. Why don't you throw us a softball?

Finn stands behind me, stone-faced and cold. Yet I can

actually physically feel the heat coming off of him, and it makes me want to curl against his side. Swallow my pride, say whatever I need to say to get us past this fight and on better terms. Cuddling terms. Kissing terms.

"It's about to be a long, lonely night for each of you." *Well, then.* After grumpily tucking away my scheme to regain any FDA (Finn Displays of Affection), I register what Burke has said. Lonely? My stomach sinks. He doesn't mean . . .

"This challenge is called 'The Lone Wolf.' For the first part, each Co-EdVenturer will spend today and tonight alone. This will give you insight into the experiences of both early trailblazers on the AT, many of whom trekked uncharted territory on their own, as well as the modern solo thru-hiker. It might also show you what your teammate has really meant to you in this journey. After recent shake-ups, maybe this will help foster a new appreciation for your partner out here on this wild adventure. Or maybe . . . you'll find you would've been better off as individuals."

I gulp, then end up coughing as my throat feels too tight to swallow anything.

"You may divide resources however you want," Burke goes on, "and you will have fifteen minutes to converse and sort out supplies between you before you'll receive directions to your individual campsites. Your fifteen minutes begins . . . now!"

When I turn to Finn, the panic must be written all over my expression, as something in his own instantly softens. I guess I'll take pity over hate, if I have to choose from the two.

"I'll give you the tent," he says, shrugging his pack down from his shoulders and opening it up.

"Oh," is my answer, my mind already miles away, running through all the potential disasters that could come from me trying to live through the night by myself. Maybe Finn thinks I've come a long way in my time here, but does he really believe I'm at the Lone Wolf level of self-sufficient? Doubtful.

Without asking, he reaches down and unsnaps my pack's hip straps, the feeling of his hand brushing my stomach making me suck in a breath. He doesn't look up, but the way his jaw tenses makes me think he heard it anyway. He steps behind me and takes the pack from my back, setting it beside his on the ground and starting to sort out our supplies.

I'm unsettled, twitchy as he shifts provisions back and forth, but I can't even bring myself to help, starting to pace instead. My mind is a roaring cacophony of *no, why, no, I can't, I won't, don't make me, this will end badly for all involved!*

From what little I can process over my own mess of feelings, Finn seems unbothered by the prospect of a night apart. He's probably relieved to get a break from me, from everything between us. We haven't had any chance to talk this morning, or he hasn't given us one. How can we get to the making up when we can't get any time together? I don't imagine this particular absence will make his heart grow fonder.

Lord knows what's in my pack when he finally holds it up, all zipped shut again and ready for me to slide it on. I turn and slip my arms through the straps, but when I go to secure the hip belt, my hands shake too much to make the two sides of the buckle align right away. Finn notices, of course.

Behind us, producers are starting to round everyone back up, but Finn steps in front of me and puts his hands on my shoulders, keeping me firmly in place.

"Hey," he says, ducking his head so we're eye level, his earnest face filling my line of sight. "Listen. You can do this. You know everything you need to spend a night on your own. You have all the resources. You'll be safe. If sleep doesn't come easy, try reading a book. I'll see you tomorrow."

I swallow against the rising emotion in my throat, feeling the stinging at the backs of my eyes. Unable to put words to all that's rioting through me right now, I just nod.

We walk back to the group side by side, and I'm all too aware it might be the last time.

I AM *THISCLOSE* to eating dry vegetable soup powder for dinner, and *evencloser* to a complete mental breakdown.

It's unclear if this experience is making me appreciate Finn any more; I appreciated him plenty already. But it *is* giving me more empathy for the protagonists of that whole subgenre of psychological thrillers I call Morally Gray Woman Lives Alone, Watches Neighbors, Thinks Too Much.

Everything in these woods seems suspicious right now. Like the bird that's been sitting in a sugar maple at the edge of the clearing, staring at me for ten minutes straight—definitely a government spy robot. And how my camp stove won't light, even though I'm following all of the instructions that are written in French (a language I can't technically understand). Someone's obviously tampered with it to sabotage me. They knew there'd be no firepit at this campsite, so I'd have to use it.

When they fictionalize my story, it'll be called *The Girl in the Tent*.

At least I still think I'm funny, kind of, and can distract myself with humor. One of the very few things I have going for me today. Another is that I can walk in a straight line, as I found my way to my solo campsite, a backcountry spot a short walk off the AT, with no issues. I talked to the GoPro a little, assuring viewers that I was totally calm about this challenge and eager to see what was in store.

But the wins have been scarce ever since. I decided to set up the tent first, so I'd have a place to sit other than on the ground or a bear canister. There aren't any good logs in this particular clearing. I was dismayed to find that somehow, between sleeping in it last night and getting it out here, one of the clips that holds the top of the tent to the poles was broken. The thick, ostensibly sturdy plastic had snapped right in two. So one corner of the ceiling drooped in a rather sad fashion, but I decided it would be fine as long as it didn't rain.

Then the rain started. A light drizzle at first that still had me throwing myself and all my stuff I could fit under shelter. And good thing I did, as the drizzle quickly turned to a downpour. Thus, I whiled away the afternoon hours watching the rain in the glimpses I could catch through the mesh at the front of the tent, and every so often lifting the fallen section at the back to dump out the rain puddled on top of it. Trying to push away thoughts of Finn and how he's faring in this storm, alone and tentless.

Logically, I can see how none of this is my fault. But my emotions are not having it. The rain has let up this evening, leaving behind air so humid, I'm swimming through it. But the storm inside me, built up from all that's happened the past couple weeks, the past year, even longer, rages on. Sitting and thinking is never great for me.

I'm not even hungry for this soup I'm failing to make, my stomach is so unsettled. The buzzing under my skin, coursing through my whole body since this morning, has only gotten worse with each new screwup or inconvenience. My pulse seems to think I'm in the middle of a neck-and-neck footrace.

If I'm trying to outrun anything, it's my own mind. Fears. Worries. Unacknowledged grief and pain. Why is this—*Wild Adventures,* the Appalachian Trail, of all settings I've found myself in over the years—where it's all caught up with me? Not just caught up, but tackled me to the ground. I've put on a good act for so long, but reality can't wait anymore. The lights are up, the audience has left, and it's just me. Alone, on my outdoor stage.

I give up on the stove and begin packing it away. I click off the camera for the night, ending what is probably the most depressing footage captured all season, and I can only hope it ends up on the cutting room floor. I repack the pouch of soup too, even though I know I should eat something if I'm going to have the energy to make it to the checkpoint—and my partner—tomorrow.

My partner, who made me feel anything but lonely in the tiny camping nest I'm now crawling back into. I had the dream—a good, genuine guy who's seen me at my worst and still wanted me. Hell, he *was* the worst when I first met him, and I still fell for him. Despite Harper's hope for us, I can't help thinking that I ruined our chances of a romance novel–type love. We'd be the book that dedicated romance readers would throw at the wall upon finishing, yelling, *"Where's my HEA? This is bullshit!"* A brief, depressing novella that tricked people with a cutesy cartoon cover.

Of course my eyes are leaking again. It's a daily routine now, I guess. Put on my makeup in the morning, cry it off in the evening. I feel like a broken TV, frantically flipping between channels that are all playing something miserable. I'm sad about Finn. Then I'm panicking at an especially unsettling noise outside. Then I'm upset with myself for being so afraid of everything all the time, for being so tangled up in my own mind that I destroy anything good in my life. Then I'm despairing because even when I don't mess things up myself, everything can still go terribly wrong. Like Granny Star dying, which I then think about and get deeply sad all over. Repeat.

I don't know how to break myself out of this, when I'm alone and can't quiet the mess inside my mind long enough to take a full breath. I wish Finn were here, that I could look to my right and see his little smirk illuminated by his tablet's light as he reads something he finds funny.

As he *reads*.

This morning, before we parted, Finn told me I should try

reading if I can't sleep. I haven't even really tried sleeping yet, but maybe a book is just what I need. Not the AT guides, a romance novel that can sweep me in and pull my attention from everything else. Things can't really get any worse while I'm reading, can they?

After a few more minutes of shallow attempts at calming breaths while lying flat on my sleeping bag, I work up to sitting. Then I go for the pocket in my pack where I keep my e-reader. I pull out the familiar black shape, but when it's in my hands, I quickly realize there's something off about it. For one, it doesn't have my purple letter *N* sticker on the front of the case. And it *does* have something bulky stuffed under the cover.

I flip it open and a stack of orange paper goes sliding into my lap. Confusion wrinkles my forehead. These aren't just sheets of paper; they look like our challenge envelopes, but there are words scrawled all over them in black ink. I look back up to the device in my hands and realize it's not my e-reader at all. It's Finn's. Eyes flicking to the envelopes again, I see the words *Dear Natalie.*

A soft gasp escapes my lips.

With trembling hands, I pick up the orange stack and start to read.

Dear Natalie,

> *First of all, sorry for my shitty handwriting and stationery. It's worse than normal because I'm writing this with my headlamp on in my hammock at night and the pen I borrowed*

*from Zeke bleeds a lot (apparently he collects fountain pens—
I think this one's broken). This is also the only paper I could
find. I have felt especially bad at articulating my thoughts
and feelings around you, probably because what I feel for you
is different than anything I've felt before and I am completely
out of my element. But also just because I'm me, and use words
sparingly, and they're often not the right ones. So I thought
I would try writing some down. I hope this isn't a completely
ridiculous idea.*

*As you know, I've been reading a book about Grandma
Gatewood, a 67-year-old from Ohio who was the first woman
to thru-hike the Appalachian Trail. I compared the two of you
early on, and I think you thought it was an insult. Probably
because of the "grandma" part. But I meant it as a compliment
because, like you, she was a complete badass.*

*Emma Gatewood was not some hard-core outdoorswoman.
She started on the trail without telling her family she was doing
it. She wore canvas tennis shoes and carried a small sack of
stuff, didn't even bring a tent. She told anyone who asked why
she did it that she thought hiking the AT would be "a lark."
Everyone doubted her, told her she should quit, should turn
back, that she'd never make it.*

*But she wasn't a delicate little old lady either. She had 11
(!!!) kids. Lived on a farm and never had much money. Got
herself out of her marriage to an abusive husband. She had
a lot working against her, but she was strong and persistent,
determined and creative, outgoing and friendly to strangers,
and all of that helped her get through the whole AT three times.*

Any of this sound familiar? You might not think so, but I really do. You've had to deal with a lot of shit. Different shit than hers, but you've still taken on so much by yourself. People have doubted you and told you that you can't achieve your goals. I (a dumbass) doubted you, to start with. But you keep proving everyone wrong and showing that you, too, are strong, persistent, determined, creative, outgoing, friendly, and one hell of a good partner to an aforementioned dumbass. Grandma Gatewood would be proud of you, Granny Star would be proud of you, and you should be very proud of yourself.

We both have things to work on, of course, but I want to work on them with you. I'm sorry for making you feel like your baggage was somehow heavier than mine. It's not. Let's help each other carry it all. I'll fix your hip belt so your shoulders don't bruise. I'm sorry for letting you think you've held me back. You've pushed me forward, into real life again, through more fun and adventure than I ever expected to have.

I chose to stay with you as my partner and I want to stay with you as more. I want us to get to the end of this thing and win it all. Then I want to keep getting to know you and building on what we have because I think it could go far past this trail, our tent, and a double sleeping bag. I know I want it to.

Feels like I should close this with a "Do you like me?" and checkboxes for yes or no. But how about when you're ready, you come tell me. You can write it down if you need to—I'll let you borrow Zeke's pen.

Yours,

Finn

P.S. (update as of this morning—while you're pacing +
distracted + letting me repack stuff) You might have noticed
I switched our e-readers. I hope you see this note and read it
in our day/night apart. I also hope you might feel inclined
afterward to read about Grandma Gatewood—I finished
the book and left it back on pg 1. Thought you'd find her
comforting and/or inspiring, or at least see I'm not bullshitting
you about her badassery. I stole your e-reader because I
started <u>Hot on Her Trail</u> by Donna O'Hare (per your rec) and
don't want to stop—just got to the part where she meets the
handsome ranger. But if you don't want to read about GG
you're welcome to anything else on mine.

Still yours,
Finn

As soon as I finish reading it, I go back to the start and read again. Then one more time, by the end barely able to make out the words through tear-filled eyes. I'm careful not to let any of my waterworks spill onto the envelopes, though, since they're now among the most valuable things I own. I'll probably need to invest in a museum display case when I get home.

I try, in my rereads, to actually digest Finn's words. To not just read like I'm committing a script's lines to memory, but to take them to heart. He still cares about me, even knowing all he knows. I've let him in on thoughts and feelings I've kept from every other person in my life, and instead of my messiness putting him off, it seems to have drawn him in even closer. He wants to be with me, walk with me, help each other carry the heaviest, hardest stuff together. My heart feels ready to burst with the amount that I want that too. If I had even half a clue where he is right now, I'd run across mountains to fling myself at him and never let go.

As a warm, hopeful giddiness settles in my chest at Finn's romantic declarations, I let myself sit with everything else he wrote. Granny Star used to tell me that was an important skill—to own it when someone says something kind to you. So if Finn says she'd be proud of me, I know she'd want me to own that. She'd want me to try believing everything he said—reminiscent of what she used to say—about my strength and persistence and Grandma Gatewood badassery. Especially knowing that this is what he was up to in his hammock last night, when we weren't talking and I thought he was still furious. If he can believe the best in me, even when we're in a rough patch, well, it means all the more.

I hear the dull tapping on the tent ceiling and realize the rain has resumed. Light but steady, it's enough to deter me from wanting to go outside again, even as I feel my appetite making a slight comeback and the bear canister with all my food is sitting under a tree a safe distance away. I can wait.

Besides, it's not just me and my thought spirals anymore. I have Finn, at least in spirit and handwriting form. And I have Grandma Gatewood.

I lie back on my sleeping bag, swipe the tablet screen open, and start to read.

Chapter Twenty-Four

Morning comes around, sunny and beautiful, and I'm beginning to think my mood controls the weather.

From the outside, not much has changed from last night. In fact, some things are objectively worse. Like the tent, which, after I fell asleep mid-book with the e-reader open on my chest, continued to collect rain in a gigantic puddle on its roof. When I went to dump it out upon waking up, water soaked not only the rain fly, but a bunch of the regular tent material, which isn't as quick to dry. I've left it lying in a patch where the sun shines through the treetops, hoping that problem will work itself out.

Then there's the stove I still couldn't get to work this morning, hoping I could boil water for oatmeal. I ended up reading late into the night until I passed out and woke with a stomach very mad at me for its emptiness. So I've had a couple protein bars and might opt for a third.

Also, my eyes. Or the skin under them, which is so puffy

from all the crying that I can see it in my normal line of sight. I'm almost too scared to check my compact mirror—key word being *almost*. I have some kissing and making up to do today, and I'm not about to do it with my eyes swollen half shut. Except for the kissing—eyes fully shut for that part.

Fortunately, I have masks for all my facial skincare needs, and I'm hella stocked up on inspiration. As I use the mirror to apply two shiny, gold gel under-eye masks, I think about Grandma Gatewood. She would probably laugh me off the trail right now for being enough of a diva to even own these things, let alone bring them backpacking on the AT. But superficial differences aside, Finn was right about our kindred spirits.

I've never been so pulled into a nonfiction book as I was by the story of this woman's life and experiences on the trail. The AT of the 1950s was not the AT of today, well-maintained and with easy enough access to shelter, water, and towns that can provide anything you need. Easier still if you happen to be walking a small part of it on *Wild Adventures,* where your nightly accommodations are preplanned for you and a whole crew shows up most nights with a hot and ready dinner. I don't think I would have made it past the first day, doing what she did with the lack of preparation she had.

But she pushed on. She slept on strangers' porches, in ramshackle shelters. Ate whatever she could scrounge up or connected with other strangers who offered to share meals with her. Got all kinds of blisters, bruises, and other aches and pains in her flimsy sneakers and worn-out clothes. Two thousand miles on foot, sixty-seven years old, and she fucking made it.

She's everything Finn said she was. Said *I* am, which I'm still not sure is fully deserved. But if he sees that much Grandma Gatewood in me, then it's in her spirit that I'm gonna finish this thing.

I've just decided this when a producer noiselessly appears at my campsite and gives me a heart attack.

"Oh my god!" I gasp and yell at the same time. The young, nerdy-looking guy whose name I still haven't learned is a little earlier than the time we were told to expect anyone this morning. He didn't actually provoke cardiac arrest, but he did scare the ever-loving shit out of me. It appears to be mutual, at least, as he jumps back a foot when he sees my masked face.

"What's wrong with your skin?!" he asks, in my opinion, rather foolishly.

"It's called Rumpelstiltskin Disease. This monster cursed me with it, making all the skin on my body gradually turn gold until I have a firstborn child I can give to him. Normally you just see me when I've covered it with makeup."

The guy is frozen, arm half extended with the envelope he brought, presumably containing my next map and go time. I roll my eyes as I snatch it from his hand.

"Calm down, buddy. It's a face mask."

He doesn't linger after that, and I tear into the envelope and scan the contents before packing up the rest of my small camp with twenty minutes until my go time. I have a map that shows Finn's campsite and mine, and a spot where we're supposed to meet up roughly in the middle and race the other teams to the checkpoint. Partners have to arrive at the checkpoint together, so if yours isn't at the meetup spot right away, you have to wait for them.

I'm eager to get back to Finn, to tell him how much his letter meant to me, say my own apologies, and fix what's broken between us. I'm also eager to get to the checkpoint and know we've made it to the final challenge. But the tent is the last thing to pack, and it hasn't dried out yet. I don't want to fold it up and stow it in my pack to accumulate who knows what kind of gross mildewy growths. But I can't hold up our team.

In the end, my method is unconventional, but will hopefully allow our primary shelter to keep drying out even as I hit the trail again. I have the large expanse of fabric draped over my pack like a massive cape, folded in on itself only once so it doesn't quite drag on the ground, and won't get torn or collect a bunch of twigs and leaves. I feel a little like a menacing forest creature ensconced in this near-literal wet blanket, but I'll be sure to tuck it away before anyone else's camera is on me.

I almost resent the woods in daylight for how nonthreatening it all seems. As if they played a mean trick on me by being so terrifying at night, and for so much of the time I've spent out here. I can almost feel them snapping back at me, saying, "Hey, that's your own issues doing this to you! Don't blame us!"

The fact that I hear the woods talking to me definitely reinforces said issues' existence. I wonder if Grandma Gatewood talked to herself much on the AT, whether mentally or out loud. If she narrated everything she was seeing like I sometimes find myself doing. Pretty wildflowers opening up their petals to the sunlight. Peaceful breeze rustling the trees. Who gave you all the right to look so idyllic, like I'm in a fairy tale?

Yeah, that's right. I've turned over a new leaf, pun intended. I'm not scared of the forest. I'm embracing it. I am one with the trees. I am gonna find my partner, who supports me and wants to be with me. I will keep working on my issues, because if I can do everything I've done out here, I can confront my inner demons. And I'm gonna win the money, go back to Oliver paid up, my future as bright as today's sun.

I'm so swept up in my inner monologuing that I almost don't see it. But then my head snaps in a cartoonish double take. Not fifty feet off the trail I'm walking along, the living, black-fur-covered embodiment of my biggest fears is nosing around in the undergrowth.

A black bear.

I come to a stumbling stop, snapping a twig underfoot in the process, and the sound has the bear's head poking up, turning in my direction. All breath leaves my body as I look into its face for the first time, its dark, fathomless eyes sizing me up. Considering if I'm a worthwhile snack, most likely, or if it should stick to scavenging for berries and greens. What was I saying about not being scared anymore?

Every dark, pessimistic instinct in my body is back on alert, screaming that this is the end, that I had a good run, I guess, but we knew it was only a matter of time before something got to me out here. I'm trembling from my core out to all my extremities, torn between the urge to run like hell and the complete inability to move an inch. Dazedly, I reach my hand back for where the bear spray is normally clipped to my pack's side, but it isn't there. Shit, did I put it in the pack by accident?

Making the mental calculations, I figure by the time I can take off my pack and dig through it for the spray, this creature will have pounced, or whatever the bear equivalent is, latched onto my puny arm, and started dragging me off to its cave to share with the wife and kiddos. It feels like if I take my eyes off the threat for even a second, it's game over.

God, my only hope is that this bear is a vegetarian like Finn.

Finn. Finn, who told me exactly what to do if I find myself in this situation, back in the very first conversation we ever had. Distracted as I was by his sudden appearance, by the whirlwind of our first day on *Wild Adventures,* all of it, I still retained a lesson or two from that chat, didn't I?

The bear takes a slow, heavy step, then another, not really toward me but not in the opposite direction either. Its eyes stay on me, anyway. Swallowing the bile I feel rising up, blinking back the terrified beginnings of tears in my eyes, I comb through my memory.

Finn said the rules were different for black bears versus brown. This one is decidedly black. Which I think means . . . less threatening? I'm almost positive this was not the kind with which I'm supposed to drop down and play dead. That doesn't feel right. And not that I've ever seen a bear in the wild, but compared to the ones I've encountered in zoos over the years, this one doesn't seem huge.

Realistically, though, the chonker still has to weigh, like, twelve Natalies. And I can't even imagine the kind of sharp, menacing teeth hiding in its deceptively cute snout. If playing dead is most effective with the scariest bears, then it has to work on the less scary ones too, right? My knees bend, about ready to drop to the dirt below and cushion the way down for the rest of me.

But something makes me pause. If playing dead worked with all bears, why wouldn't he have just told me to do that? There was another option. I recount how the conversation went as best I can, straightening when I remember standing on my toes and lifting my arms in the air before yelling at Finn about his pockets. That was it. With black bears, you try to appear big and intimidating so they'll run away. I eye the terrifying fluffball, now stopped with its nose pointed up as if sniffing the air. Can it smell my anxiety from over there?

When its front paws leave the ground, the big head and torso slowly rising, the time for floundering is over. Before I think it through any more, I grab on to the pieces of tent fabric hanging at my sides, clutch a handful in each fist, and raise my arms in the air as I rise onto my toes.

"HEY!" I yell, projecting to the back row of the biggest theater I can imagine. "WHAT CAN I TELL YOU THAT WILL GET YOU TO RUN OFF WITHOUT EATING ME TODAY?"

The bear freezes in a half-upright stance. I wonder what they think of this human-sized, nylon-winged butterfly that's just appeared and started yelling at them. Does anything about me right now say "bigger, stronger predator"? I don't want to insult this animal's intelligence.

"WE BOTH KNOW YOU WOULD WIN IF THIS AC-TUALLY CAME DOWN TO A FIGHT. BUT I'M SCRAPPY WHEN I NEED TO BE." Nothing is happening. Why isn't any-thing happening? "I PROBABLY WOULDN'T TASTE GREAT EITHER. TOO MANY ARTIFICIAL INGREDIENTS. LIKE, ON MY FACE. ALL KINDS OF CHEMICALS. SOME PURPLE DYE IN MY HAIR, TOO. DO YOU EVEN EAT HAIR? THAT SOUNDS DISGUSTING."

The bear must agree. Its front legs drop to the ground again while it continues to eye me. This feels like major points on my side of the scoreboard.

"THAT'S RIGHT. WALK AWAY, NOW. YOU DON'T WANT TO SEE ME WHEN I'M ANGRY." I think that's some-thing the Hulk says, isn't it? I feel a little bit like the Hulk right now, with this whole big-and-scary act. Mentally, I pat my-self on the back for pulling off "intimidator" so well. "IS IT JUST ME, OR IS THE HULK KIND OF A SUPERHERO-Y GLORIFICATION OF TOXIC MASCULINITY? LIKE, OH, I'M SUPPOSED TO SEE THIS GUY'S ANGER ISSUES AS A *POSITIVE*? I'D NEVER SAY IT IN MIXED COMPANY, 'CAUSE I HAVEN'T SEEN THE MOVIES AND DON'T ACTUALLY KNOW ANYTHING ABOUT THE HULK OTHER THAN RAGE AND MUSCLES AND GREEN MARK RUFFALO, AND I DON'T NEED DIE-HARD MARVEL FANS ROASTING ME OVER A CAMPFIRE. BUT I TRUST YOU TO KEEP IT BETWEEN US."

Okay, so it's good the bear doesn't seem to understand En-glish. But even better is that, after only a little more of my rambling medium-hot takes on popular media, the bear looks away. My yelling voice shakes with a wave of relief that rolls through me, but I know I'm not safe yet, so I keep talking. And ever so slowly, one paw at a time, the large animal turns itself around and lumbers in the other direction from me.

Still yelling nonsense, still holding up my tent cape around me, still stretching myself as tall as possible, I backward walk on down the trail.

". . . SO PINE WAS ALWAYS THE BEST CHRIS. I'VE NEVER HEARD ANYTHING TO CONVINCE ME OTHER- WISE. LIKE, HE READS BOOKS! HE HAS A FLIP PHONE! I'VE ONLY RECENTLY REALIZED THAT A GUY BEING KINDA ANTI–MODERN CONVENIENCES IS A TURN-ON FOR ME, BUT I'M NOT ASHAMED TO ADMIT IT. AND THE MORE HE LEANS INTO THE SILVER FOX THING, HOT DA—"

"Natalie," comes a sharp whisper from behind me, and I let out a garbled shriek as I whirl around, tangling myself up in a blanket of damp blue tent and tripping on my own feet in the process. I pitch forward, smashing nose-first into a hard chest.

"What the fuck!" I wheeze, but muffled in the woodsmoke- scented cotton of Finn's T-shirt, it comes out as more of a "Wrrrtthwfrrrh."

It's only when his steady hands clamp down on my shoulders and push me to stand back up that I realize my whole body is shaking like a leaf. That new leaf I allegedly turned over, before getting scared shitless again.

"Shhh," he soothes, starting to unravel the tent from around me with a furrow between his stern brows. "You're okay. You're safe now. You can stop running bear defense."

"Y-you saw it too? The bear? Th-that was a bear back there. I . . . I ran into a bear." My words are choppy, my breaths sawing unevenly out of my lungs. I didn't notice any of this while I was yelling—or maybe it wasn't happening, didn't start till my adrenaline crashed. When Finn, having fully detached the tent from my person and tossed it to the ground beside us, brings his hands up to frame my face and his thumbs to swipe tears from my cheeks, it dawns on me that I've been crying. Who knows how long that's been going on, either? It's ahead of schedule today.

"I saw it," he confirms, lips forming a flat line as he watches me warily. "Our meetup spot's just back there. I saw you coming this way, then you froze, so I started toward you to see what was up. Then stopped when I saw the bear. Then I was like, 'Hey, jackass, maybe you should go help your partner somehow.' But then you started talking." The corner of his mouth twitches. "It was clear you had it under control."

In an instant, I'm doubled over, my whole body heaving in hysterical laugh-sobs. I feel my backpack jostle and let Finn remove it for me, vaguely registering through bleary eyes that he turns both of our GoPros off. Then his hands return to my back, my shoulders, gently patting around. His voice floats down to me, murmuring assurances that I'm safe and did a great job, and I can't form the words to let him know I'm not, in fact, having a total breakdown.

Until I can. Straightening back up after a few minutes, I

swipe under my own eyes and meet his gaze. "I fucking *did that*! I looked like an absolute nutjob and said things that hopefully never leave this forest, but I faced down a bear and walked away just fine! Can you believe it?"

This is followed by a rather witchy cackle. Finn continues to eye me for a moment before his expression eases, a slow smile forming. "Hell yeah, you did. You did that, Natalie."

"I did that!"

"Your biggest fear since we started this thing, and you just handled it like a pro."

"Bears fear *me* now!"

"Not sure what the whole tent cape was about, but it worked in your favor."

"Long story, but you're right, it did!"

"I'm so proud of you."

My response to those soft, sincere words is to throw my arms around his neck and claim his lips with mine. Finn catches me against him, tightening his arms around my back to hold me up as he quickly matches my fervor with his own, kissing me like it's the first time all over again. In a way, it feels like it is. Like it's my first kiss *ever,* or at least the first one with someone who's truly known me—the best of me but also my least flattering, darkest, messiest sides, and he still wants every bit of it. Every bit of me.

Our kiss is frantic, devouring at first, then melts into the slow, deep kind that could go on for minutes or hours. Each pull of his lips on mine, trace of my tongue to his, feels like an answer to one of the questions still hanging over us.

Are we doing this? Yes.

Even though I can be difficult? Yes.

And you can lose patience? Yes.

You're sure that—? Yes. Shut up. Just kiss me.

But I know there are still words to be said, and in time, I pull back, letting my forehead rest against his as our panting breaths mingle. Finn lowers me to the ground but keeps his head bent close to mine. I'm about to begin when he gets there first.

"Did you read my note?"

I frown, tip my head to the side. "Note?"

Finn's face flushes even redder than it was from the kissing and he starts to step back, but I can't let him. I grab his T-shirt in my fist and hold him in place. "I didn't get any mere *note*. I got a letter, a tome, my new favorite work of literature that has ever existed, a masterpiece on orange envelopes—"

"Okay, you're evil," he says.

I giggle like the smitten little bear conqueror I am. "I'm a better actress than I thought, apparently. But Finn . . ." I continue with nothing but sincerity. "I'm sorry. For everything—for trying to push you away, and not trusting everything you've said to me, how cared for you've made me feel. I know it comes from my own shit I need to deal with, and I've put things on you that aren't fair—"

"It's okay," he says, shaking his head quickly. "I know I'm not the best at being supportive or encouraging. Or, well, the easiest to be around in general. I'm working on it."

"No," I cut back in. "You're super supportive. I know you've worked on it and you've changed so much, even in the short time I've known you. But I have plenty of work to do too, and like you wrote, I want to work on things with you in my corner. Start dealing with things that scare me." I gesture back in the direction of the showdown. "I guess I've already started, just now."

"Hell yeah, you have," Finn says, brushing a soft kiss across my forehead.

I lean in and wrap my arms around him, resting my chin on his chest. "Are there more forehead kisses in it for me? Like, as motivation. Confront some anxiety or unprocessed trauma, get a forehead kiss afterward?"

"I think that can be arranged." He plants another one on me. "That one was a freebie."

Laughing, I stand on my toes and bring my lips to his again. When, still lip-locked, he leans forward, picks me up with a hand on the back of each of my thighs, I startle at first then go along with it as he guides my legs to wrap around his waist. But then he starts walking, and I pull back.

"Where are we going?" I ask breathily, dropping quick kisses on his cheeks, nose, chin.

"I've been reading this book . . . ," he says, a sultry, teasing note to his voice that sends a chill down my spine. My spine, which is then gently pressed against the trunk of a tree, Finn's perfect body caging me in. "*Hot on Her Trail.* You might know it?"

I nod, biting down on my smile, and his eyes zero in on my lower lip.

He continues, "It's convinced me of the merits of making out against a tree."

My laugh is caught by his mouth on mine again. And I have to say, he's on to something. Or the fictional sexy forest ranger is. But I'll take this real-life, sometimes grumpy, always gorgeous partner of mine any day.

We kiss each other senseless. Kind of literally, as we both seem to forget where we are, what we're in the middle of, that we've probably used up all ten camera-free minutes for this hour. The only thing that breaks us apart in the end is a loud wolf whistle and a shout of "That's my boy!"

Finn's head whips around, body still pinning me in place, and I peek over his shoulder to see Zeke in the distance at what I assume is the meetup spot, one victorious fist in the air. Next to him, Enemi looks characteristically displeased, smacking his arm.

"Zeke! Are you even trying to win? You shouldn't have stopped them!" She stomps a foot, then turns and breaks into a jog. "Come *on*, we've got to hurry now."

Zeke looks unrepentant, giving us a huge smile and double thumbs-up before he follows. Finn steps back, hands gently guiding me back to my feet as he gives me a rueful smile.

"Yeah, so we should probably get back to the challenge." He pulls our envelope out of his pocket, starting to speed-walk backward and reaching up to turn his camera back on. "Last one there's out of a hundred thousand dollars?"

My heart sinks, even as it's still pounding from the thrill of being with him like this. "Do you really think we can catch up to them?"

Finn steps to the side, revealing that Evan is still standing at the meetup spot, no Harper in sight. "We don't necessarily have to."

My jaw drops. I would've thought surely we'd gotten sidetracked long enough for both of the other teams to get ahead. Even as I put my pack on, balling up the tent for Finn to stuff it in the bag, and start on down the trail, I worry about Harper.

But Evan gives us a friendly, if a little tired, wave. "Go on," they call out. "Win it for us, okay?"

Finn and I start for the second to last checkpoint, jogging as fast as our newly reinvigorated bodies will allow, only stopping for a short break to catch our breath, drink water, and, okay, share another quick kiss or two. And when, a couple miles later, we run up to a gaggle of producers, a couple of cameras, and Burke Forrester to get the good news, we do so hand in hand.

Chapter Twenty-Five

I'll get up, I think before I've even opened my eyes, *just as soon as the boat stops rocking.* It takes a beat for the follow-up thought to occur. *Why am I on a boat?*

I blink slowly, squinting against the bright strip of sunlight pouring through the gap in the red fabric overhead. And it all comes back to me in a rush.

It's not a boat that's been gently rocking me from side to side, but a hammock. Finn's hammock, and our double sleeping bag, both of which we slept in together. Slept, but also cuddled, kissed, held each other, gazed up at the stars, gazed more at each other, kissed some more, too, and just . . . more. I smile as the images flash through my mind, feeling my cheeks flush. He really is an excellent kisser. A wonderful cuddler. And I'm obsessed with his hands—how they fit against mine, how he plays with the purple strands of my hair while my head is on his chest, how they quest and explore down my back, hips, everywhere else that's never been touched with such care and reverence as he shows me.

It's because of that care—how confident he makes me, with everything he says and does, that he is mine—that I'm not concerned he's not in the hammock with me. This isn't some shaky ground, what-happens-next morning after. Nope, it's the day we see if we each win $100,000.

In other words, his ass isn't going anywhere without me.

An unexpected perk of hooking up with someone while stranded in a forest together in singularly bizarre circumstances where both your futures are in each other's hands. But even if we didn't have that ahead of us today, I'd feel confident by now that Finn's a sure thing.

When I eventually tumble out of the hammock with all the grace of a newborn giraffe learning what its legs are for, he still looks at me like I just fixed global warming, and I know I'm right to have that confidence. A smile that goes all the way to his eyes lights up his face. He's crouched by the camp stove, and takes in my rumpled morning self with nothing but warmth and affection in his deep brown gaze.

"Good morning," I say as I shuffle toward him in boots with the laces left untied.

"Morning." Finn stands, arms outstretched to pull me into the sweetest embrace. I tip my chin up to meet his kiss, the minty freshness from his lips reminding me I haven't brushed my teeth yet, nor done my skincare routine or applied a smidge of makeup. We did make a stop at another creek last night for a bit of swimming (him), hair washing (me), and an excuse to kiss out in the open with minimal clothing on (both), so I don't feel as gross as I could. And he is so unconcerned it's almost funny. The guy should have higher standards, bless his heart.

"Doing okay?" he asks as he pulls back and returns to whatever he's up to with the stove.

"More than," I answer, plopping down next to him right on the dirt. It's true. Yesterday was a whirlwind—the bear, making up with my main man, saying goodbye to Harper and Evan. I'd gotten weepy on my other best friend here as we prepared to part ways, surprising us both with the level of emotion. She'd patted me awkwardly on the back. "My aunt lives in Boston. I will definitely see you again," she'd said. "Now go get the rest of your HEA."

She and Evan left as good friends too, sharing with Burke Forrester and the cameras that they plan to do more of the AT together in the not-too-distant future.

In the present, Finn gives me a saucy little grin and wink that has my stomach doing a somersault. We start what is sure to be a fast-paced, chaotic day with the most peaceful final morning of camping that I could imagine. Finn makes us oatmeal *and* hot tea with the camp stove and insists he didn't do any dark magic to get it working. I'm not convinced. We both go to get ready, and by the time I'm back, he has our whole campsite packed up. Leaving no trace, like we were never here at all. I'm grateful for his effort, of course, but also a little sad, seeing how quickly it can all be packed away, swept from existence. I don't want the same to happen to us at the end of filming.

But he continues to reassure me through his actions and words that this relationship has staying power. His thumb sweeps across the back of my hand as he holds it, both of us walking with packs on to the checkpoint from last night by the designated arrival time. We click on our GoPros for the hike, and I take mine out of its holster to film the two of us together for potentially the last time. The two teams in the final challenge and episode are usually covered the whole way by camera operators.

"Good morning, adventure lovers," I begin, then hold up our linked hands for the viewing public, "from these adventurous lovers!"

Finn lets out a choked laugh, and I snicker. "Excuse him, he's allergic to cuteness. We're gonna have to get him some antihistamines, though, because I simply have no intentions of stopping!"

"I— You—" Finn sighs with a weary shake of his head. "Carry on, I guess."

As if I needed his permission. I smile into the camera. "You might have noticed Finn and I soft launching our coupledom at the checkpoint yesterday, what with the hand-holding. But Houston, we are ready to hard launch this sucker. Three, two, one, blast off and all that."

Finn agreed to said hard launch last night, both of us deciding we don't want to be a secret—and that the cat was out of the bag after several stolen kisses during our hike to the checkpoint. Our GoPros probably didn't capture actual lips locking, but the simultaneous footage from Finn's camera of the view over my shoulder and my footage of his chest—and any accompanying audio—probably said it all. With filming almost over, there's limited time for others to be in our business anyway, and we want to like each other out loud. He probably didn't realize just how loud I can get.

"In all seriousness, we've been through so much together on the trail. All kinds of ups and downs, both metaphorical feelings-y and literal mountain-y in nature. And *in* nature. God, even when I'm not trying, I'm punning."

Finn laughs, the smallest glimpse of a jolly *ho-ho-ho* but the only one I've gotten so clearly on camera. Viewers don't know how lucky they are for that. It takes effort to bring my focus back to what I was saying.

"I've grown so much, and I think Finn would agree he has too"—I look to him and he nods—"and I feel lucky that by random chance, I could do this with him by my side. Falling for Finn was the easiest part of *Wild Adventures*. I didn't even have to try, and I couldn't have stopped it if I wanted to."

With that, I lean over and kiss his cheek. He unlinks our hands and throws his arm over my shoulders to pull me in to his side, dropping a kiss atop my head. I squeak and probably angle the camera at our shoes for a second before righting it. I plan to fix the camera back onto my pack now, but before I can, Finn speaks, looking right into the lens.

"With anyone but Natalie as my partner, you wouldn't be seeing me here right now. I'm sure I would've taken my ass home quite a few challenges ago, along with whichever poor soul got stuck with me. But instead I got her, and whether we win today or not, it's the luckiest thing that's ever happened to me."

I turn to him with my entire heart in my eyes, finding that he's already looking at me the same way. Without breaking our gaze, or his stride, he adds, "But if it wasn't already clear, we're going to win today."

"**FOR THE LAST** time," Burke Forrester announces with all the importance he can imbue with the words. "Ready . . . set . . . adventure!"

Hand in hand once again, Finn and I set off on our last leg of the Appalachian Trail. While Enemi sprints away, a weary Zeke following shortly after and an even wearier camera operator and producer behind them both, we pace ourselves with a jog. *You're welcome, film crew assigned to Team Finnatalie.* The crew with us will switch off with a new producer and camera operator pairing every so often throughout today's journey, as they haven't gotten as used to jog-hiking as the competitors have.

I wish Finn and I had the option to periodically tag out with fresh, energized Finns and Natalies. We're supposed to be hiking about six miles in total, mostly along a side trail separate from the other team's with an unknown number of stops and challenges along the way. It's going to be a long, strenuous day, and I feel as ready as I'll ever be.

Which is not very ready, but more than I would've been

when we started this whole thing, in my un-broken-in boots that destroyed my poor feet. Now, these puppies are callused. Rugged. They've seen some shit. Six miles is child's play.

Finn and I each keep our eyes peeled as we go, switching between watching our steps and looking for an orange envelope on the right side of the trail. That was the only instruction we were given to start out with—to continue north on the AT and watch out for two envelopes hanging from trees, marking where each team's side trail begins. As is generally the case in a *Wild Adventures* finale, Burke didn't give a whole spiel with a theme, nor any other hint at what obstacles we'll meet today. Because the greatest adventure of all, apparently, is to fumble around in the dark and hope your team is the first to run smack into $100,000. All he really emphasized, with ominous precision, was to *carefully* read each instruction given and follow them *to the letter*. Even though we have a camera operator and producer with us for the journey, they definitely won't be helping out or holding our hands.

Good thing reading and hand-holding are two of Team Finnatalie's passions.

"Here we go," Finn says, and I look up to see him nod toward our right, steering us to the edge of the trail where an envelope hangs from a branch. Leaning against the tree is what I'm pretty sure is a saw, one long piece of metal with sharp teeth down one side and a handle on either end. Beside it is an opening in the undergrowth, a less trodden path than the main AT but clearly the beginning of a side trail.

I take down the envelope and tear it open, then pull out

the couple folded papers inside and begin to read the top one. "'Finn and Natalie, your path to the final checkpoint continues this way. Take your saw and follow the enclosed map to your next stop, where another envelope awaits with next steps. Happy trails!'" I look up. "Well, that's cute. Why haven't we been saying that more?"

"An oversight," Finn agrees, indulging me. He reaches down and picks up the saw by one handle, hefting it in a way that makes me think it's heavier than it looks. He nods to the papers in my hands, the second of which is our map. "Lead the way."

The words are music to my ears. I guide us down the narrow trail for about a half mile, most of it steep and dizzyingly curvy, before we get to the end of the map and the next orange envelope. I'd worried the envelope would be easy to miss, but I shouldn't have—it rests atop a "fallen" tree that completely blocks our path.

"So we're obviously cutting this thing up," Finn says from the other side of the downed tree trunk he's easily climbed over in the time it's taken me to open the new envelope and scan the instructions.

"Slow down there, Paul Bunyan. We're supposed to . . ." I trail off, holding out a hand to still his progress. Then dropping it when I reach the end of the page. "Okay, yeah, we're cutting it up."

No matter how much Finn likes me, I think he still likes being right a little more.

The instructions say to cut up the section of tree blocking the trail—marked at either end in orange paint—into at least three pieces. We will need to roll the smaller log sections all the way to our next stop, however, so we should cut them as small as we need to in order to transport them as quickly as possible, making as many trips as we choose.

"These things are always heavier than you think they're gonna be," Finn says once I've explained this, his voice straining as he bends to pick up the saw again after a break from holding it. "Let's start with three pieces, then try out rolling them around. I bet we'll need to do at least four or five. You about ready?"

"Ready?" I ask dubiously, not trusting his easy-breezy tone.

He swings the saw up onto the top of the downed tree, and it lands with a reverberating clang. "What, you thought I was doing all the work? Crosscut saw, Hart. Take your handle."

If my parents could see me now, I find myself thinking a while later, not for the first time since I've been on the trail, and likely not the last, *they would shit themselves.*

"How did you get to be such a princess?" I can hear Mom chastising.

"Guess you like 'em high-maintenance, huh?" Dad "joked" with the first boyfriend I ever introduced to him, an accident never to be repeated. The two of them had made countless comments about me not knowing what real work is, false wishes of good luck making a living at playing dress-up. They'd even put down Granny Star for "spoiling me rotten."

But here I am, standing Burke Forrester only knows where in the Appalachian backcountry, yanking a tool I'd never seen in real life before today back and forth across an entire tree trunk.

It's brutal, intense work. It felt nearly impossible when we first got started that I'd even be able to lightly score the bark, let alone cut clean through the whole thing. Finn talked me through it, told me how capable I was yet again, probably pulled more than his weight to begin with, but gradually, I found the rhythm. Two cuts down and halfway through another, I feel unstoppable.

This princess can work her ass off. I've got dirt so deep in my fingernails, it might be there forever, an AT souvenir. New blisters and bumps and scrapes every day. I also still have perfect winged eyeliner, if I haven't sweat it off. I might be high-maintenance, but I can maintain it all myself. I'm strong and clever and still like to look good. And I've found someone who sees and appreciates all these facets of me. It's an incredible feeling.

"Damn," Finn pants between pulls on our saw. "I think," pull, push, "you've got," pull, push, "more power left," pull, push, "in you than I do."

"C'mon, Markum!" I taunt like I'm a cross between his playground bully and personal trainer. "Use those sexy muscles or lose 'em! Don't embarrass me! Find that second wind! It's a hundred grand! I'll kiss your boo-boos later!"

"I can't tell . . . if I'm really . . . attracted to you . . . right now or . . . afraid of you." The fire in his eyes is giving the former, but I'll let him pretend it's a real question.

"Why not both! You can have it *allllll*!!!" The excessive exclamation points are audible in my frantic yelling.

When we get through the third cut, Finn and I work together to push the sections out and roll them a few feet, but it's quickly apparent that they need to be about half their current size if we're to push them more than spitting distance. So we roll and wedge them back into place between the two ends of the tree, as Finn says that'll be easier than trying to cut each section when it's out on its own.

It could take hours more or days—I can't be sure, and I think checking a clock would make me cry—for us to halve the three sections. Finn lets go of his saw handle and collapses to the ground when we finish the last cut, breathing as heavy as I've ever seen from him. But I can't be stopped. Drawing on stores of energy or adrenaline or pure survival instinct, I don't even know, I move to the first section we cut. I make sure Finn isn't sprawled in the path of it, then start to push, letting out the roar of a wild beast. The weight of this section is much less a threat to my aging nineteen-year-old back than the first ones we tried rolling, of course, but it's still a lot for any reasonable person to push alone. Alas, reason has no place in the *Wild Adventures* finale.

"What the hell, Natalie?" Finn calls as I roll the log piece past him and he scrambles to his feet. "I just needed a break for two seconds, then I would've helped you!"

"No time to rest!" my inner she-beast shouts back as I keep shoving the log down the path indicated on our new map. It's less than a quarter mile, but on a steady incline. "Only *push*!"

"Yeah, I've decided on afraid," he says before settling in to help me push on.

And on, and on, and on.

Chapter Twenty-Six

"Are we having fun yet?" Finn has the audacity to say an hour or twelve later, the most gorgeous, infuriating smile splitting his glistening face as I feel like I'm near death's door. Not only have we rolled all six logs to the top of the hill, but, as our next instructions then laid out, we've stacked them into a staircase-like structure like the one I made of hay bales at the stables.

In other words, we reassembled the tree we'd just hacked up, just a little differently shaped.

"We're *having* a great story to tell in couples therapy one day," I snipe back. A rather wheezy snipe. I hear the camera operator snort-laugh, and it feeds the shameless attention-seeker within.

Then Finn lifts the hem of his T-shirt to wipe at his sweaty face, and it's my turn to collapse. Unfortunately for me, the guy even perspires attractively.

Maybe all this exertion was worth it, I think to myself, in my exhausted, mildly disgruntled daze. *Hundred thousand dollars or not. I have a hot partner, with arms that flex beautifully and a back that strained the confines of his T-shirt as he stacked the hell out of some logs, and isn't that the real prize of it all?*

Finn waves a hand in front of my face, looking at me like he's worried I've come down with heatstroke.

"What?" I ask breathlessly.

"I asked if you're ready for this," he replies.

"Yes."

A pause, in which I watch a drop of sweat travel down his neck. A nice neck. A—

"For climbing to the platform?" The impatience in his voice snaps me out of my stupor.

"Oh. Yes, that too."

With Finn right behind me, I carefully work my way up our wobbly log stairs to the platform they lead to, affixed to a tree about ten feet off the ground. Waiting there is a tray of graham crackers, marshmallows, chocolate bars, and an orange envelope, all held by an official-looking person I don't recognize.

"How are those hands doing right about now?" Finn asks once he's torn open the next envelope, his eyes darting across the page of instructions. I look down at my palms, still bearing signs of the rope burn from a few days ago, but they're more dirty than anything.

"Depends," I answer warily. "Are they about to have to haul a log down this zip line?"

Fortunately, we get to leave the logs behind us from here on out. The long, scarily skinny wire looming like a specter behind the official stranger only needs to carry me and a small plate of s'mores on a relatively gentle but still terrifying descent to a platform farther down the trail. My hands' job is to hold the plate steady enough to get to the other end with my s'mores completely intact, a task made much more difficult by the fact that we have no way to toast the marshmallows first. The three stacks—graham cracker on the bottom, chocolate bar, marshmallow, and graham cracker on top—are precarious enough without any sticky melted sugar goo holding them together.

In a way, I decide as the stranger who turns out to be the zip line attendant gets me all harnessed up and clipped to the wire, I find these uncooked s'mores relatable. What am I, if not a stack of shaky ingredients, barely holding it together, but made a little stronger every time I face the fiery intensity of my anxiety and fears, or every time Finn melts my insides a little by reminding me how great he thinks I am?

It's possible I'm coming down with heatstroke after all.

When there's nothing left for me to do but step off the platform, I take the—exceedingly careful and balanced—leap. It's not as terrifying as I expected, flying over treetops with nothing but a flimsy metal string keeping me from becoming a splat on the forest floor. It's not the fastest zip line, nor the steepest, only angled down enough to keep propelling me forward. And I'm too focused on keeping the plate still to feel anything but a nervous exhilaration, the wind whipping the sweaty wisps of hair at my temples into my eyes, chilling my skin all the way through my harness and damp tank top.

My eyes are so laser-focused on my kinda-s'mores that I barely notice the next platform is coming up in time to ready my feet for as soft a landing as I can manage. I don't take another breath until I'm standing up straight again, processing what I see on my plate.

"IT'S GOOD!" I shout, like a commentator on all the football games my dad watches.

Finn, when he lands a couple minutes after me, is not so lucky, with all three graham cracker tops falling over. I can hear his creative, expletive-filled grumblings about how much he hates graham crackers for half his hike back up the hill, where he has to climb our stairs to the first platform and try again. His second trip down, the crackers redeem themselves, earning us the next envelope from the second zip line attendant.

From there, it's clear we can both feel our team hitting our stride. I see it flash in Finn's eyes as I hand over more lip balm–covered cotton pads assembled from my toiletry kit, and he uses them to quickly get a fire going in one of the familiar metal fire rings. It's in the smile I can't suppress while we toast the marshmallows as instructed.

When we get our next instructions, after speed-hiking to the end of our side trail where it meets back up with the AT, Finn reads them aloud, a smile stretching wider across his face with each word. " 'Co-EdVenturers, this is your last leg—use it to make some trail magic for your fellow hikers. You'll do this by handing out the six s'mores you've made, each to a different hiker you meet. You must find hikers willing to consume the s'more then and there, and they must finish it before you continue on. You have three miles from here to the checkpoint in which to distribute all your s'mores. See you at the finish line!' "

I meet his hopeful grin with a gasp, raising the little storage container of s'mores I've been holding onto for reasons unknown until now. "I get to talk to people?!"

"Unless you want me to take the lead on this one," he teases.

My laugh echoes off the trees as I begin to jog. "Here I was, thinking you wanted to win!"

I'm probably a little too confident in my sweet-talking abilities, and the universe decides it needs to humble me. It only takes interacting with the first few strangers to cross our path for team morale to sink.

"Where the fuck did all these hikers with food sensitivities come from?!" I screech when the latest guy to reject our s'mores is barely out of earshot. "Which is worse, *Steve*—you getting a wittle tummy ache from one square of chocolate, or me *dropping out of college*!"

The stifled snicker from the production crew peanut gallery is less gratifying in this instance. Finn takes my hand and squeezes as we resume our brisk pace.

"Plenty of trail left," he says with a confidence I'm not quite feeling after three failed "trail magic" attempts. "We can absolutely do this."

I definitely frighten every person I talk to from then on out, jumping down their throats with enough enthusiasm behind my "let me watch you eat my s'more" plea. They definitely think there's s'more than just chocolate and marshmallows inside. But when I explain our situation as briefly as I can, the big TV camera beside me backing up my story, I start to get takers.

Turns out, making anyone stand there and let you watch

them eat a room-temperature s'more you assembled a while ago is not the kind of beautiful connection with my fellow humans and hikers that I'd longed for when I first started walking the AT. Reviews aren't glowing.

"Why is it kind of damp?" asks a decently good-looking twentysomething guy. Attractive or not, I don't want to explain to him the concept of condensation when you put hot things in less-hot containers.

"I think this has some ash in it," says a nice older woman a few minutes later, delivering the news apologetically.

"Thank god we don't have a Yelp page," I tell Finn after giving our third s'more out to a middle-aged man whose dismayed expression spoke volumes. "Why is torturing innocent hikers considered 'trail magic'?"

"I'm sure if they understood the scope of the good deed they did today, it would feel more magical," he offers.

I'm tired, and filthy, and sore in places I didn't know could get sore. I know Finn is too. But he doesn't complain. He stays patient with me when I have to slow down a little because of a stitch in my side or when I want to gripe about a total stranger's gluten intolerance keeping them from eating graham crackers.

I know it's a conscious effort to stay calm and positive. I'm acutely aware of what's on the line, so much that I can't let myself think about it, about all I have to lose. About the fact that we still haven't seen Zeke and Enemi, and I have no clue if that's a good or bad thing.

"I have to say," Finn says while we speed-walk onward, apparently reading my mind, "it's getting a little weird that we haven't spotted the other team once since this morning. Like, did they only decide to cut their log in three pieces and do it in half the time we did? Or did they catch all six marshmallows on fire?"

"Yeah," I agree. "Did a tree fall on Enemi, totally unrelated to the challenge, and crush all but the ruby slippers on her feet?"

"You sound a little too hopeful with that one."

I shrug. Finn bumps his shoulder to mine with a laugh. "Point is, we don't have a clue how close of a race we're in."

He doesn't say it, but I'm sure we're thinking the same thing—it feels closer by the minute.

It turns out I'm right about this, as we turn on a ridge that gives us a clear view of a section of trail we walked about ten minutes ago.

"NO!" Enemi's shriek, coming only seconds after I've spotted her and Zeke back there and they've realized we're in the lead, could probably be heard clear across the country. Hikers on the Pacific Crest Trail will be left wondering what kind of bird that far-off, irregular call came from.

"Is that the last guy we gave a s'more to?" Finn asks, referring to the familiar middle-aged man shaking his head—and holding out his hands defensively, for good measure—as he passes our competitors.

My laugh is delirious, a little unhinged, and too hopeful to be contained. "It is. Looks like he didn't want seconds."

This peek into the others' progress, or lack thereof, reinvigorates us both. We begin jogging again, determined to keep our lead. Our fresh enthusiasm is rewarded when the trail magic fairies smile upon us, sending the two friendliest backpack-ers I've ever encountered straight into our path—and into our hearts forever when they take and eat our last two s'mores.

"Thank you so much!" I call as I walk backward toward the checkpoint and my two new best friends continue in the other direction, laughing and waving over their shoulders. It's only the twelfth time I've said those words to them. "I'll never forget you! Love you!"

Finn, a few feet ahead of me as he's begun our final push to the finish with significant speed, lets out a funny combina-tion of a laugh and a cough. "Wow," he says, clearing his throat while I return to facing forward and speed-hike up to his side. "Should I have given you three some space?"

I sigh dreamily through my quickening breaths. "No, no. If it's meant to be, we'll find our way back to each other. And I need you around for the money we're about to win!"

And it's that single sentence that curses us. It must be, be-cause not even half a second later, mid-laugh, Finn goes pitch-ing forward, landing on all fours with a ground-shaking thud. I gasp as he rolls to his side, reaching toward his left foot then seeming to think better of it.

"Finn!" I drop to my knees beside him, gut twisting at the look of pain on his face. "Are you okay? What happened?"

"I"—he sucks in a sharp breath as he tries to bend his foot forward—"tripped on something. Think I hurt my ankle."

I look back as our crew rushes closer. The producer starts asking him about pain levels from one to ten and if she needs to call medical backup. I'm frantic, replaying the last couple minutes in my head like I can roll them back and get a redo.

"I jinxed us!" I cry when the producer steps away to make a call on her sat phone. "The words 'about to win' had no business crossing my lips until we got to the checkpoint!"

He grimaces. "No, it's obviously my fault. I should have watched where I was walking."

"Well, I was distracting you by talking," I argue.

"Uh, yeah, because I was talking too? We always are?"

How dare he insist on absolving both of us of guilt in this freak incident? If we're about to lose the whole competition over this, I want something other than bad luck to blame.

"So is this it?" I say meekly. The producer has stepped away with her satellite phone to her ear, presumably to call for that elusive medical backup team.

But to my surprise, Finn sits up. "No way."

"What?" I squeak. "How?"

Very carefully, almost in slow motion, he starts to stand. I make a bunch of incoherent noises of half-hearted protest, even as hope blooms inside me. Then he goes to put weight on his injured ankle and almost falls over, letting out a pained yelp.

Hope crashes to the ground, bursting into flames on impact.

"Nope, sit your sweet ass back down," I command, even as it hurts like a sprained ankle.

"No," he says, sharper than he's been with me all day. Than ever, maybe. Softening his voice, he takes my chin to make me meet his serious gaze. "We're ahead of Zeke and Alli, got rid of all our s'mores. We can't give up, not when we've made it this far. All we've gotta do is hoof it to the finish line."

"Yeah, with one busted hoof!" I retort.

Finn puts both hands on my shoulders, melting my insides with his molten chocolate stare. "What did Renée do when Wilder was losing consciousness from a snake bite, and the bad guys were closing in?"

My eyes widen. "What did who and who do when *what?*"

"*Hot on Her Trail!*" He snaps his fingers in front of my face and realization dawns. I've created a monster. "Keep up. Desperate to outrun their evil pursuers and get him to a doctor because, you know, snake bite, she found her inner strength to haul his mostly incapacitated body in a firefighter's carry. Just in time, they made it to the safe house that happened to belong to a hot doctor–slash–Navy SEAL, who administered antivenin and kept them hidden from the bad guys until Wilder regained consciousness and could fight alongside him. They really set up Doctor SEAL as a future romantic hero, by the way—is the next book in the series about him?" Before I can answer, or really catch up to these ramblings, Finn shakes his head. "Not important right now. What *is* is that we don't give up. Find that inner strength like Renée. Or like the you who was hauling logs twice your body weight like it was nothing. Help me hobble my way to the end of this thing." He shrugs. "You never know when a surprise safe house is gonna appear."

I can only look at him slack-jawed for a moment. But when he gives my shoulders a gentle shake and widens his pleading eyes, I feel his urgency and it moves me to action. "Okay, sexy forest ranger. Give me your pack."

It's the slowest race to a finish line *Wild Adventures* has ever seen. Or that any race has ever seen, really, except perhaps for that fabled tortoise-and-hare situation where slow and steady won. We are highly unsteady. With two packs strapped to my shoulders and hips like the most abstract, unwieldy butterfly costume ever made, I'm already top-heavy. Add my giant partner using me as his crutch, sending me swaying with every hop-step he takes, we're a barely walking threat to public safety.

"At least this'll be funny to watch back," I offer, trying to lift my own spirits. I won't let the full weight of this failure, this crushing loss, sink in until it's official. But probably best to start easing into the impending letdown.

Finn squeezes my shoulders. "I'm telling you. The snake bite hasn't killed me yet. Hot Dr. Forrester could be just around the corner."

I laugh because the only other thing to do is cry, and I don't want Finn to feel bad.

I feel fate catching up with us—or Zeke and Enemi, at the very least. I try to keep focusing on the good that's come from this journey as we hop-step along. For example, Finn discovering his love of romance novels. I'll have so much to share with him as he enters this exciting new chapter in his reading life.

It's as I've started mentally crafting him a reading list that a few things happen at once. First, I hear them. Voices behind us, and not from the film crew.

"Zeke, if you don't pick up the *fucking* pace, I *swear*—"

"Alli, if I keep hearing your voice in my nightmares for the rest of my life, you won't even get to keep the hundred thousand, 'cause I'm suing you for emotional distress."

Then we literally round a corner in the trail and I see it in the distance. A flash of orange waving between the trees, the exact shade and size of a *Wild Adventures* flag.

"Oh my god," I whisper at the same time Finn says, "Is that . . . ?"

"Oh my god!" Enemi shrieks once again, and I hate that we had the same reaction. "They're right there, they're right there, we can overtake them!"

"Does she think we can't hear her?" I ask Finn, who is noticeably quickening his hop-stepping. I hurry to keep up.

Pounding footsteps get closer and closer, the curses I'm saying in my head get louder and louder.

Enemi zips by us, a witchy cackle echoing in her wake. "Wow, Natalie. Your clumsiness is contagious, huh?"

A menacing growl answers her, and it takes me a moment to register it's coming from me, not Finn. No, he's trying to whisper reassuring words in my ear, even as Zeke jogs past us too.

Still, Finn won't let me just throw in the quick-dry camp towel. He moves from hop-steps to straight-up hopping, these bizarrely energetic, powerful, one-footed leaps, and it's all I can do to shakily scurry alongside him.

The finish line flag grows more defined, Burke Forrester coming into view along with more crew around him. And when Enemi and Zeke run up to him, arms thrown into the air, we have front-row seats to their victory celebration.

"We were *so close*," I say for Finn's ears only, my voice already more of a whimper. We're really less than a minute's walk away. Maybe a little more as we slow to hop-steps again.

Finn presses a kiss to my temple. "I know. I'm so sorry, Nat."

I want to drop these heavy bags we no longer need, just throw my arms around him and cry into his chest. Let him comfort me in our loss. But I also want to finish this thing with some dignity, and without either of us saying it, I know he wants that too.

When we finally get to the finish line, I expect Zeke and Enemi to step aside, if not to be humble in success then at least to get a better view of Burke telling us we're losers. But they stay put, and if I'm not mistaken, they don't look so over the moon just yet. They look antsy, expectant. Like they're still waiting for the final verdict.

Seems a little weird, but I don't remember at the moment how the show normally does this. If they always wait for both the final two teams to arrive, stand them together to say what everyone already knows—who got there first and who goes home with nothing. It's harsh, but I guess I shouldn't expect anything else.

I make sure Finn is steady, still not putting much weight on his injured ankle, before unclipping our packs and letting them both drop to the ground. That's a relief, at least. I don't have to carry one of these big-ass backpacks ever again if I don't want to. It's not the massive college scholarship that would change my life, but cold comfort is still comfort, right?

Free to do so, I nestle into Finn's side. As his arm tugs me close, I wrap one of mine around his back. I reach up and put my other hand on his chest, right over his pure, beautiful, fiercely beating heart.

"Co-EdVenturers," Burke Forrester begins, that higher-than-on-TV voice doing its best to be low and serious. "You've come so far on this journey, on foot and in your hearts . . ."

He loses me there. I tune out the platitudes, close my eyes, and listen to Finn's heartbeat. Deep breath in, slow exhale. Think about the positives again.

It works fine enough, but tears still build up behind my shut eyelids and slowly make tracks down my cheeks. *We were so. Close.*

"What the *FUCK*?"

The eardrum-shattering scream interrupts my peaceful, almost meditative state. I jump and feel Finn's whole body tense and stiffen. When I whip my head to the side, Enemi's face shows nothing but rage. I think her eyes are actually shooting lasers at Burke Forrester. Next to her, Zeke is stunned, a hand frozen in his hair, pushing the strands in all directions.

I look to Burke, seeing if he'll give me any clues as to what I missed here.

"Zeke, Alli. I'm sorry," he says. And now I'm hearing my own heartbeat in my ears, my pulse quickly picking up. Is he saying what I think he is? "Per the rules of our competition, it isn't only about making it here first, but correctly completing all parts of the challenge. When one of the s'more recipients did not eat the entire s'more, Alli threw what remained into the woods, in violation of the challenge's instructions. As such, your team has not won *Wild Co-EdVentures*."

While Enemi sputters like a malfunctioning cassette tape and Zeke gapes at her, apparently learning alongside the rest of us what she did, Burke angles himself toward Finn and me.

"Finn, Natalie," he begins, a grin spreading across his orange face that I could actually kiss right now, if this is real. "As you successfully completed all parts of the challenge and made it here as a team, on top of an amazing performance throughout the whole season of *Wild Co-EdVentures*, you are the winners! Congratulations!"

I don't have time to scream, cry, or even really think before Finn is kissing me. It's a kiss I feel everywhere, from my fingertips at the nape of his neck down to my toes pressing grooves into the soles of my hiking boots. In every inch of my messy, emotional, beautiful insides.

It's a kiss that shows everyone else what we already knew— that we won long before we got to the finish line.

Epilogue

Four Months Later

"You . . ." I manage between panting breaths. "Are lucky . . . I love you."

Instead of my darling boyfriend, at whom the comment is directed, it's Benny Beneventi who replies.

"I don't love Finn yet. Someone remind me why I'm here?"

Reese's boyfriend is less outdoorsy than I was, pre–*Wild Adventures*. I think Finn expected they'd bond over all the activities he planned for our fall break in Vermont, fooled by Benny arriving at the Burlington airport already wearing a flannel and hiking boots. Finn didn't realize that was only the city boy's Rugged Outdoorsman cosplay, the exact same outfit he'd worn the first time he and Reese ever hiked together.

"Basic safety protocol, Norberto," I say, speech coming easier now as we get to a flatter part of the trail. "When planning a camping trip, you always invite at least one person you can out-run. You know, in case of a bear encounter."

Benny scoffs. "Joke's on you. I watched this show where a girl came across a bear in the wild, and now I know you're not supposed to run from them. You just start yelling a bunch of pop culture opinions and annoy the bear into running from *you*."

The whole group laughs while I groan. But when I catch Finn's knowing look, I give him a wink. We both know I have no shame about my now-infamous black bear showdown.

We also know that as much as I complain any time he drags me out hiking or camping, I love this shit.

I thought it was a long shot to get everyone into this trip idea, back in the summer when I proposed it. No more than a month into Finn's and my long-distance relationship, it was ambitious to look at fall break plans together. But my new financial aid and scholarship setup had just been finalized, ensuring that not only could I afford to go back to Oliver College, but I wouldn't have to worry about money for the rest of my time there. My nightly video call dates with my beautiful grumpy man were going splendidly. I was feeling grand and making plans.

My childhood besties, Reese and Clara, were immediately interested in spending a long weekend in Finn's hometown, eager as they were to meet the boyfriend they'd watched me become a lovesick fool for on TV. Benny goes where Reese goes. More surprising, though, was being able to get Harper, Evan, and Zeke here. Harper and I have talked regularly since *Wild Adventures* ended, and through her, I've gotten to know Evan more. The two of them live only a state apart and have stayed true to their plans to keep hiking together.

Zeke was more of a wild card. I think the guy needed someone to talk to after the show was over, to parse out the overwhelming experience of it all, and he and his partner didn't leave on the best terms, after she cheated them out of a win. Enter Finn. Borrow a guy's fountain pen one time, become his amateur therapist for life. But the other guy's grown on him, enough that Finn asked another month or so later if he could extend a fall break invite to Zeke.

No regrets so far. Not on the invite list, anyway. Minor regrets about giving Finn such free rein over the itinerary. We're staying in his mom's basement most of the weekend, because she is an actual angel on earth and hostess with the mostest *delicious* homemade cinnamon rolls. But tonight, we're revisiting our relationship's roots—and giving some of the group a more rustic experience than they bargained for.

"It's beautiful out here," Reese says, looking around at the leaves in all shades of red, orange, yellow. A few lingering green, some brown too. All of it combining to create a ridiculously picturesque Fall In Vermont Experience.

Hopefully that'll cushion the blow when I have to tell her about packing out your used toilet paper.

"Yeah, you all came at the perfect time," Finn says. "Pretty colors to see, but we won't need to put heat packs in our sleeping bags just yet."

"If anyone does get too cold tonight, you can borrow Reese," Benny calls out. "She's an actual furnace in her sleep."

"I can't help it!" Reese smacks her guy on the arm. He blows a kiss to her.

"And if anyone can't fall asleep in total silence, you can borrow Natalie," Finn adds, letting out an obnoxious fake snore I'm sure is like no sound I've ever made.

"My allergies have improved, I'll have you know!" I shoot him a glare as the group dissolves into laughter.

Harper, Evan, Zeke, Finn, and I all carry the sleeping bags, tents, and almost everything else in our fancy backpacking packs that we got to keep after *Wild Adventures*. We're only camping for one night, but eight people require a lot of stuff. And when I'd asked the other three what kind of luggage they were bringing, it was suitcases and small, school-size backpacks. So they've been responsible for their clothes and personal items, with the former Co-EdVenturers taking the bulk of the equipment and food.

Backcountry backpacking is not the easiest way to introduce my indoorsy friends to camping. But it *is* a fitting introduction to Finn Markum as a human.

A human who suddenly appears at my side, sliding his palm against mine and interlacing our fingers. I pretend I'm not going to accept after that snoring callout, but he isn't fooled. The fun thing about being long distance most of the time is that small moments of real, tangible connection like this still give me butterflies.

"Hey." He presses a quick kiss to my cheek, and I'm pretty sure I hear Reese let out a swooning sigh a few steps behind us. "We're almost there. I promise you're going to love it. I brought stuff for mushroom carbonara over the campfire for dinner."

I raise a brow, impressed at this news. "Wow, throwback. Did you forage the shrooms yourself?"

He smirks. "Not this time. But I also brought heat packs in case temps do drop after all, and there's plenty of water, and some decks of cards if anyone gets bored, and—"

"Hey," I whisper, leaning in to his side as I give his hand a squeeze. "I'm supposed to be the anxious one here. Stop trying to steal my role."

Finn huffs a soft laugh, still a little startled every time I poke fun at my own anxiety. A thing I've been doing more and more as I've come to terms with it. I've actually started to treat it with one of the college counseling center's therapists since returning to school, and more recently, an outside psychiatrist she referred me to. I'm not on any meds yet, but it's a possibility I'm exploring. And working with Lora, my therapist, has already changed the whole game.

I'm talking about things I never have with a professional, barely have with anyone but a select few who are all on this camping trip. My parents and difficult childhood, Granny Star, freshman year, the brain spirals and panic and ever-mounting list of worries all come up. Our biweekly sessions, covered in my tuition and fees, lessen the weight I've been carrying like twelve completely full backpacking packs at once, for all these years.

And make it easier for me to find a way to laugh through it, like I do with everything in my life, good or bad. No longer am I laughing to hide the hard stuff.

Finn shakes his head. "I just want everyone to have a good time. I wouldn't say I'm anxious about it. Just . . ."

"Nervous," I fill in.

He grunts.

"Worried."

An unintelligible grumble.

"Unsettled."

Before he can make another one of his growly noises and get me way too hot and bothered in the company of guests, I cut him off with a firm, quick kiss.

"Should we give you all privacy?" Harper asks from the back of the group in her usual monotone. But I can hear the snark. "Long distance is hard. Not getting to do all this touchy-feely stuff often. Don't let us stop you. If the tent's a-rockin'—"

"Harps, you're going to make Finn's head explode," I cut her off, giving my guy a pat on his blushing cheek. "All this blood rushing to his face and ears can't be good for him."

"I'm resisting a really suggestive joke right now, even though you set it up perfectly, and I'm doing that for you, Finn. I hope you're happy," she says.

"Very," Finn calls back, overly loud and turning to face her.

"Please feel free to share the joke with me individually," Zeke pipes up. "I'm free all night and also forever."

His Harper crush hasn't gone away, but I think he also just enjoys making her squirm with declarations like that. The group keeps bantering back and forth as we continue our hike through the gorgeous Green Mountains, which I'm so glad to be seeing at last. Finn has visited me in Boston since we both went back to school, driving the almost four hours down on a Friday and back on a Sunday each time. But I don't have a car and haven't quite figured out a reasonable way to get up here for a weekend. I can't afford plane tickets like the ones I splurged on for this trip very often, though my scholarship and the raise I've earned since being back at Body Wonderland have made it way more possible.

So much feels possible now, it's almost jarring. Amazing what tending to your crumbling mental health and accepting help will do. My classes are even going pretty well this semester, and I have a small role in an upcoming show on campus.

The only area that hasn't seen significant change is my relationship with my parents. When I returned after *Wild Adventures,* there was no celebration of my having won a $100,000 scholarship on a reality show. Said scholarship was still going toward a school and program that is a bad idea in their eyes, and probably always will be. But I'm becoming better at accepting that this is their issue, not a reflection of the value of me or my choices.

This is another therapy lesson, of course. But it's also a Finn lesson. A part of being with someone who owes me nothing, has nothing tying me to him through biology or history. Nothing keeping him in my life but the fact that he really, really wants to be here. Really, really likes me—loves me, even, a feeling we both finally admitted to last month—for everything I am, good and bad, messy and put-together. It's revolutionary. It's eye-opening.

It's the wildest adventure I've ever been on.

We reach our campsite, a spot where Finn and his dad stayed multiple times throughout his childhood. I'm honored that he'd bring us here, share this piece of his life and the special bond he had with his father. He doesn't seem to feel sad about it, though I'm watching closely all evening. Looking for a flicker of grief—depression, anger, any of its associated emotions—as we set up tents, build a fire, make dinner, then s'mores, and talk and laugh together. Nighttime sets in, sunset fading into a star-covered sky.

It's only when the stars are brightest, when the fire has almost burned out, and all our tired friends have said goodnights and split off for our respective sleeping quarters, that I catch Finn alone. I know I'll get him to myself the rest of the night, when we crawl into our tent together just like the good old days of four months ago. But when I'm walking back from brushing my teeth and doing the rest of my nightly routine, I spot his familiar silhouette standing alone, head tipped back.

I drag my feet a little, making sure not to accidentally sneak up on him. When I'm almost at his side, he doesn't even turn to see that it's me. Just holds his arm out, ready for me to tuck myself under it.

"What if I'd been Zeke?" I tease, my whisper sounding too loud in the peaceful night. It feels quieter here than it did on the AT. Or maybe that's just my own mind.

"Then I would've heard your thundering elephant walk from half a mile away and kindly pointed you toward your tent," he whispers back, eyes still on the stars.

I smile and look up too, taking in the sparkling tapestry that, no matter where I'm looking at it, will always take me back to that night in the Smokies with Finn.

"Have you found the Big Dipper yet?" I ask.

He points to it right away, like I knew he would. I track its shape with my eyes from star to star, corner to corner of the "dipper" piece, then on out to the handle. The very same stars a tiny Finn and his hero used to gaze at, sometimes from this very same spot.

I tighten my arms where they're looped around Finn's middle, holding him as close as I can.

"You know," Finn says after we've been here so long I'm nearly dizzy, the twinkling dots overhead blurring together before my eyes. "I *am* lucky you love me."

I tip my chin down a little, let it rest on his chest so I'm looking only as far up as his face. The strain in my neck from all the time it was tipped back is apparent now, and before I've so much as winced at it, Finn brings his hand up and massages my nape. At last, he brings his gaze down to meet mine.

"I'm lucky to love you," I reply. "And lucky you love me too."

"Even though I make you go camping when you're trying to have a restful weekend with your friends?" he teases, eyes tracing my face with so much affection, it makes my heart ache in the best way.

"Especially because you take me camping," I say, standing on tiptoes to brush my lips over his. "I actually do my best resting in sleeping bags." *Kiss.* "When two are zipped together." *Kiss.* "And there's a devastatingly handsome man in there to wrap me in his arms and keep me warm."

Finn cups my face then and claims my lips with his, deep, slow, all-consuming. Perfect.

"So, beautiful," he murmurs, barely a breath between us. "My tent or yours?"

I glance at the single tent we were granted by the *Wild Adventures* gods in the backpack Hunger Games. Finn superglued its one broken clip back together after filming, and it looks good as new, but also like an old friend I haven't visited in too long.

With a smirk, I answer, "Both."

Acknowledgments

I have a lot to be grateful for in the wild adventure (have I over-used that yet?) of creating this book! So many people have supported me in getting here, including every reader who's picked up my first two books, and I wish I could thank you all individually. Alas, that's a lot of ink and pages we don't have, so I'll start with:

My agent, Laura Crockett, and editor, Hannah Hill. Thank you both for being so enthusiastically on board with everything I've wanted to write and helping make those ideas way better than I could on my own. You always know how to lift my spirits at the low points of this journey, and I feel luckier to be on your team with each book we work on together.

My publicist, Lili Feinberg. Thank you for your tireless work for my books and always being down for reality TV ramblings.

The rest of the team at Delacorte Press and Random House Children's Books, my wonderful publishing home. Special thanks to Beverly Horowitz, Wendy Loggia, Tamar Schwartz, Colleen

Fellingham, Shannon Pender, Natali Cavanagh, Stephania Villar, Erica Stone, Katie Halata, Natalie Capogrossi, Angela Carlino, Michelle Crowe, and Ana Hard.

So many friends and family members who offered knowledge and insight as I drafted this story. Thanks to Aaron Cambron for being a super-fun gi who also knows a lot about mushrooms; to Elora Ditton and Nolan Meier, my Vermont insiders and two of my very favorite people in the world; Jamie Vescio for naming my French restaurant and being a delight of a human and friend; and my cousin Liv for being the coolest, smartest Horse Girl I know. I'm also extremely grateful for the books that helped my research, including *Hiking Trails of the Smokies* by the Great Smoky Mountains Association, *Nature of the Appalachian Trail* by Leonard M. Atkins, and *Grandma Gatewood's Walk* by Ben Montgomery. All of these are wonderful reads, and any errors, intentional or not, in depicting the AT and the Smokies are mine alone.

My writing friends for solidarity, laughs, and inspiration. Thanks to Elora Ditton (again) because I'm obsessed with your magical self; Claire Ahn and Thais Vitorelli, my sweet and talented first writing friends; Mazey Eddings, my fellow Anxious Girl; Ava Wilder, Sam Markum, and Rachel Runya Katz, the Totani survivors; Anita Kelly, LC Milburn, Chandra Fisher, Anna Sortino, Briana Miano, Katie Bohn, and the rest of the Fork Fam; and so many others whose friendship has kept me going in this difficult industry, including Brian Kennedy, Martha Waters, Ellen O'Clover, Gwenda Bond, Elizabeth Kilcoyne, Rachel Lynn Solomon, Torie Jean, Auriane Desombre, and Susan Lee.

All the booksellers, teachers, and librarians who have found my work and gotten it into readers' hands—thank you so much for all you do!

The "real life" friends who somehow haven't abandoned me after years of bringing my publishing life shenanigans into your lives, and in fact continue to be nice and supportive. Thank you to Katie Cambron, Daniel Cambron, Sydney Norman, Megan Wall, Lee Kiefer, Gerek Meinhardt, Barton Lynch, Trevor McNary, Abby Slucher, Maggie Garnett, and Jillian Madden.

My family. Thank you to my parents, Michelle, Brad, Ginny, and Ron, for your endless support; my siblings, Brianna, Julian, Grant, Reagan, and Max—I love each of you even more all the time; and all the other Hills, Tudors, and Parsonses. I'm lucky to have a family so big and so wonderful!

Finally, my Stephen. Thank you for being my live-in hiking/camping/backpacking/Great Outdoors expert, and the other main character in my all-time favorite love story.

Want more of Reese and Benny's love story?
Don't miss . . .

"Sweet and satisfying."
—JENNA EVANS WELCH, *New York Times*
bestselling author of *Love & Gelato*

Love from Scratch

KAITLYN HILL

Turn the page for a sneak peek!

Chapter One

The man in front of me has a bee in his bonnet and cat hair on his coat. I know these things because from where I stand— smooshed into the back of a crowded elevator in the downtown Seattle skyscraper where my internship is located—the sleeve of his suit is only inches from my face. As such, I can see the white strands plain as day against the black fabric while he grunts at the phone in his hand—plus feel the tickle in my nose that says I'm dangerously close to a sneeze.

Lordhavemercy, I think, one big compound, catchall word I inherited from my mamaw and so many other Southerners, religious or not. It's what you say when you're in company too polite to say something worse.

Mr. Business is testing my limits, though. He just couldn't be bothered to use a lint roller, could he? Nor to give me any personal space back here, in the midst of whatever turmoil he's dealing with in his email inbox. I hope my nose breath is making him hot. I press my tongue to the roof of my mouth, a trick I saw online somewhere to help put off sneezing, watching the floor numbers tick higher.

Finally, the *ding ding* is for my floor and I adjust my grip on the tray of to-go cups I'm balancing in the crook of my arm, reaching for my badge to swipe into the office with the other hand as I make the quiet, "pardon me, sorry" noises required to edge my way out of the crush of bodies. It's made a little easier today by the human Grumpy Cat, whose office must also be on floor forty-two, thus allowing me to slink through the wake left by his wide frame.

That plan is working flawlessly, right up until he steps off the elevator and—I don't know—needs a moment to collect himself, or realizes he forgot to feed Fluffy or something. He stops short, with no regard for my or anyone else's presence a half step behind him.

And because I do not stop short, I run smack into his cat-hair-covered backside, coffee tray first, sending hot brown lava into the air, onto the floor, and all over myself.

"Whoa, careful there," the man grumbles with an errant glance over his shoulder. He's already turning to head down the hall toward the entrance of some investment firm, leaving me gaping and covered in gourmet bean water.

I should be careful? Oh, for the love of—

"Reese! Oh my God, are you okay?"

Teagan, receptionist at Friends of Flavor, comes rushing out of the glass double doors that face the elevators, through which I guess she just witnessed the accident.

"I'm fine," I say in the least grumbly voice I can manage, peeling my once-lavender shirt away from where it's clinging to my stomach and chest. I'm never dressed in the blacks and grays of most of the businesspeople who work in our building, but of course I had to go all-pastel today. "Can't say the same for the drinks, though."

I peer over the to-go cups, which have all miraculously stayed in their designated slots, and to my relief find that my own hot tea might be the only total loss. *Gourmet leaf water,* I mentally correct myself, with regard to what's soaked me. I've never felt so betrayed by my favorite beverage. The bean waters kept their lids on and lost a little foam at most. Small victories.

"What an asshole," Teagan blurts, nodding in the direction of my new nemesis, who has by now disappeared. I nod my agreement but keep my mouth shut; she's been here a couple of years and is so well liked that I don't think anyone would bat an eye at her outburst. I've been here less than two weeks and would rather not be tossed out on my tea-soaked rear for losing my temper.

"You go on in, I'll wipe the rest of this up," she continues, shooing me away. I would argue, but she probably knows the time and therefore realizes that I'm already cutting it close, so I thank her profusely and get on my way.

Rounding the lobby corner, I shift the ill-fated tray to my other hand just in time to hold it out of the way of someone passing with a wheel of cheese so massive he nearly has to walk sideways to fit it through the hall. I pass by one of the ingredient pantries and catch a guy who looks like he stepped straight out of the Discovery Channel dropping live crabs into a tank. When I've almost reached the little alcove off Prep Kitchen 2 where my team works, a cooked strand of spaghetti sails just past the end of my nose and sticks to the wall beside me.

"Sorry! Didn't see you there," calls out an embarrassed kitchen assistant. I wave him off and bite my bottom lip to keep myself from saying something snippy. Not seeing me there seems to be the theme today, doesn't it? But honestly, they seldom "see me there," and that's fine. So long as I'm noticed by the people who matter—the people with my future in their hands.

This is how it goes at Friends of Flavor. It's the second full week of my internship, and I'm only just getting used to the organized chaos that characterizes these "culinary content creators." There is constant hustle and bustle, chefs and kitchen assistants and art directors and camera crews and more rushing around to get the next recipes made, the next episodes shot for the various series, the kitchens cleaned so it can start all over. I'm merely a background player, an intern on the marketing team, and I have no desire to be anything more attention-grabbing—for now. If I can just keep my head down, work hard, learn from the pros, and do a good job on the tasks I'm given this summer, it could be the beginning for me. My entry into their flagship semester-long culinary internship in the fall, and from there . . . who knows what else? Once I have my degree, I'm angling for something full time in marketing or maybe on the production side—wherever my skills can be best put to use. If all goes according to plan, hopefully I'll have a chance to stay in this weird and wonderful world long term.

Working at FoF has been my dream for years now, ever since my best friends back home in Kentucky, Natalie and Clara, pulled me out of a seriously self-pitying funk our freshman year of high school and into the home theater at Clara's house with a dozen FoF videos queued up. It was the start of our shared obsession with the channel and the charismatic chefs who make its culinary magic. On countless nights when our schoolmates went to parties and football games, we stayed in, smooshed together on someone's bed or couch, catching up on all the episodes of FoF's cooking series. We fell in love with Katherine's easygoing competence on *Fuss-Free Foodie*. We got to travel the US with Rajesh in *Cross-Country Cookery*. We dreamed of one day competing against other amateur chefs on *Good Chef/Bad Chef*. The prep kitchens and studio where most shows took place seemed like Narnia to us, as aspirational and dreamy and seemingly out of reach as that wonderland through the wardrobe.

I never imagined Narnia having quite so many copy machines, though. After rounding the corner near one of the mechanical beasts, I'm finally in the marketing team nook. I hand off the surviving cups to each of the team members I work with, who mumble their under-caffeinated thanks, then take a seat at my makeshift TV-tray desk. If anything, I suppose I can be thankful that the shock of the hot liquid down my front has given me the jolt of energy that I won't be getting from a beverage this morning. I see a lock of dripping blond hair hanging in my periphery and try my best to discreetly wring it out above the trash can before pushing it back into place. I snap a quick picture of the results of the spill to Natalie and Clara with the caption "#OOTD #professional." Their responses come quickly and are highly on-brand.

> **Clara:** yikes! hope you have stain-fighting detergent. my mom uses tide

> **Natalie:** Wet t-shirt contest?? LOVE that for you!

Laughing as I pocket my phone, I decide to put the annoyance of the coffee-tea-tastrophe to rest so I can get on with my day. I take out my laptop and open it, tucking my backpack neatly against the wall—as neatly as it will go, anyway, in a space barely big enough for a small trash can, let alone a whole human and her possessions.

Dream internship, I remind myself. Living the dream.

The dream that wasn't so out of reach, as it turns out. Friends of Flavor is a real business, with real offices, where they hire real people to do real work. I had no idea the extent of the labor it takes behind the scenes to make twelve minutes of "Rajesh Prepares Chef Grant's Deconstructed Chicken Cordon Bleu" look so clean and flawless. But the world of food media is complex, with many cogs that keep the machine running. It's appealed to me since I first started watching FoF's shows, and they're producing the best work in the business. I love food and enjoy cooking, but my culinary chops are mostly collected from time spent in my mamaw's kitchen throwing extra butter into everything and learning her recipes and techniques by example. Without any professional kitchen experience, I always figured that my graphic design skills from years on the school newspaper staff would have to be my in.

And when I started browsing internships for the summer before college and saw that the big streaming service that hosts Friends of Flavor had a spot open in its marketing department for a recent high school grad with minimal experience to their name? A chance to get away from my hometown and to my new city as soon as possible before I go to the University of Washington in the fall, to start anew away from all the people and baggage of my past, to work with some of my favorite creators in the whole wide web? I barely even considered what the day-to-day would look like, or that it might be anything other than a dream come true. Truly, I don't think I've ever clicked a button so fast in my life.

I've done quite a bit of clicking buttons since then, though, like I do now as I open up the usual tabs in my browser. Button clicking is one of my main responsibilities here, along with getting morning coffee when the boss decides to splurge on some from outside the staff break room. Every Friends of Flavor social media page is at the ready on my computer, waiting for me to tend to the replies and reposts and favorites appropriately. In other words, to click some buttons.

On Instagram, I like everyone's comments that I can. This is a never-ending task, as there are thousands of comments per post and they are constantly multiplying. Half of them are just people tagging their friends so they'll see the post, but as my boss Margie says, we still have to show that we "appreciate their engagement." I reply to a handful that I deem reply-worthy, like if they ask a genuine question to which I can find an answer—

> **@sw3et.c4rolin3e3:** What brand of brown sugar did Nia use in her drop cookies?
>
> **@friendsofflavor:** Domino, but any kind will do!

—or if they say something that gives me a chance to be quippy—

> **@MrZtoA1:** I accidentally melted my butter instead of softening it OOPS
>
> **@friendsofflavor:** BUTTER luck next time! ;)

Quippy comments always get more engagement and are the most fulfilling for me personally. My food pun repertoire is vast and always growing. Those almost balance out all of the comments I have to delete and users I have to block for inappropriateness. Why anyone would come to a page for a *cooking channel* to post racial slurs is beyond me, but then so is posting that garbage anywhere. I think of it as my daily taking out the trash, and it's sort of cathartic. Block, delete, block, delete, block, block, block.

Twitter and Facebook are more of the same, though the latter is increasingly bogged down with accidental comments by older folks who were clearly trying to type in the search bar, bless their hearts. Where we get the most engagement, and therefore where I spend the bulk of my time, is in the comments on our actual video content.

It's impossible to keep up with all of the comments on the Friends of Flavor channel on our host streaming service, Ulti-Media. The UltiMedia website is busy as it hosts a wide variety of original scripted and unscripted content on its different channels. There are channels for every interest—sitcoms, dramas, romantic movies. But Friends of Flavor's culinary reality series make it one of the most popular channels of all. Everyone likes food, right? And honestly, most people seem to like our videos.

UltiMedia has a comments section under each video, and each channel has an account that can monitor and reply to comments—a lot of my job is managing Friends of Flavor's. But there are so many episodes within each of the different series getting a minimum of thousands of new views daily, it's all I can do to give the occasional "Thanks for watching!" to every 217th commenter. Anything to show we care, I guess. It's one of

Friends of Flavor's biggest priorities to remain as approachable to the over four million viewers of each new video as they were to the first fourteen, and as a loyal longtime fan myself, I appreciate it.

I've been at it for a couple of hours when I hear Margie abruptly scoot her chair back behind me. I peek over my shoulder, though I know she's likely only taking a bathroom break. But to my surprise, she's gazing at her cell phone as she gets to her feet and gestures for me to get up, too.

"Aiden texted. Impromptu meeting in PK 1. Why don't you join me, see what's up?"

I nod, knowing it's more of an order than a suggestion, and close my laptop. I fight the urge to tuck in the flyaway strands of Margie's long, gray-brown braid as I trail her down the hall. While Margie has her shit together more than most people I know, the state of her braid always suggests otherwise. And somehow, I seem to be the only one who notices. It's like these people didn't grow up with a mama who would lick her fingers and pat into submission any individual hair that dared to step out of line.

When we reach Prep Kitchen 1, I'm pulled out of my hair reverie by the tall, stressed-out head of operations of Friends of Flavor—and cohost of *Good Chef/Bad Chef*—looking even paler than usual. Aiden, whose blond-haired, surfer-bro looks I might find attractive if not for every word that comes out of his mouth, paces back and forth. He has one hand on his hip and the other scratches aggressively at his neck, his intense gaze snapping toward us—well, toward Margie—when we enter.

"We have a problem," he announces.

"So I gathered," Margie replies coolly. She has at least a couple of decades of age and experience on Aiden and the rest of the Friends, and it mostly stands out when anything has gone wrong.

"The six of us have to fly to Chicago this afternoon. Jules Veronique had an opening in his schedule come up for tonight, and his assistant just called me, and they've finally agreed to let us film the crossover episode at his new restaurant. Everyone's schedule is cleared, the suits okayed it, and flights are booked, so we're going. Because we have to go, right? So we're going. We need to leave any minute."

He pauses, giving Margie an opening. "So . . . what's the issue?"

Aiden sighs, pulling a hand through short, platinum locks. "We were going to film a regular episode of *Piece of Cake* this afternoon, but Nia will be with the rest of us in Chicago. We have advertisers already scheduled and expecting an episode tomorrow, but now we won't have our pastry chef here to *film that episode*. Since you're marketing and have experience in the saving-face stuff, I thought you might . . . I don't know, have an idea."

Margie nods slowly, sucking her cheeks in. I feel a bit touchy on her behalf at the clipped way Aiden talks to her. Maybe it's my respect-your-elders upbringing. Maybe I'm still thinking of Mr. Cat Suit and I'm projecting onto Aiden. Or maybe it's just that I'm over men's condescension toward women who are their equals—not that I'd ever express such opinions to these two.

After a moment of staring blankly into mid-distance, Margie opens her mouth to speak.

"Yo, A, was this the sourdough starter you were looking for? It kinda looks like a baby vommed in this bowl. Kinda smells like it, too, but—"

The speaker who isn't Margie stops short and sets the bowl he's holding on the counter, looking at our small crowd in confusion. I haven't seen him before. He's definitely an intern; if the fact that he looks about my age hadn't given him away, the general air of doesn't-know-what's-going-on-in-this-office-or-the-world would.

"He could do it."

It's Margie who speaks this time, and it feels like all eyes in the room turn to her in surprise.

"Our *intern?*" sputters Aiden.

Sourdough Guy crosses his thick arms over his apron-clad chest, looking a little defensive even though he doesn't know why yet. He's significantly shorter than Aiden, barely my height, but a lot bulkier. It'd be hard not to notice that he clearly works out when he's not in the kitchen. I try not to judge appearances, but muscles combined with the backward baseball cap on his head are making it difficult. Another dude-bro.

Margie shrugs. "Sure. It'll be different. '*Piece of Cake* Makes Macarons, Featuring the Intern.' Better than nothing."

Aiden steps closer and lowers his voice nowhere near enough to keep Sourdough Guy from hearing him. "I don't think so. He really—he's not ready to do a video. Not on his own, anyway."

"Reese can do it with him."

I don't even register at first that Margie is talking about me. The stressed-out chef doesn't either, but that's because he hasn't bothered to learn my name.

"Who?" he asks.

"Reese. Marketing intern." Margie puts a hand on my shoulder and nudges me forward as if presenting me for inspection. I open my mouth to protest, but I can't seem to produce any sound.

Aiden barely glances at me before wiping a hand over his face. "Margie. Please. Intern plus intern does not equal chef."

She matches Sourdough Guy's stance, though it looks less aggressive on her. "No, but it does equal a solution to your problem, which is what you asked me for. It'll be fun and different, and if it's a bomb, we'll never have to try it again. Don't you have a plane to catch?"

The expression on Aiden's pale face is grim, and I'm sure my own is similar, because what the *devil*? After another tense moment, Aiden sighs heavily. "I'm trusting you with this, all right? Can you manage this for me?"

In spite of my reluctance to do what Margie has suggested,

I'm secondhand offended again when he speaks to her like a child. But she just pulls her braid over her shoulder and starts smoothing it with her hand like she has all the patience in the world.

"I've got it. Give Jules my best."

Two best friends.
One reality dating show.
And some very
un-best-friend-like feelings . . .

NOT HERE TO STAY FRIENDS

KAITLYN HILL

AVAILABLE NOW!

About the Author

KAITLYN HILL is a writer who lives to tell love stories and make people laugh. While books make up most of her personality, Kaitlyn also enjoys messy reality TV, has never met a tea she didn't like, and thrives on overly ambitious home improvement projects. She resides in Kentucky with her real life romance hero.